D1071801

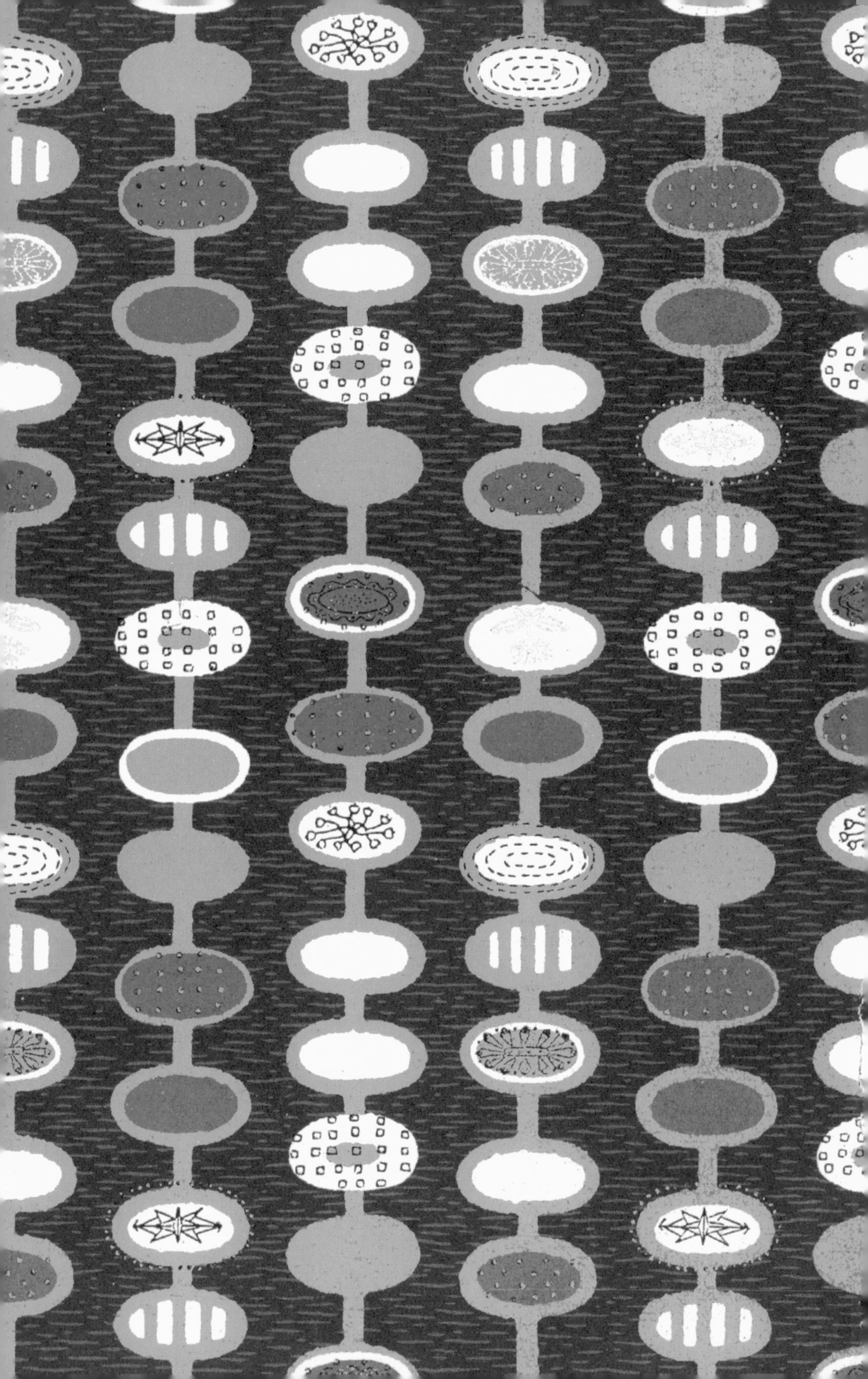

THE OUTFIT

IDW PUBLISHING

OPERATIONS:
TED ADAMS, CEO & PUBLISHER • GREG GOLDSTEIN, CHIEF OPERATING OFFICER
MATTHEW RUZICKA, CPA, CHIEF FINANCIAL OFFICER • ALAN PAYNE, VP OF SALES
LORELEI BUNJES, DIRECTOR OF DIGITAL SERVICES • JEFF WEBBER, DIRECTOR OF ePUBLISHING
ANNAMARIA WHITE, DIR., MARKETING AND PUBLIC RELATIONS • DIRK WOOD, DIR., RETAIL MARKETING
MARCI HUBBARD, EXECUTIVE ASSISTANT • ALONZO SIMON, SHIPPING MANAGER
ANGELA LOGGINS, STAFF ACCOUNTANT • CHERRIE GO, ASSISTANT WEB DESIGNER

EDITORIAL:
CHRIS RYALL, CHIEF CREATIVE OFFICER & EDITOR-IN-CHIEF • SCOTT DUNBIER, SENIOR EDITOR, SPECIAL PROJECTS
ANDY SCHMIDT, SENIOR EDITOR • BOB SCHRECK, SENIOR EDITOR • JUSTIN EISINGER, SENIOR EDITOR, BOOKS
KRIS OPRISKO, EDITOR/FOREIGN LIC. • DENTON J. TIPTON, EDITOR • TOM WALTZ, EDITOR • MARIAH HUEHNER, EDITOR
CARLOS GUZMAN, ASSISTANT EDITOR • BOBBY CURNOW, ASSISTANT EDITOR

DESIGN:
ROBBIE ROBBINS, EVP/SR. GRAPHIC ARTIST • NEIL UYETAKE, SENIOR ART DIRECTOR
CHRIS MOWRY, SENIOR GRAPHIC ARTIST • AMAURI OSORIO, GRAPHIC ARTIST
GILBERTO LAZCANO, PRODUCTION ASSISTANT • SHAWN LEE, GRAPHIC ARTIST

www.idwpublishing.com
ISBN: 978-1-60010-762-7 • 13 12 11 10   1 2 3 4

RICHARD STARK'S
PARKER

the *Outfit*

A Graphic Novel

BY
Darwyn Cooke

EDITED by SCOTT DUNBIER

IDW PUBLISHING

San Diego　　2010

This one's for Cal.

RICHARD STARK'S PARKER:

Outfit

MIAMI BE

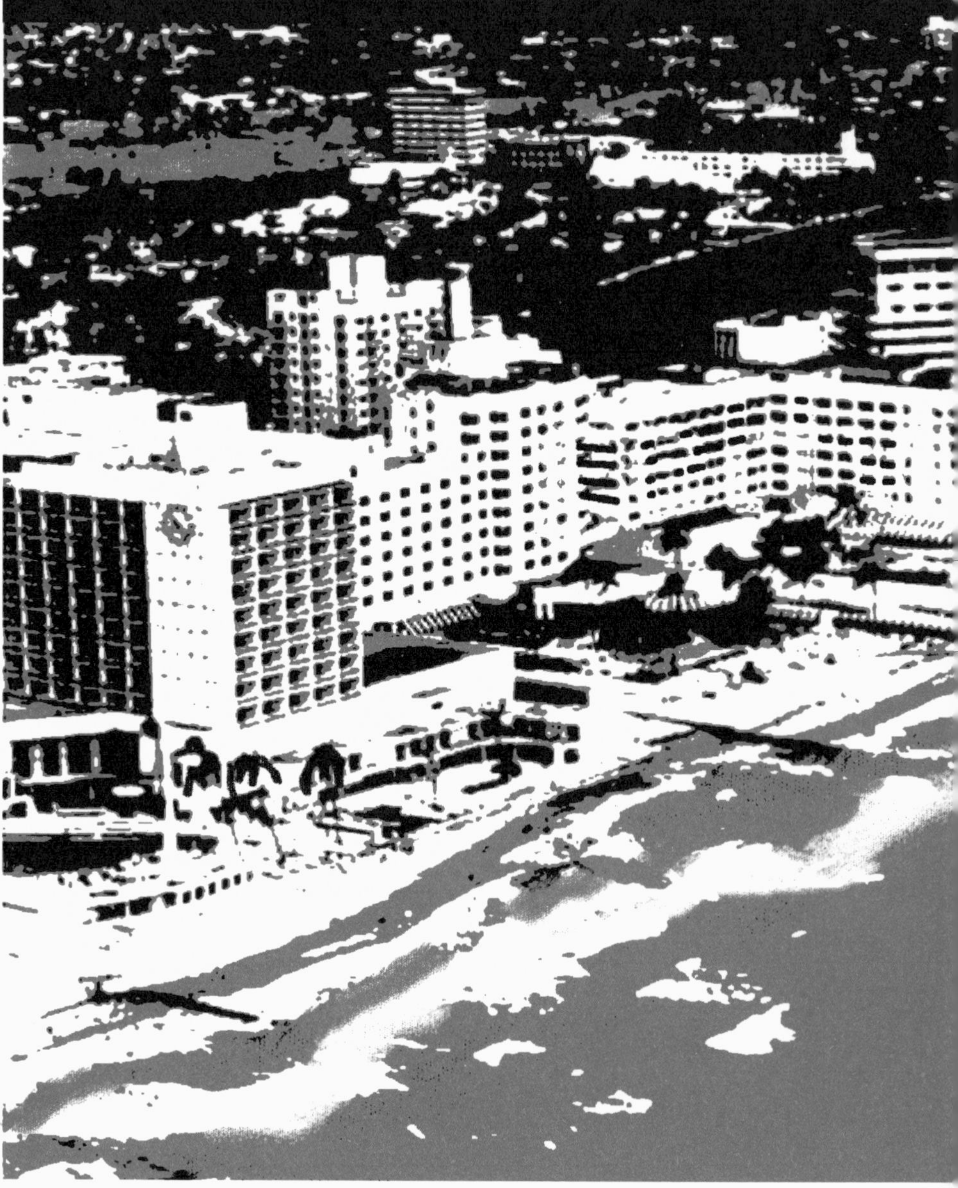

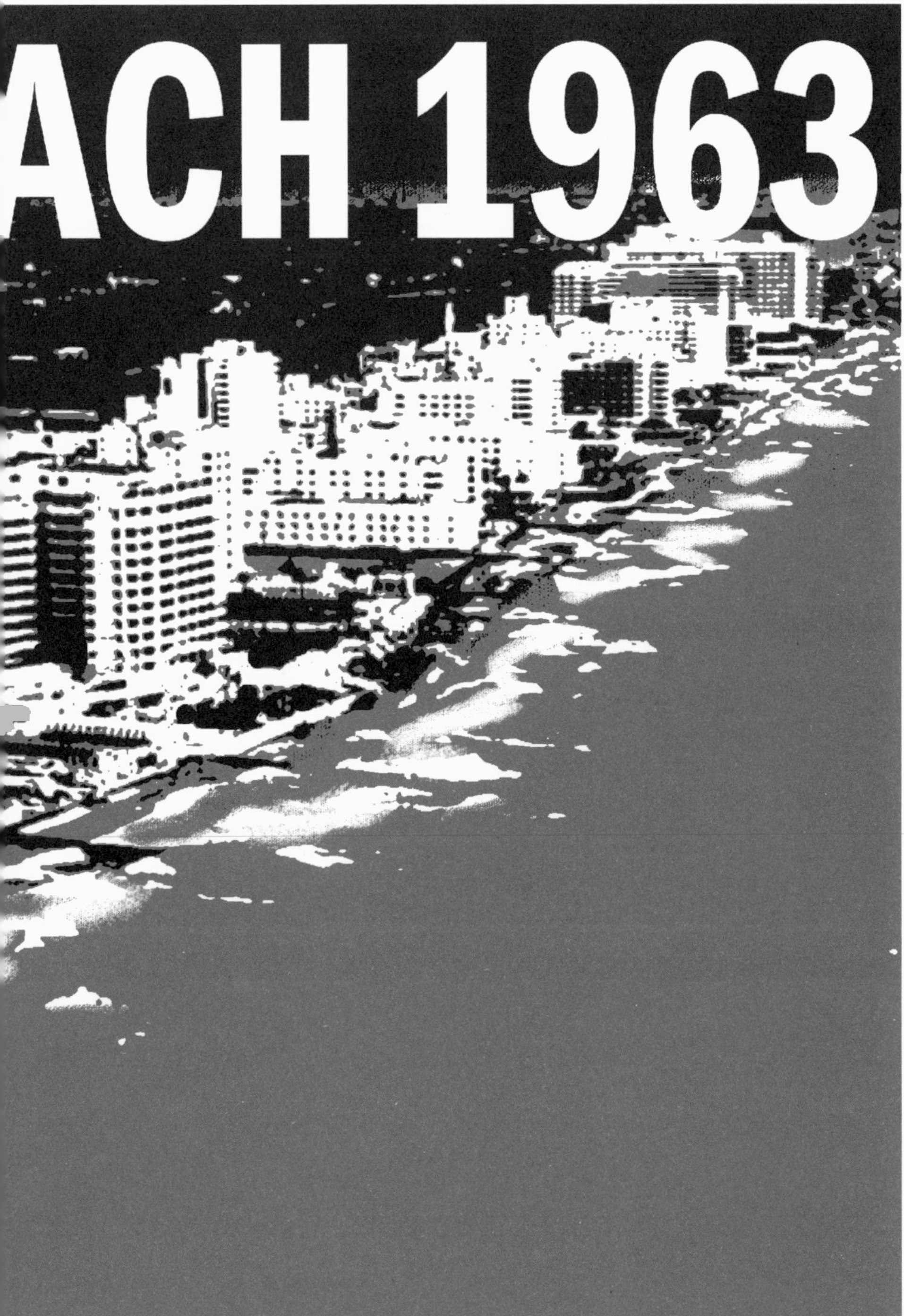
ACH 1963

BOOK ONE

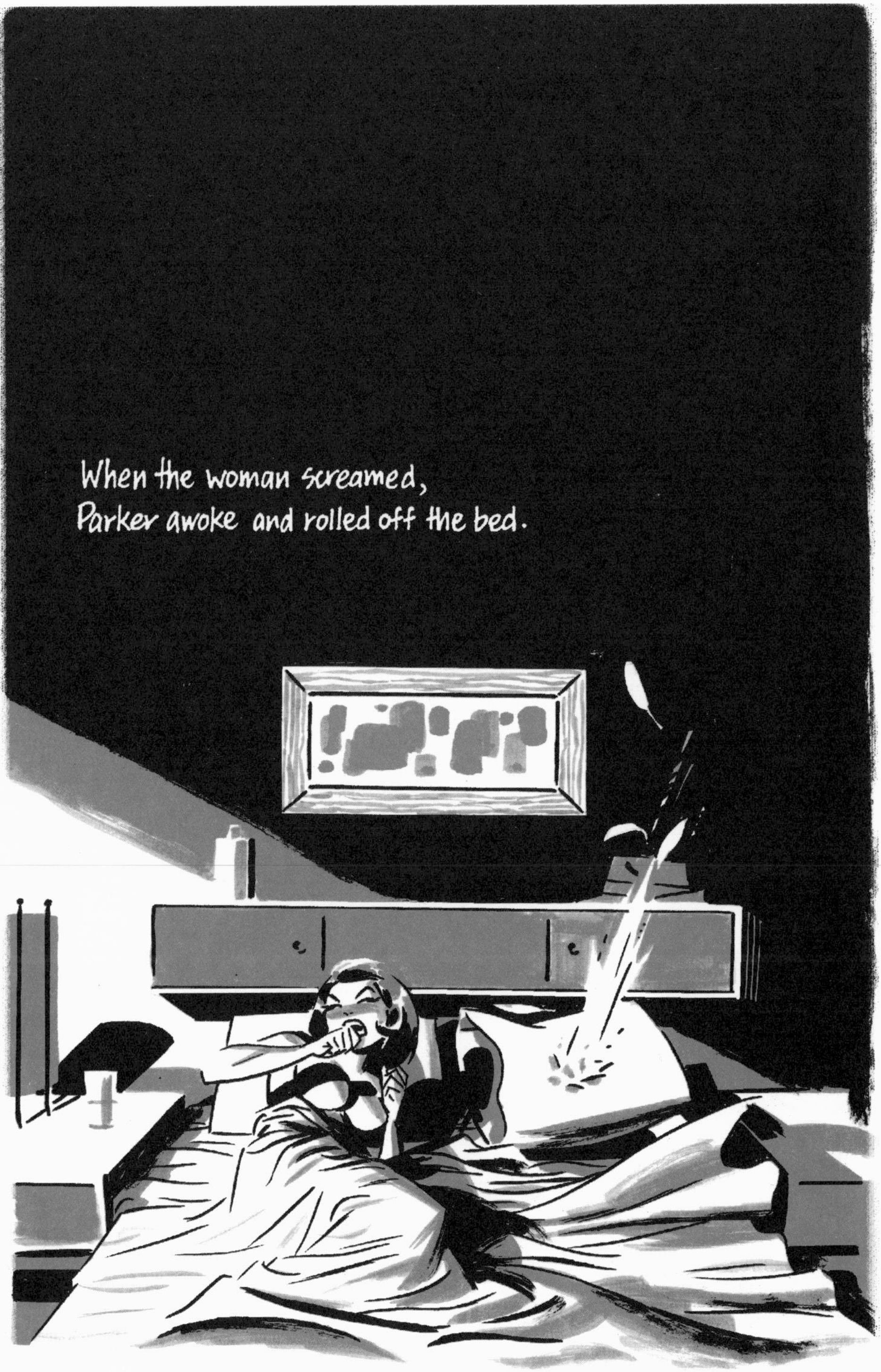
When the woman screamed,
Parker awoke and rolled off the bed.

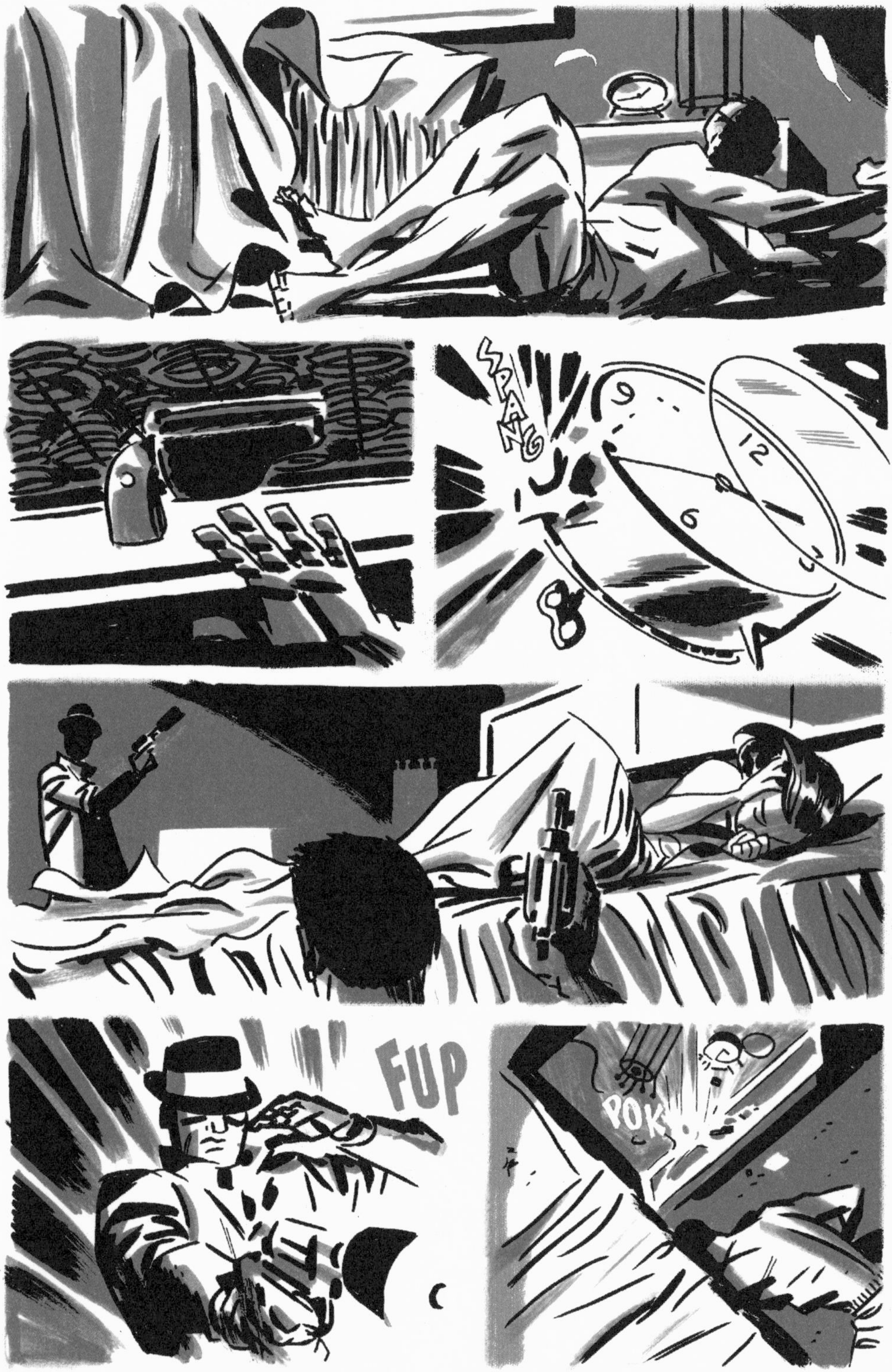
SPANG
FUP
POK

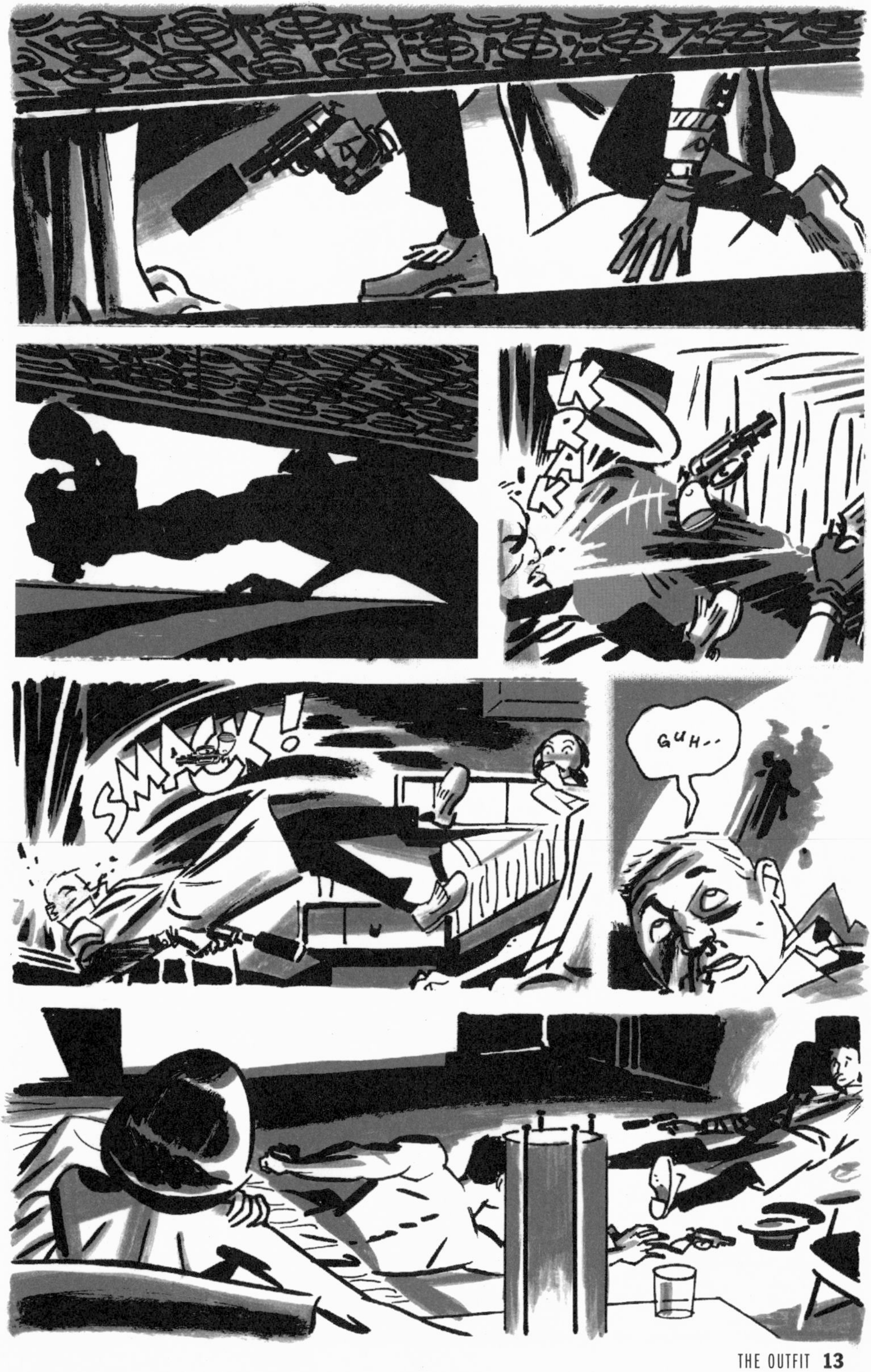
KRAK
SMACK!
GUH...

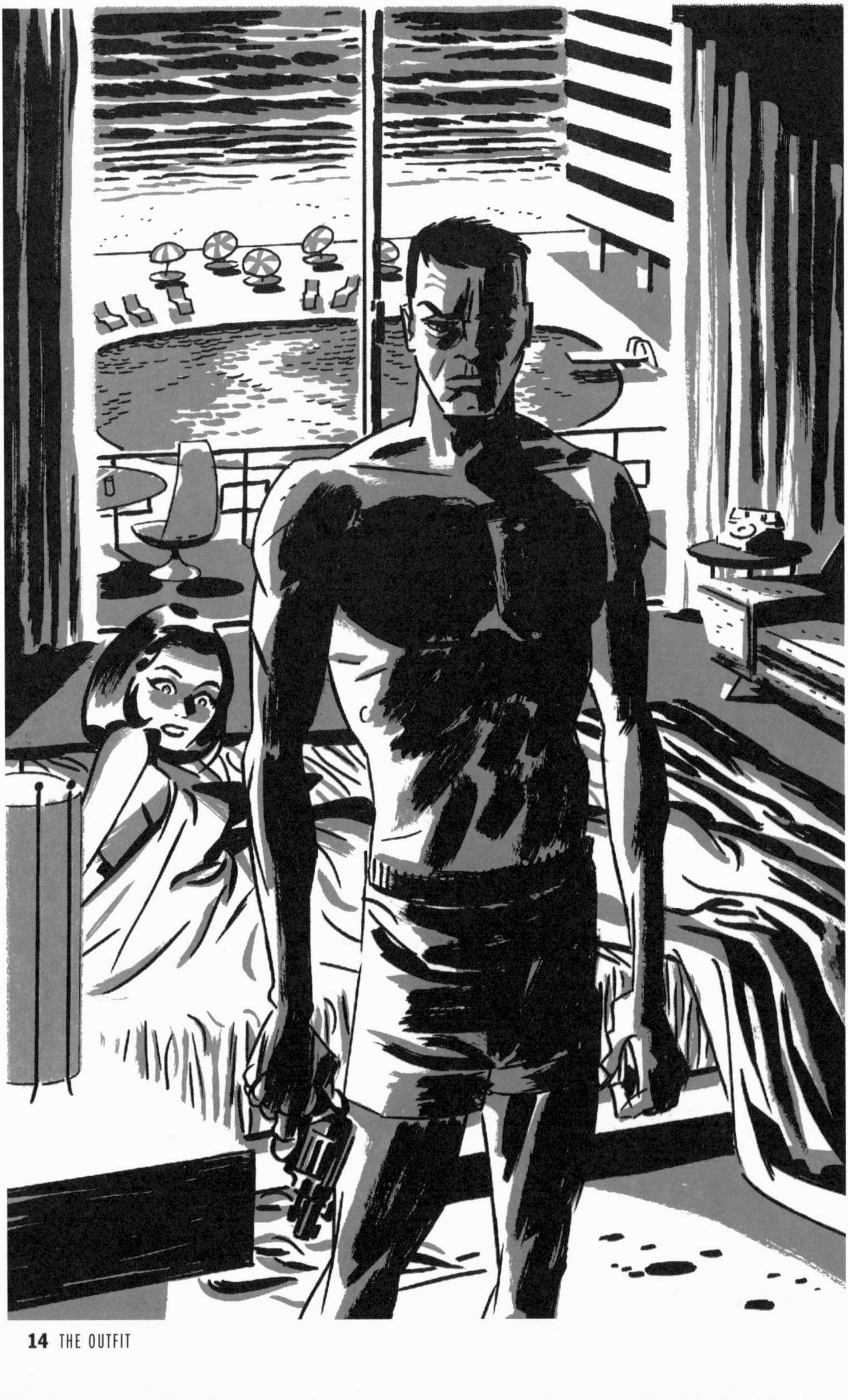

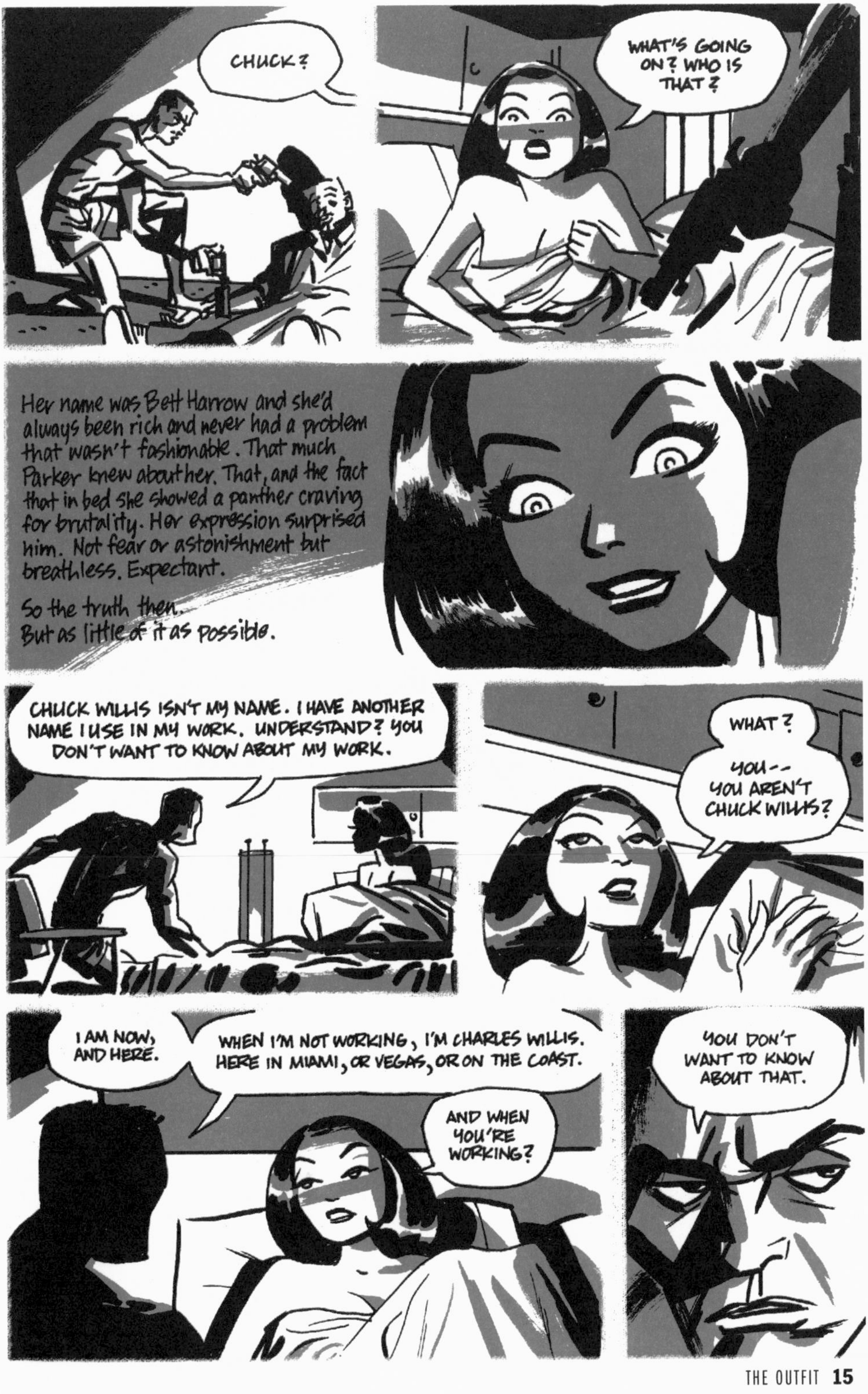
CHUCK?
WHAT'S GOING ON? WHO IS THAT?
Her name was Bett Harrow and she'd always been rich and never had a problem that wasn't fashionable. That much Parker knew about her. That, and the fact that in bed she showed a panther craving for brutality. Her expression surprised him. Not fear or astonishment but breathless. Expectant.
So the truth then. But as little of it as possible.
CHUCK WILLIS ISN'T MY NAME. I HAVE ANOTHER NAME I USE IN MY WORK. UNDERSTAND? YOU DON'T WANT TO KNOW ABOUT MY WORK.
WHAT?
YOU-- YOU AREN'T CHUCK WILLIS?
I AM NOW, AND HERE.
WHEN I'M NOT WORKING, I'M CHARLES WILLIS. HERE IN MIAMI, OR VEGAS, OR ON THE COAST.
AND WHEN YOU'RE WORKING?
YOU DON'T WANT TO KNOW ABOUT THAT.

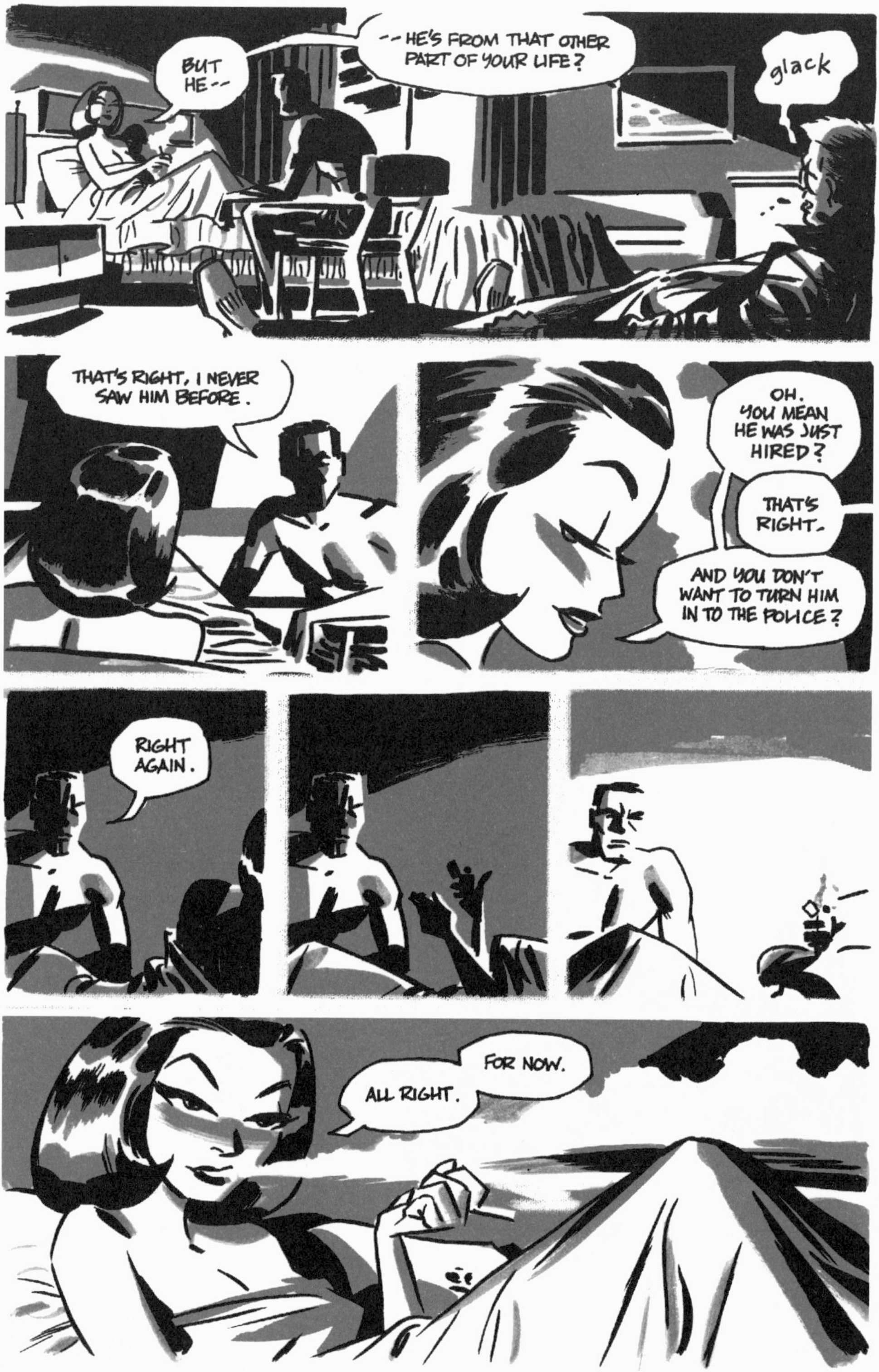
BUT HE--
--HE'S FROM THAT OTHER PART OF YOUR LIFE?
glack
THAT'S RIGHT, I NEVER SAW HIM BEFORE.
OH. YOU MEAN HE WAS JUST HIRED?
THAT'S RIGHT.
AND YOU DON'T WANT TO TURN HIM IN TO THE POLICE?
RIGHT AGAIN.
ALL RIGHT.
FOR NOW.

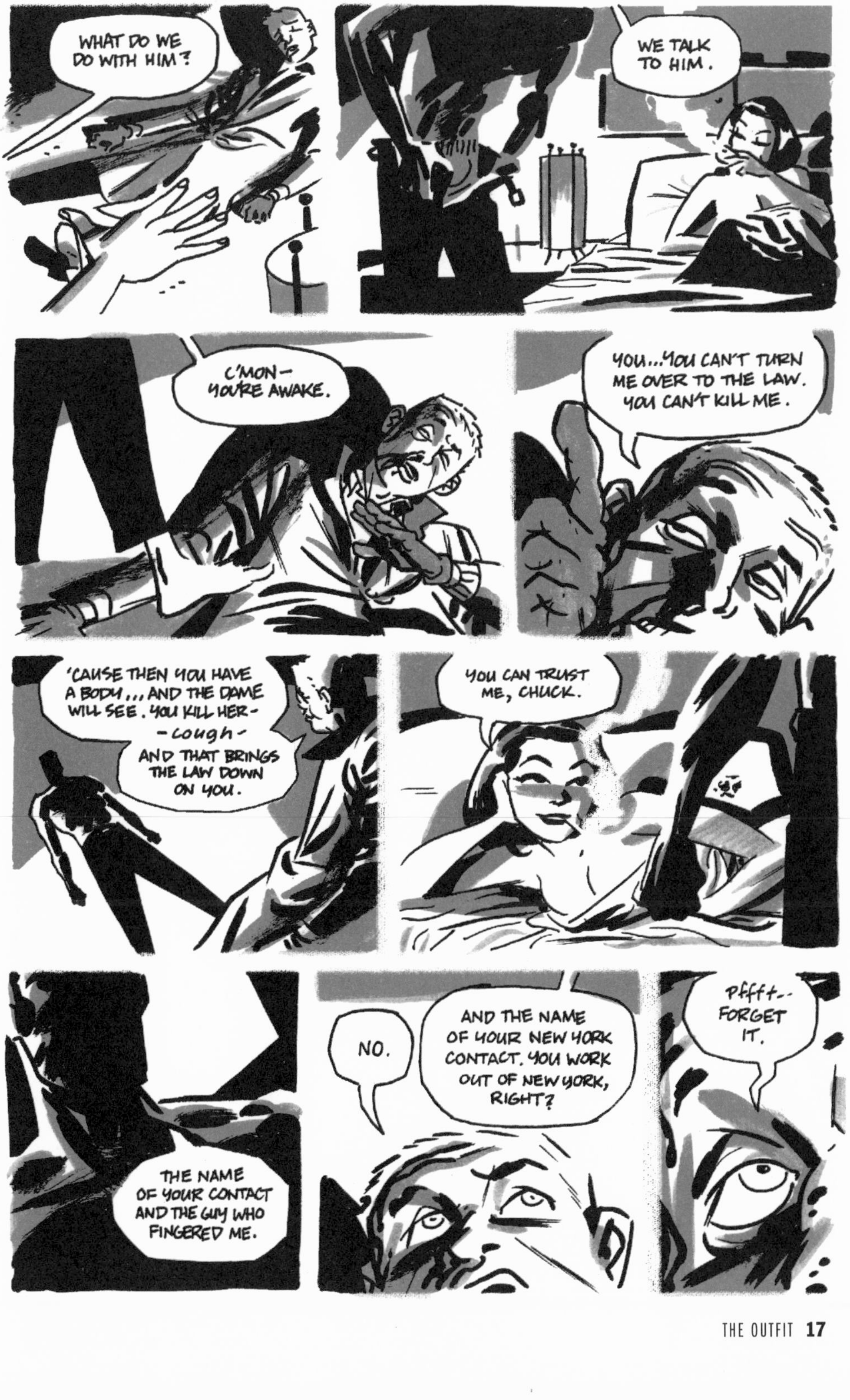
WHAT DO WE DO WITH HIM?
WE TALK TO HIM.
C'MON— YOU'RE AWAKE.
YOU...YOU CAN'T TURN ME OVER TO THE LAW. YOU CAN'T KILL ME.
'CAUSE THEN YOU HAVE A BODY... AND THE DAME WILL SEE. YOU KILL HER- -cough- AND THAT BRINGS THE LAW DOWN ON YOU.
YOU CAN TRUST ME, CHUCK.
THE NAME OF YOUR CONTACT AND THE GUY WHO FINGERED ME.
AND THE NAME OF YOUR NEW YORK CONTACT. YOU WORK OUT OF NEW YORK, RIGHT?
NO.
Pffft.. FORGET IT.

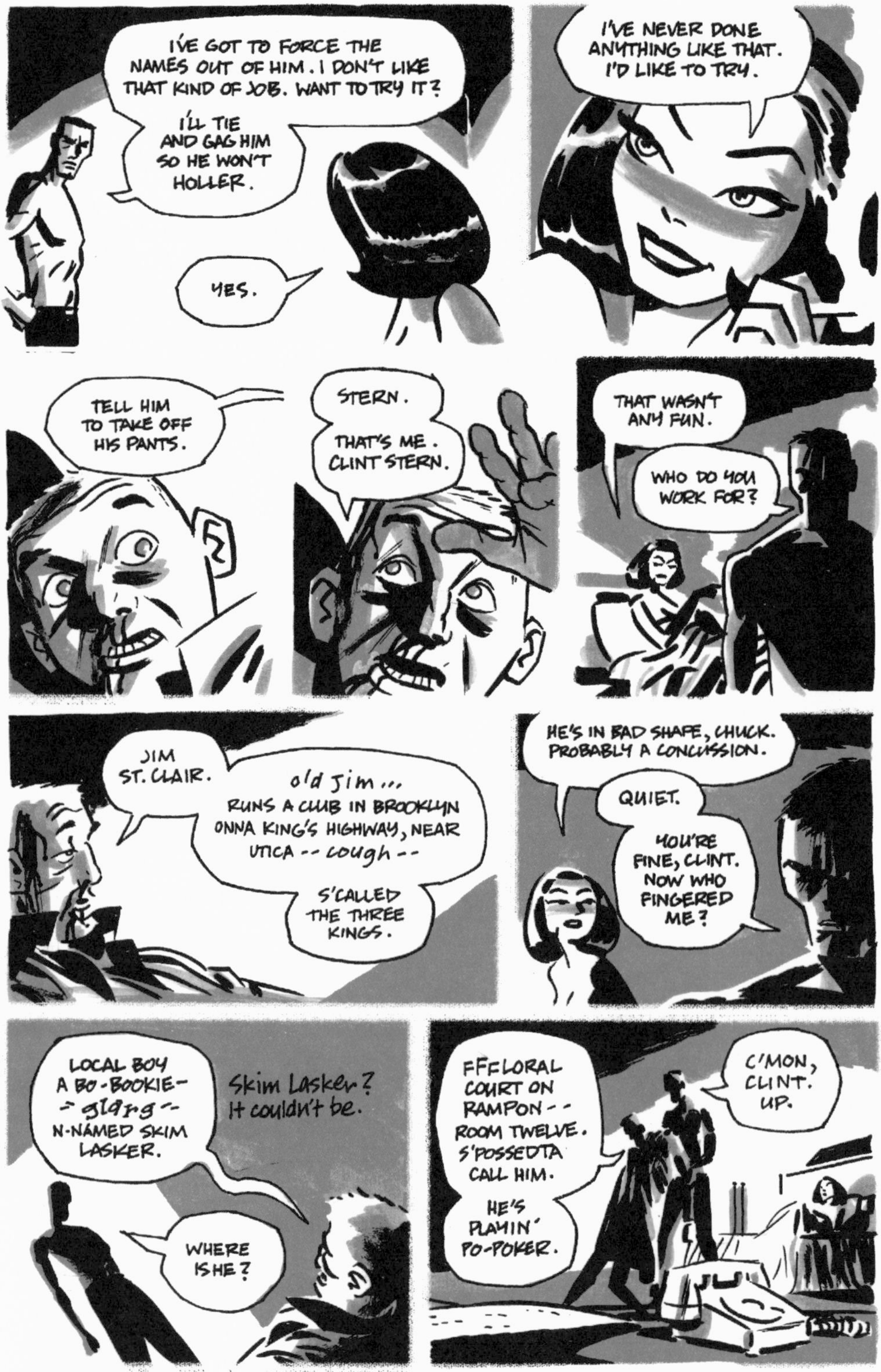

I'VE GOT TO FORCE THE NAMES OUT OF HIM. I DON'T LIKE THAT KIND OF JOB. WANT TO TRY IT?
I'LL TIE AND GAG HIM SO HE WON'T HOLLER.
YES.
I'VE NEVER DONE ANYTHING LIKE THAT. I'D LIKE TO TRY.
TELL HIM TO TAKE OFF HIS PANTS.
STERN.
THAT'S ME. CLINT STERN.
THAT WASN'T ANY FUN.
WHO DO YOU WORK FOR?
JIM ST. CLAIR.
old Jim... RUNS A CLUB IN BROOKLYN ONNA KING'S HIGHWAY, NEAR UTICA -- cough --
S'CALLED THE THREE KINGS.
HE'S IN BAD SHAPE, CHUCK. PROBABLY A CONCUSSION.
QUIET.
YOU'RE FINE, CLINT. NOW WHO FINGERED ME?
LOCAL BOY A BO-BOOKIE- -glarg- N-NAMED SKIM LASKER.
Skim Lasker? It couldn't be.
WHERE IS HE?
FFFLORAL COURT ON RAMPON -- ROOM TWELVE. S'POSSEDTA CALL HIM.
HE'S PLAYIN' PO-POKER.
C'MON, CLINT. UP.

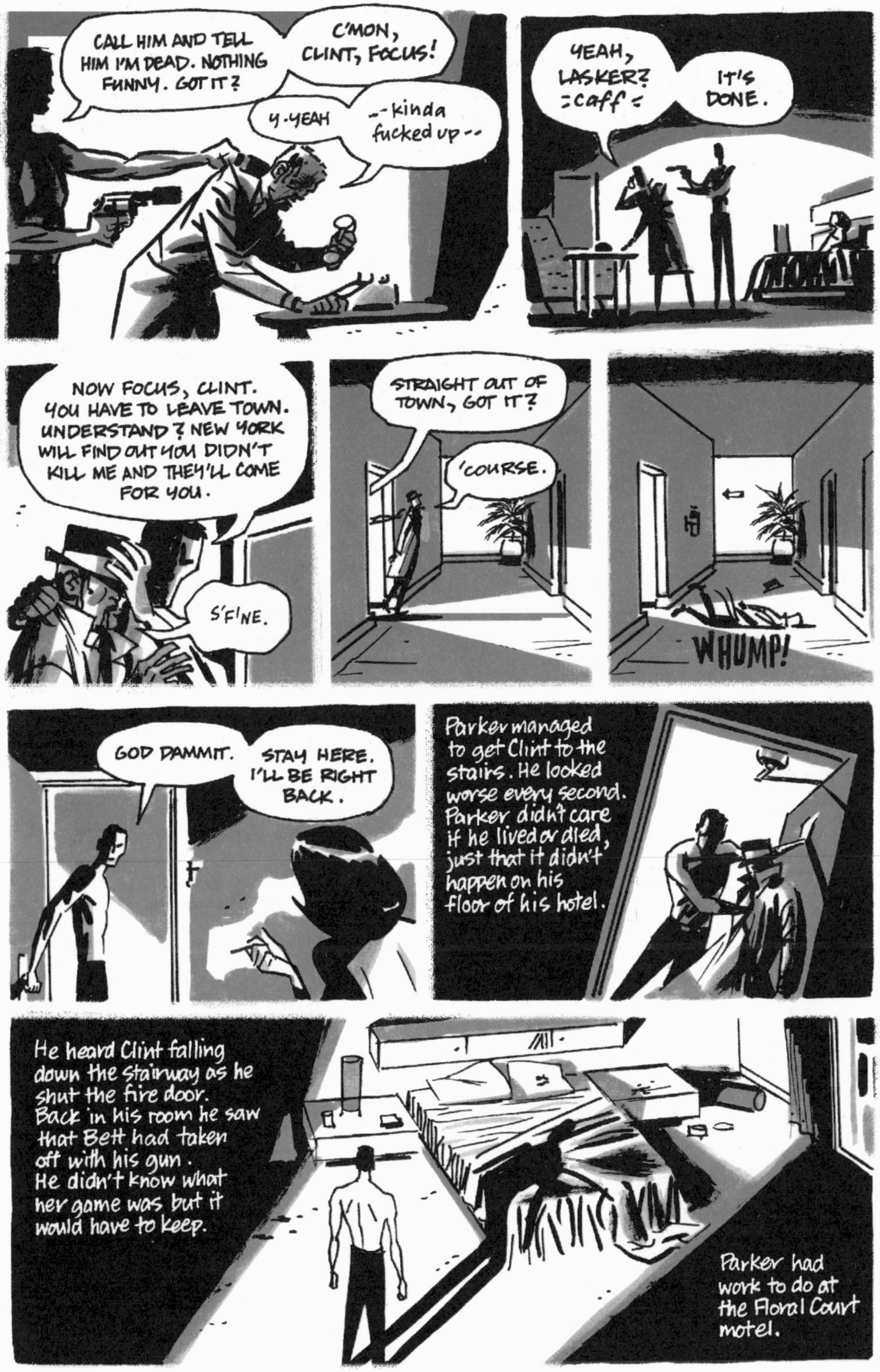

CALL HIM AND TELL HIM I'M DEAD. NOTHING FUNNY. GOT IT?
C'MON, CLINT, FOCUS!
Y-YEAH
--kinda fucked up--
YEAH, LASKER? =caff=
IT'S DONE.
NOW FOCUS, CLINT. YOU HAVE TO LEAVE TOWN. UNDERSTAND? NEW YORK WILL FIND OUT YOU DIDN'T KILL ME AND THEY'LL COME FOR YOU.
S'FINE.
STRAIGHT OUT OF TOWN, GOT IT?
'COURSE.
WHUMP!
GOD DAMMIT.
STAY HERE. I'LL BE RIGHT BACK.
Parker managed to get Clint to the stairs. He looked worse every second. Parker didn't care if he lived or died, just that it didn't happen on his floor of his hotel.
He heard Clint falling down the stairway as he shut the fire door. Back in his room he saw that Bett had taken off with his gun. He didn't know what her game was but it would have to keep.
Parker had work to do at the Floral Court motel.

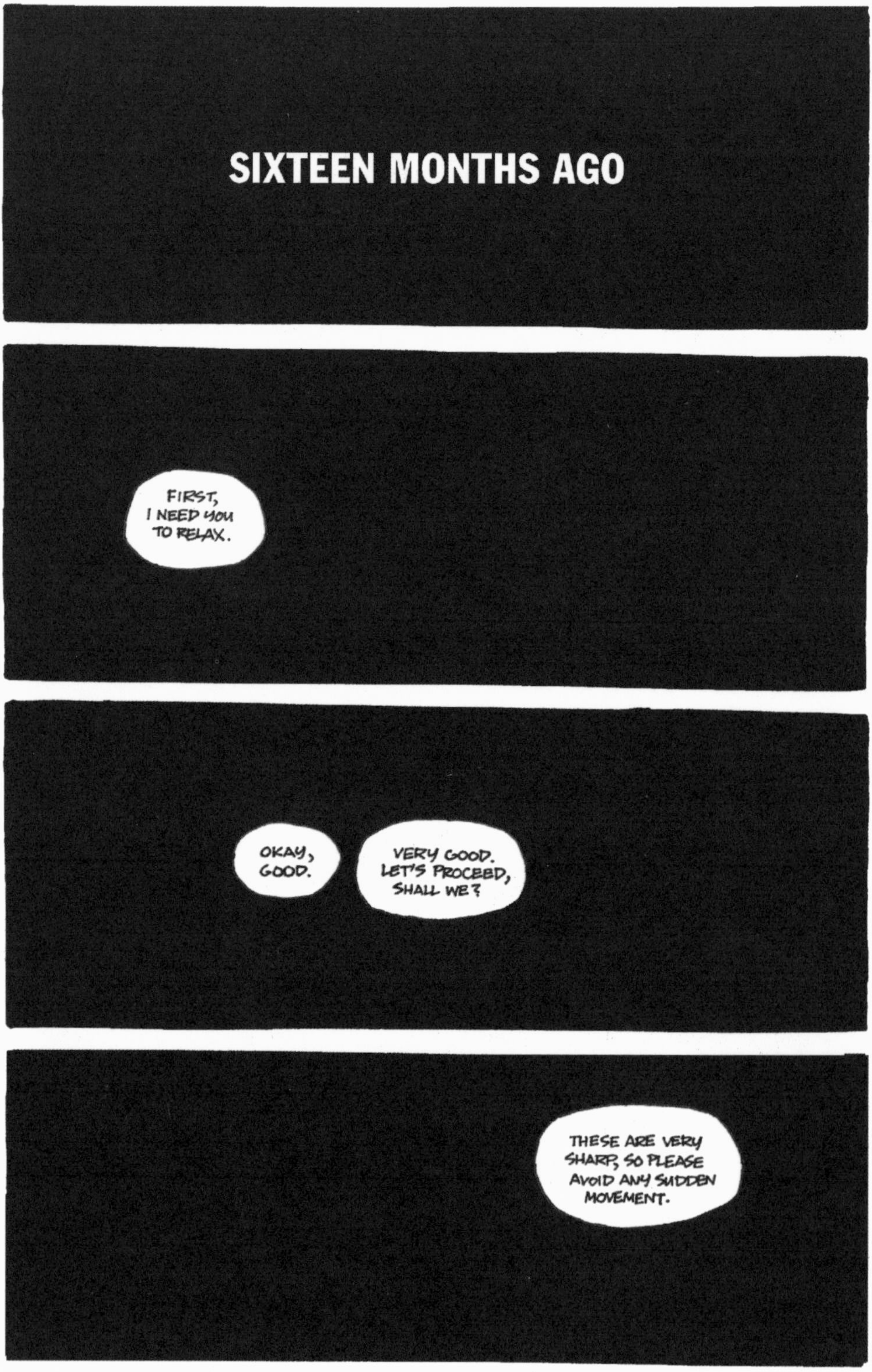
SIXTEEN MONTHS AGO
FIRST, I NEED YOU TO RELAX.
OKAY, GOOD.
VERY GOOD. LET'S PROCEED, SHALL WE?
THESE ARE VERY SHARP, SO PLEASE AVOID ANY SUDDEN MOVEMENT.

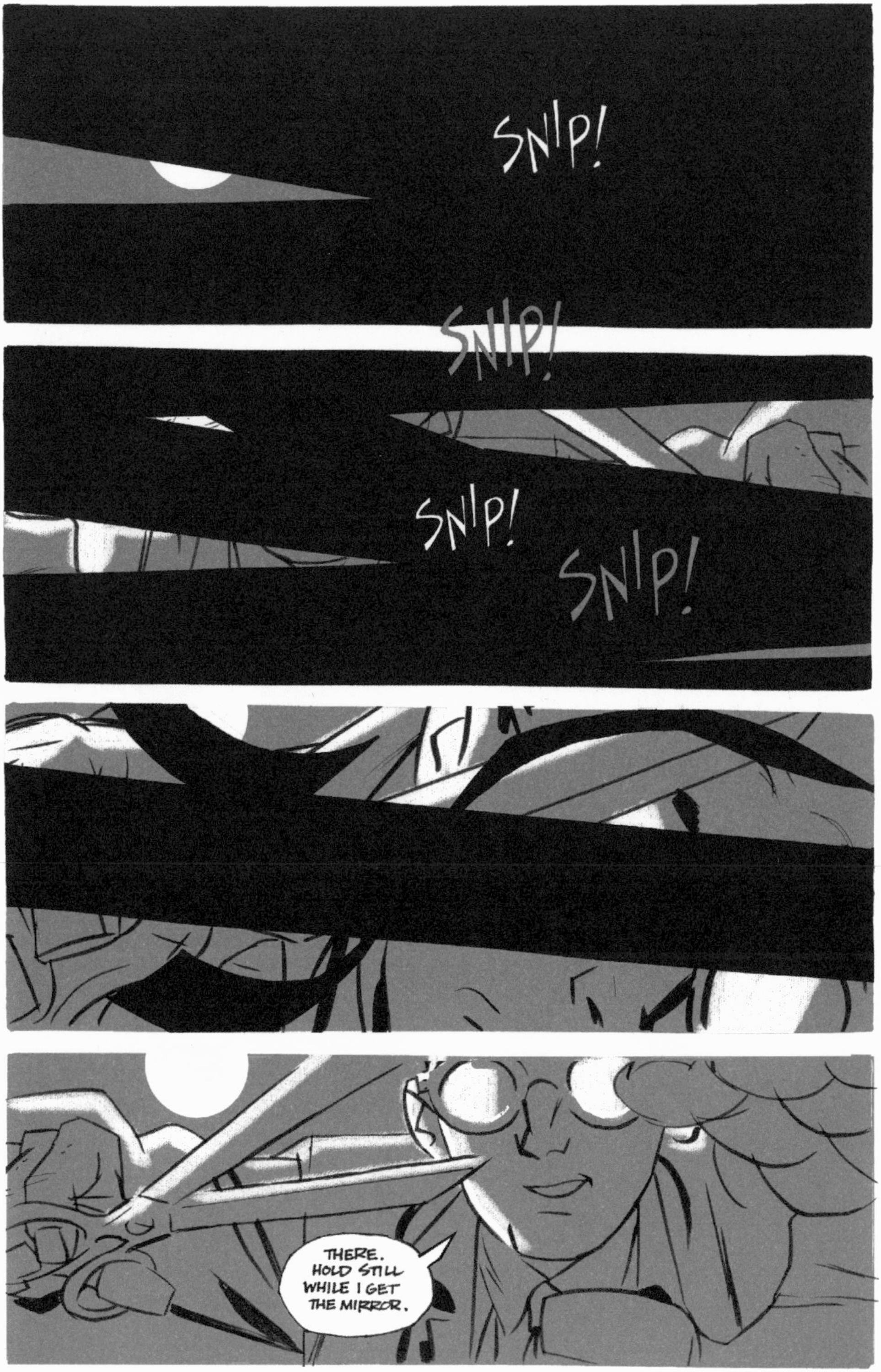
SNIP!
SNIP!
SNIP!
SNIP!
THERE. HOLD STILL WHILE I GET THE MIRROR.

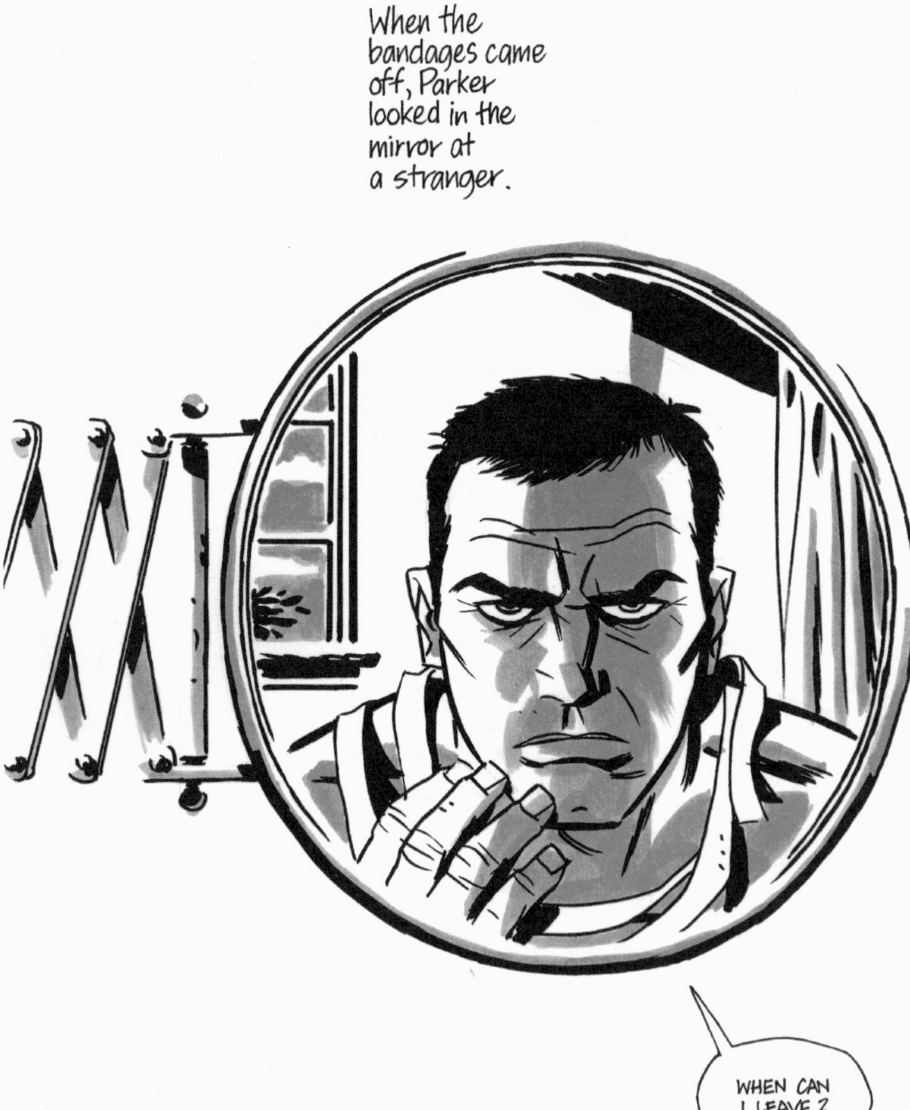
When the bandages came off, Parker looked in the mirror at a stranger.
WHEN CAN I LEAVE?

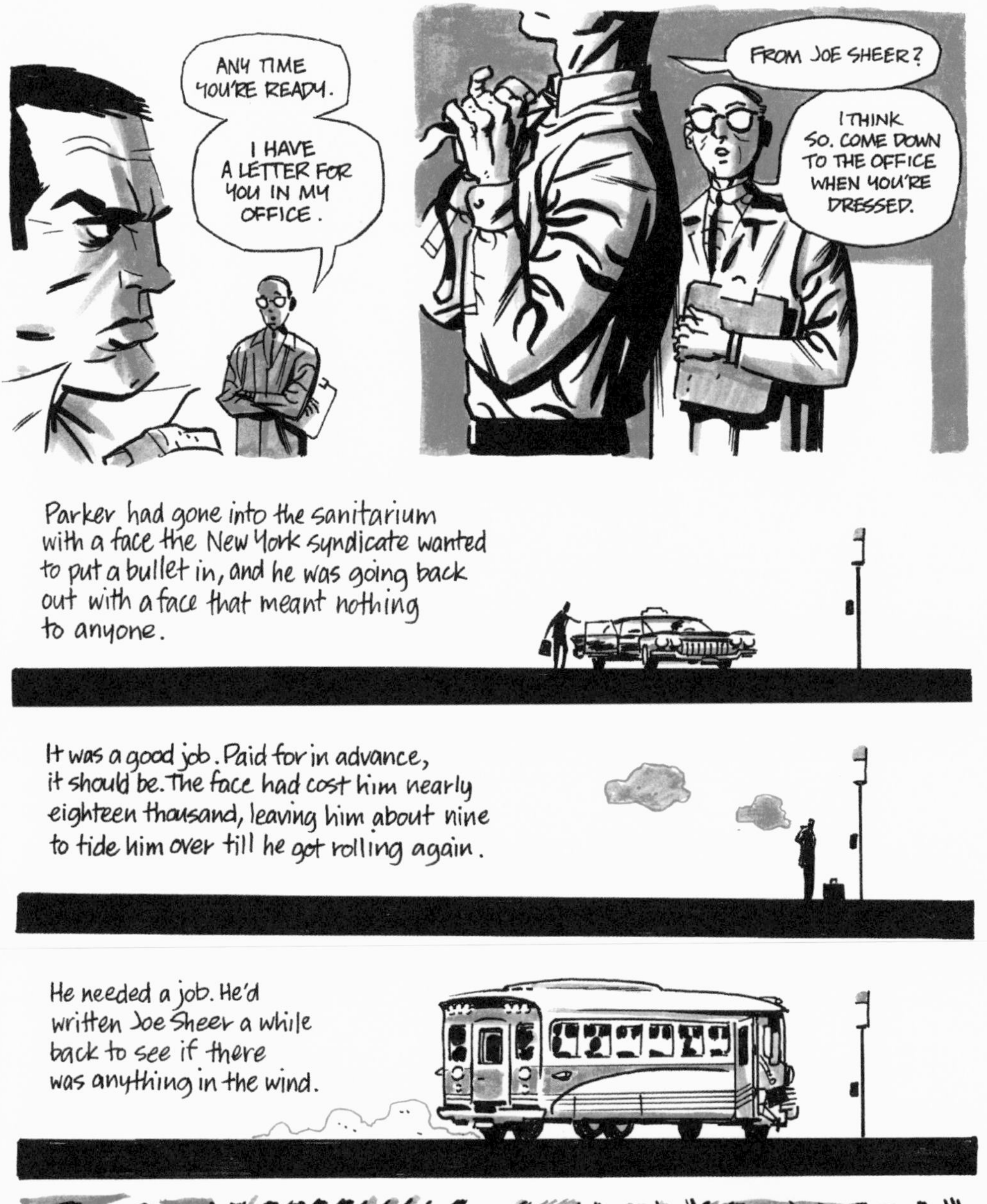
ANY TIME YOU'RE READY.
I HAVE A LETTER FOR YOU IN MY OFFICE.
FROM JOE SHEER?
I THINK SO. COME DOWN TO THE OFFICE WHEN YOU'RE DRESSED.
Parker had gone into the sanitarium with a face the New York syndicate wanted to put a bullet in, and he was going back out with a face that meant nothing to anyone.
It was a good job. Paid for in advance, it should be. The face had cost him nearly eighteen thousand, leaving him about nine to tide him over till he got rolling again.
He needed a job. He'd written Joe Sheer a while back to see if there was anything in the wind.
STEP

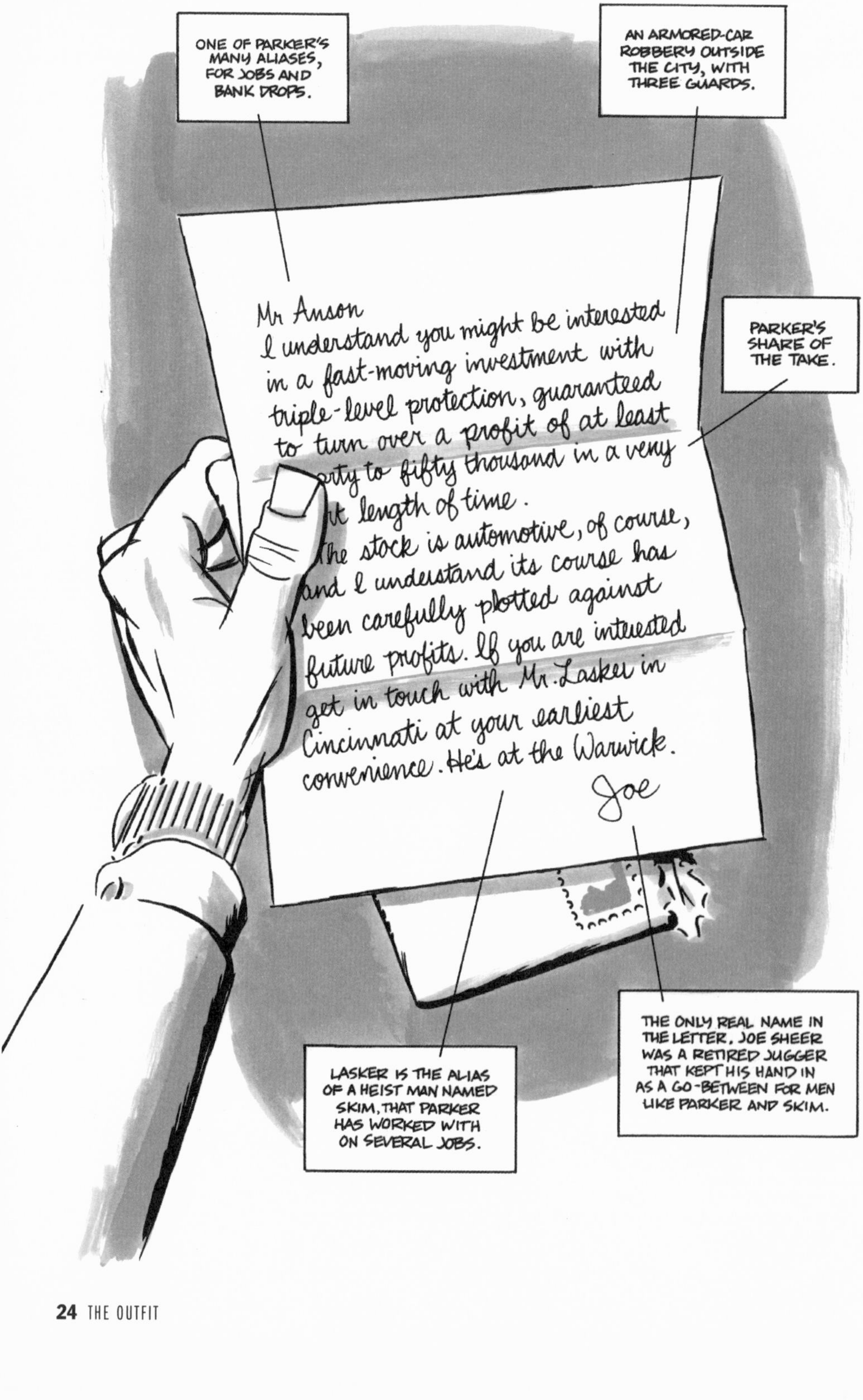

ONE OF PARKER'S MANY ALIASES, FOR JOBS AND BANK DROPS.
AN ARMORED-CAR ROBBERY OUTSIDE THE CITY, WITH THREE GUARDS.
Mr Anson
I understand you might be interested
in a fast-moving investment with
triple-level protection, guaranteed
to turn over a profit of at least
orty to fifty thousand in a very
rt length of time.
he stock is automotive, of course,
and I understand its course has
been carefully plotted against
future profits. If you are interested
get in touch with Mr. Lasker in
Cincinnati at your earliest
convenience. He's at the Warwick.
Joe
PARKER'S SHARE OF THE TAKE.
LASKER IS THE ALIAS OF A HEIST MAN NAMED SKIM, THAT PARKER HAS WORKED WITH ON SEVERAL JOBS.
THE ONLY REAL NAME IN THE LETTER. JOE SHEER WAS A RETIRED JUGGER THAT KEPT HIS HAND IN AS A GO-BETWEEN FOR MEN LIKE PARKER AND SKIM.

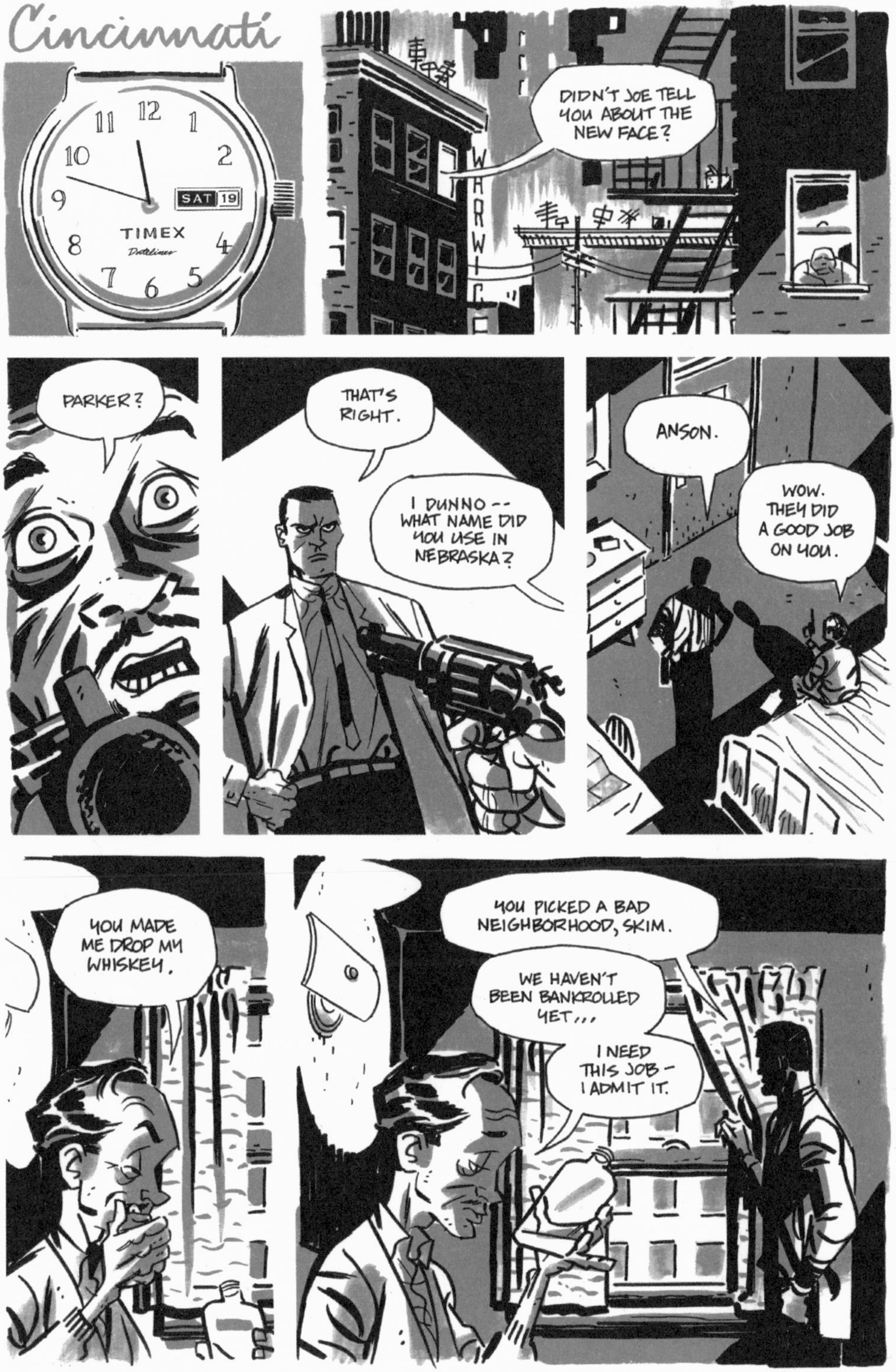
Cincinnati
11 12 1
10 2
9 3
8 4
7 6 5
SAT 19
TIMEX
Datelines
WARWICK
DIDN'T JOE TELL YOU ABOUT THE NEW FACE?
PARKER?
THAT'S RIGHT.
I DUNNO -- WHAT NAME DID YOU USE IN NEBRASKA?
ANSON.
WOW. THEY DID A GOOD JOB ON YOU.
YOU MADE ME DROP MY WHISKEY.
YOU PICKED A BAD NEIGHBORHOOD, SKIM.
WE HAVEN'T BEEN BANKROLLED YET...
I NEED THIS JOB - I ADMIT IT.

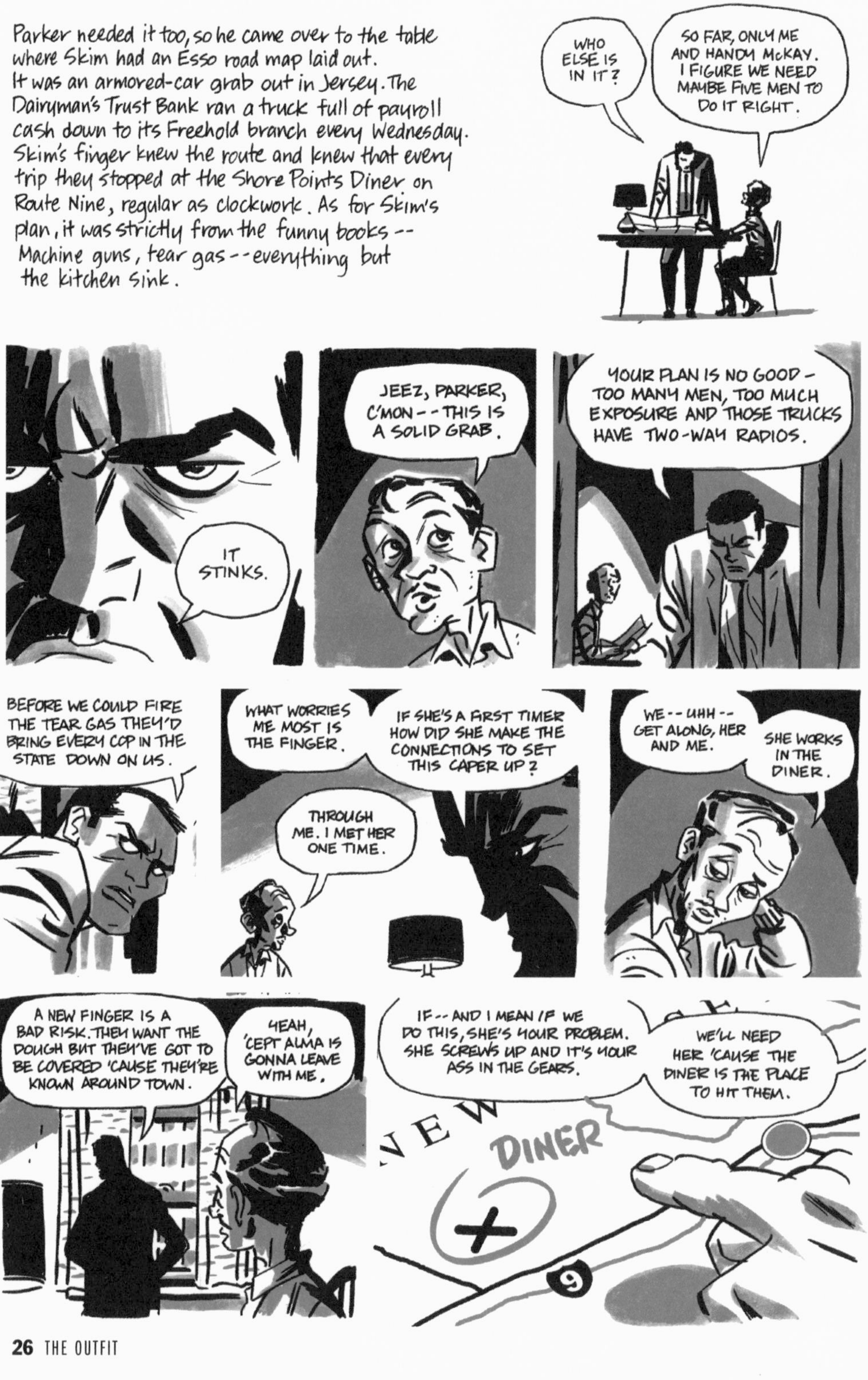
Parker needed it too, so he came over to the table where Skim had an Esso road map laid out. It was an armored-car grab out in Jersey. The Dairyman's Trust Bank ran a truck full of payroll cash down to its Freehold branch every Wednesday. Skim's finger knew the route and knew that every trip they stopped at the Shore Points Diner on Route Nine, regular as clockwork. As for Skim's plan, it was strictly from the funny books -- Machine guns, tear gas -- everything but the kitchen sink.
WHO ELSE IS IN IT?
SO FAR, ONLY ME AND HANDY McKAY. I FIGURE WE NEED MAYBE FIVE MEN TO DO IT RIGHT.
IT STINKS.
JEEZ, PARKER, C'MON -- THIS IS A SOLID GRAB.
YOUR PLAN IS NO GOOD - TOO MANY MEN, TOO MUCH EXPOSURE AND THOSE TRUCKS HAVE TWO-WAY RADIOS.
BEFORE WE COULD FIRE THE TEAR GAS THEY'D BRING EVERY COP IN THE STATE DOWN ON US.
WHAT WORRIES ME MOST IS THE FINGER.
IF SHE'S A FIRST TIMER HOW DID SHE MAKE THE CONNECTIONS TO SET THIS CAPER UP?
THROUGH ME. I MET HER ONE TIME.
WE -- UHH -- GET ALONG, HER AND ME.
SHE WORKS IN THE DINER.
A NEW FINGER IS A BAD RISK. THEY WANT THE DOUGH BUT THEY'VE GOT TO BE COVERED 'CAUSE THEY'RE KNOWN AROUND TOWN.
YEAH, 'CEPT ALMA IS GONNA LEAVE WITH ME.
IF -- AND I MEAN IF WE DO THIS, SHE'S YOUR PROBLEM. SHE SCREWS UP AND IT'S YOUR ASS IN THE GEARS.
WE'LL NEED HER 'CAUSE THE DINER IS THE PLACE TO HIT THEM.
NEW
DINER
9

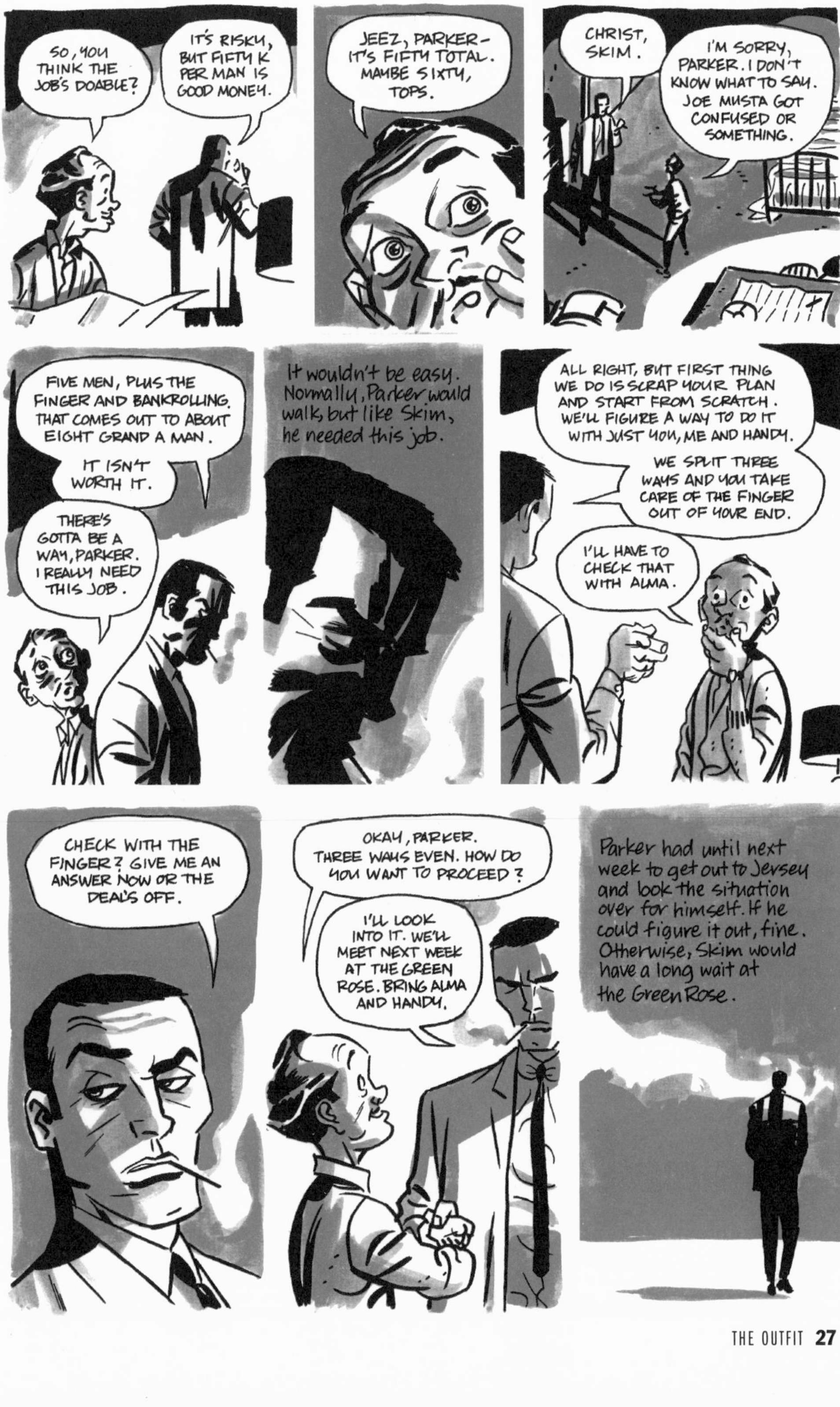
SO, YOU THINK THE JOB'S DOABLE?
IT'S RISKY, BUT FIFTY K PER MAN IS GOOD MONEY.
JEEZ, PARKER- IT'S FIFTY TOTAL. MAYBE SIXTY, TOPS.
CHRIST, SKIM.
I'M SORRY, PARKER. I DON'T KNOW WHAT TO SAY. JOE MUSTA GOT CONFUSED OR SOMETHING.
FIVE MEN, PLUS THE FINGER AND BANKROLLING. THAT COMES OUT TO ABOUT EIGHT GRAND A MAN.
IT ISN'T WORTH IT.
THERE'S GOTTA BE A WAY, PARKER. I REALLY NEED THIS JOB.
It wouldn't be easy. Normally, Parker would walk, but like Skim, he needed this job.
ALL RIGHT, BUT FIRST THING WE DO IS SCRAP YOUR PLAN AND START FROM SCRATCH. WE'LL FIGURE A WAY TO DO IT WITH JUST YOU, ME AND HANDY.
WE SPLIT THREE WAYS AND YOU TAKE CARE OF THE FINGER OUT OF YOUR END.
I'LL HAVE TO CHECK THAT WITH ALMA.
CHECK WITH THE FINGER? GIVE ME AN ANSWER NOW OR THE DEAL'S OFF.
OKAY, PARKER. THREE WAYS EVEN. HOW DO YOU WANT TO PROCEED?
I'LL LOOK INTO IT. WE'LL MEET NEXT WEEK AT THE GREEN ROSE. BRING ALMA AND HANDY.
Parker had until next week to get out to Jersey and look the situation over for himself. If he could figure it out, fine. Otherwise, Skim would have a long wait at the Green Rose.

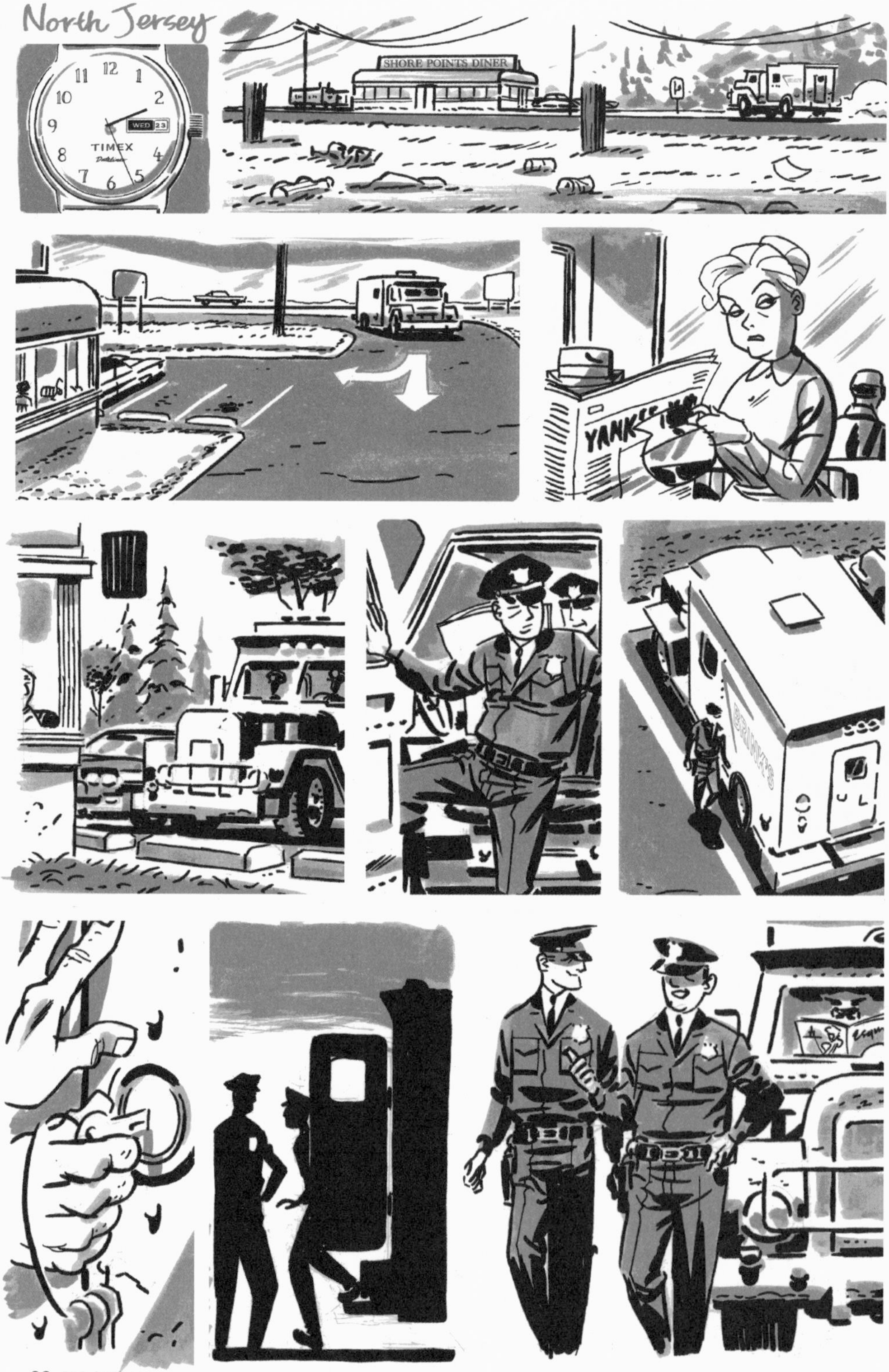
North Jersey
SHORE POINTS DINER
TIMEX
WED 23
YANK
BRINK'S

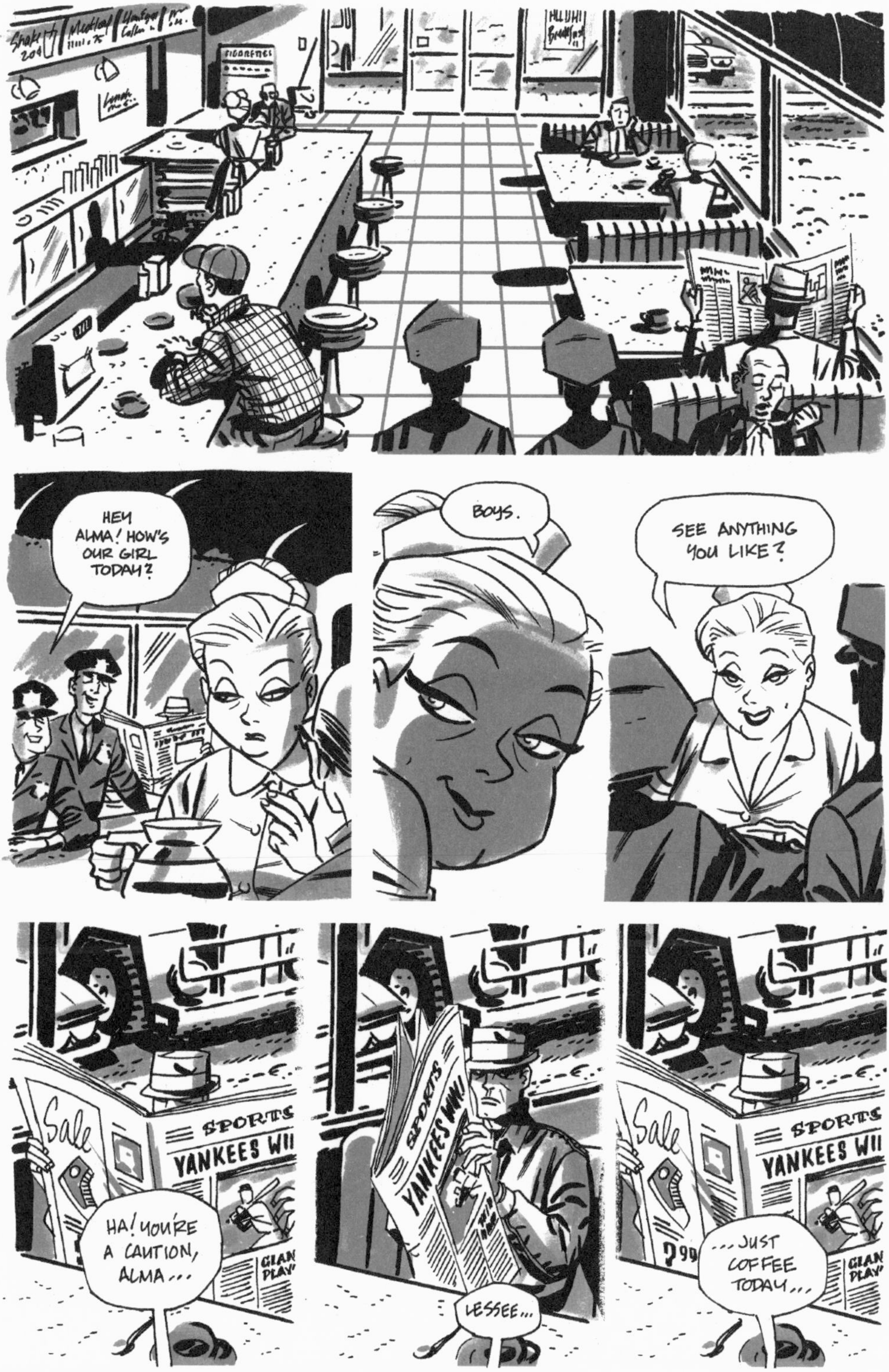
HEY ALMA! HOW'S OUR GIRL TODAY?
BOYS.
SEE ANYTHING YOU LIKE?
SPORTS
YANKEES WI
HA! YOU'RE A CAUTION, ALMA...
LESSEE...
...JUST COFFEE TODAY...

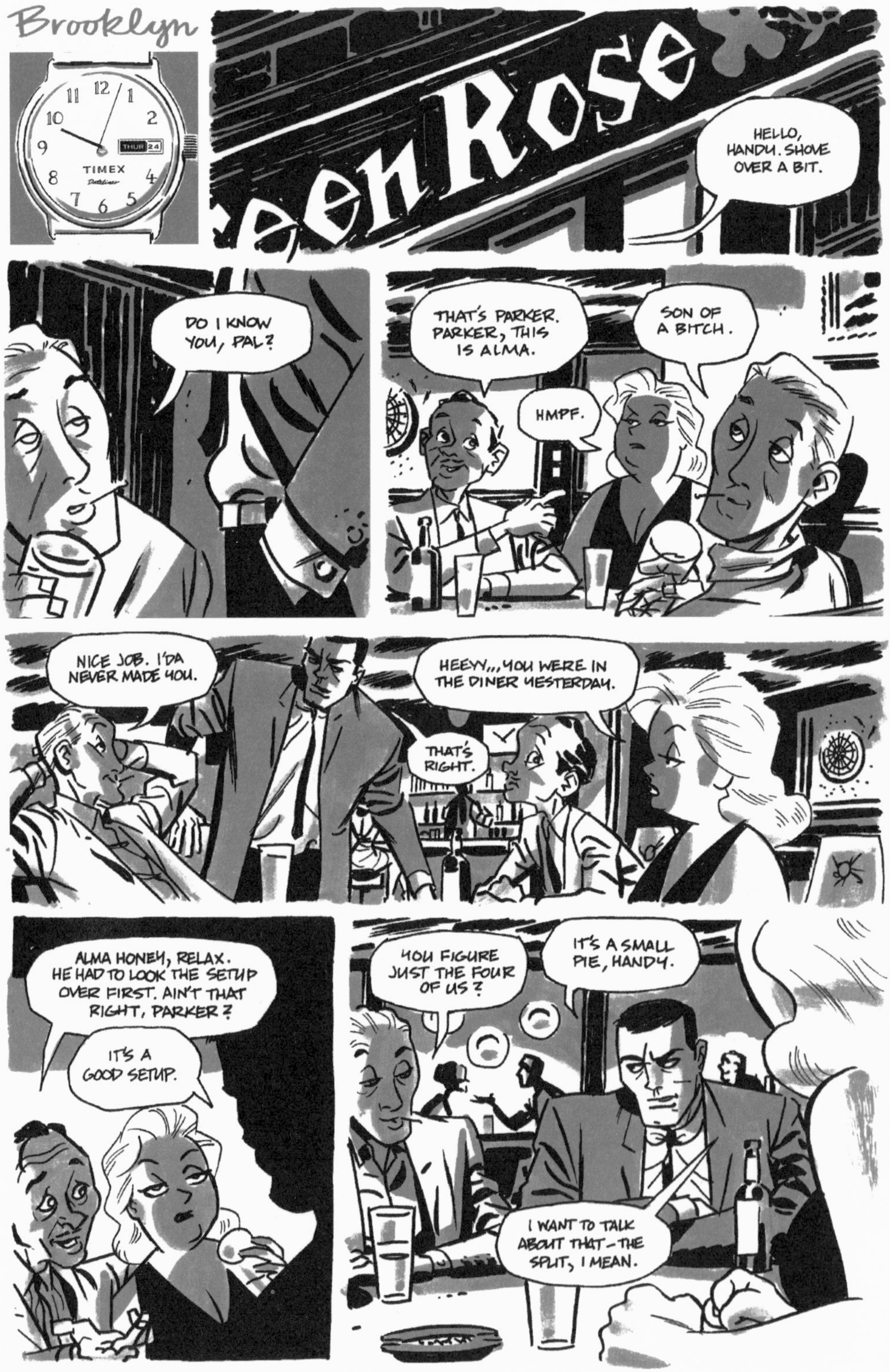
Brooklyn
TIMEX
THUR 24
een Rose
HELLO, HANDY. SHOVE OVER A BIT.
DO I KNOW YOU, PAL?
THAT'S PARKER. PARKER, THIS IS ALMA.
SON OF A BITCH.
HMPF.
NICE JOB. I'DA NEVER MADE YOU.
HEEYY,,, YOU WERE IN THE DINER YESTERDAY.
THAT'S RIGHT.
ALMA HONEY, RELAX. HE HAD TO LOOK THE SETUP OVER FIRST. AIN'T THAT RIGHT, PARKER?
IT'S A GOOD SETUP.
YOU FIGURE JUST THE FOUR OF US?
IT'S A SMALL PIE, HANDY.
I WANT TO TALK ABOUT THAT—THE SPLIT, I MEAN.

OKAY, SLOW DOWN. WHO'S RUNNING THIS SHOW? IT AIN'T ME, I'M NOT THE TYPE.

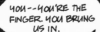

YOU -- YOU'RE THE FINGER. YOU BRING US IN.

YOU RUNNING IT, SKIM?

I NEVER WORKED AN ARMORED CAR BEFORE.

Parker laid out the plan.

1/ Box armored car into its parking spot with two trucks.
2/ When driver opens back of truck to let out guard 2, get drop on them.
3/ Sap guard 2. Use fake uniform and driver to lure guard 3 out of cab.
4/ Sap both and tie up all three, locking them in the back of one of the trucks.
5/ Block back with getaway car and transfer cash to trunk.

NO GUNPLAY, NO ONE GETS HURT. WE SHOULD HAVE MORE THAN ENOUGH TIME TO GET CLEAR BEFORE ANYONE FINDS THE GUARDS.

WE'LL USE ALMA'S CAR FOR THE GETAWAY.

THAT'S THE PART I DON'T LIKE. I THINK WE SHOULD LEAVE IN SEPARATE CARS TO THROW OFF THE LAW.

NOW, ALMA --

IT'S OKAY, SKIM.

THAT'S GOOD, ALMA. HANDY AND I CAN USE ONE OF THE TRUCKS. WE'LL NEED TO FIND A SAFE PLACE FOR THE SPLIT.

I'M HEADING TO BALTIMORE TOMORROW TO ARRANGE OUR BANKROLL.

SKIM, YOU SET UP THE GUNS. TWO PISTOLS, ONE SHOTGUN.

ALMA, SEE IF YOU CAN FIND A GOOD SPOT FOR THE SPLIT.

YOU GOT IT, PARKER.

I SHOULD BE BACK SUNDAY. YOU NEED A LIFT, HANDY?

SOUNDS GOOD.

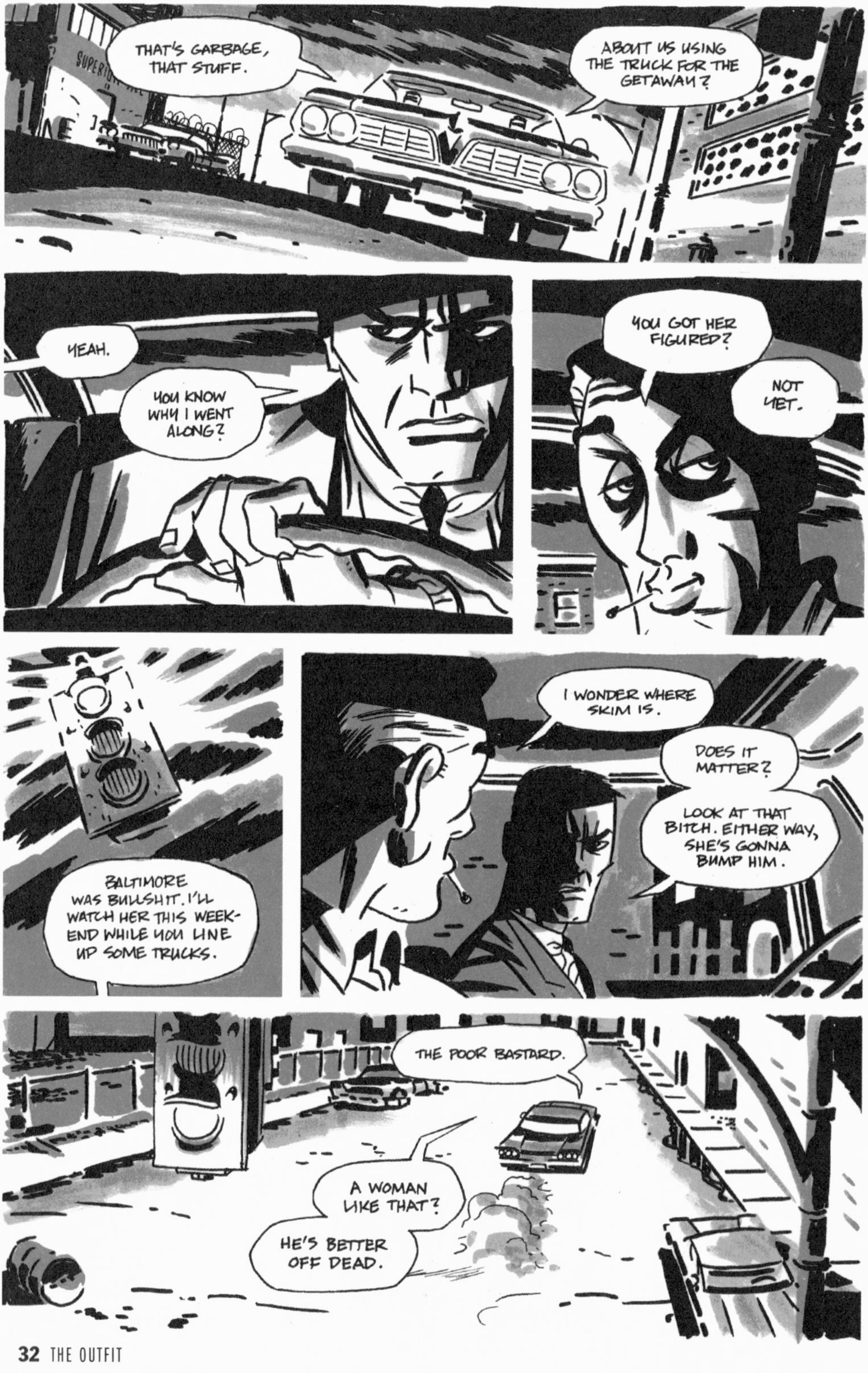

THAT'S GARBAGE, THAT STUFF.
ABOUT US USING THE TRUCK FOR THE GETAWAY?
YEAH.
YOU KNOW WHY I WENT ALONG?
YOU GOT HER FIGURED?
NOT YET.
BALTIMORE WAS BULLSHIT. I'LL WATCH HER THIS WEEK-END WHILE YOU LINE UP SOME TRUCKS.
I WONDER WHERE SKIM IS.
DOES IT MATTER?
LOOK AT THAT BITCH. EITHER WAY, SHE'S GONNA BUMP HIM.
THE POOR BASTARD.
A WOMAN LIKE THAT?
HE'S BETTER OFF DEAD.

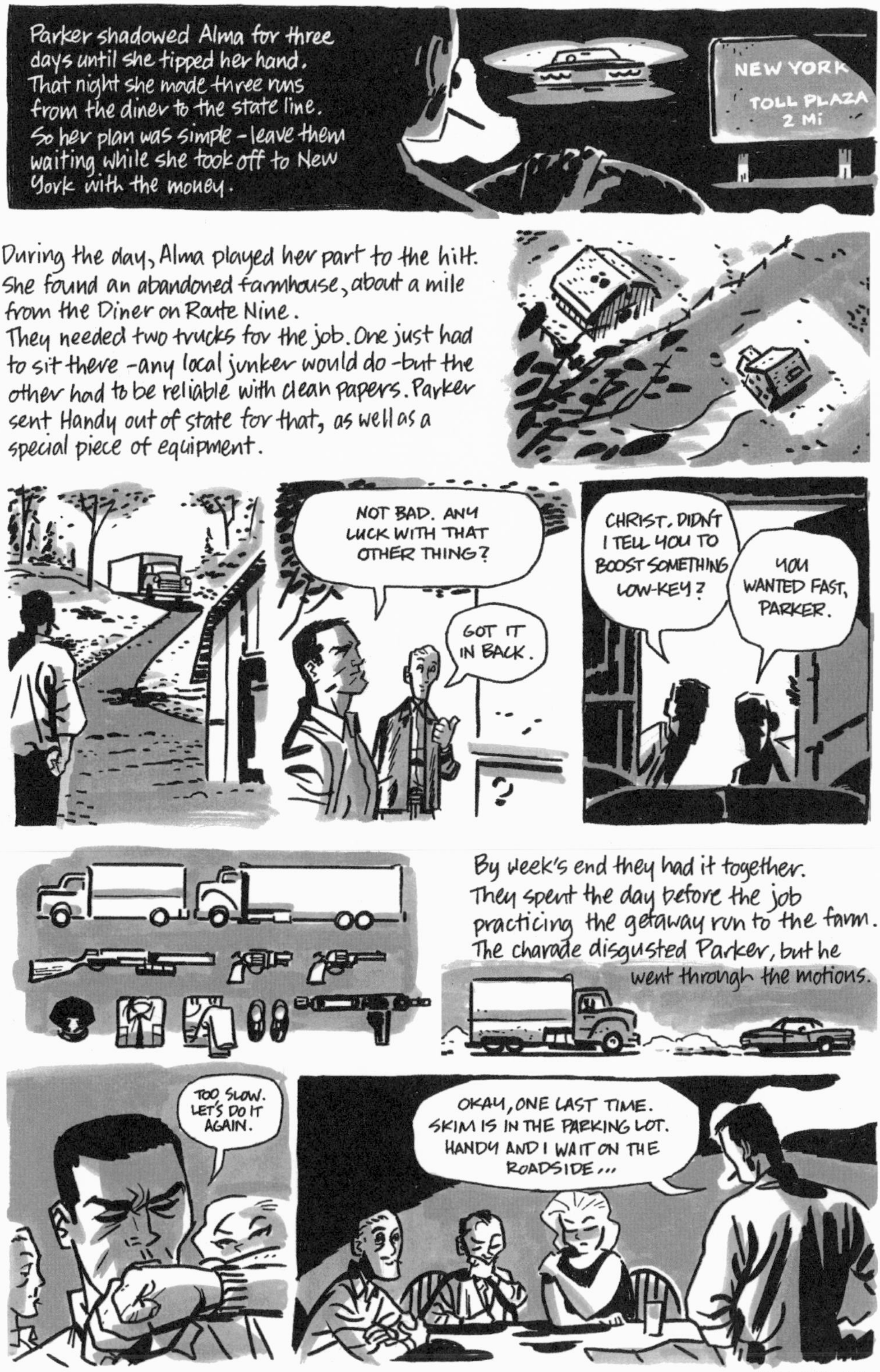
Parker shadowed Alma for three days until she tipped her hand. That night she made three runs from the diner to the state line. So her plan was simple - leave them waiting while she took off to New York with the money.
NEW YORK
TOLL PLAZA
2 Mi
During the day, Alma played her part to the hilt. She found an abandoned farmhouse, about a mile from the Diner on Route Nine. They needed two trucks for the job. One just had to sit there - any local junker would do - but the other had to be reliable with clean papers. Parker sent Handy out of state for that, as well as a special piece of equipment.
NOT BAD. ANY LUCK WITH THAT OTHER THING?
GOT IT IN BACK.
CHRIST. DIDN'T I TELL YOU TO BOOST SOMETHING LOW-KEY?
YOU WANTED FAST, PARKER.
By week's end they had it together. They spent the day before the job practicing the getaway run to the farm. The charade disgusted Parker, but he went through the motions.
TOO SLOW. LET'S DO IT AGAIN.
OKAY, ONE LAST TIME. SKIM IS IN THE PARKING LOT. HANDY AND I WAIT ON THE ROADSIDE...

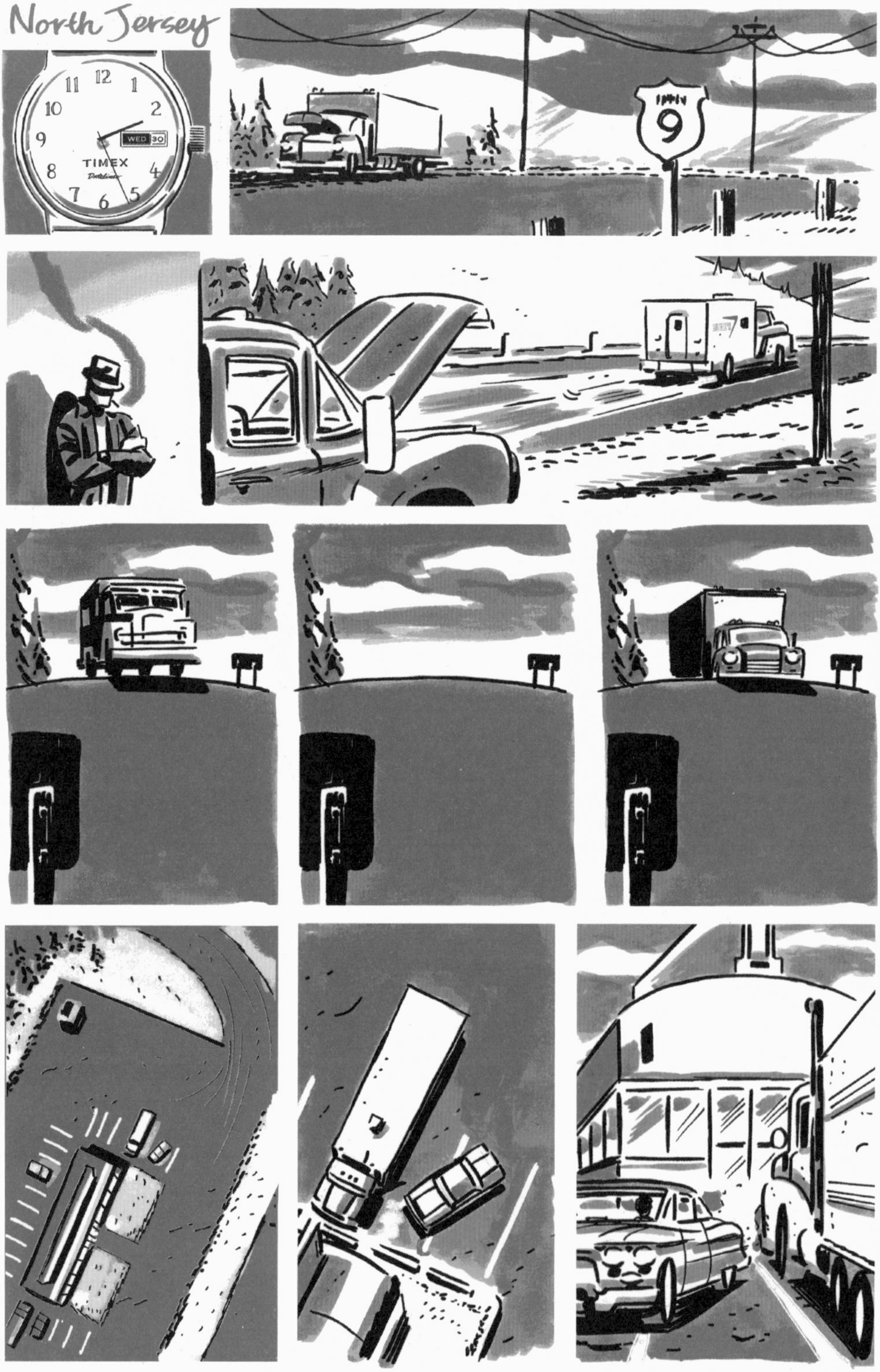
North Jersey
TIMEX
WED 30
9

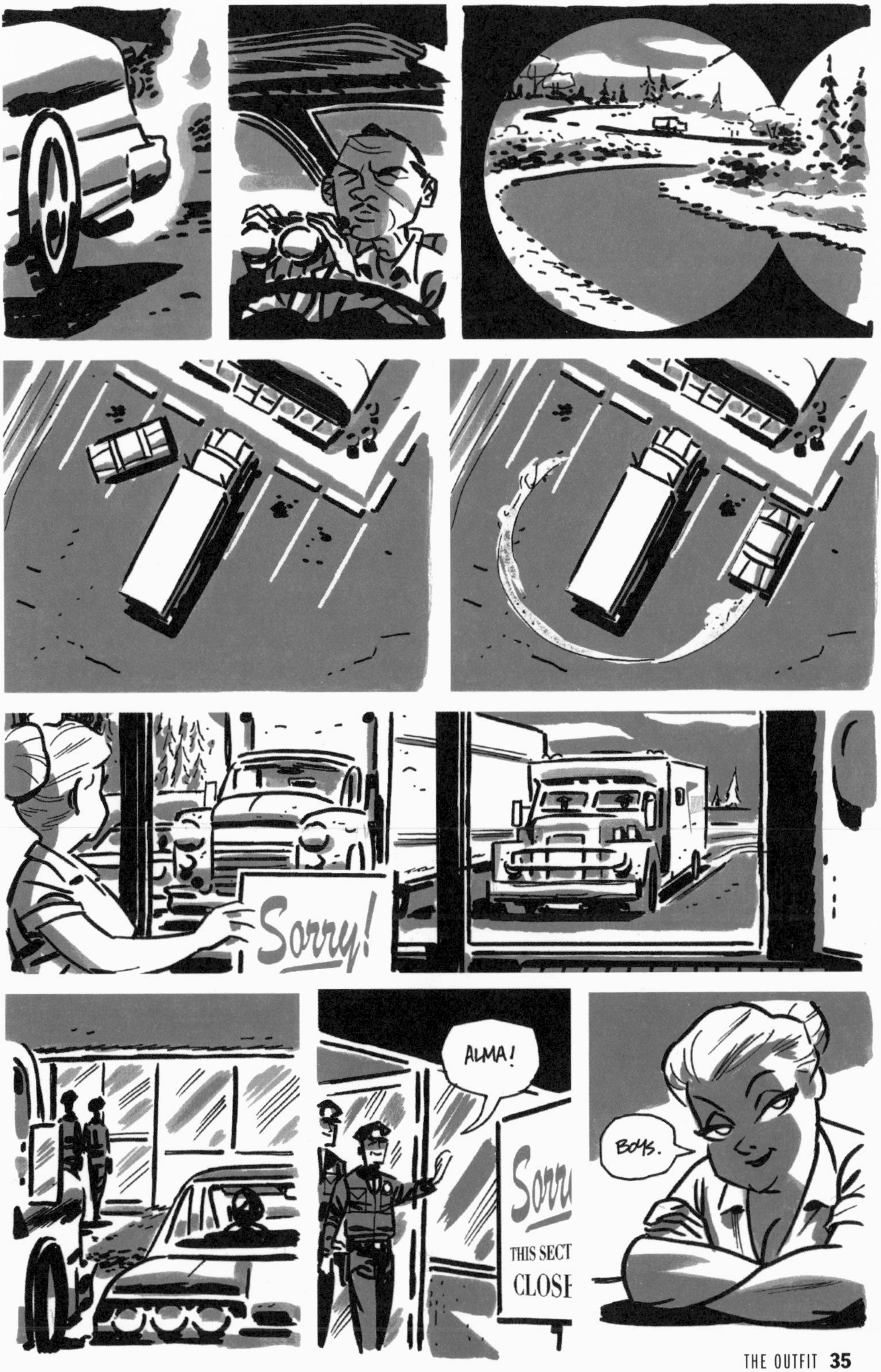
Sorry!
ALMA!
Sorry
THIS SECT
CLOSE
BOYS.

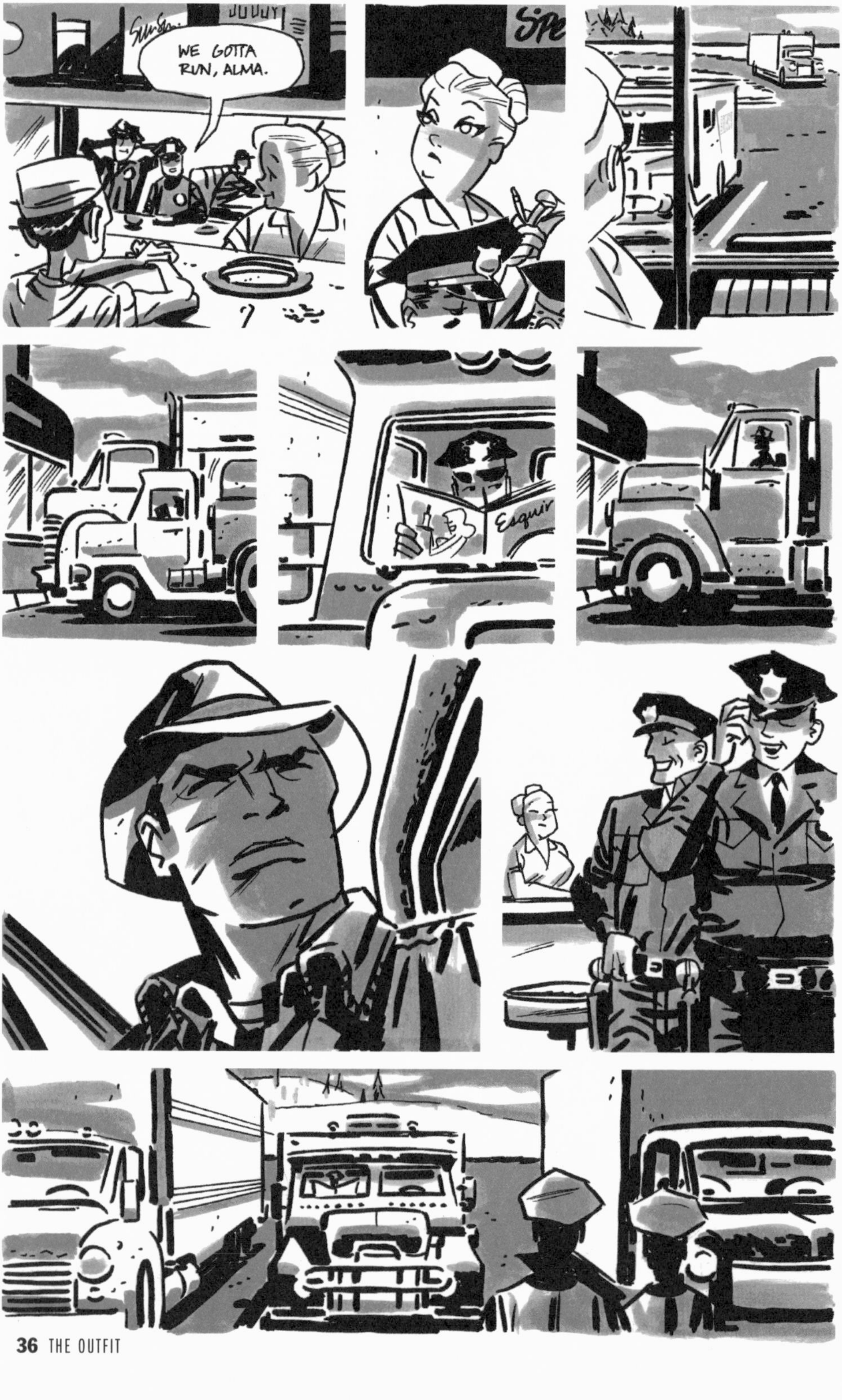
WE GOTTA RUN, ALMA.
Esquir

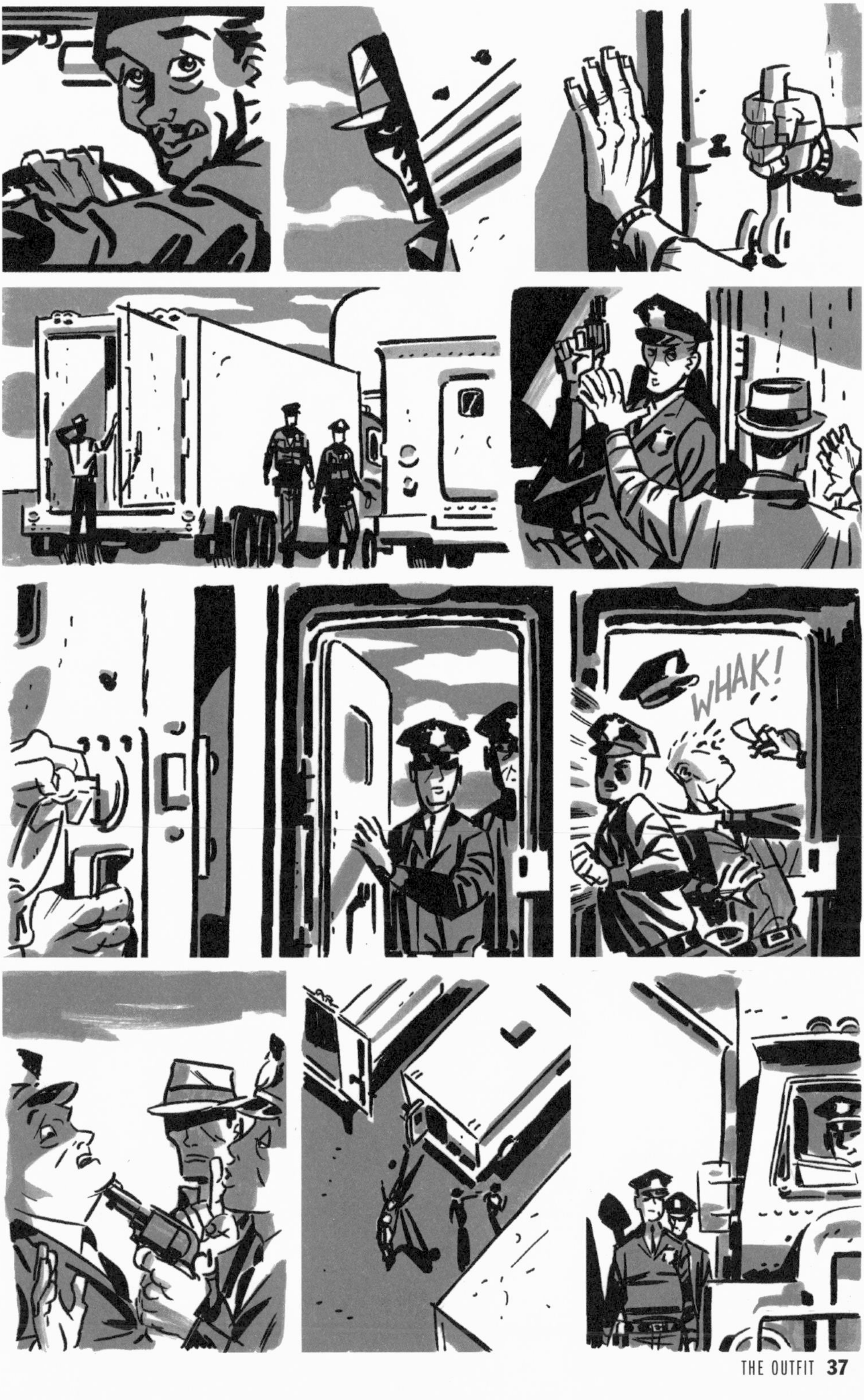
WHAK!

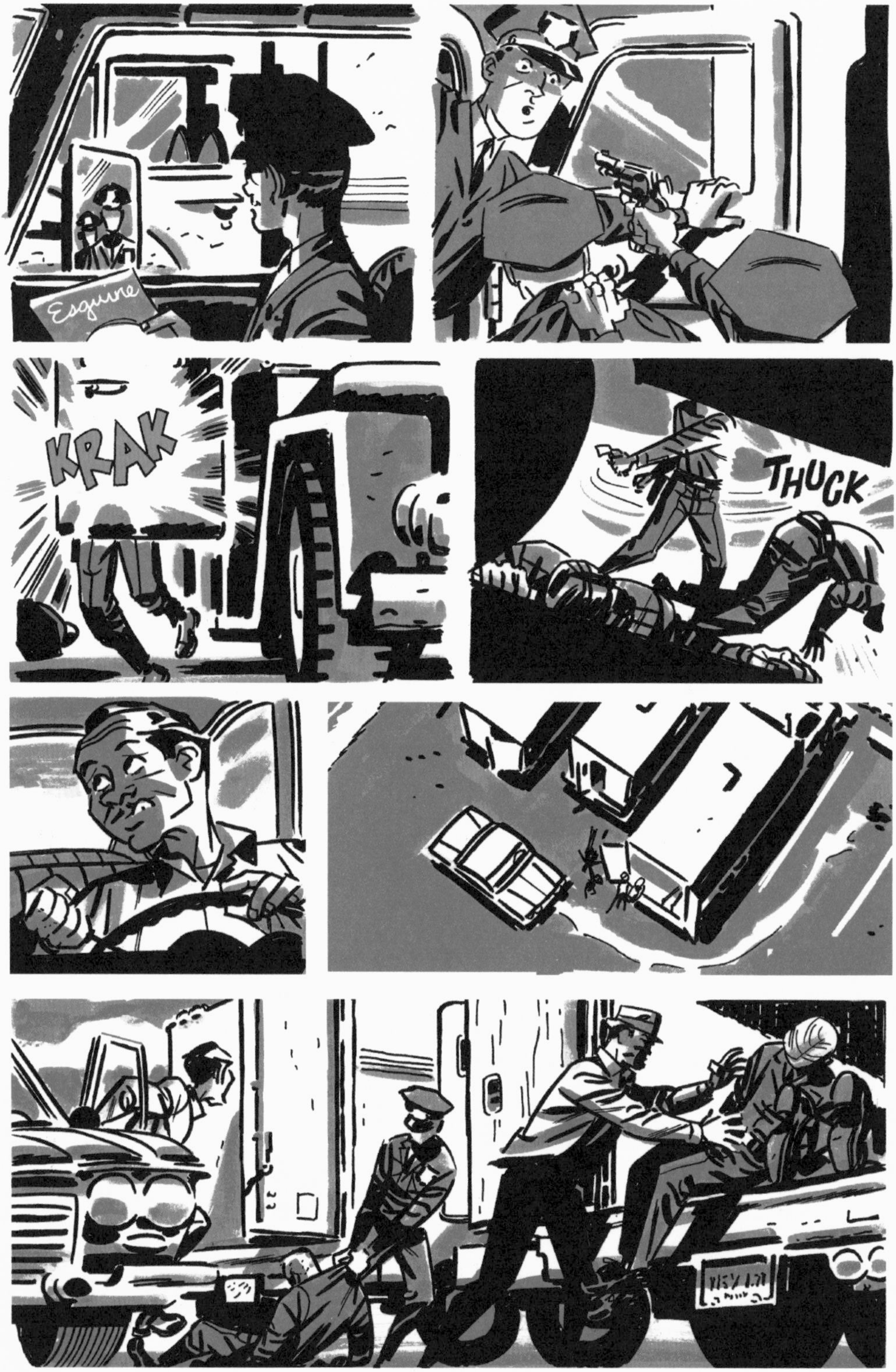
Esquire
KRAK
THUCK

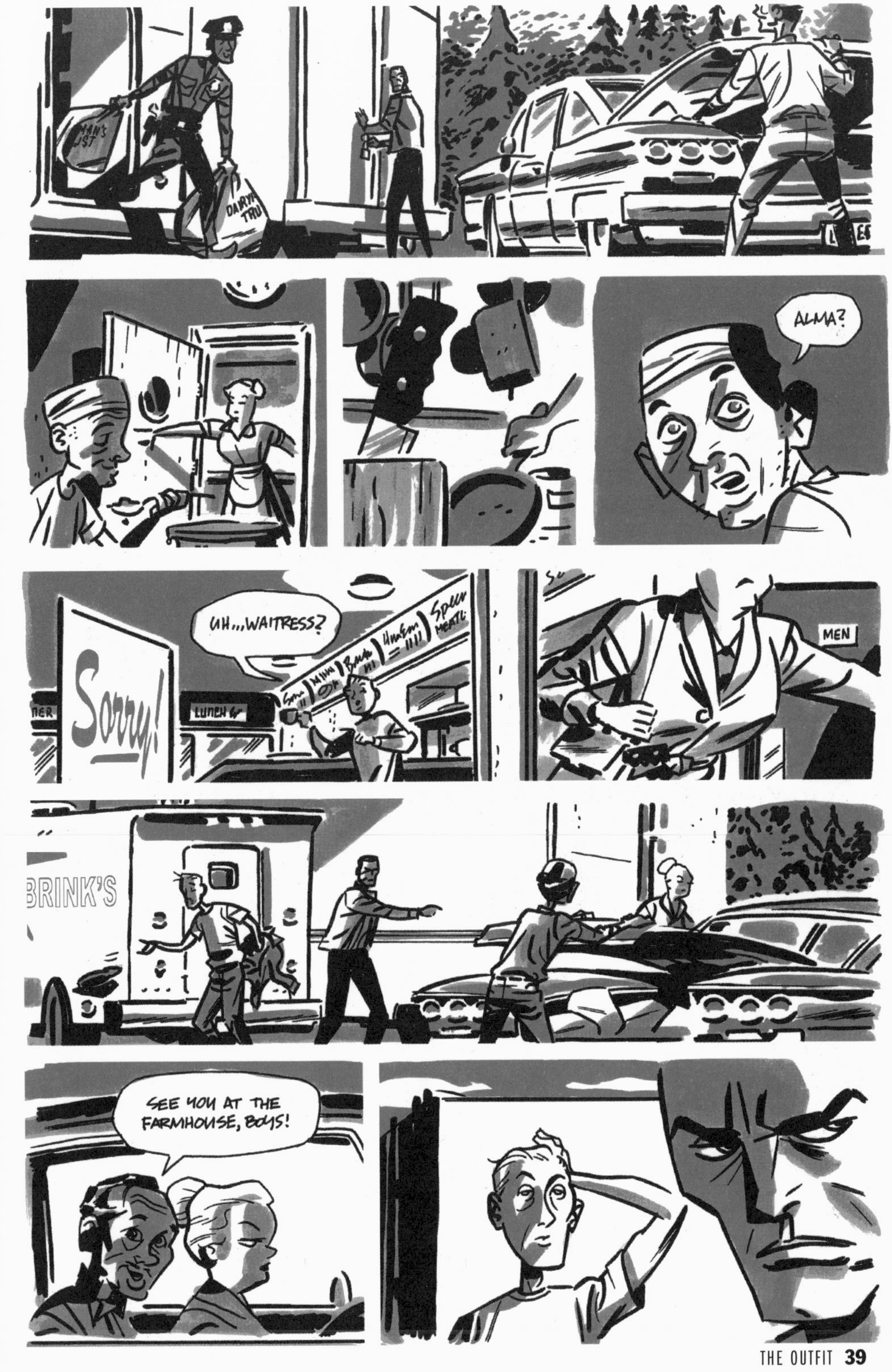
ALMA?
UH... WAITRESS?
Sorry!
MEN
BRINK'S
SEE YOU AT THE FARMHOUSE, BOYS!

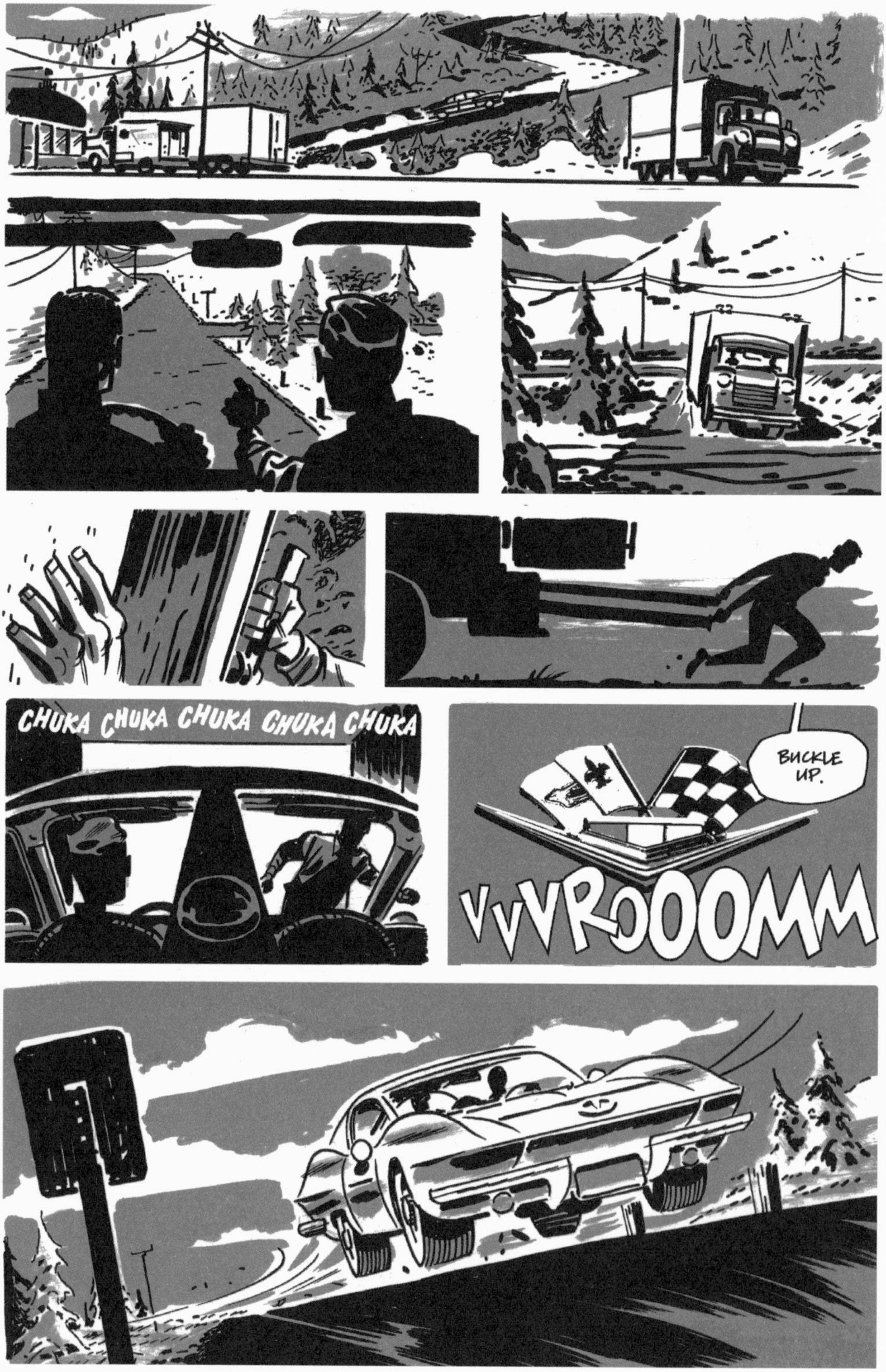
CHUKA CHUKA CHUKA CHUKA CHUKA
BUCKLE UP.
VVVROOOMM

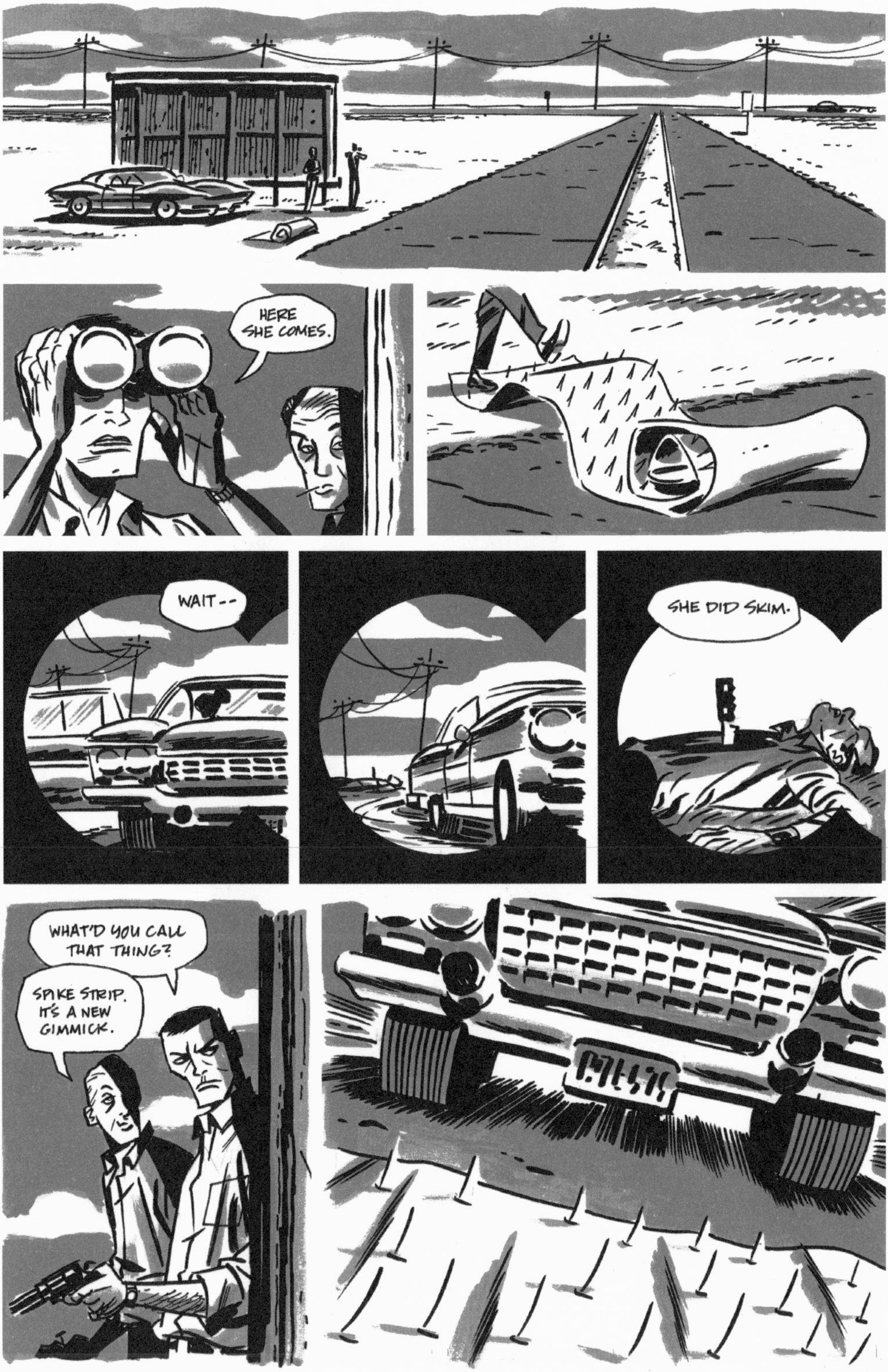
HERE SHE COMES.
WAIT--
SHE DID SKIM.
WHAT'D YOU CALL THAT THING?
SPIKE STRIP. IT'S A NEW GIMMICK.

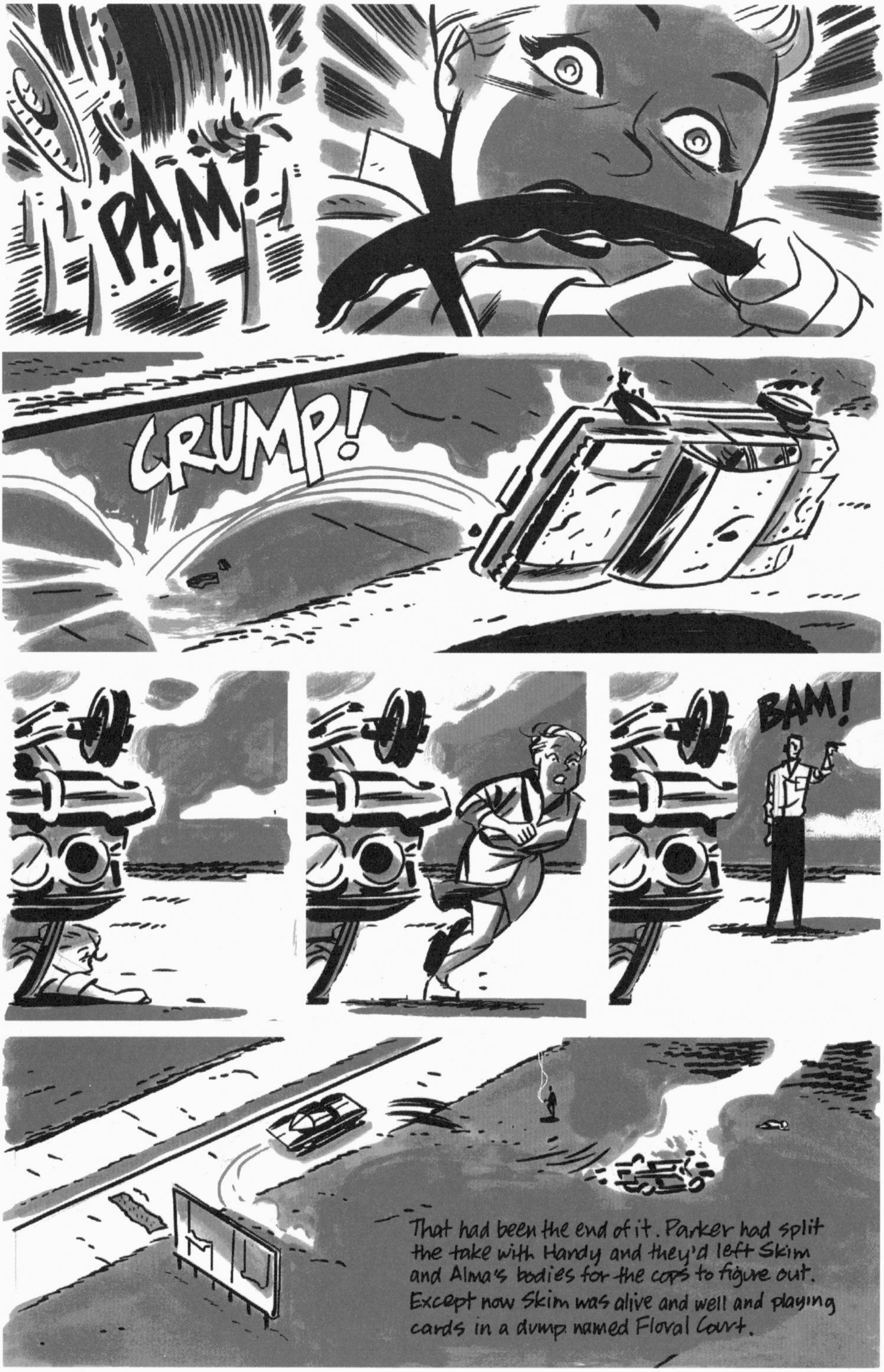
PAM!
CRUMP!
BAM!
That had been the end of it. Parker had split the take with Hardy and they'd left Skim and Alma's bodies for the cops to figure out. Except now Skim was alive and well and playing cards in a dump named Floral Court.

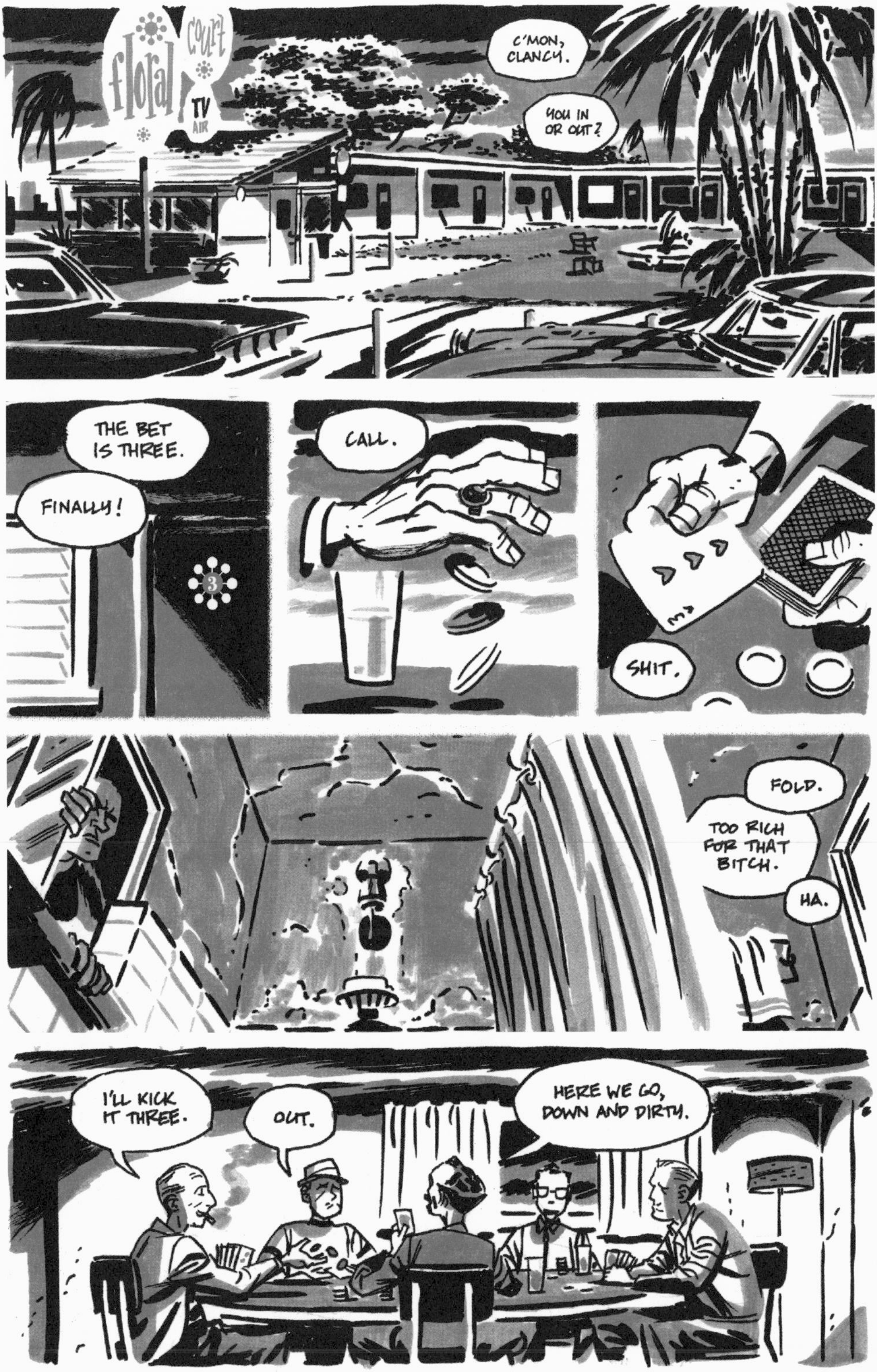
floral court
TV
AIR
C'MON, CLANCY.
YOU IN OR OUT?
THE BET IS THREE.
FINALLY!
3
CALL.
SHIT.
FOLD.
TOO RICH FOR THAT BITCH.
HA.
I'LL KICK IT THREE.
OUT.
HERE WE GO, DOWN AND DIRTY.

MAK GOOD

OY.

CHRIS THIS H

ALL OF YOU — KEEP YOUR HANDS ON THE TABLE.

oh no.

CHRIST.

MONEY AND WALLETS ON THE TABLE.

NOW.

LISTEN, PAL --

SHUT UP.

YOU — PICK 'EM UP AND FILL YOUR COAT.

EASY, PAL. JUST TAKE IT AND GO.

QUIET.

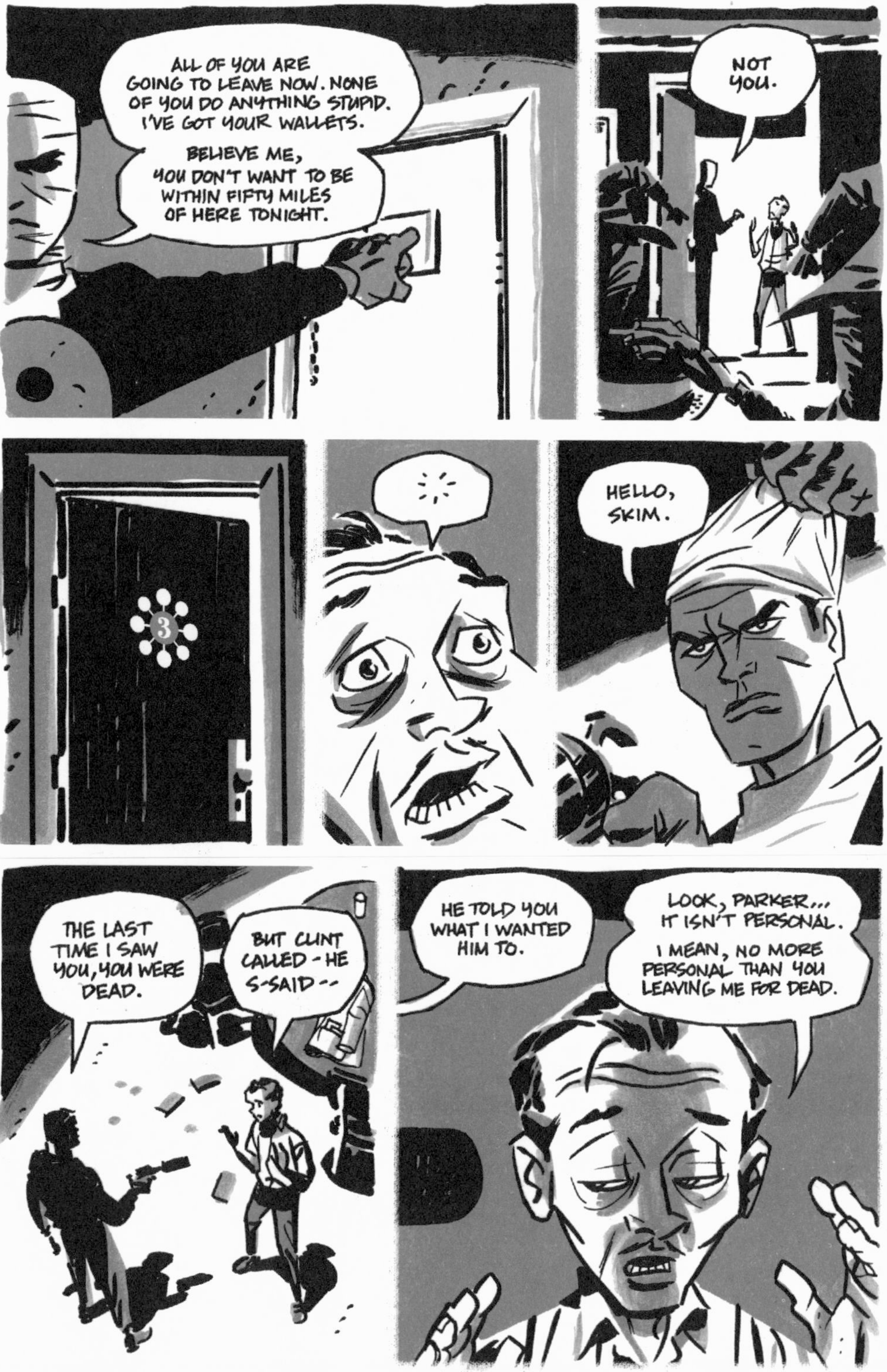
ALL OF YOU ARE GOING TO LEAVE NOW. NONE OF YOU DO ANYTHING STUPID. I'VE GOT YOUR WALLETS.
BELIEVE ME, YOU DON'T WANT TO BE WITHIN FIFTY MILES OF HERE TONIGHT.
NOT YOU.
HELLO, SKIM.
THE LAST TIME I SAW YOU, YOU WERE DEAD.
BUT CLINT CALLED - HE S-SAID --
HE TOLD YOU WHAT I WANTED HIM TO.
LOOK, PARKER... IT ISN'T PERSONAL.
I MEAN, NO MORE PERSONAL THAN YOU LEAVING ME FOR DEAD.

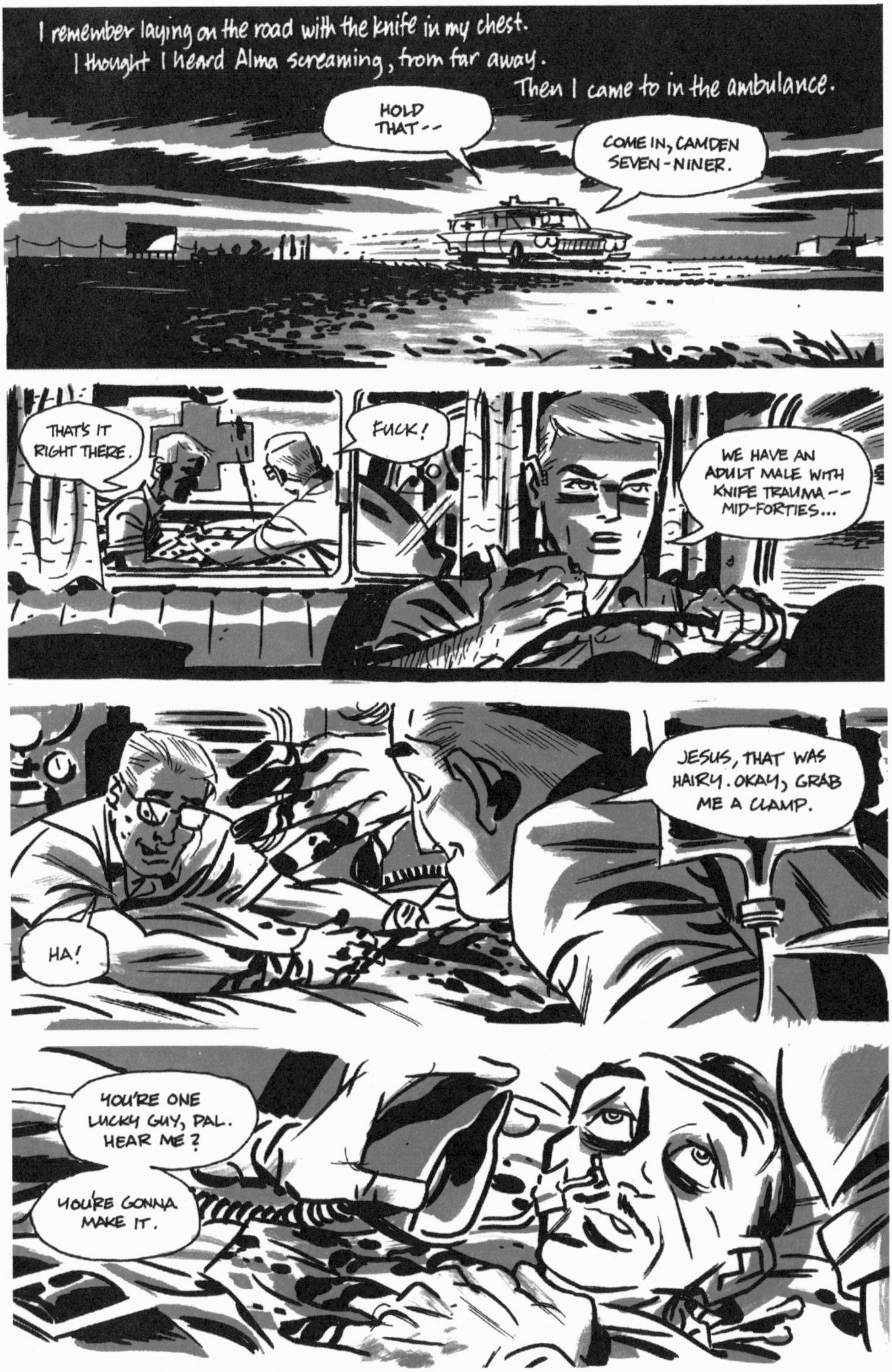
I remember laying on the road with the knife in my chest.
I thought I heard Alma screaming, from far away.
Then I came to in the ambulance.
HOLD THAT--
COME IN, CAMDEN SEVEN-NINER.
THAT'S IT RIGHT THERE.
FUCK!
WE HAVE AN ADULT MALE WITH KNIFE TRAUMA-- MID-FORTIES...
JESUS, THAT WAS HAIRY. OKAY, GRAB ME A CLAMP.
HA!
YOU'RE ONE LUCKY GUY, PAL. HEAR ME?
YOU'RE GONNA MAKE IT.

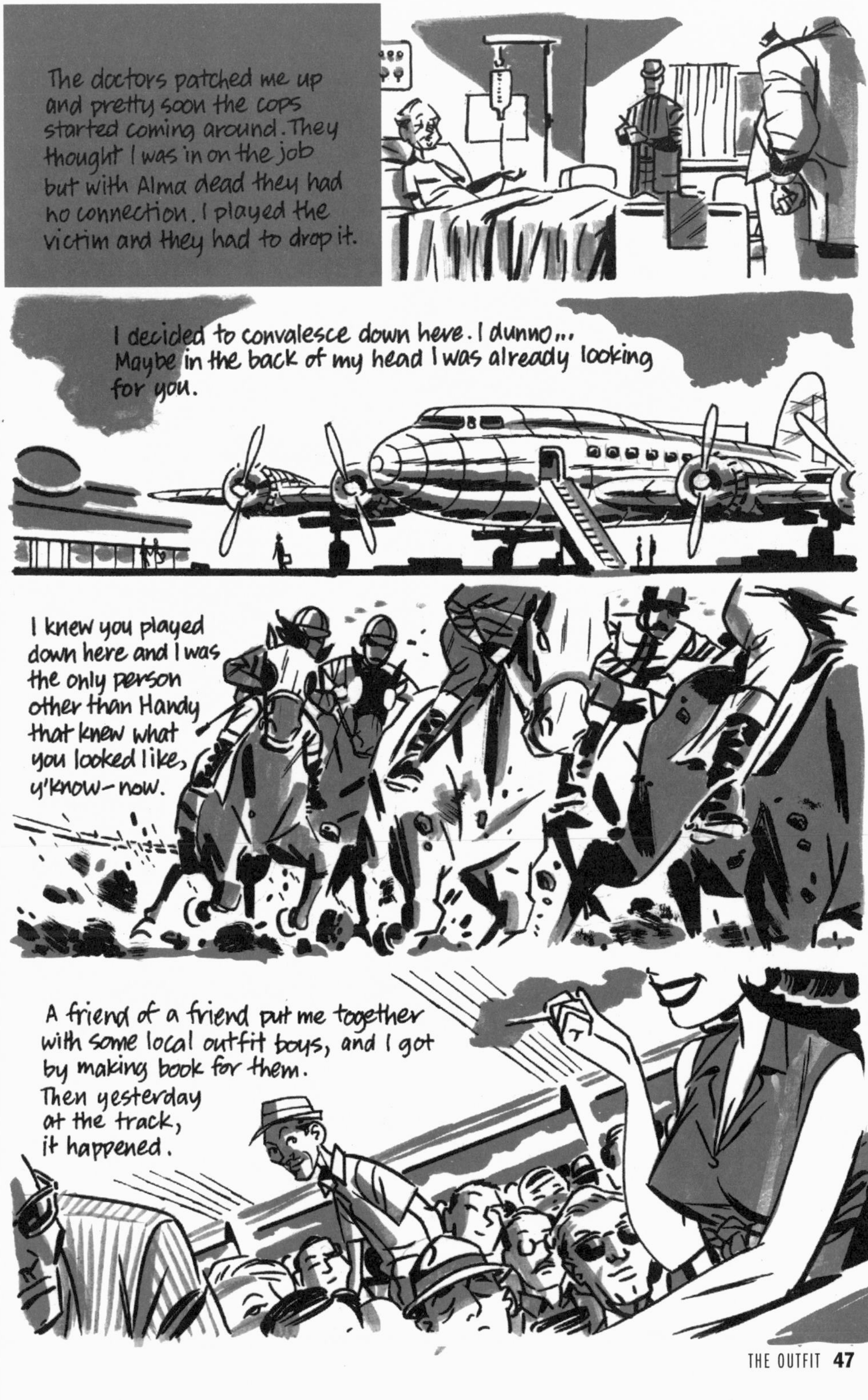
The doctors patched me up and pretty soon the cops started coming around. They thought I was in on the job but with Alma dead they had no connection. I played the victim and they had to drop it.
I decided to convalesce down here. I dunno... Maybe in the back of my head I was already looking for you.
I knew you played down here and I was the only person other than Handy that knew what you looked like, y'know—now.
A friend of a friend put me together with some local outfit boys, and I got by making book for them.
Then yesterday at the track, it happened.

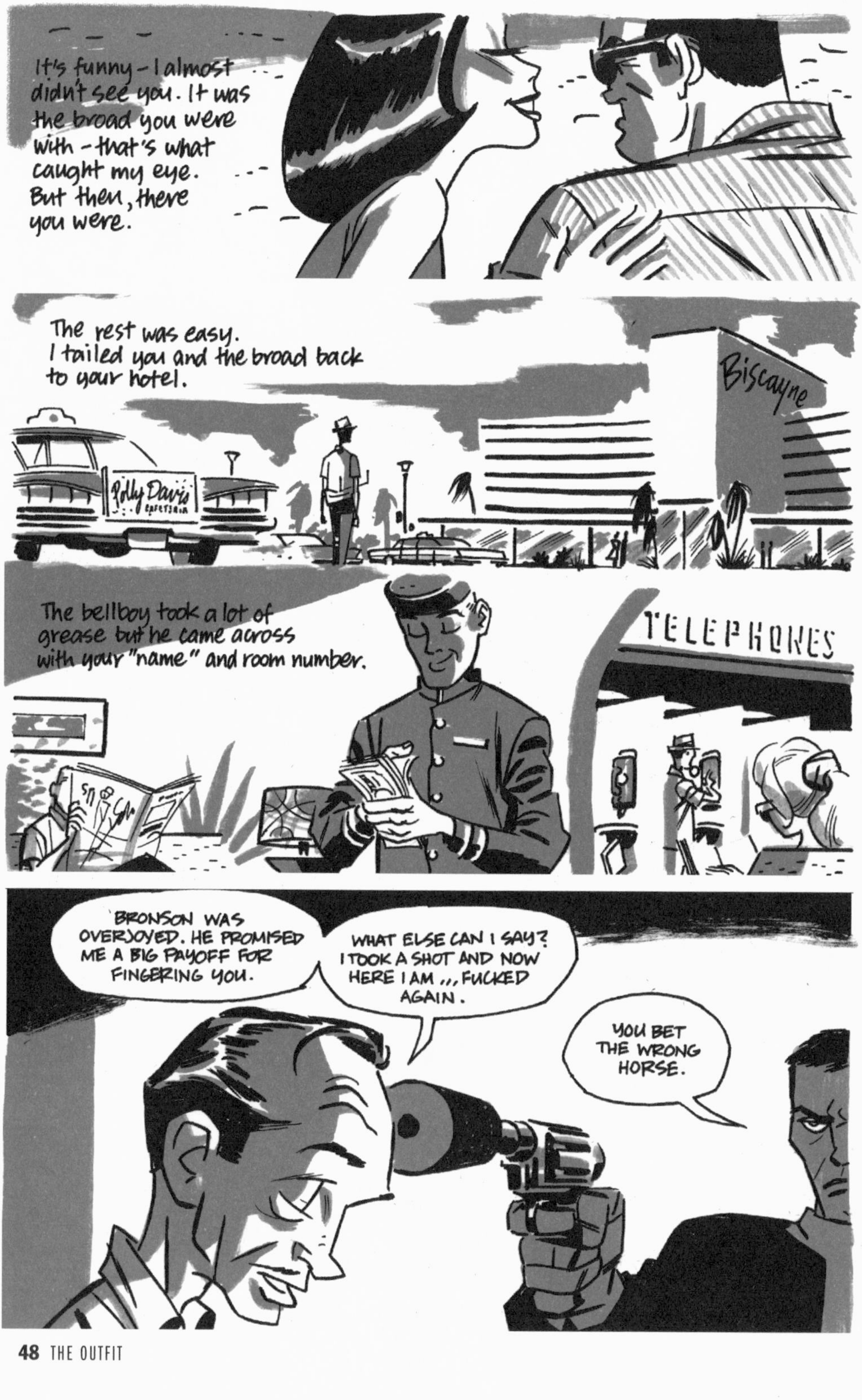
It's funny - I almost didn't see you. It was the broad you were with - that's what caught my eye. But then, there you were.
The rest was easy. I tailed you and the broad back to your hotel.
Biscayne
Polly Davis
The bellboy took a lot of grease but he came across with your "name" and room number.
TELEPHONES
BRONSON WAS OVERJOYED. HE PROMISED ME A BIG PAYOFF FOR FINGERING YOU.
WHAT ELSE CAN I SAY? I TOOK A SHOT AND NOW HERE I AM ,,, FUCKED AGAIN.
YOU BET THE WRONG HORSE.

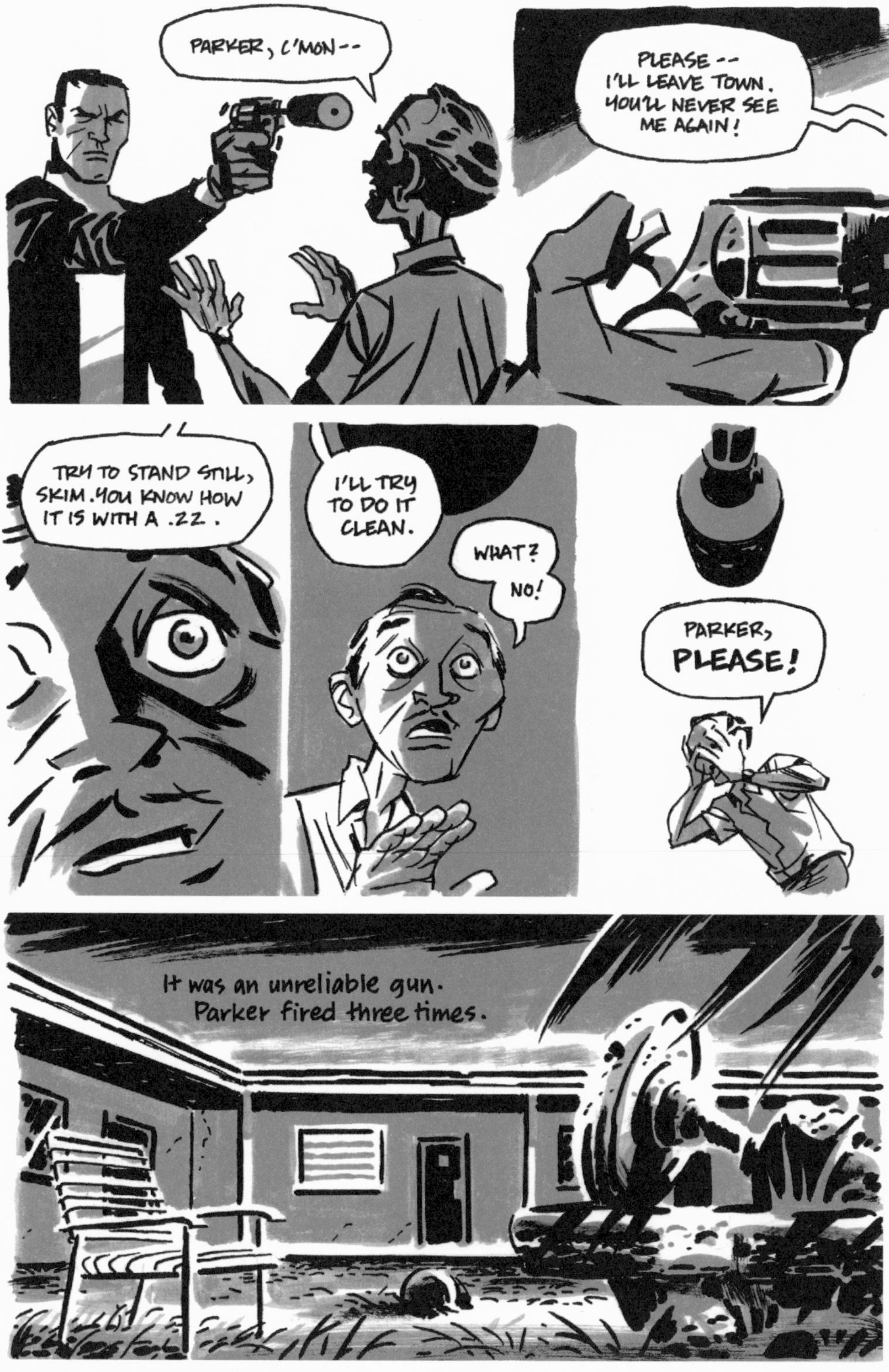
PARKER, C'MON--
PLEASE-- I'LL LEAVE TOWN. YOU'LL NEVER SEE ME AGAIN!
TRY TO STAND STILL, SKIM. YOU KNOW HOW IT IS WITH A .22.
I'LL TRY TO DO IT CLEAN.
WHAT?
NO!
PARKER, PLEASE!
It was an unreliable gun. Parker fired three times.

Parker sat at the table fumbling with pen and paper, frowning. He wasn't used to writing letters.

It took three drafts to get it right and a call to the operator to check the spelling of the word "grievance." Satisfied, he wrote six letters, with the only changes being the names and the particular job.

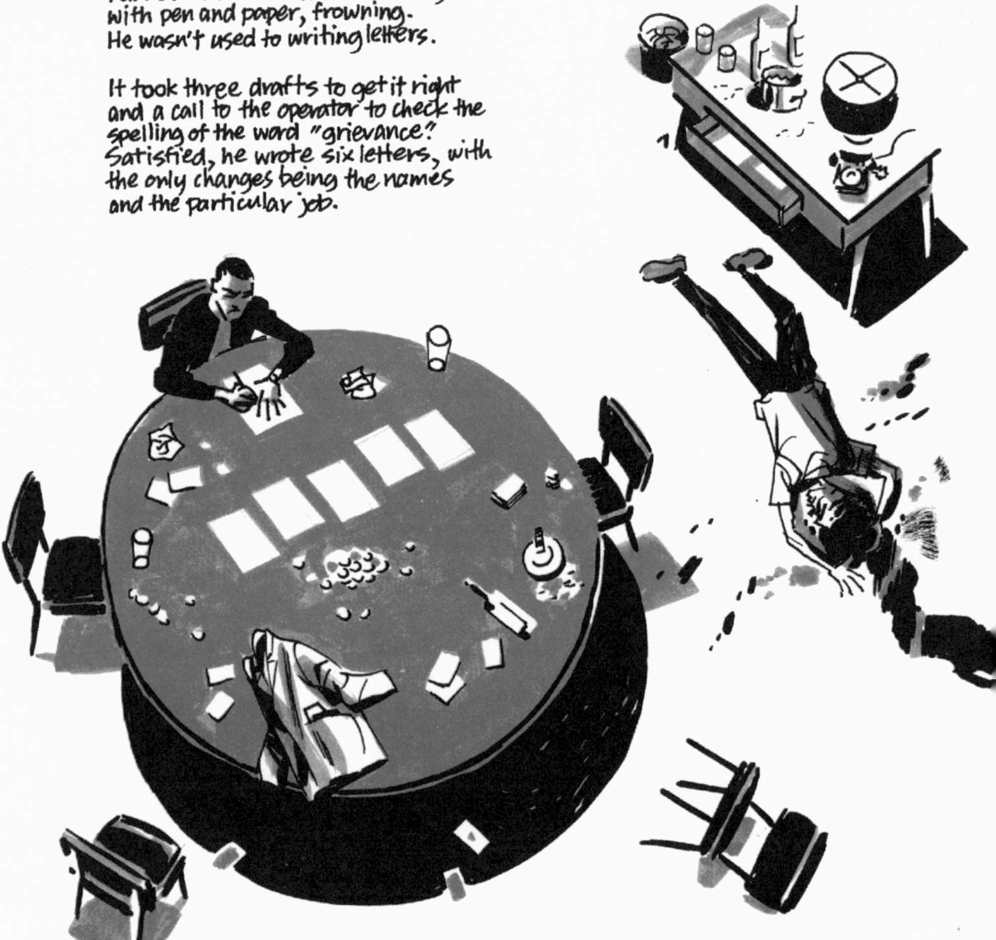

Frank-

The Outfit thinks it has a grievance with me. It doesn't.
But it keeps sending its punks around to make trouble.
I told their headman I'd give them money trouble if
they didn't quit, and they didn't quit.
You told me once about a lay you worked out for that
gambling place outside Boston and you'd be doing me a favor
if you knocked it off in the next couple weeks. I'm writing
some of the other boys, too, so you can be sure they'll
be too busy to look for you special. I don't want a cut
and can't come in on it because I'll be busy hitting them
myself. You can reach me through Joe Sheer.
Maybe we'll work together again someday. PARKER

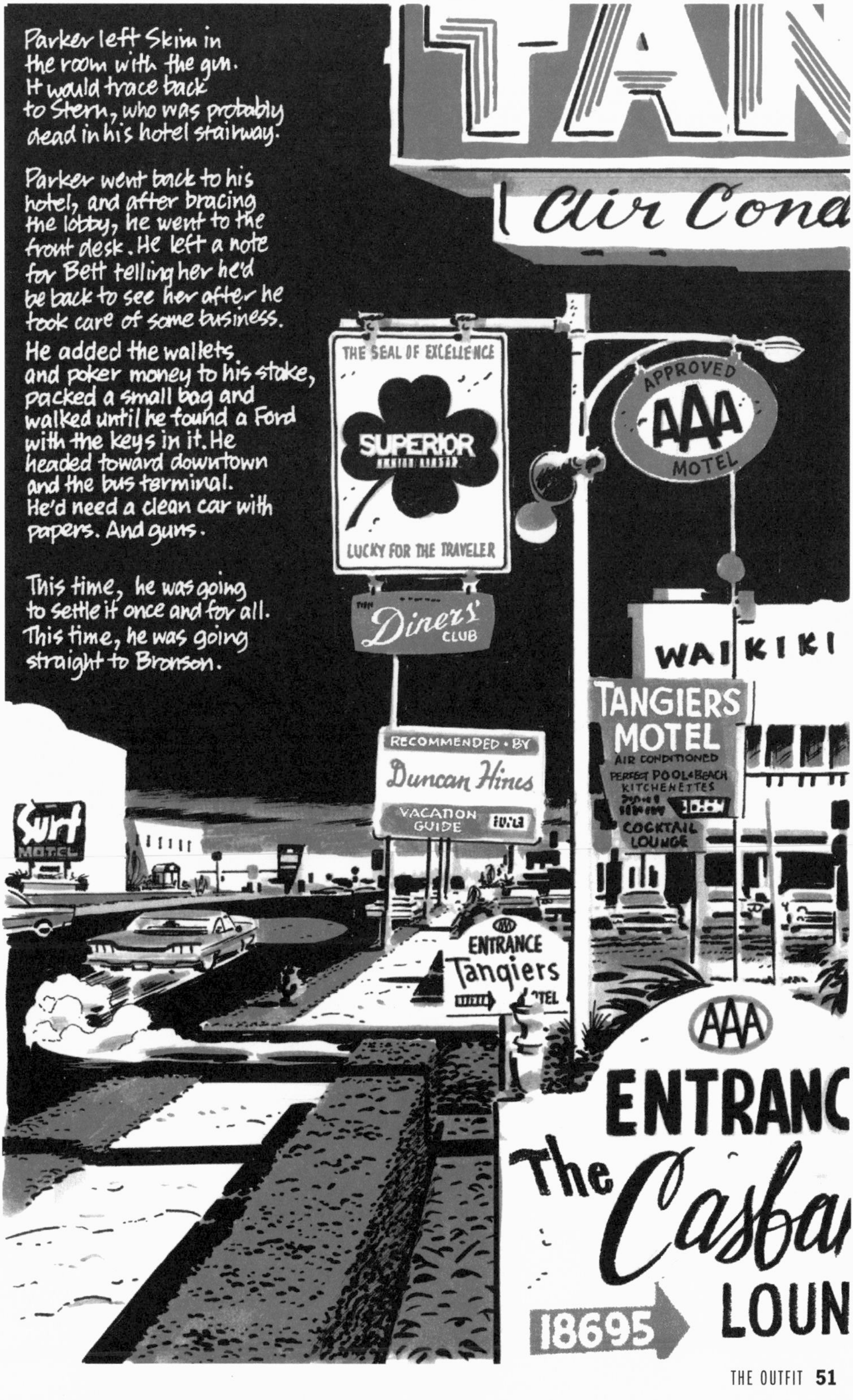

Parker left Skim in the room with the gun. It would trace back to Stern, who was probably dead in his hotel stairway.
Parker went back to his hotel, and after bracing the lobby, he went to the front desk. He left a note for Bett telling her he'd be back to see her after he took care of some business.
He added the wallets and poker money to his stake, packed a small bag and walked until he found a Ford with the keys in it. He headed toward downtown and the bus terminal. He'd need a clean car with papers. And guns.
This time, he was going to settle it once and for all. This time, he was going straight to Bronson.
Air Cond
THE SEAL OF EXCELLENCE
SUPERIOR
LUCKY FOR THE TRAVELER
APPROVED
AAA
MOTEL
Diners' CLUB
WAIKIKI
TANGIERS MOTEL
AIR CONDITIONED
PERFECT POOL & BEACH
KITCHENETTES
COCKTAIL LOUNGE
RECOMMENDED • BY
Duncan Hines
VACATION GUIDE
Surf
MOTEL
ENTRANCE
Tangiers
AAA
ENTRANC
The Casba
LOUN
18695

BOOK TWO

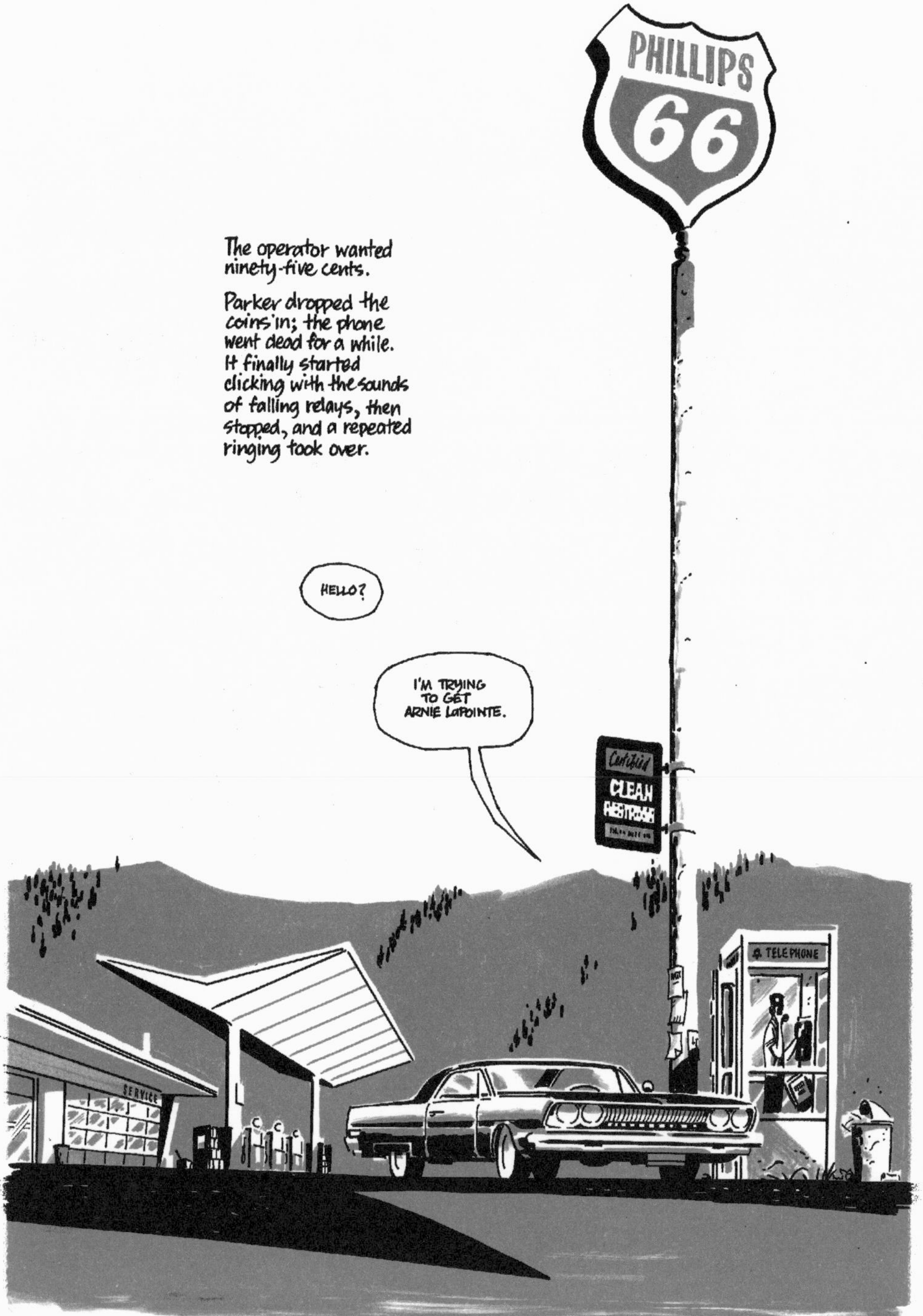
PHILLIPS
66
The operator wanted ninety-five cents.
Parker dropped the coins in; the phone went dead for a while. It finally started clicking with the sounds of falling relays, then stopped, and a repeated ringing took over.
HELLO?
I'M TRYING TO GET ARNIE LAPOINTE.
Certified
CLEAN
TELEPHONE
SERVICE

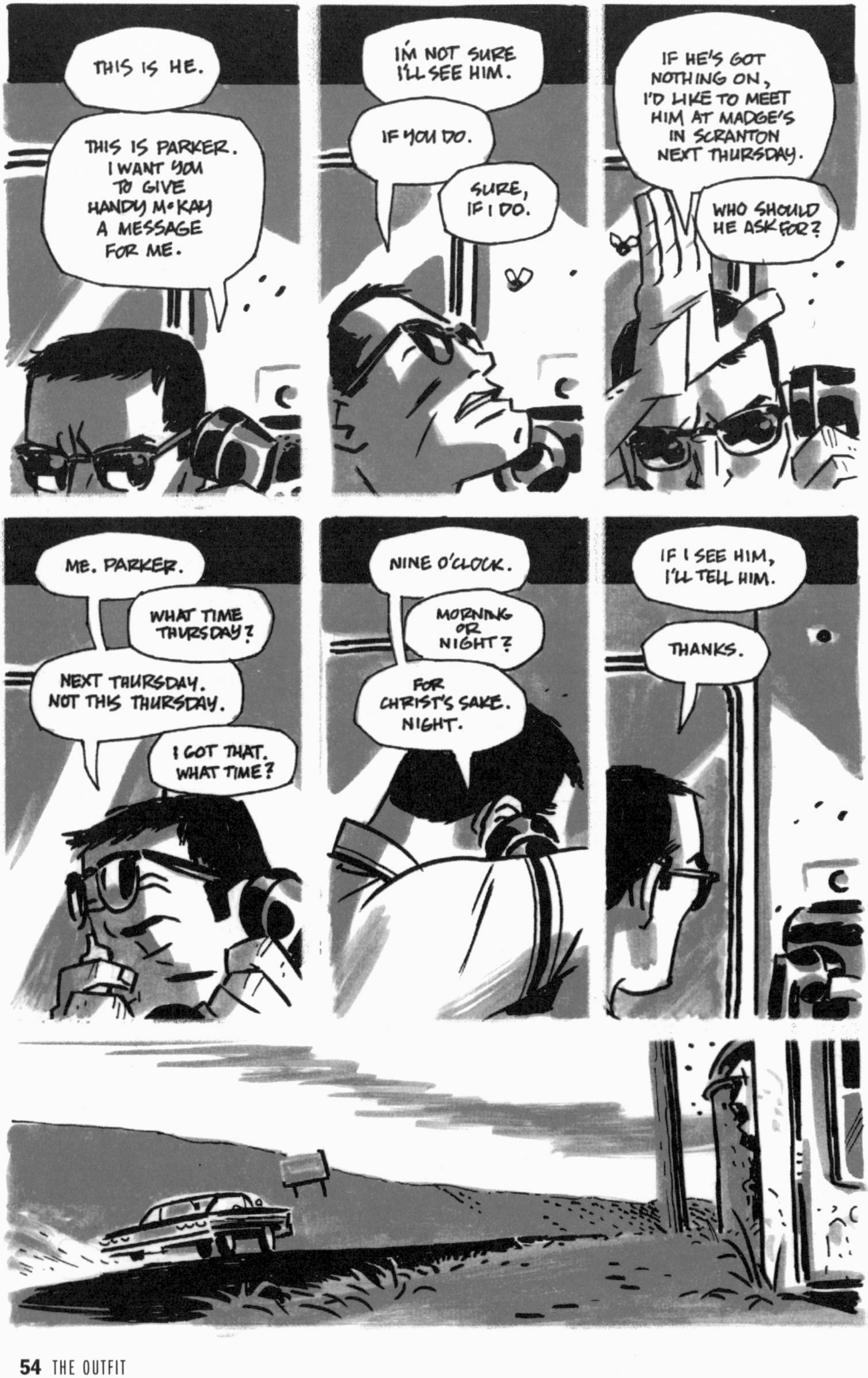
THIS IS HE.
THIS IS PARKER. I WANT YOU TO GIVE HANDY McKAY A MESSAGE FOR ME.
I'M NOT SURE I'LL SEE HIM.
IF YOU DO.
SURE, IF I DO.
IF HE'S GOT NOTHING ON, I'D LIKE TO MEET HIM AT MADGE'S IN SCRANTON NEXT THURSDAY.
WHO SHOULD HE ASK FOR?
ME. PARKER.
WHAT TIME THURSDAY?
NEXT THURSDAY. NOT THIS THURSDAY.
I GOT THAT. WHAT TIME?
NINE O'CLOCK.
MORNING OR NIGHT?
FOR CHRIST'S SAKE. NIGHT.
IF I SEE HIM, I'LL TELL HIM.
THANKS.

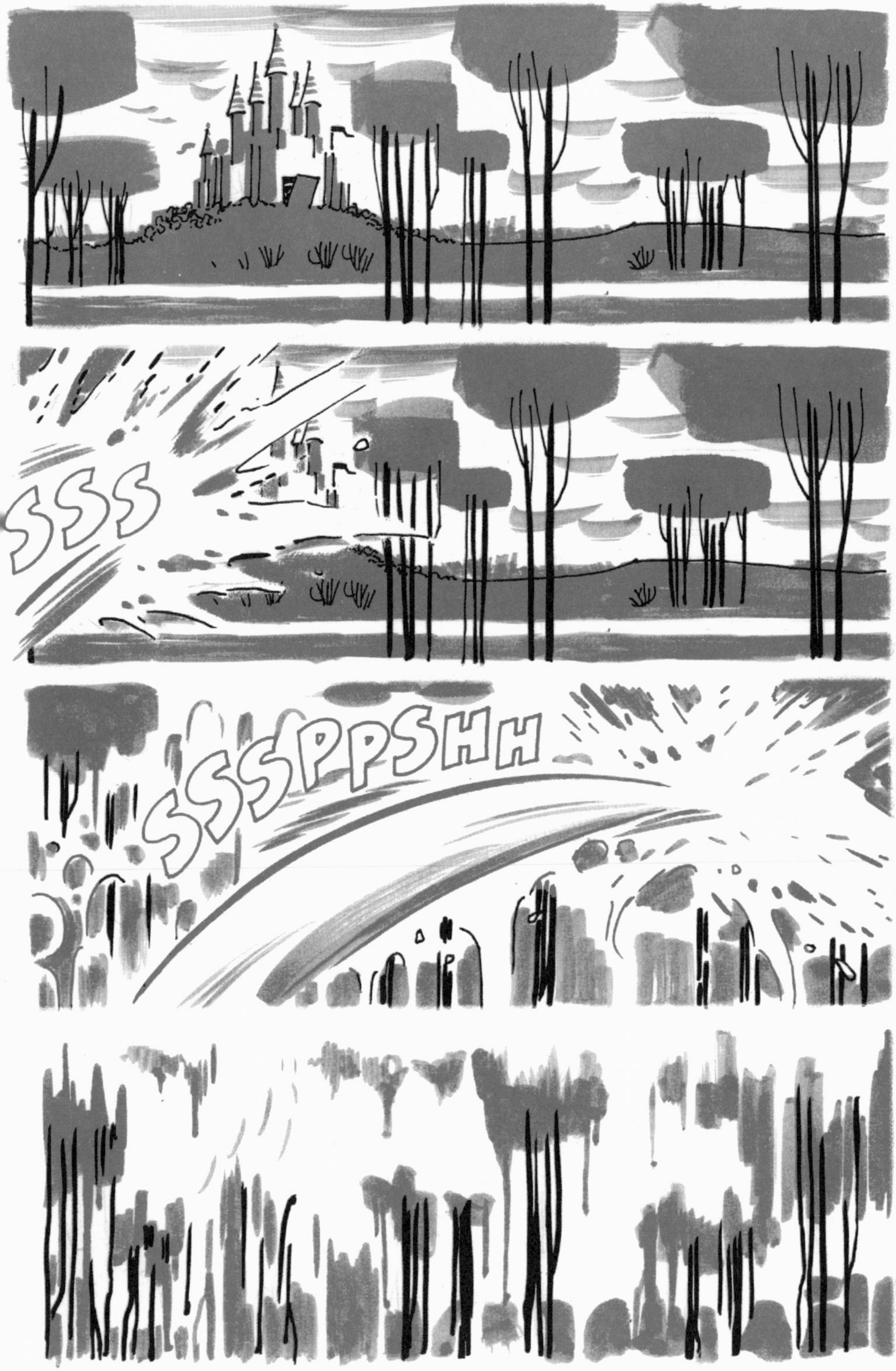
SSS
SSSPPSHH

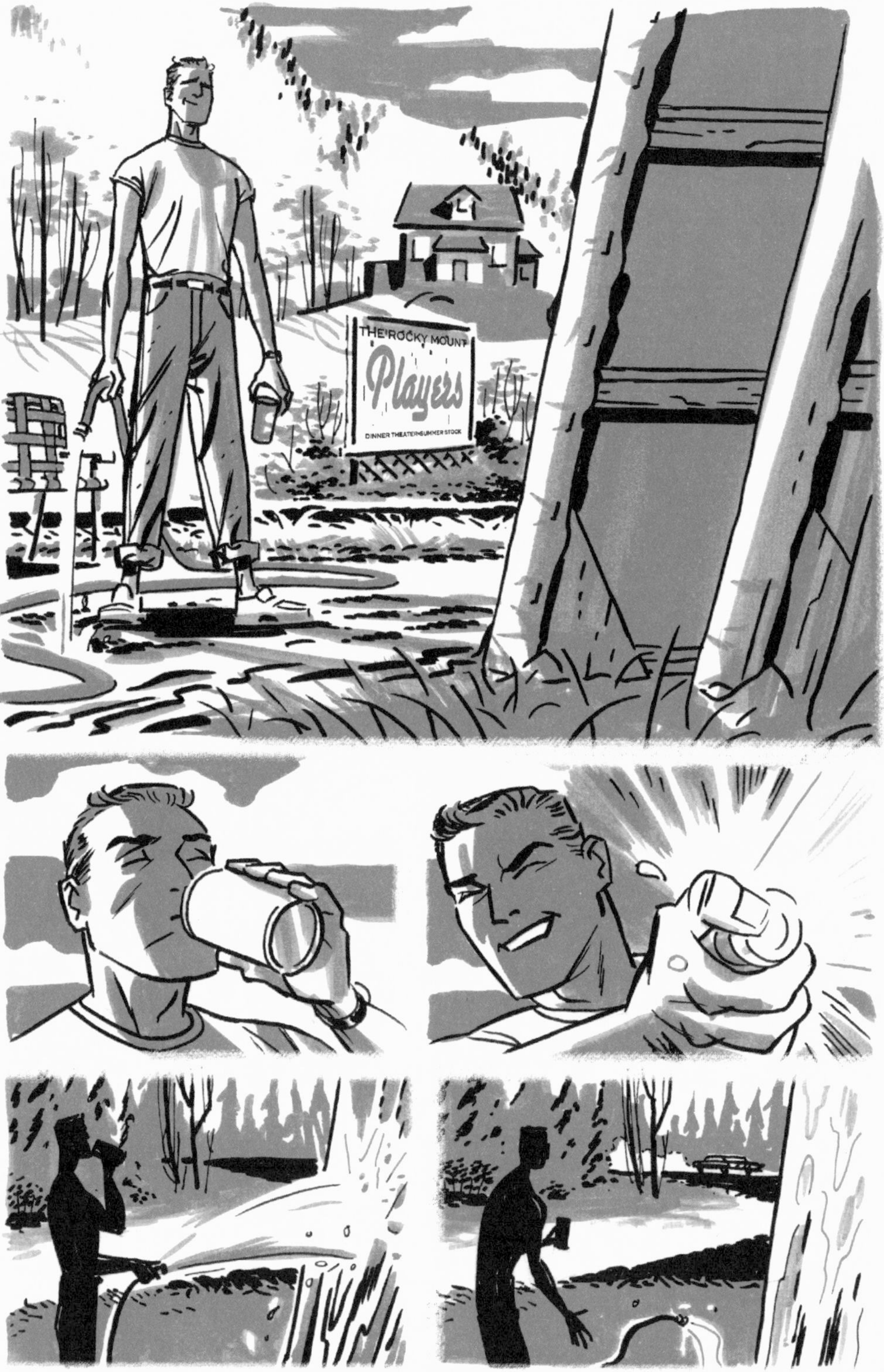
THE ROCKY MOUNT
Players
DINNER THEATER•SUMMER STOCK

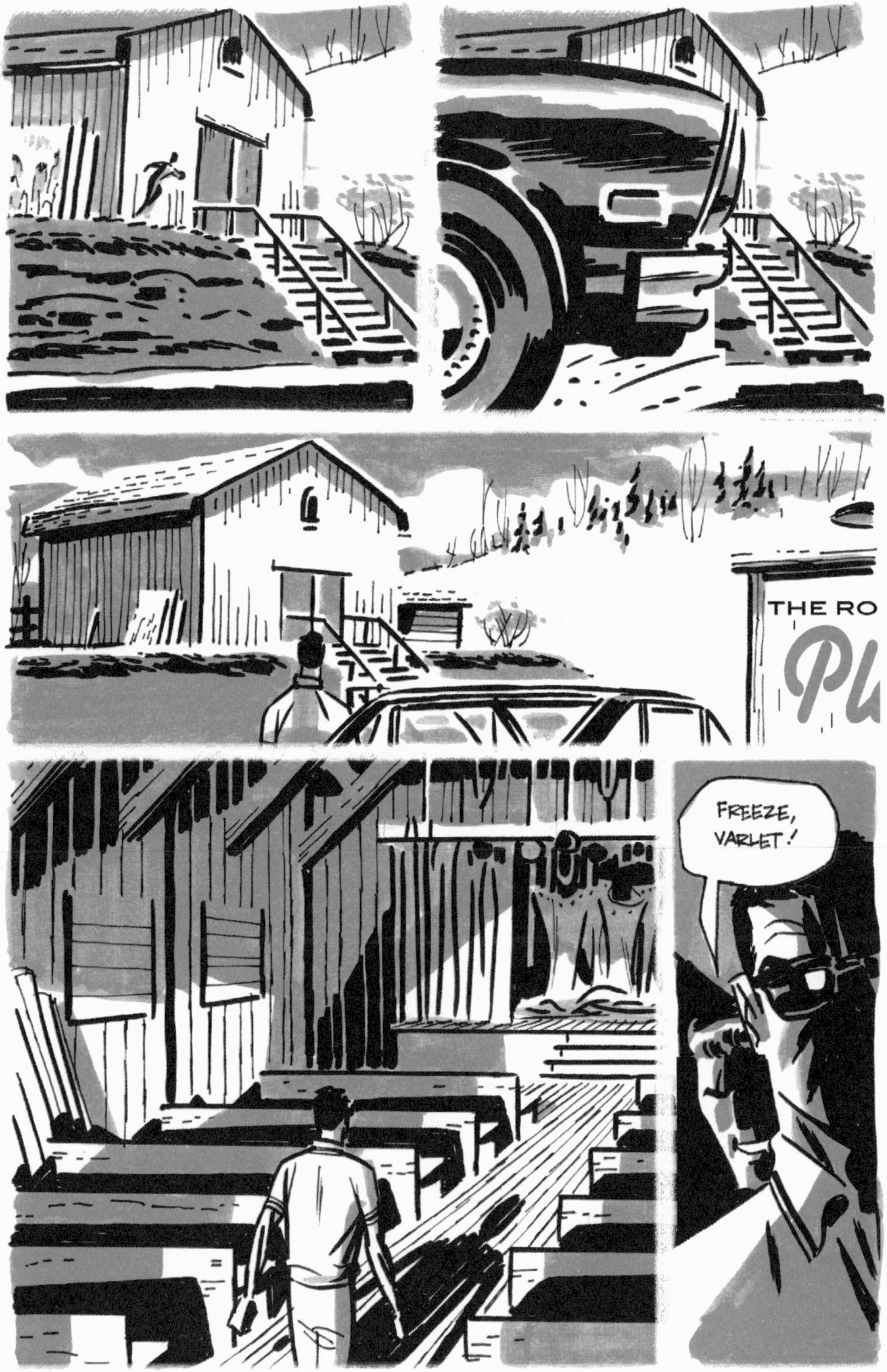
THE RO
PL
FREEZE, VARLET!

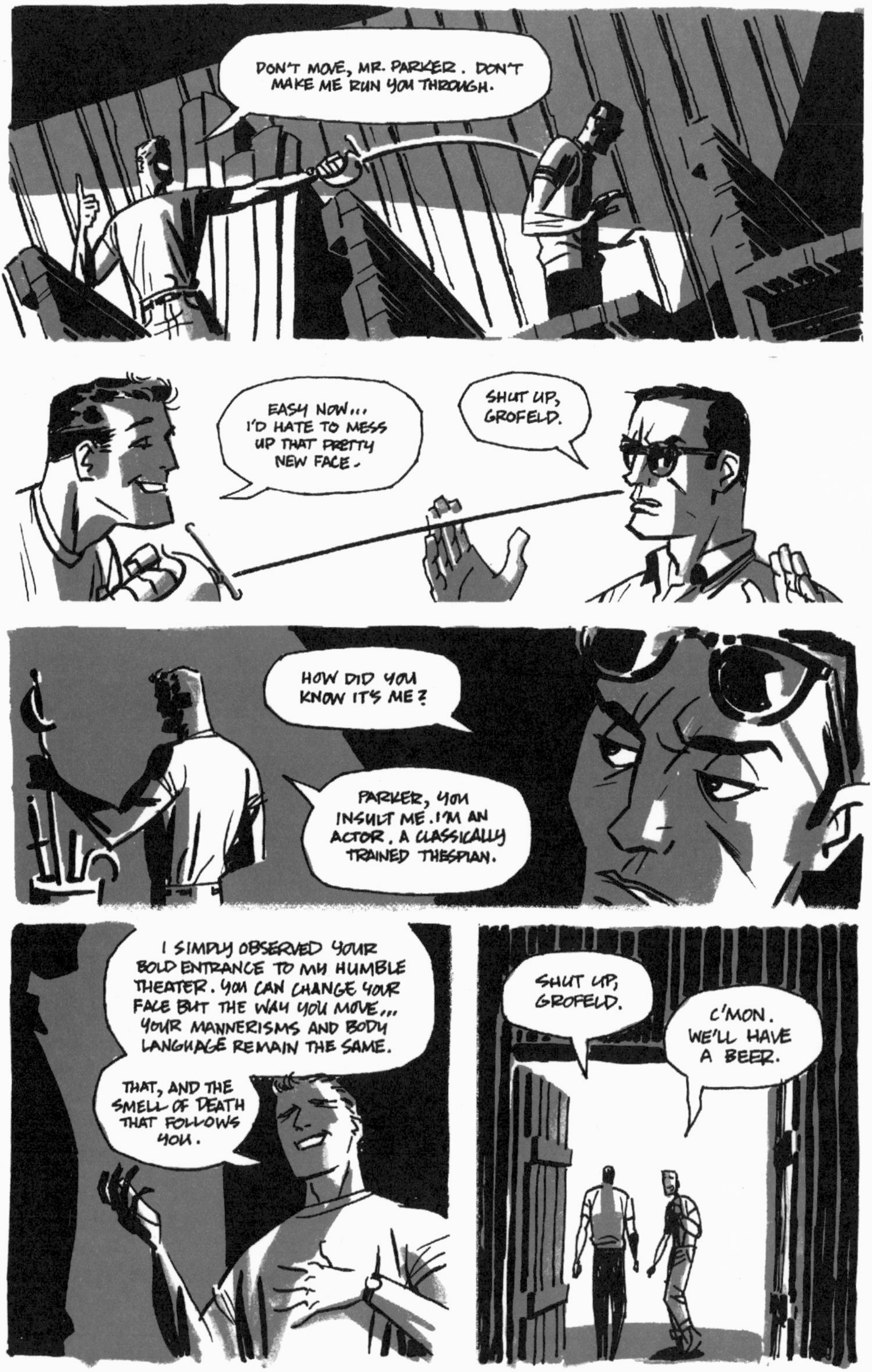
DON'T MOVE, MR. PARKER. DON'T MAKE ME RUN YOU THROUGH.
EASY NOW... I'D HATE TO MESS UP THAT PRETTY NEW FACE.
SHUT UP, GROFELD.
HOW DID YOU KNOW IT'S ME?
PARKER, YOU INSULT ME. I'M AN ACTOR. A CLASSICALLY TRAINED THESPIAN.
I SIMPLY OBSERVED YOUR BOLD ENTRANCE TO MY HUMBLE THEATER. YOU CAN CHANGE YOUR FACE BUT THE WAY YOU MOVE... YOUR MANNERISMS AND BODY LANGUAGE REMAIN THE SAME.
THAT, AND THE SMELL OF DEATH THAT FOLLOWS YOU.
SHUT UP, GROFELD.
C'MON. WE'LL HAVE A BEER.

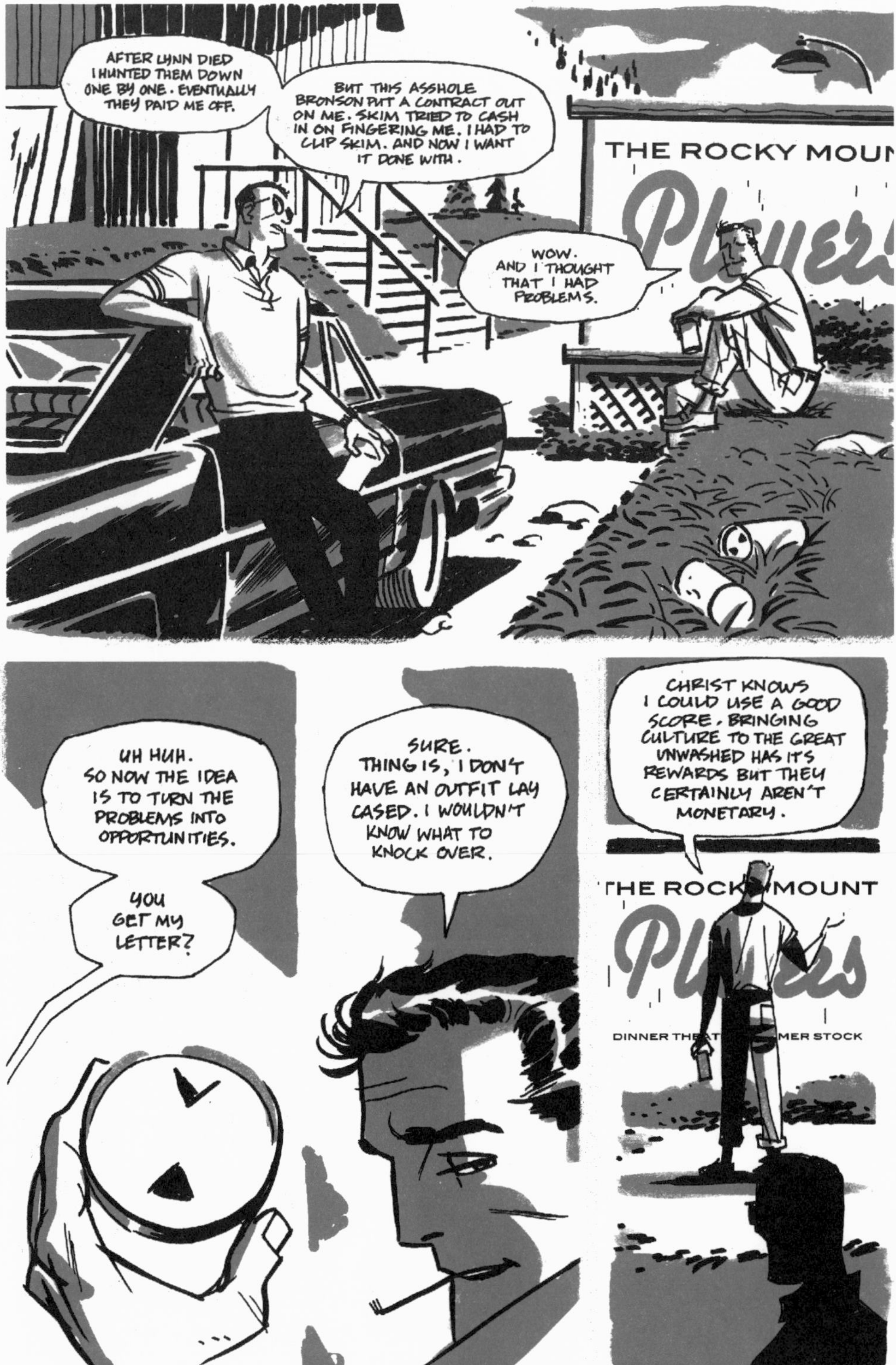
AFTER LYNN DIED I HUNTED THEM DOWN ONE BY ONE. EVENTUALLY THEY PAID ME OFF.
BUT THIS ASSHOLE BRONSON PUT A CONTRACT OUT ON ME. SKIM TRIED TO CASH IN ON FINGERING ME. I HAD TO CLIP SKIM. AND NOW I WANT IT DONE WITH.
THE ROCKY MOUN
WOW. AND I THOUGHT THAT I HAD PROBLEMS.
UH HUH. SO NOW THE IDEA IS TO TURN THE PROBLEMS INTO OPPORTUNITIES.
YOU GET MY LETTER?
SURE. THING IS, I DON'T HAVE AN OUTFIT LAY CASED. I WOULDN'T KNOW WHAT TO KNOCK OVER.
CHRIST KNOWS I COULD USE A GOOD SCORE. BRINGING CULTURE TO THE GREAT UNWASHED HAS IT'S REWARDS BUT THEY CERTAINLY AREN'T MONETARY.
THE ROCK MOUNT
DINNER THE MER STOCK

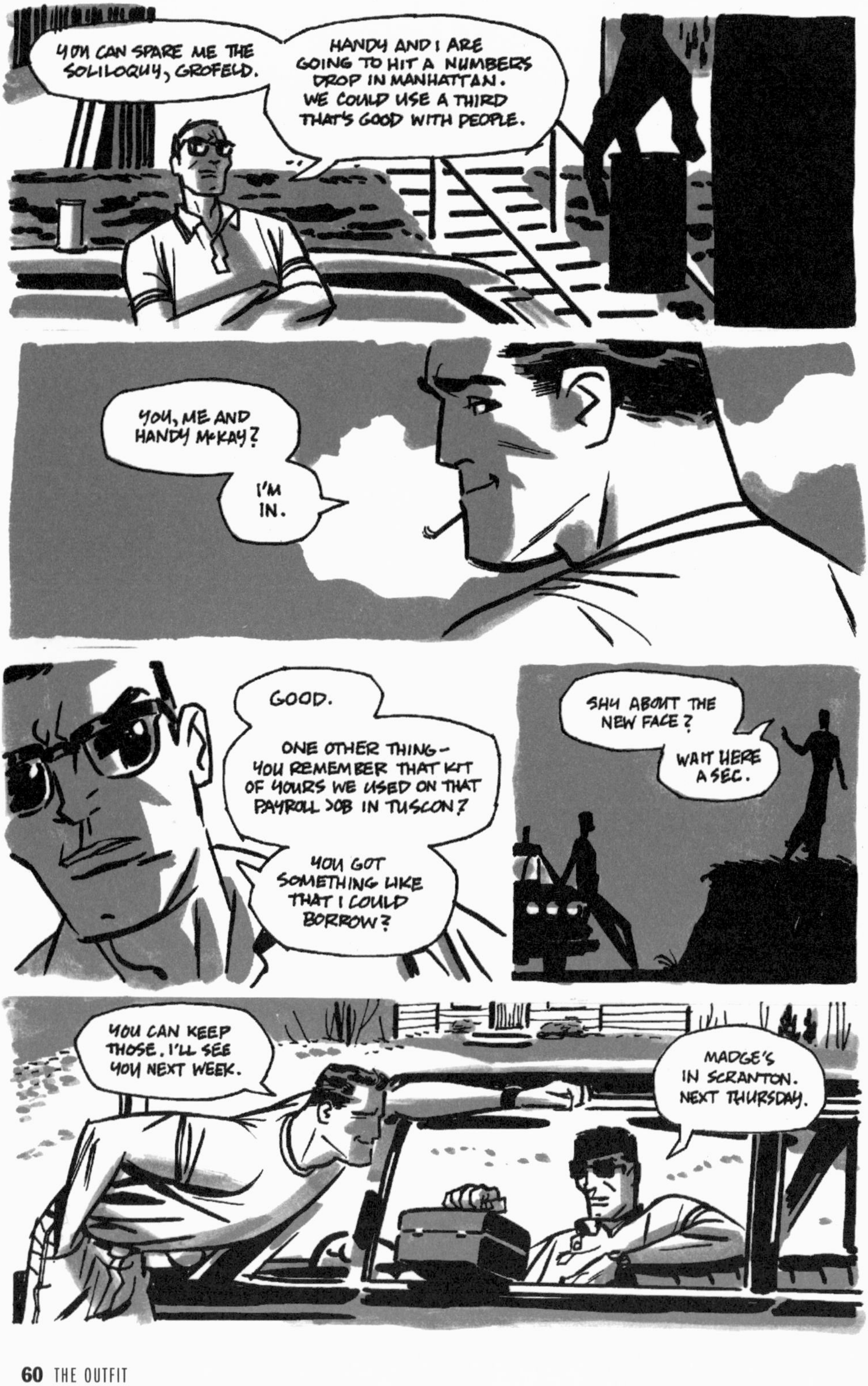
YOU CAN SPARE ME THE SOLILOQUY, GROFELD.
HANDY AND I ARE GOING TO HIT A NUMBERS DROP IN MANHATTAN. WE COULD USE A THIRD THAT'S GOOD WITH PEOPLE.
YOU, ME AND HANDY McKAY?
I'M IN.
GOOD.
ONE OTHER THING- YOU REMEMBER THAT KIT OF YOURS WE USED ON THAT PAYROLL JOB IN TUSCON?
YOU GOT SOMETHING LIKE THAT I COULD BORROW?
SHY ABOUT THE NEW FACE?
WAIT HERE A SEC.
YOU CAN KEEP THOSE. I'LL SEE YOU NEXT WEEK.
MADGE'S IN SCRANTON. NEXT THURSDAY.

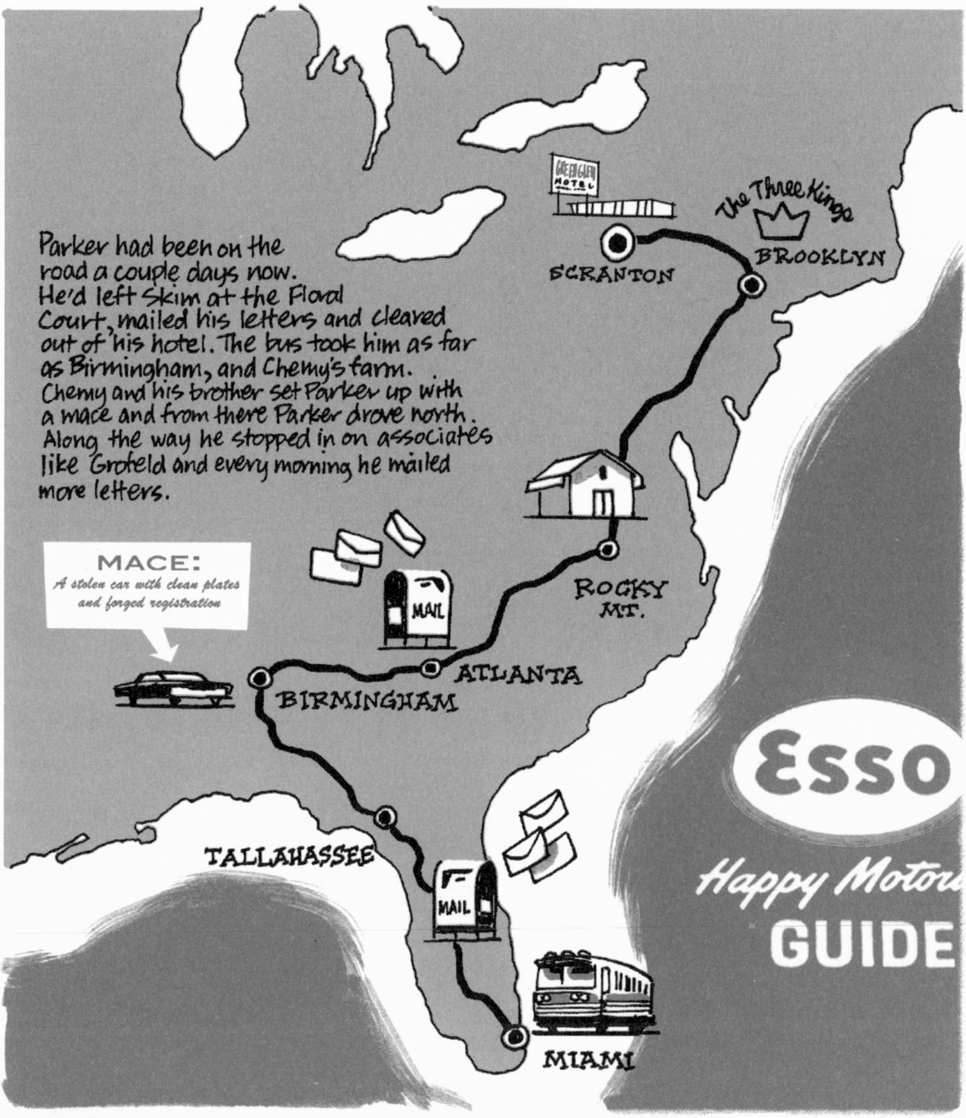
Parker had been on the road a couple days now. He'd left Skim at the Floral Court, mailed his letters and cleared out of his hotel. The bus took him as far as Birmingham, and Chemy's farm. Chemy and his brother set Parker up with a mace and from there Parker drove north. Along the way he stopped in on associates like Grofeld and every morning he mailed more letters.
MACE:
A stolen car with clean plates and forged registration
The Three Kings
SCRANTON
BROOKLYN
ROCKY MT.
ATLANTA
BIRMINGHAM
TALLAHASSEE
MIAMI
MAIL
MAIL
Esso
Happy Motor
GUIDE

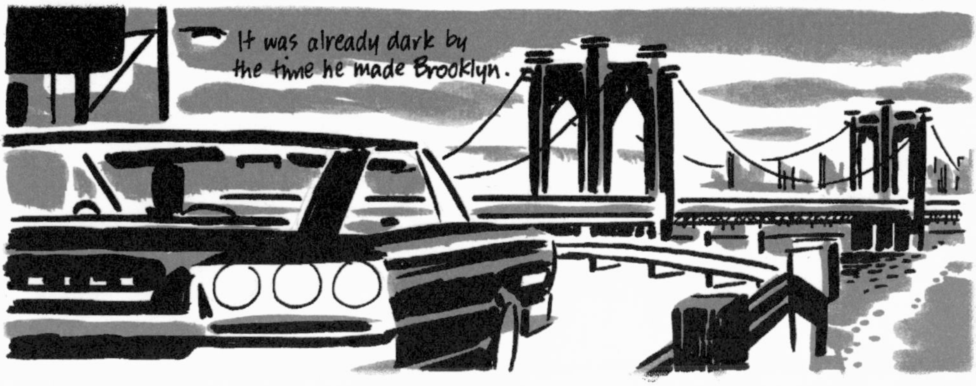
It was already dark by the time he made Brooklyn.

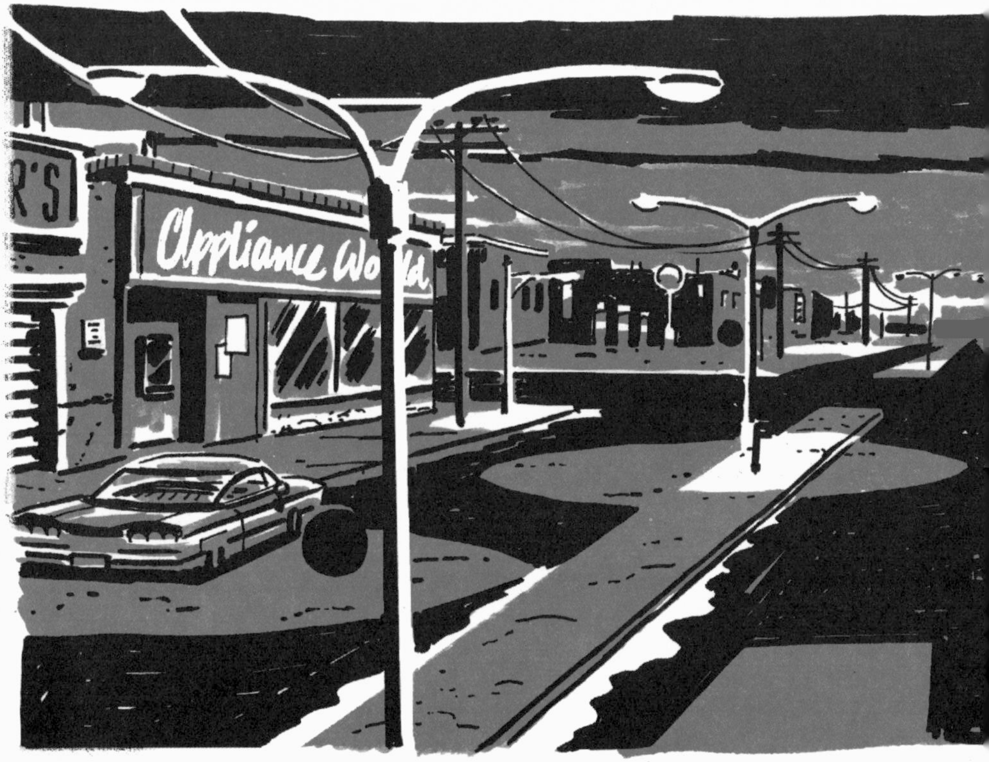
Appliance World

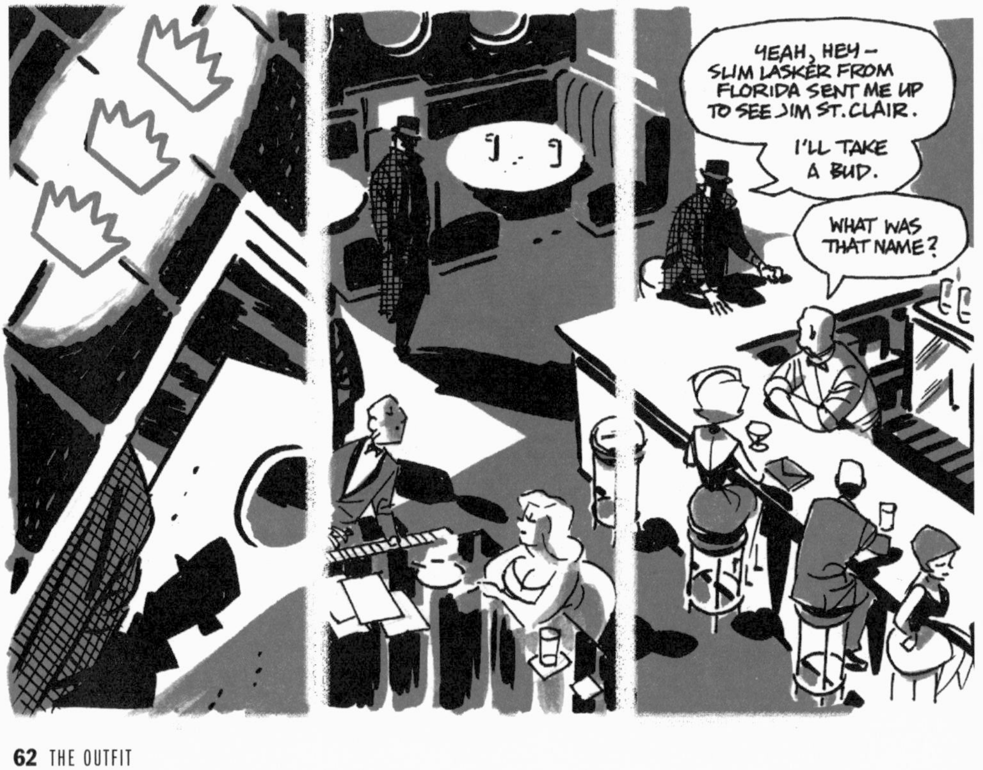
YEAH, HEY—
SLIM LASKER FROM FLORIDA SENT ME UP TO SEE JIM ST. CLAIR.
I'LL TAKE A BUD.
WHAT WAS THAT NAME?

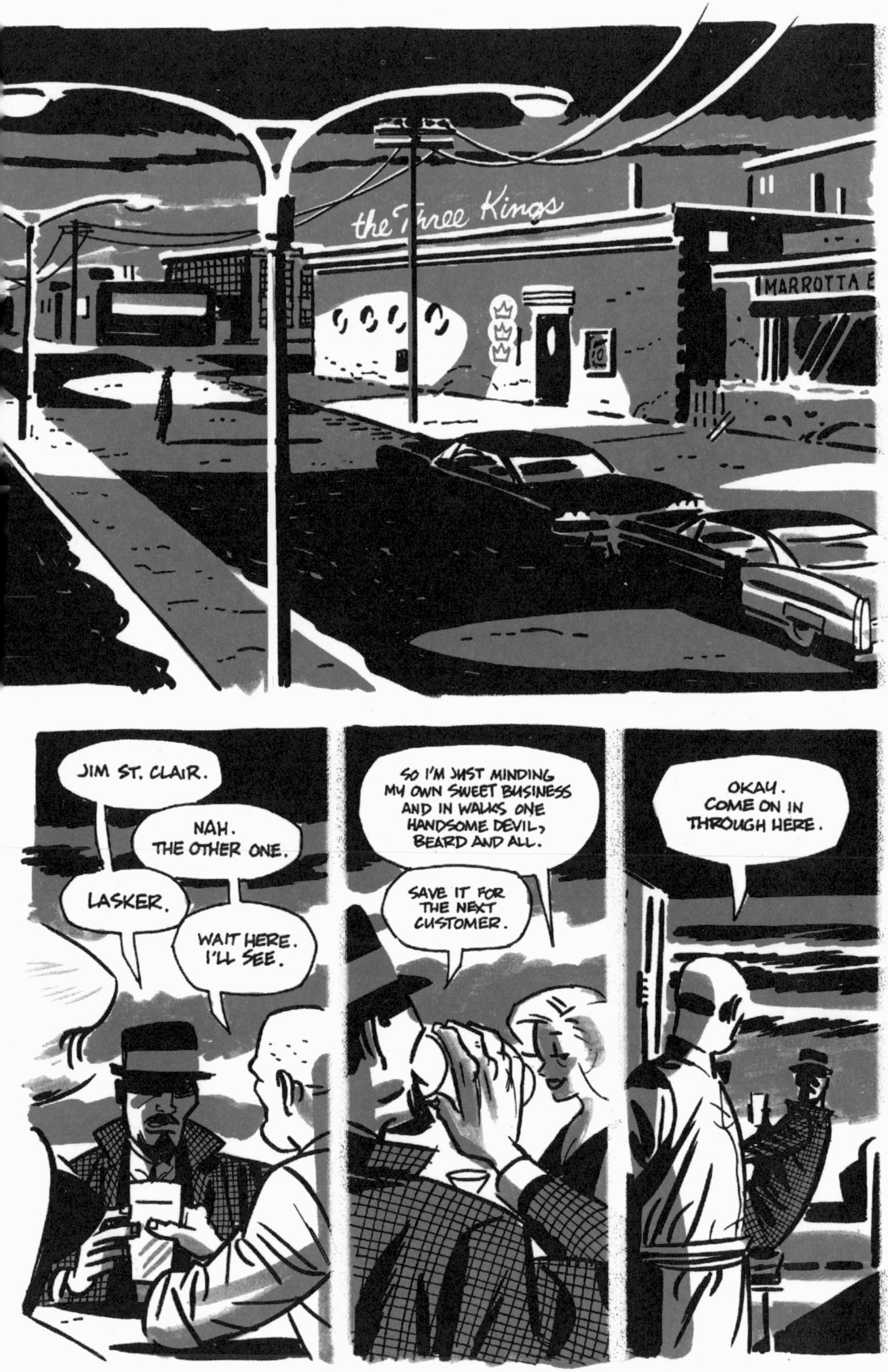
the Three Kings
MARROTTA E
JIM ST. CLAIR.
NAH. THE OTHER ONE.
LASKER.
WAIT HERE. I'LL SEE.
SO I'M JUST MINDING MY OWN SWEET BUSINESS AND IN WALKS ONE HANDSOME DEVIL, BEARD AND ALL.
SAVE IT FOR THE NEXT CUSTOMER.
OKAY. COME ON IN THROUGH HERE.

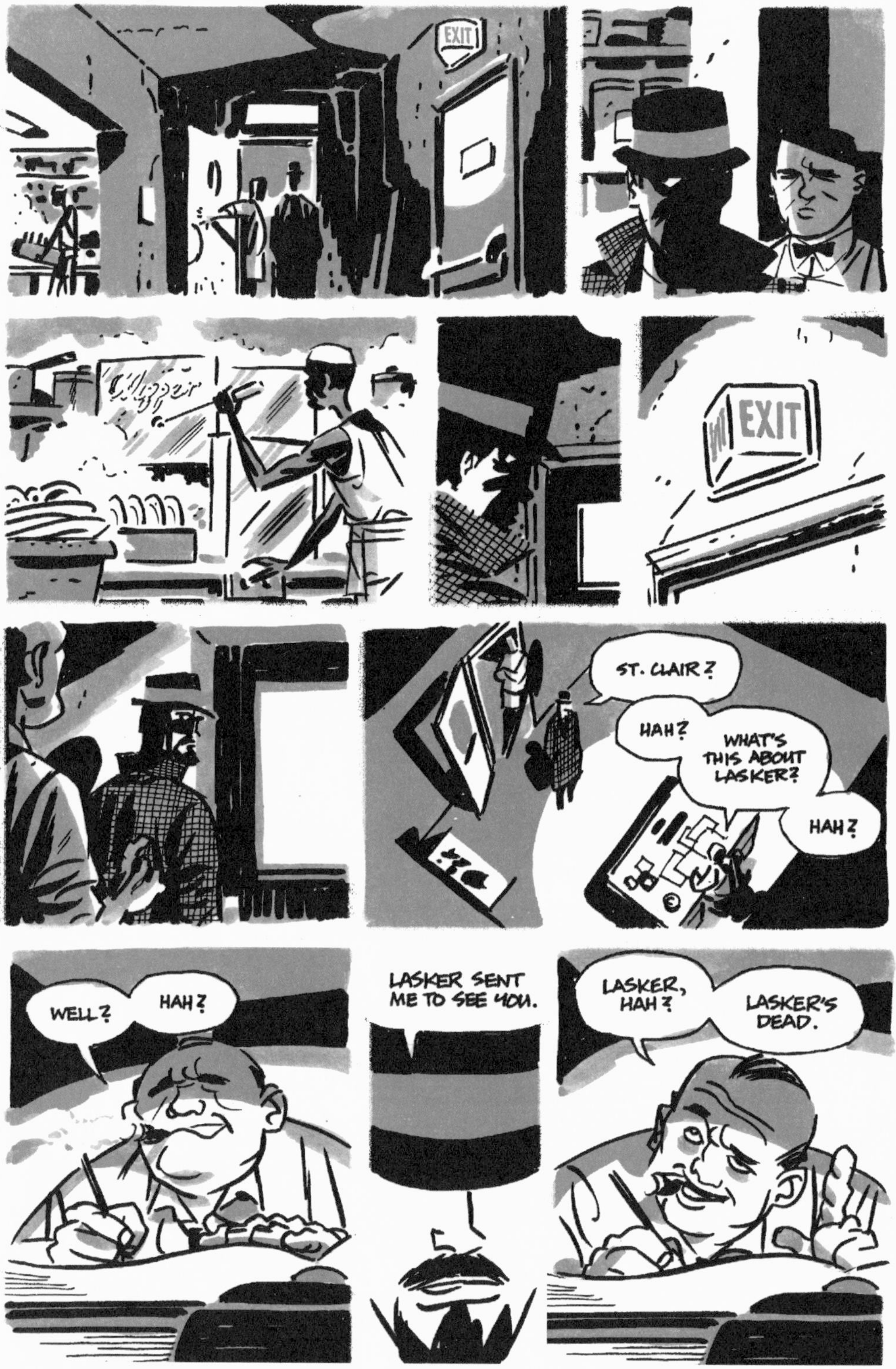
ST. CLAIR?
HAH?
WHAT'S THIS ABOUT LASKER?
HAH?
WELL?
HAH?
LASKER SENT ME TO SEE YOU.
LASKER, HAH?
LASKER'S DEAD.

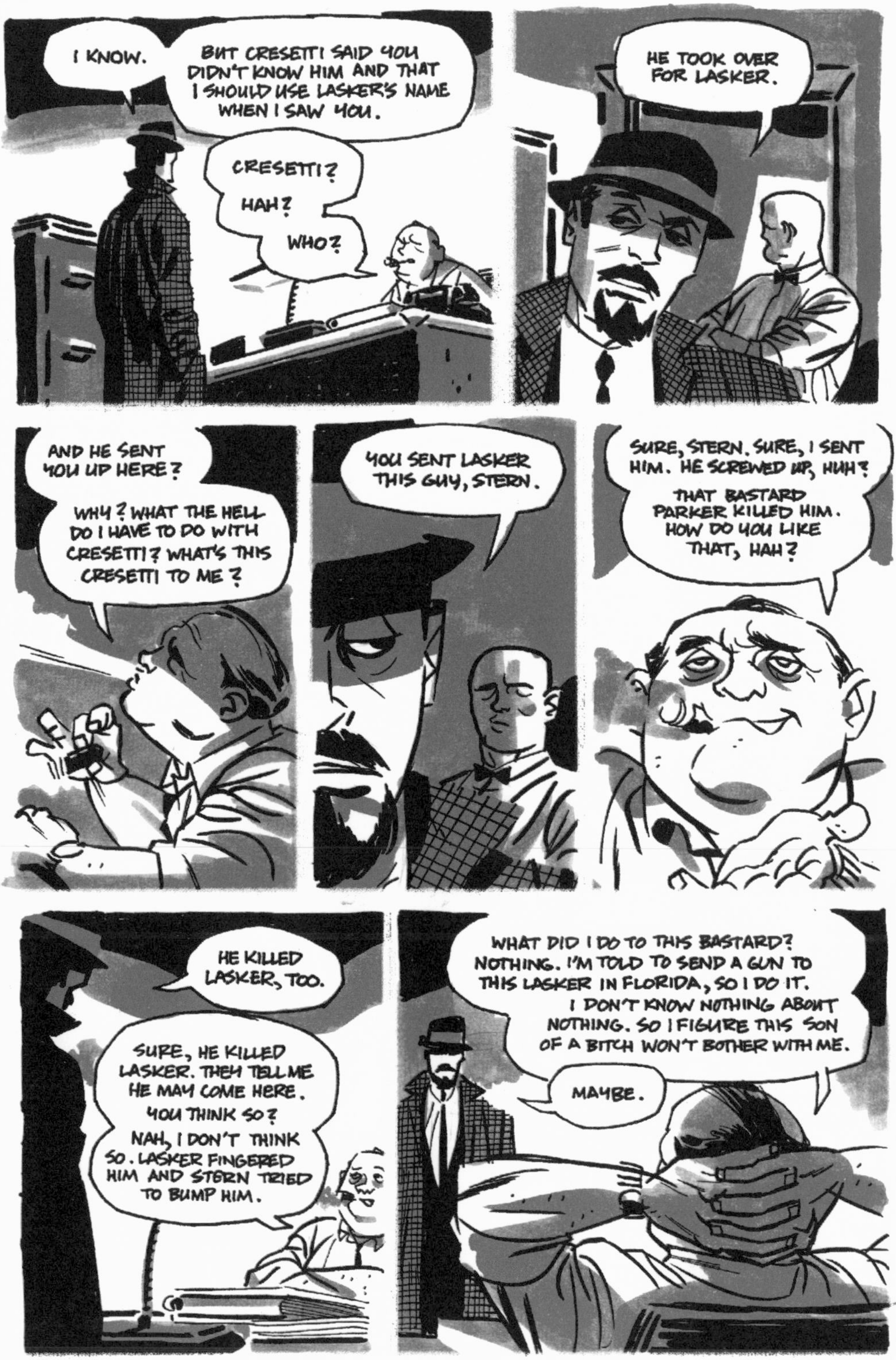
I KNOW.
BUT CRESETTI SAID YOU DIDN'T KNOW HIM AND THAT I SHOULD USE LASKER'S NAME WHEN I SAW YOU.
CRESETTI?
HAH?
WHO?
HE TOOK OVER FOR LASKER.
AND HE SENT YOU UP HERE?
WHY? WHAT THE HELL DO I HAVE TO DO WITH CRESETTI? WHAT'S THIS CRESETTI TO ME?
YOU SENT LASKER THIS GUY, STERN.
SURE, STERN. SURE, I SENT HIM. HE SCREWED UP, HUH?
THAT BASTARD PARKER KILLED HIM. HOW DO YOU LIKE THAT, HAH?
HE KILLED LASKER, TOO.
SURE, HE KILLED LASKER. THEY TELL ME HE MAY COME HERE.
YOU THINK SO?
NAH, I DON'T THINK SO. LASKER FINGERED HIM AND STERN TRIED TO BUMP HIM.
WHAT DID I DO TO THIS BASTARD? NOTHING. I'M TOLD TO SEND A GUN TO THIS LASKER IN FLORIDA, SO I DO IT.
I DON'T KNOW NOTHING ABOUT NOTHING. SO I FIGURE THIS SON OF A BITCH WON'T BOTHER WITH ME.
MAYBE.

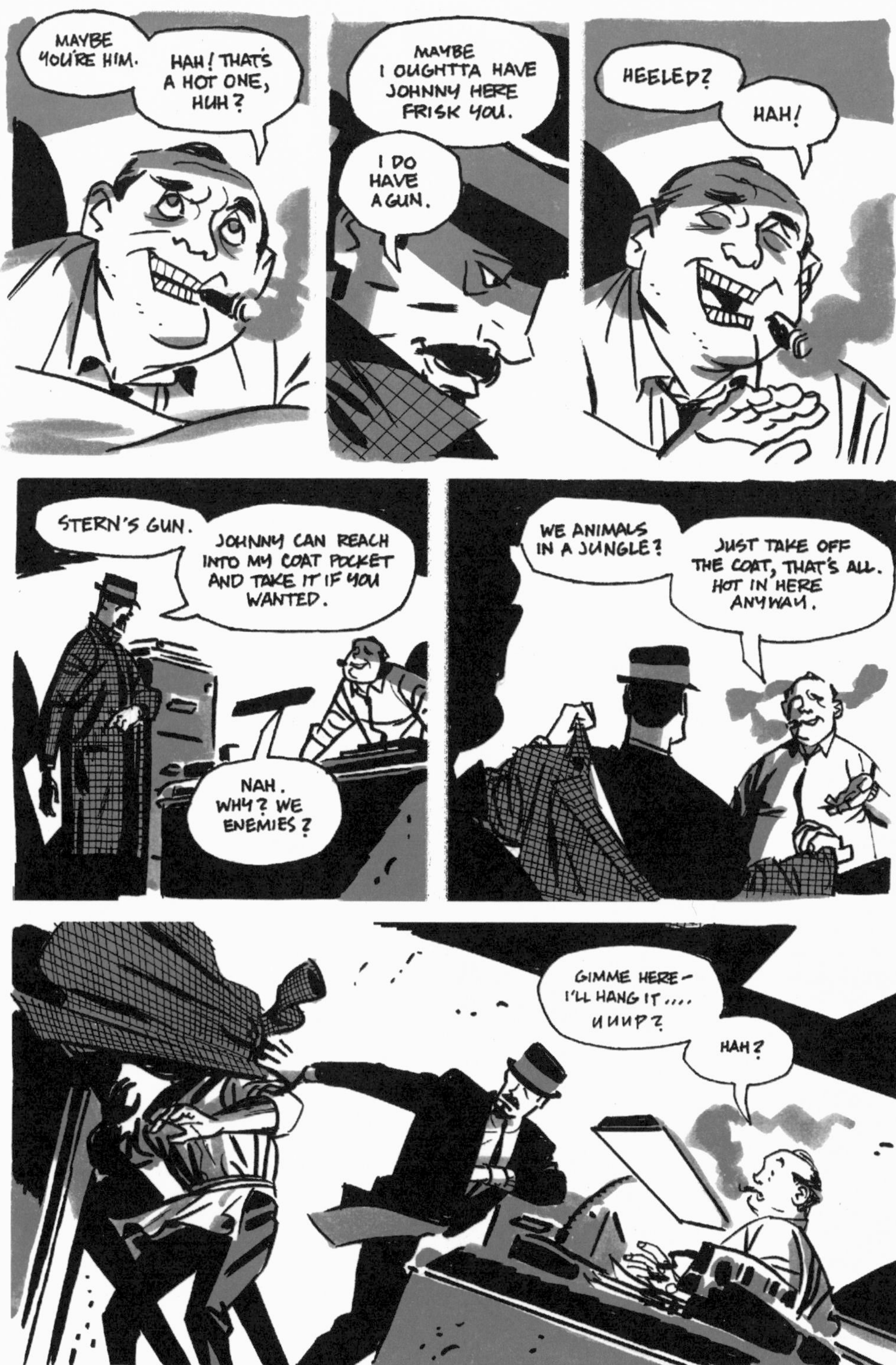
MAYBE YOU'RE HIM.
HAH! THAT'S A HOT ONE, HUH?
MAYBE I OUGHTTA HAVE JOHNNY HERE FRISK YOU.
I DO HAVE A GUN.
HEELED?
HAH!
STERN'S GUN.
JOHNNY CAN REACH INTO MY COAT POCKET AND TAKE IT IF YOU WANTED.
NAH. WHY? WE ENEMIES?
WE ANIMALS IN A JUNGLE?
JUST TAKE OFF THE COAT, THAT'S ALL. HOT IN HERE ANYWAY.
GIMME HERE - I'LL HANG IT.... UUUP?
HAH?

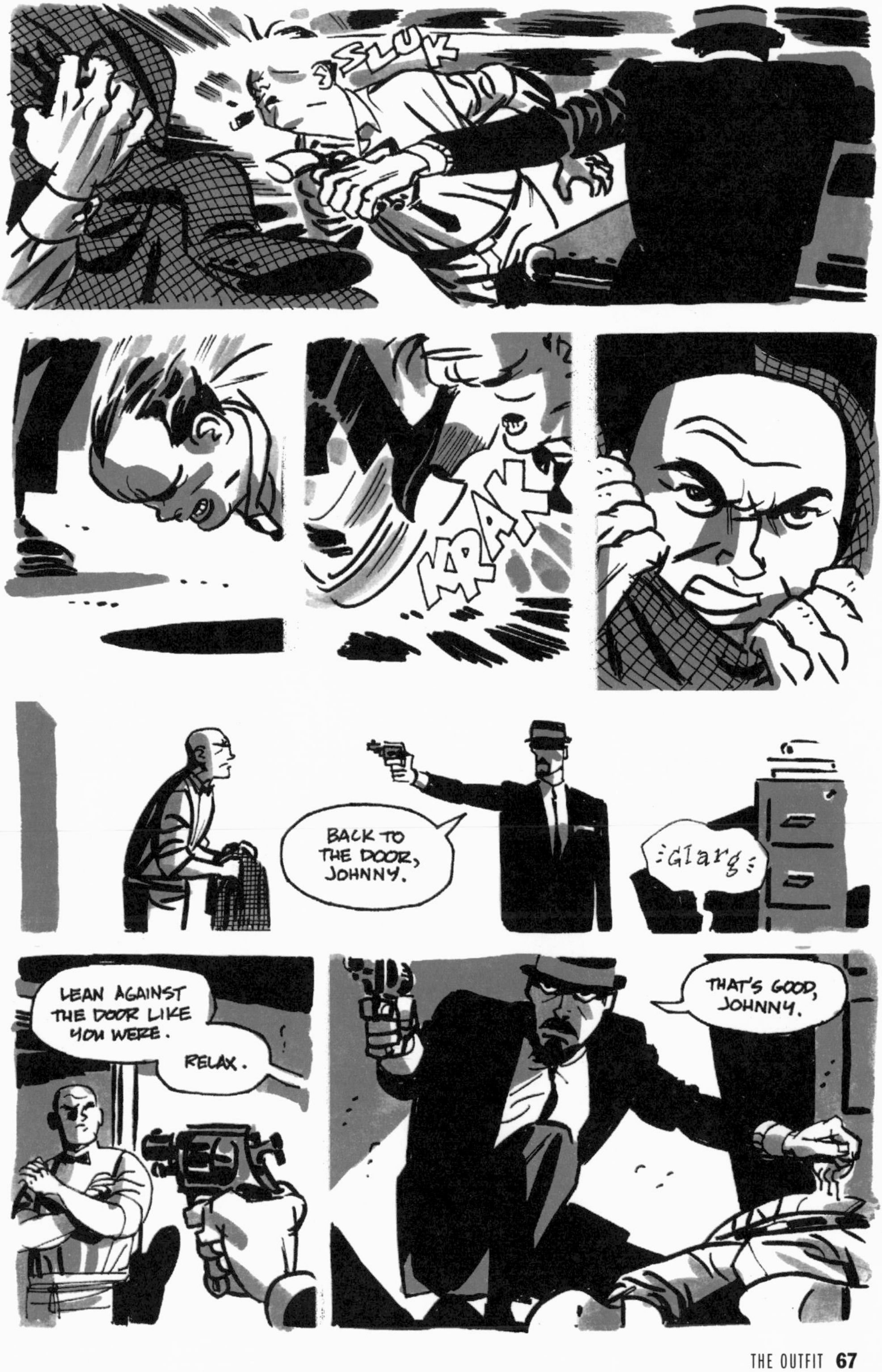
SLUK
KRAK
BACK TO THE DOOR, JOHNNY.
Glarg
LEAN AGAINST THE DOOR LIKE YOU WERE.
RELAX.
THAT'S GOOD, JOHNNY.

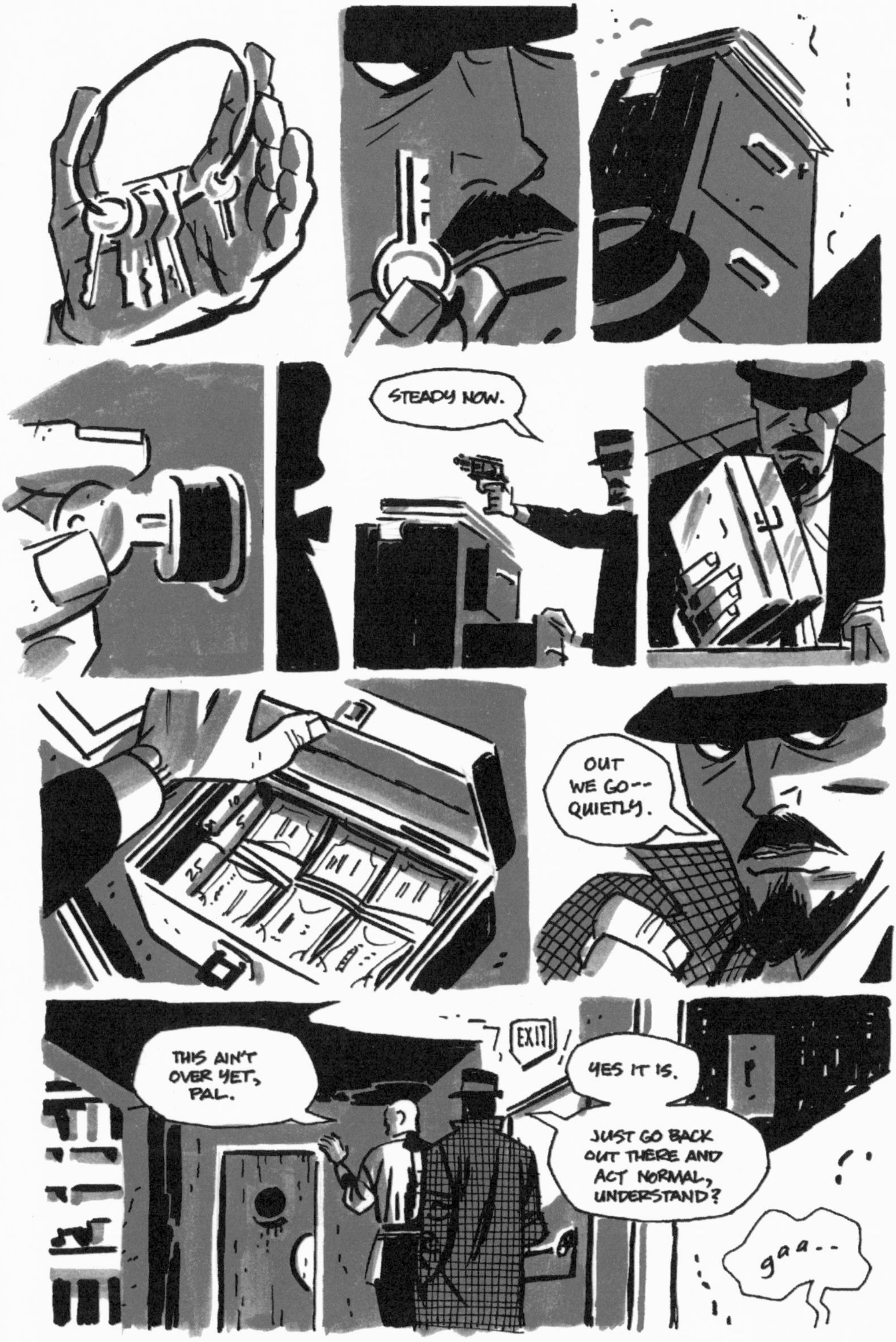
STEADY NOW.
OUT WE GO-- QUIETLY.
THIS AIN'T OVER YET, PAL.
EXIT
YES IT IS.
JUST GO BACK OUT THERE AND ACT NORMAL, UNDERSTAND?
gaa..

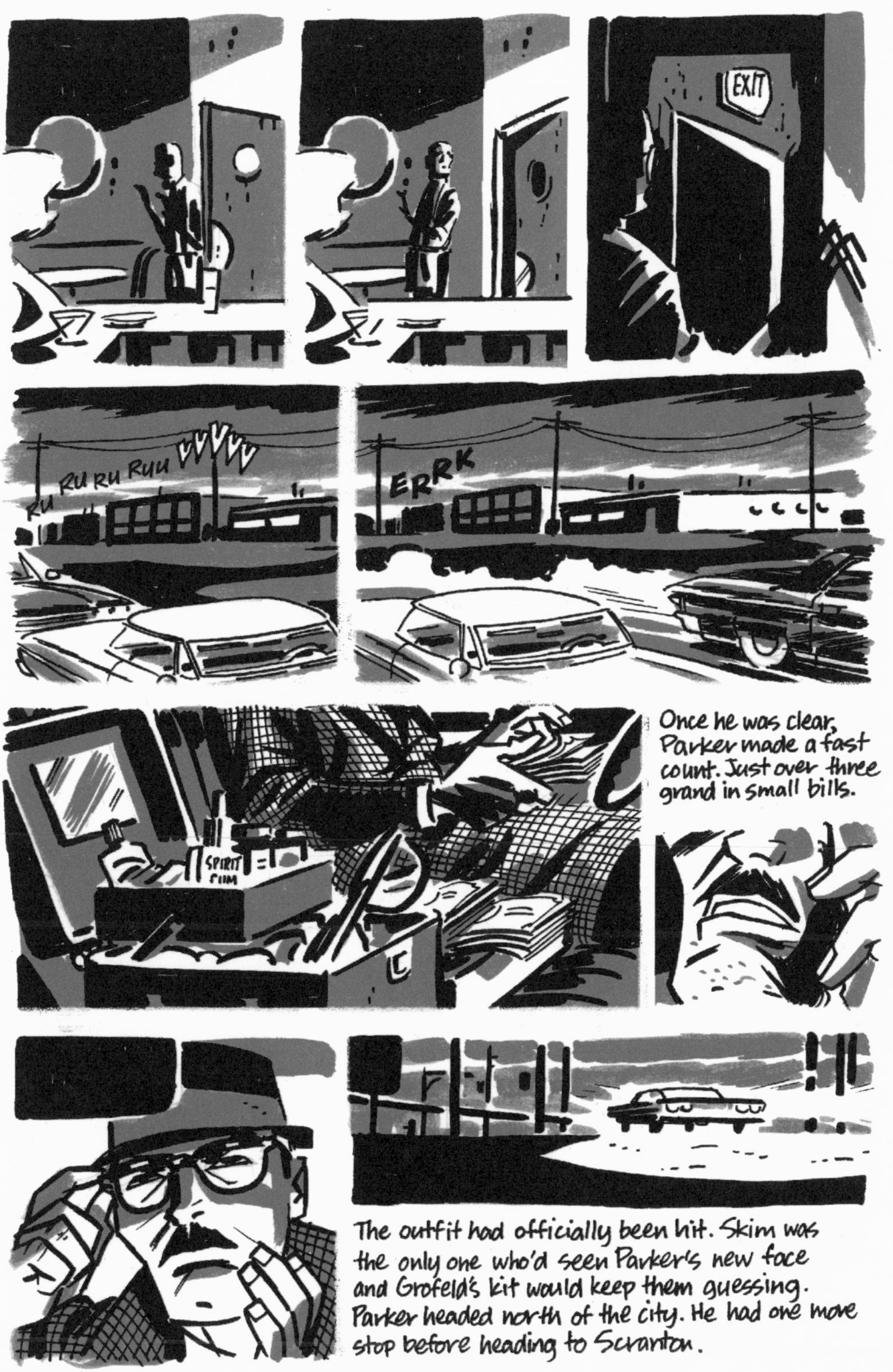
EXIT
RU RU RU RUU VVVV
ERRK
SPIRIT GUM
Once he was clear, Parker made a fast count. Just over three grand in small bills.
The outfit had officially been hit. Skim was the only one who'd seen Parker's new face and Grofeld's kit would keep them guessing. Parker headed north of the city. He had one more stop before heading to Scranton.

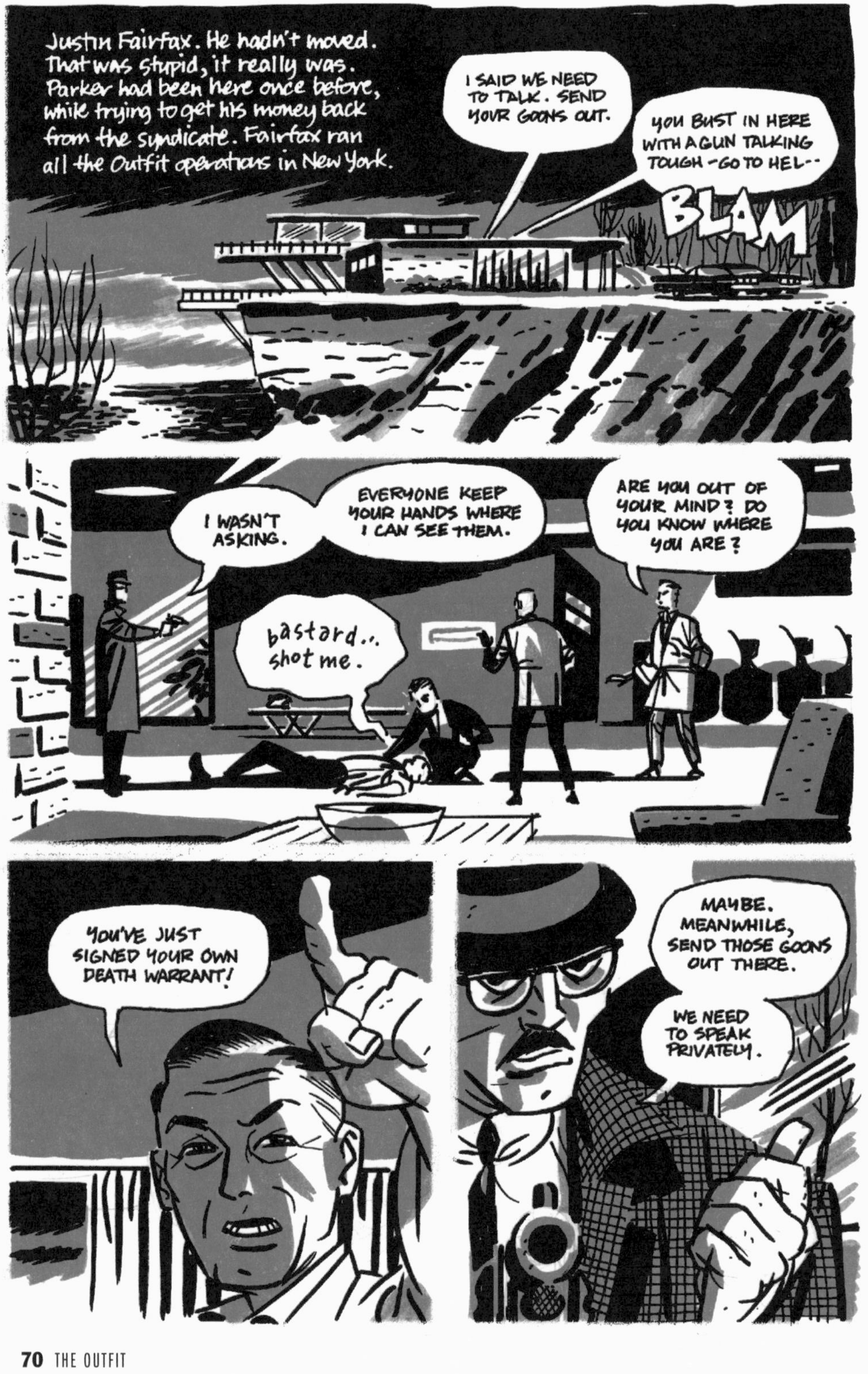

Justin Fairfax. He hadn't moved. That was stupid, it really was. Parker had been here once before, while trying to get his money back from the syndicate. Fairfax ran all the Outfit operations in New York.
I SAID WE NEED TO TALK. SEND YOUR GOONS OUT.
YOU BUST IN HERE WITH A GUN TALKING TOUGH -GO TO HEL--
BLAM
I WASN'T ASKING.
EVERYONE KEEP YOUR HANDS WHERE I CAN SEE THEM.
ARE YOU OUT OF YOUR MIND? DO YOU KNOW WHERE YOU ARE?
bastard... shot me.
YOU'VE JUST SIGNED YOUR OWN DEATH WARRANT!
MAYBE. MEANWHILE, SEND THOSE GOONS OUT THERE.
WE NEED TO SPEAK PRIVATELY.

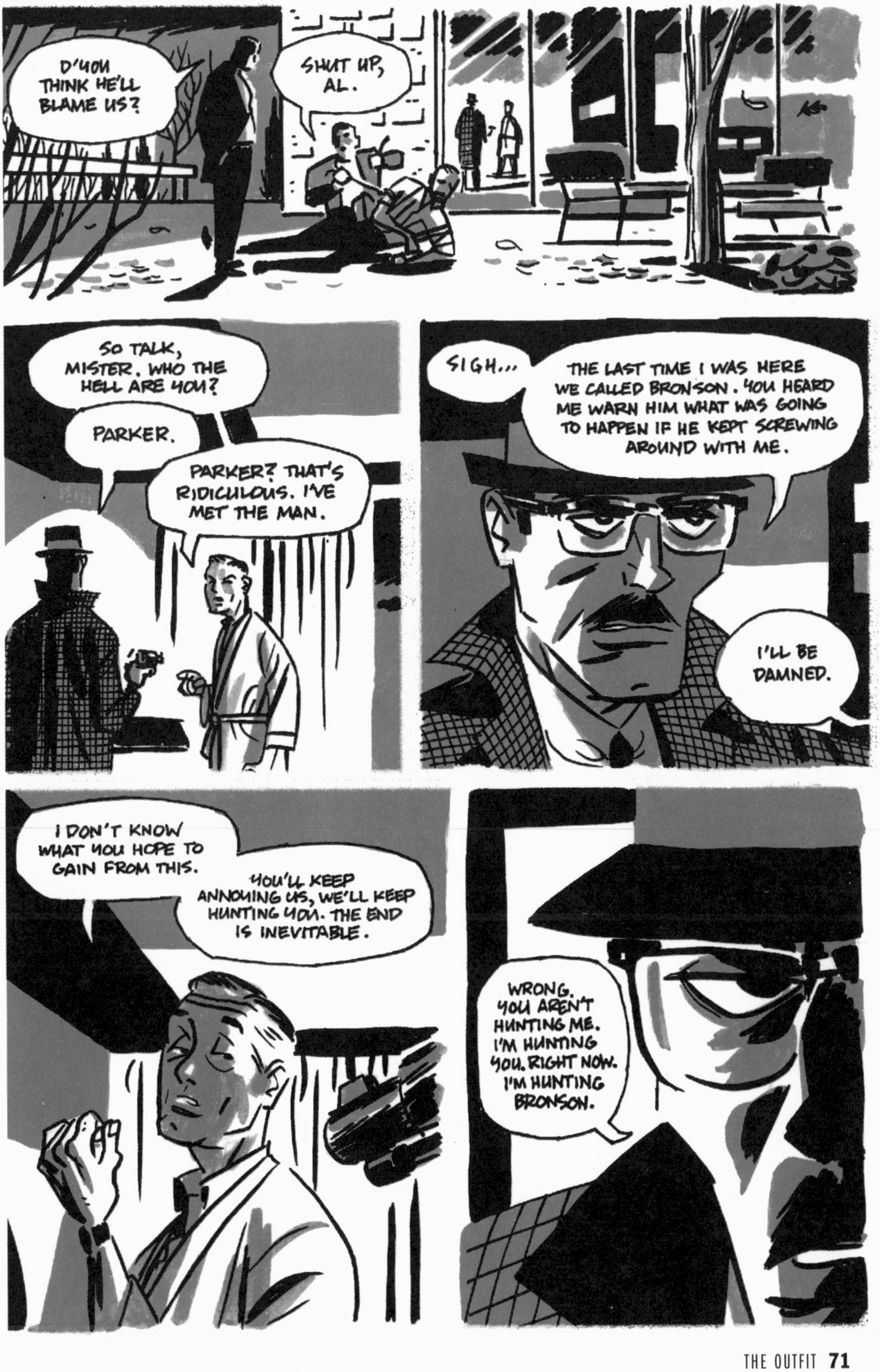
D'YOU THINK HE'LL BLAME US?
SHUT UP, AL.
SO TALK, MISTER. WHO THE HELL ARE YOU?
PARKER.
PARKER? THAT'S RIDICULOUS. I'VE MET THE MAN.
SIGH...
THE LAST TIME I WAS HERE WE CALLED BRONSON. YOU HEARD ME WARN HIM WHAT WAS GOING TO HAPPEN IF HE KEPT SCREWING AROUND WITH ME.
I'LL BE DAMNED.
I DON'T KNOW WHAT YOU HOPE TO GAIN FROM THIS.
YOU'LL KEEP ANNOYING US, WE'LL KEEP HUNTING YOU. THE END IS INEVITABLE.
WRONG. YOU AREN'T HUNTING ME. I'M HUNTING YOU. RIGHT NOW. I'M HUNTING BRONSON.

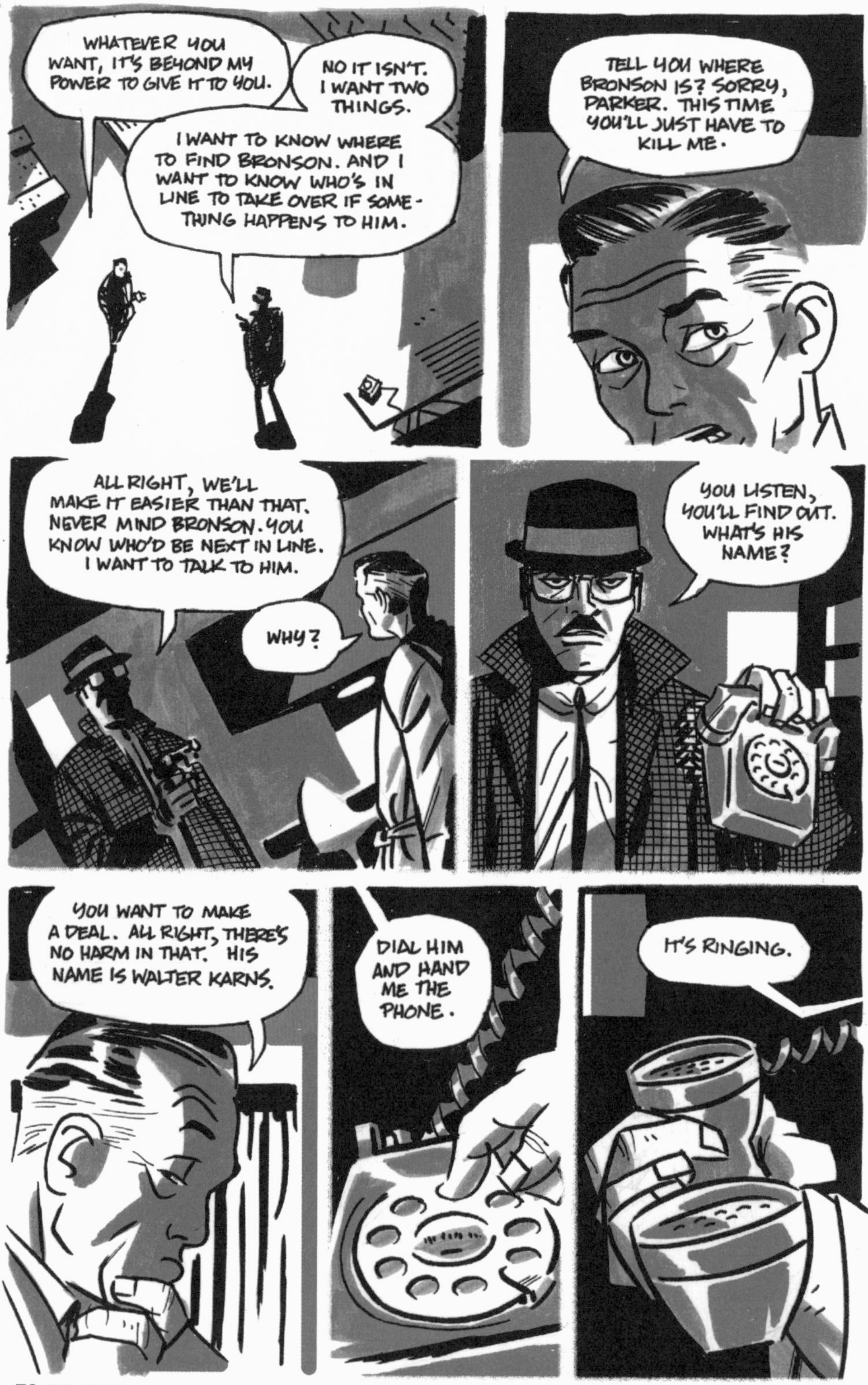
WHATEVER YOU WANT, IT'S BEYOND MY POWER TO GIVE IT TO YOU.
NO IT ISN'T. I WANT TWO THINGS.
I WANT TO KNOW WHERE TO FIND BRONSON. AND I WANT TO KNOW WHO'S IN LINE TO TAKE OVER IF SOME-THING HAPPENS TO HIM.
TELL YOU WHERE BRONSON IS? SORRY, PARKER. THIS TIME YOU'LL JUST HAVE TO KILL ME.
ALL RIGHT, WE'LL MAKE IT EASIER THAN THAT. NEVER MIND BRONSON. YOU KNOW WHO'D BE NEXT IN LINE. I WANT TO TALK TO HIM.
WHY?
YOU LISTEN, YOU'LL FIND OUT. WHAT'S HIS NAME?
YOU WANT TO MAKE A DEAL. ALL RIGHT, THERE'S NO HARM IN THAT. HIS NAME IS WALTER KARNS.
DIAL HIM AND HAND ME THE PHONE.
IT'S RINGING.

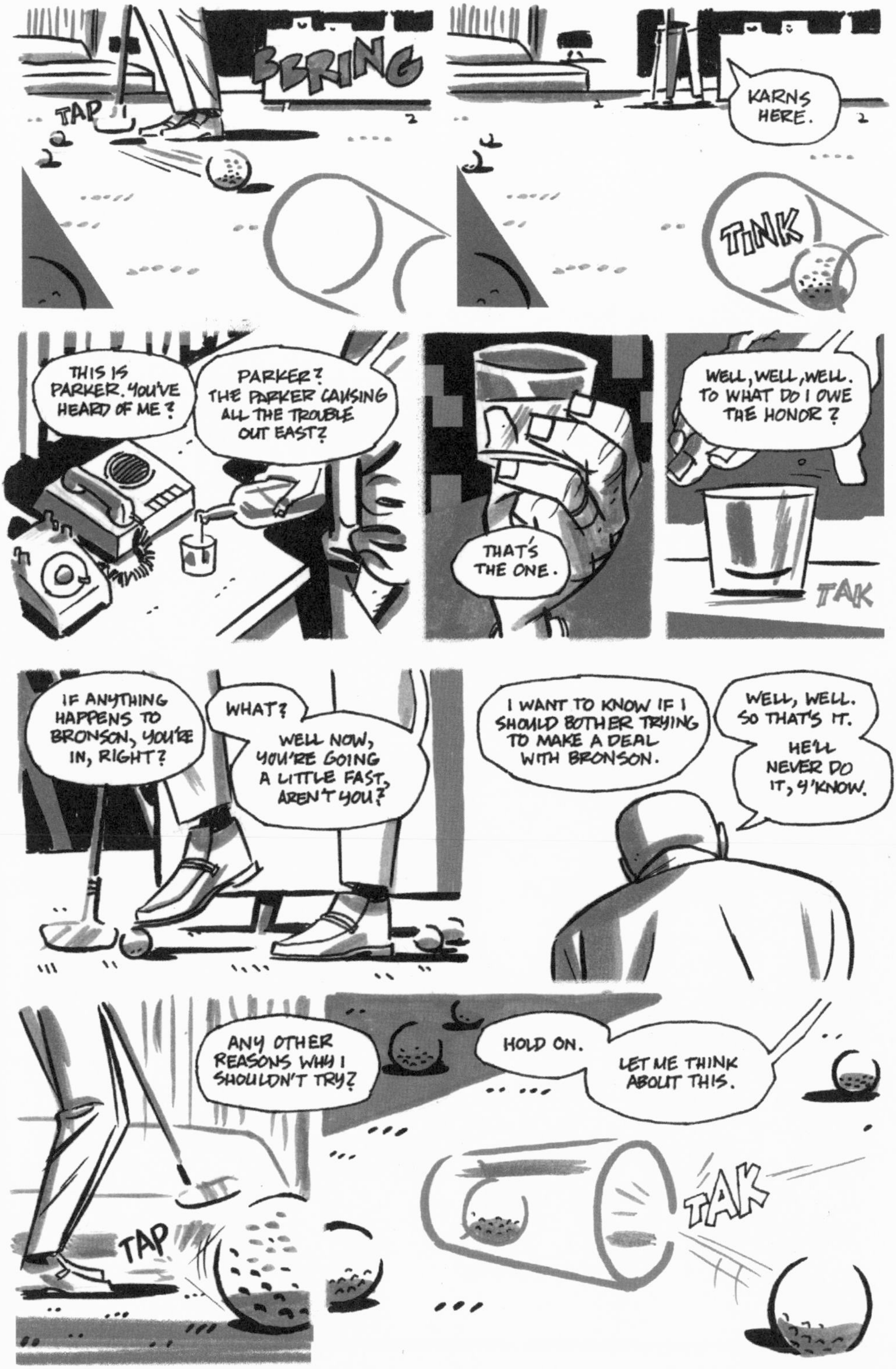
BRING
TAP
KARNS HERE.
TINK
THIS IS PARKER. YOU'VE HEARD OF ME?
PARKER? THE PARKER CAUSING ALL THE TROUBLE OUT EAST?
THAT'S THE ONE.
WELL, WELL, WELL. TO WHAT DO I OWE THE HONOR?
TAK
IF ANYTHING HAPPENS TO BRONSON, YOU'RE IN, RIGHT?
WHAT?
WELL NOW, YOU'RE GOING A LITTLE FAST, AREN'T YOU?
I WANT TO KNOW IF I SHOULD BOTHER TRYING TO MAKE A DEAL WITH BRONSON.
WELL, WELL. SO THAT'S IT.
HE'LL NEVER DO IT, Y'KNOW.
ANY OTHER REASONS WHY I SHOULDN'T TRY?
HOLD ON.
LET ME THINK ABOUT THIS.
TAP
TAK

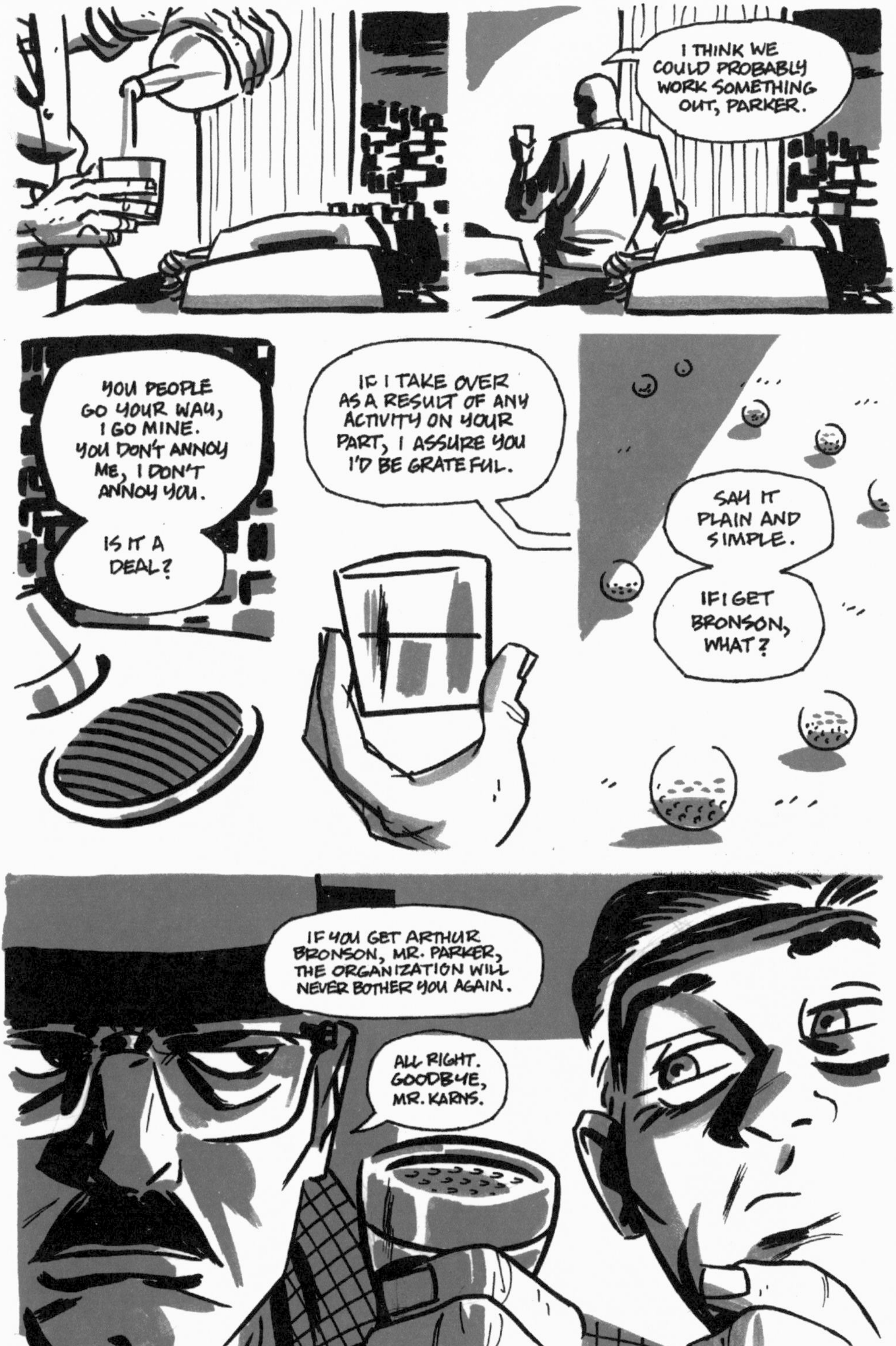
I THINK WE COULD PROBABLY WORK SOMETHING OUT, PARKER.
YOU PEOPLE GO YOUR WAY, I GO MINE. YOU DON'T ANNOY ME, I DON'T ANNOY YOU.
IS IT A DEAL?
IF I TAKE OVER AS A RESULT OF ANY ACTIVITY ON YOUR PART, I ASSURE YOU I'D BE GRATEFUL.
SAY IT PLAIN AND SIMPLE.
IF I GET BRONSON, WHAT?
IF YOU GET ARTHUR BRONSON, MR. PARKER, THE ORGANIZATION WILL NEVER BOTHER YOU AGAIN.
ALL RIGHT. GOODBYE, MR. KARNS.

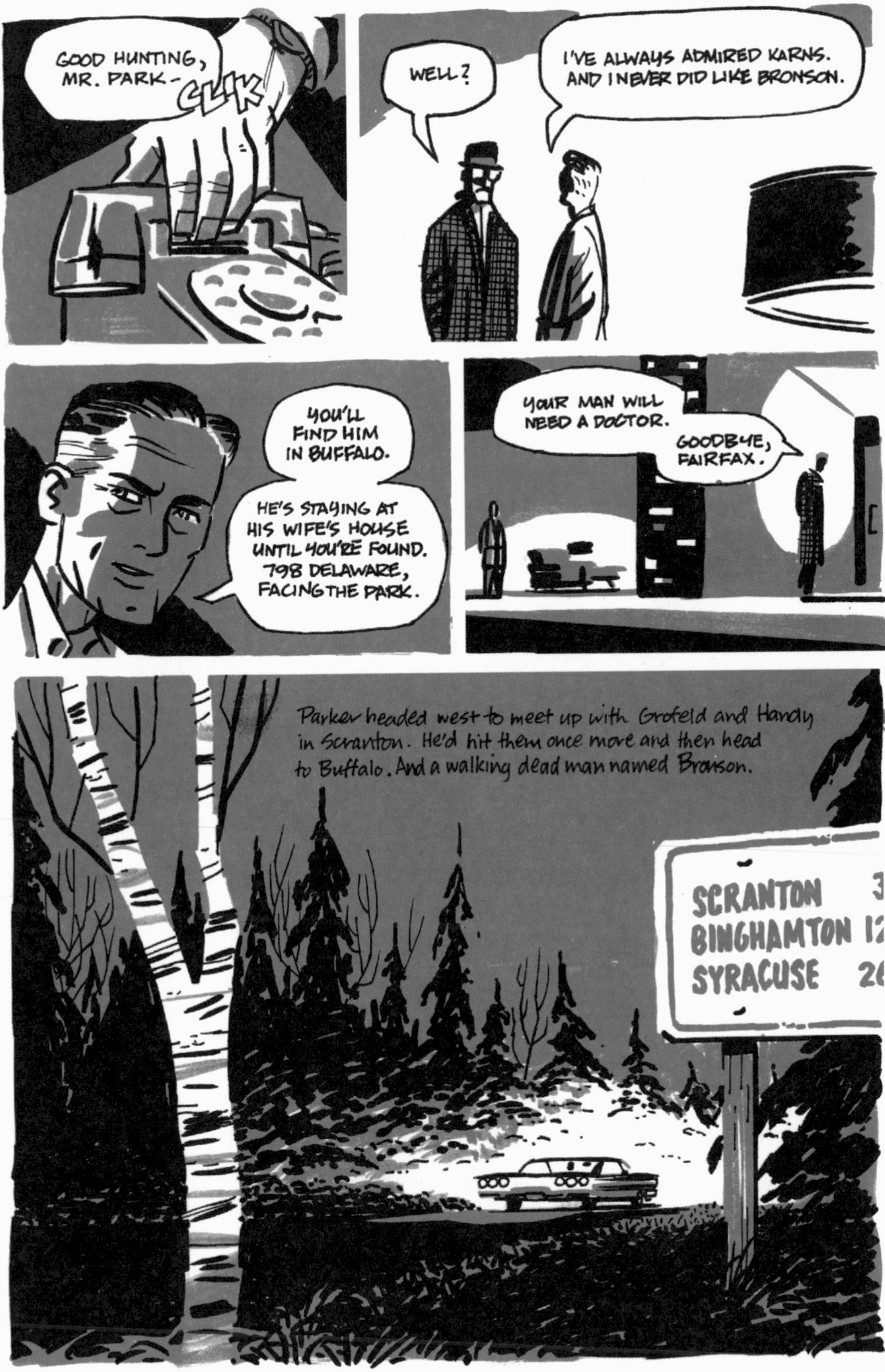
GOOD HUNTING, MR. PARK -
CLIK
WELL?
I'VE ALWAYS ADMIRED KARNS. AND I NEVER DID LIKE BRONSON.
YOU'LL FIND HIM IN BUFFALO.
HE'S STAYING AT HIS WIFE'S HOUSE UNTIL YOU'RE FOUND. 798 DELAWARE, FACING THE PARK.
YOUR MAN WILL NEED A DOCTOR.
GOODBYE, FAIRFAX.
Parker headed west to meet up with Grofeld and Handy in Scranton. He'd hit them once more and then head to Buffalo. And a walking dead man named Bronson.
SCRANTON 3
BINGHAMTON 1
SYRACUSE 2

BOOK THREE

GO TO JAIL.
GO DIRECTLY
TO JAIL.
DO NOT PASS GO.
DO NOT COLLECT
TWO HUNDRED
DOLLARS.

As far as
Arthur Bronson
was concerned,
he already was
in jail.

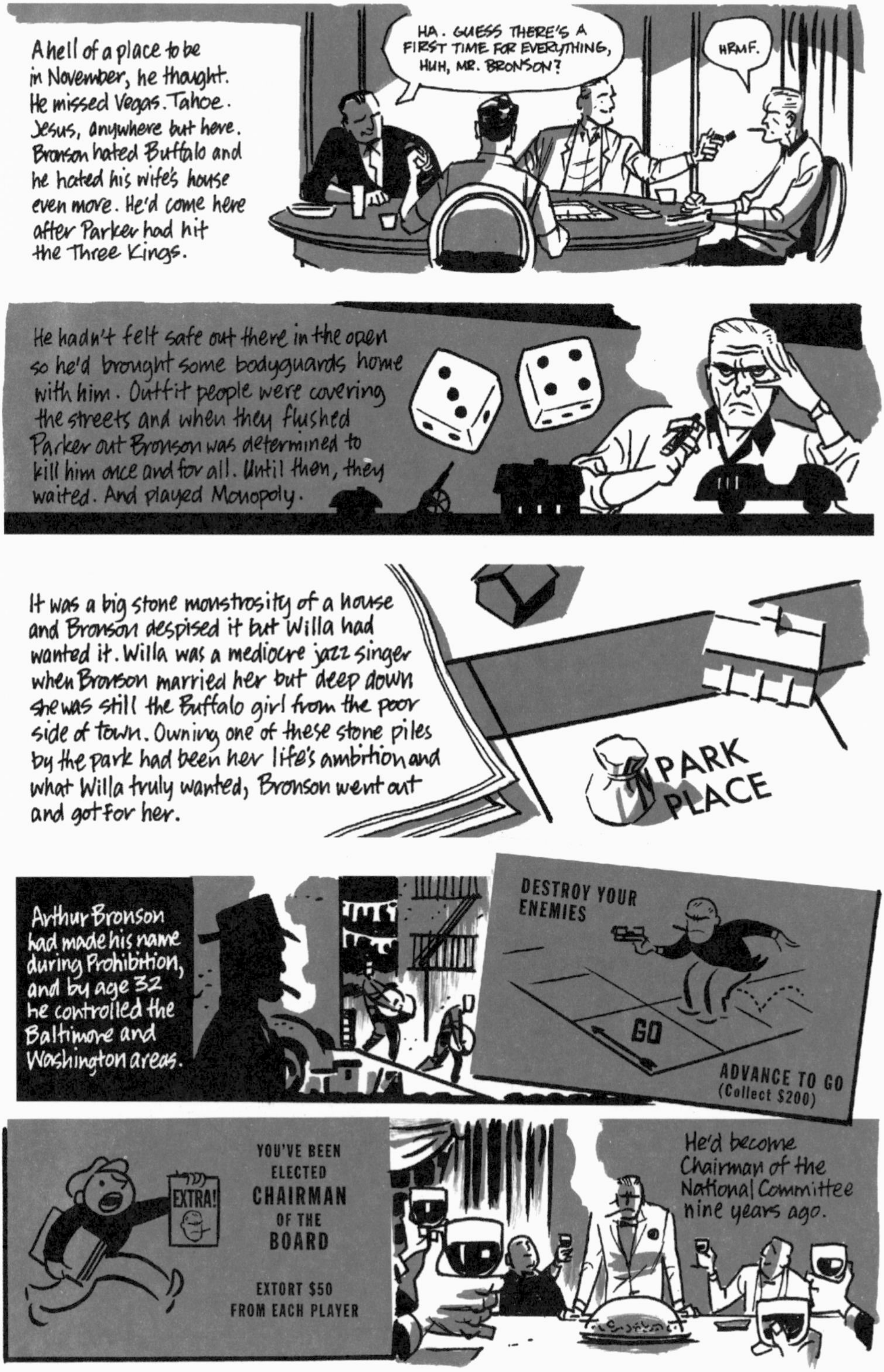
A hell of a place to be in November, he thought. He missed Vegas. Tahoe. Jesus, anywhere but here. Bronson hated Buffalo and he hated his wife's house even more. He'd come here after Parker had hit the Three Kings.
HA. GUESS THERE'S A FIRST TIME FOR EVERYTHING, HUH, MR. BRONSON?
HRMF.
He hadn't felt safe out there in the open so he'd brought some bodyguards home with him. Outfit people were covering the streets and when they flushed Parker out Bronson was determined to kill him once and for all. Until then, they waited. And played Monopoly.
It was a big stone monstrosity of a house and Bronson despised it but Willa had wanted it. Willa was a mediocre jazz singer when Bronson married her but deep down she was still the Buffalo girl from the poor side of town. Owning one of these stone piles by the park had been her life's ambition and what Willa truly wanted, Bronson went out and got for her.
PARK PLACE
Arthur Bronson had made his name during Prohibition, and by age 32 he controlled the Baltimore and Washington areas.
DESTROY YOUR ENEMIES
GO
ADVANCE TO GO
(Collect $200)
EXTRA!
YOU'VE BEEN ELECTED
CHAIRMAN
OF THE
BOARD
EXTORT $50 FROM EACH PLAYER
He'd become Chairman of the National Committee nine years ago.

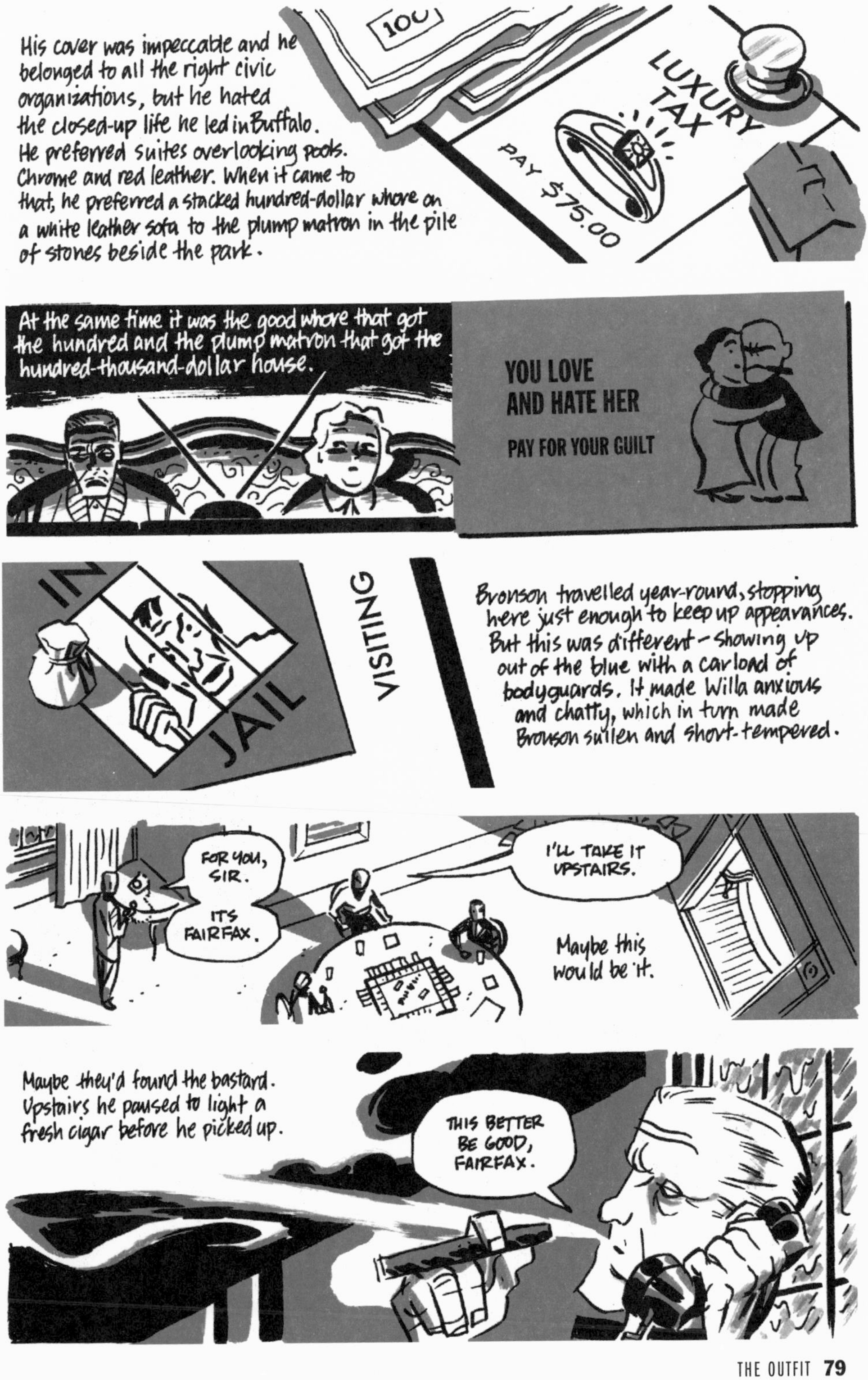
His cover was impeccable and he belonged to all the right civic organizations, but he hated the closed-up life he led in Buffalo. He preferred suites overlooking pools. Chrome and red leather. When it came to that, he preferred a stacked hundred-dollar whore on a white leather sofa to the plump matron in the pile of stones beside the park.
100
LUXURY TAX
PAY $75.00
At the same time it was the good whore that got the hundred and the plump matron that got the hundred-thousand-dollar house.
YOU LOVE AND HATE HER
PAY FOR YOUR GUILT
IN JAIL
VISITING
Bronson travelled year-round, stopping here just enough to keep up appearances. But this was different—showing up out of the blue with a carload of bodyguards. It made Willa anxious and chatty, which in turn made Bronson sullen and short-tempered.
FOR YOU, SIR.
ITS FAIRFAX.
I'LL TAKE IT UPSTAIRS.
Maybe this would be it.
Maybe they'd found the bastard. Upstairs he paused to light a fresh cigar before he picked up.
THIS BETTER BE GOOD, FAIRFAX.

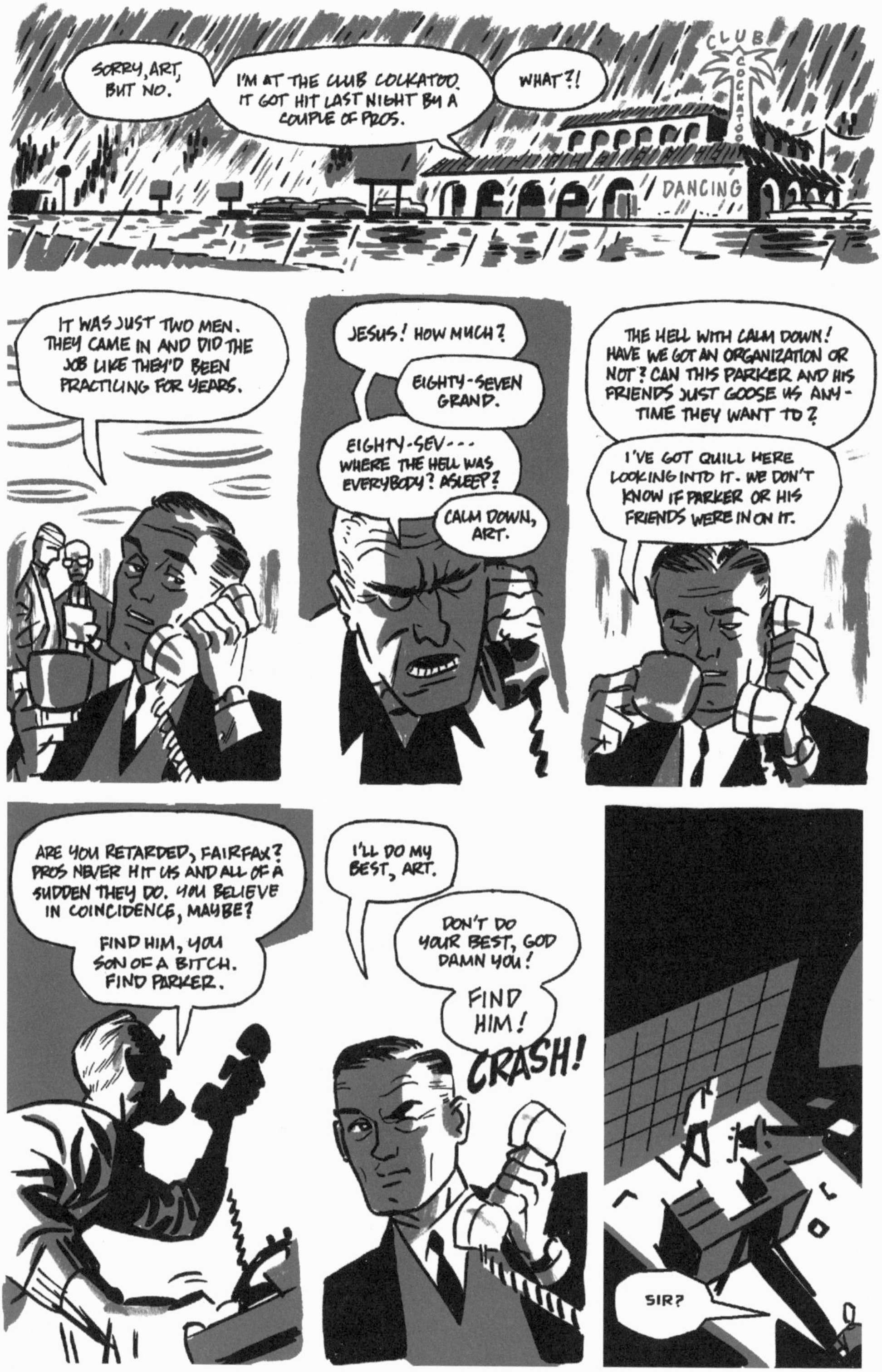

CLUB
COCKATOO
DANCING
SORRY, ART, BUT NO.
I'M AT THE CLUB COCKATOO. IT GOT HIT LAST NIGHT BY A COUPLE OF PROS.
WHAT?!
IT WAS JUST TWO MEN. THEY CAME IN AND DID THE JOB LIKE THEY'D BEEN PRACTICING FOR YEARS.
JESUS! HOW MUCH?
EIGHTY-SEVEN GRAND.
EIGHTY-SEV--- WHERE THE HELL WAS EVERYBODY? ASLEEP?
CALM DOWN, ART.
THE HELL WITH CALM DOWN! HAVE WE GOT AN ORGANIZATION OR NOT? CAN THIS PARKER AND HIS FRIENDS JUST GOOSE US ANYTIME THEY WANT TO?
I'VE GOT QUILL HERE LOOKING INTO IT. WE DON'T KNOW IF PARKER OR HIS FRIENDS WERE IN ON IT.
ARE YOU RETARDED, FAIRFAX? PROS NEVER HIT US AND ALL OF A SUDDEN THEY DO. YOU BELIEVE IN COINCIDENCE, MAYBE?
FIND HIM, YOU SON OF A BITCH. FIND PARKER.
I'LL DO MY BEST, ART.
DON'T DO YOUR BEST, GOD DAMN YOU!
FIND HIM!
CRASH!
SIR?

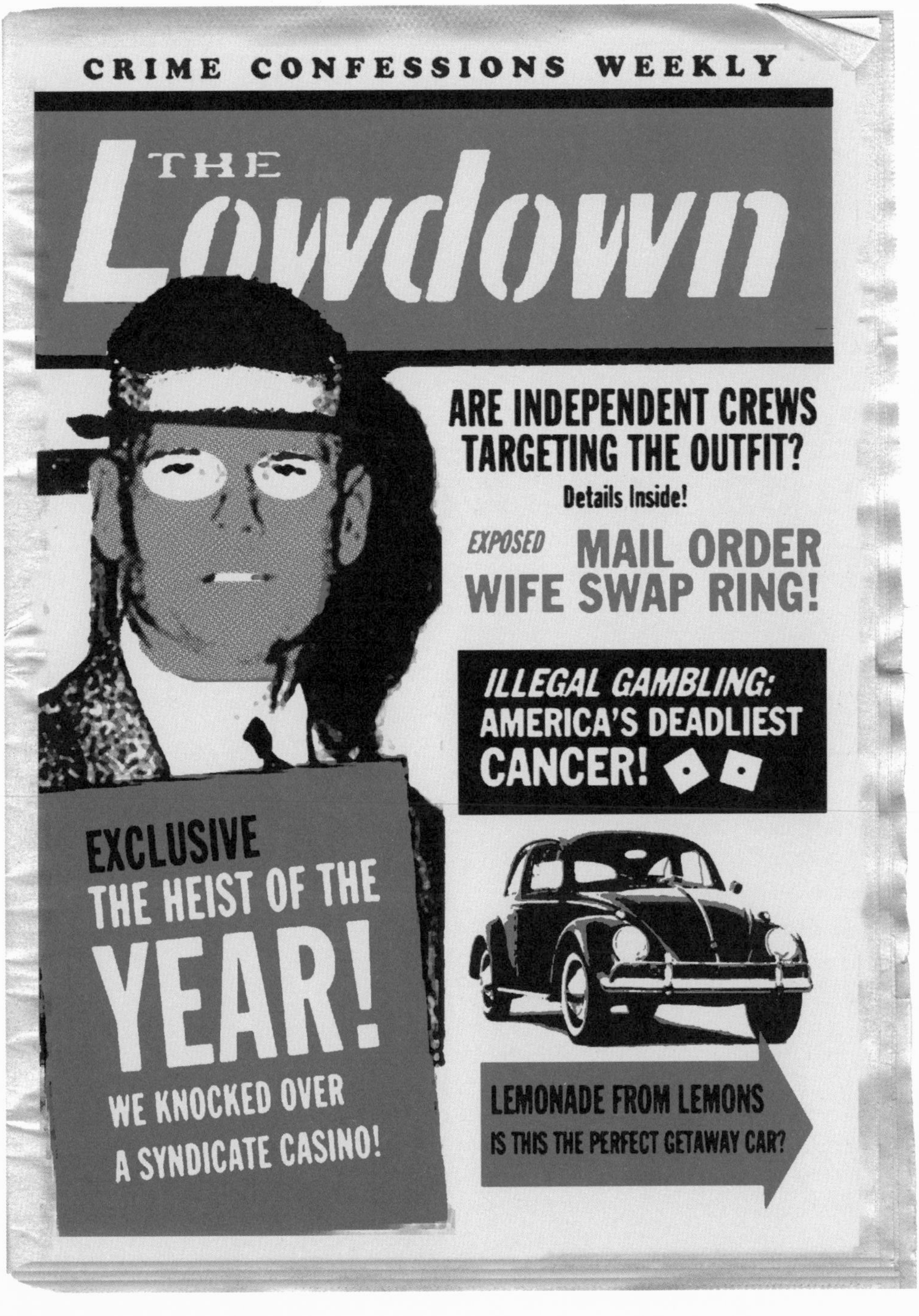
CRIME CONFESSIONS WEEKLY
THE Lowdown
ARE INDEPENDENT CREWS TARGETING THE OUTFIT?
Details Inside!
EXPOSED MAIL ORDER WIFE SWAP RING!
ILLEGAL GAMBLING: AMERICA'S DEADLIEST CANCER!
EXCLUSIVE
THE HEIST OF THE YEAR!
WE KNOCKED OVER A SYNDICATE CASINO!
LEMONADE FROM LEMONS
IS THIS THE PERFECT GETAWAY CAR?

THE
CLUB COCKATOO
RAID

THE THRILLING STORY OF THE YEAR'S
BIGGEST HEIST AND THE TWO DARING MEN
WHO PULLED IT OFF.

by Richard Stark

The neon sign which hung out by the road was green. It said: Club Cockatoo Dancing.

The way it works is this: This was an Outfit operation, a rambling cream stucco structure two stories high. The only legal activity going on in the Club Cockatoo was dancing. On the first floor was the bar, where every drink ever heard of in New York City was available – at a price a little higher than in New York City. The waiters and bartenders had decks of marijuana for sale; the stronger drugs had never really caught on in that part of the country. Upstairs were the beds, and the maidens who manned them. And downstairs were the games. It was a good operation, profitable and safe. The local law was well-greased, and there had been no problems. Not until tonight.

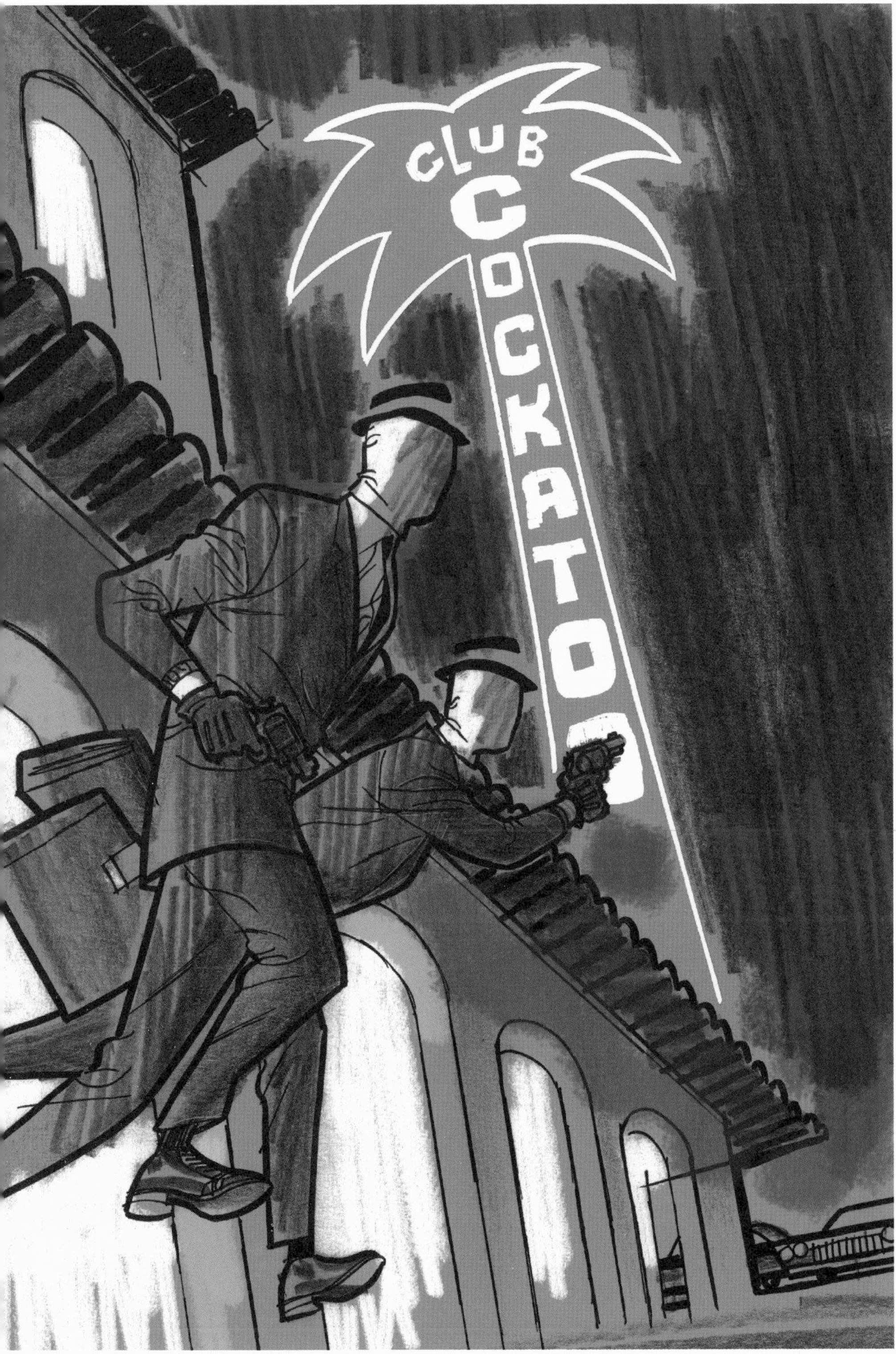
CLUB
COCKATOO

Town was five miles away to the east, along the two-lane black-top road, moving gradually down the decline into the valley where the city was situated. From that direction came an orange Volkswagen. It putted by the Club Cockatoo, with the characteristic cough of the VW. A mile and a half further along there was an Esso station, closed for the night. The VW putted in there and stopped. The lights were shut off. The low, small silhouette of the car could hardly be seen in the dark – couldn't be seen at all unless you knew it was there. The driver, a short thin man named Rico, got out and walked back down the road toward the Club Cockatoo.

THEY WORE DARK SUITS AND TIES, AND TOOK THEIR HATS OFF AS THEY STEPPED THROUGH THE ENTRANCE.

It was a Saturday night, so the parking lot was crowded. Rico walked through the ranks of cars to the line parked facing the side of the building. There was a door on the side, near the rear, and Rico headed for that. The car nearest that side door was a black Buick.

The driver was alone in the Buick. He was tall and slender, about forty, with a pock-marked face. His name was Terry. He nodded when he saw Rico.

Terry got out and they both walked around to the front and entered the club. They wore dark suits and ties, and took their hats off as they stepped through the entrance.

No building is safe from robbery, if a professional can get his hands on the blueprints. There were a few basic flaws in this particular building – from a robbery-proof viewpoint – that the Outfit had never considered before, but would have an opportunity to consider tonight.

The side door. It led to a short hallway, which, in turn, led to the bar. This hallway also opened onto a flight of stairs which led down to the gambling room. A man going down these stairs would find himself in another hallway with the main gambling room to his right. Directly across the hall, he would see the doors to the restrooms. Turning to his right and entering the main room, he would see that it was filled with tables of various kinds, and that along one wall there was a wire wicket, like a teller's cage in a bank, except that the wire enclosure extended to the ceiling. Behind this were the cashiers, with drawers full of money and chips. And behind the cashiers was a wall with a door in it. Turning around and going back to the hallway and thence the men's room, he would discover that the men's room and the cashiers' space shared a wall, and that the door he had already noticed led into the men's room. This door was kept locked; it could be unlocked from either side only by a key. Each cashier had a key which he was required to turn in when going off duty.

And the office. It was behind the cashiers' wicket, to the left of the men's room. The door to the office was about eight feet to the left of the private door to the men's room. This door was not kept locked; because the cashiers use it fairly often, clearing checks, bringing money in or taking money out, coming on or going off duty. The office was windowless, having an air-conditioner high on the outside wall, and the door to the cashiers' space was its only entrance. The three men who worked in the office were armed.

Rico and Terry entered the club and stopped at the bar long enough for a bottle of beer, then they went downstairs to the gambling room. They entered the men's room. Each went quickly into a stall and closed the door, and then they both put on rubber masks which covered their faces completely. They put their hats on over the masks and waited. Patrons came and went.

They waited forty minutes before they heard the sound of a cashier's key. They heard a door open and close, they heard footsteps on the floor. They came out of the stalls.

They each had guns now – stubby English .32s. The cashier was a small, bald man with spectacles which reflected the light. He wore a white shirt with the sleeves rolled up, and his forearms were thin and pale and almost hairless.

Rico went over to the cashier. "Turn around. Put your palms against the wall." Then he patted pockets till he found the key.

They marched the cashier into a stall and made him kneel down. Rico sapped him and lowered him gently to the tile floor. If there were no killings and no injuries needing hospital care, there would probably be no official squawk from this job. The club wouldn't be making any reports to the law if it could avoid it. If the job was clean and quiet, the law would never hear about it at all.

They closed the stall doors and went to the private door. Rico unlocked it and led the way through. They had the guns in their pockets now, their right hands tucked into the same pockets.

To the left was a long table. Beyond that table was the door to the office. In front stretched the counter and the wire cage. All but one of the cashiers had their backs to them. This one sat at the table to the left, running an adding machine. He looked over when Rico and Terry came through the doorway, and his eyes widened. He was the only one who could see the masks; the other cashiers were facing away and the customers and stickmen beyond the mesh were too far away to see what was happening. Anyone looking through the wicket toward the dim area by the back wall wouldn't realize that those pale expressionless faces weren't faces at all.

RICO PULLED OUT THE GUN AND SHOWED IT TO HIM. "MY PARTNER HAS ONE, TOO."

Speaking softly, Rico said to the man at the adding machine, "Come here. Be nice and quiet." There was a steady flow of noises from beyond the wire, the rustle of conversation and the clatter of chips. None of the cashiers heard Rico's voice.

The man at the adding machine got to his feet. He understood now, and he was terrified. He was blinking rapidly behind his glasses, and his hands gripped each other at his waist. He came over slowly.

Rico said "Stand in front of me." Rico pulled out the gun and showed it to him. "My partner has one, too."

The man nodded convulsively.

"What's your name?" That was part of his pattern, Rico always wanted to know the name. He said it was psychological, it calmed the victim down and made him less likely to do something stupid out of panic, but that was just an excuse. He wanted to know the name, that was all.

"Stewart. Rob – Robert Stewart."

"All right, Bob. We're cleaning this place. We want to do it quiet, we don't want your customers all shook up. And we don't want the cops coming down here and seeing all the wheels and everything. You don't want that either, right?"

Stewart nodded again. He was staring at Rico's mouth, watching the lips move behind the rubber mask, making it tremble.

"Now, Bob, the three of us are going to walk into the office. Smile, Bob, I want to see you smile."

Stewart stretched his lips. From a distance, it might look like a smile.

"That's the way. Now keep smiling while we go into the office." Rico tucked the gun into his pocket again, but kept his hand on it. "Here we go, Bob."

They walked into the office, Stewart smiling his strained smile, and Terry closed the door and leaned against it. Rico pulled his gun out again, shoved Stewart to the side, and said, "I'm looking for heroes."

A man was squatting in front of the safe, his hands full of stacked bills. A second man was at the desk, a pencil in his right hand. A third man was at a table entering figures in a ledger. They all looked up and froze. The man at the safe kept licking his lips and glancing at the safe door. He was trying to build up the courage to slam the door. Rico pointed the gun at him. "You – what's your name?"

"What?" He'd been concentrating on the gun and the safe door, and he couldn't understand the question.

"Your name. What's your name?"

"J-Jim."

"All right, Jim. Stand up straight. That's good. Take two steps to your left. Very nice, Jim." Rico took two canvas sacks from under his coat and handed them to Stewart. "What you do, Bob," he said, "you go over and empty that safe. Put all the loot in these sacks. Jim, you give Bob that money you're holding. You-" he pointed the gun again at the man at the desk. "What's your name?"

"Fred Kirk." He was a heavy, florid man, probably the manager since he was the only one who didn't seem frightened.

"All right, Fred. If that phone rings, say you can't talk now. You've got a problem here. You'll call back."

"You won't get three miles."

"Quiet now, Fred."

"Don't you know who runs this place? You guys are crazy."

"No more talk, Fred. Don't make me put you to sleep. You-" he turned to the man at the ledger. "What's your name, partner?"

"Kelway. Stanley Kelway." His quavering voice was high and thin.

"Now, don't get upset, Stan. Just sit there easy."

Stewart came back with the two canvas sacks, both bulging now, nearly too heavy for him to carry. He held them out to Rico, but Rico shook his head. "Oh no, Bob, you'll carry them. Fred, you'll wait till Bob gets back before you make a fuss or Bob won't be coming back. You wouldn't want a corpse on the property, would you, Fred?"

Kirk glowered.

"All right, Bob, let's go."

Terry went first, opening the door and stepping out quickly, looking both ways. The cashiers still worked along, unconcerned, their backs on the action. Beyond the mesh, the customers and stickmen concentrated on their own business. Terry moved to the right. Stewart followed him, carrying the sacks. Rico backed out, closed the door and pocketed the gun.

There were two customers in the men's room and when they saw the masked men they raised their hands without being asked. Rico closed the door and said, "Bob here is an employee. Aren't you, Bob?"

Stewart nodded.

"Bob will come back in a minute and explain the whole thing. In the meantime, he'd like you to stay right here and not raise any sort of fuss. For your own good, that is. And for his. Isn't that right, Bob?"

Stewart nodded again.

"You don't have to keep your hands up like that, boys. Just stay here and wait. It'll only be a couple of minutes. But if you try to leave here too soon, you might just possibly get shot."

Terry, Rico and Stewart left the men's room, crossed the hall, and went up the stairs. Terry opened the side door and checked outside, then nodded to Rico. He never talked during a job, unless it was absolutely necessary. Rico did all the talking for both of them.

Rico took the two sacks from Stewart. "All right, Bob," he said. "You did that real well. You can go back downstairs now."

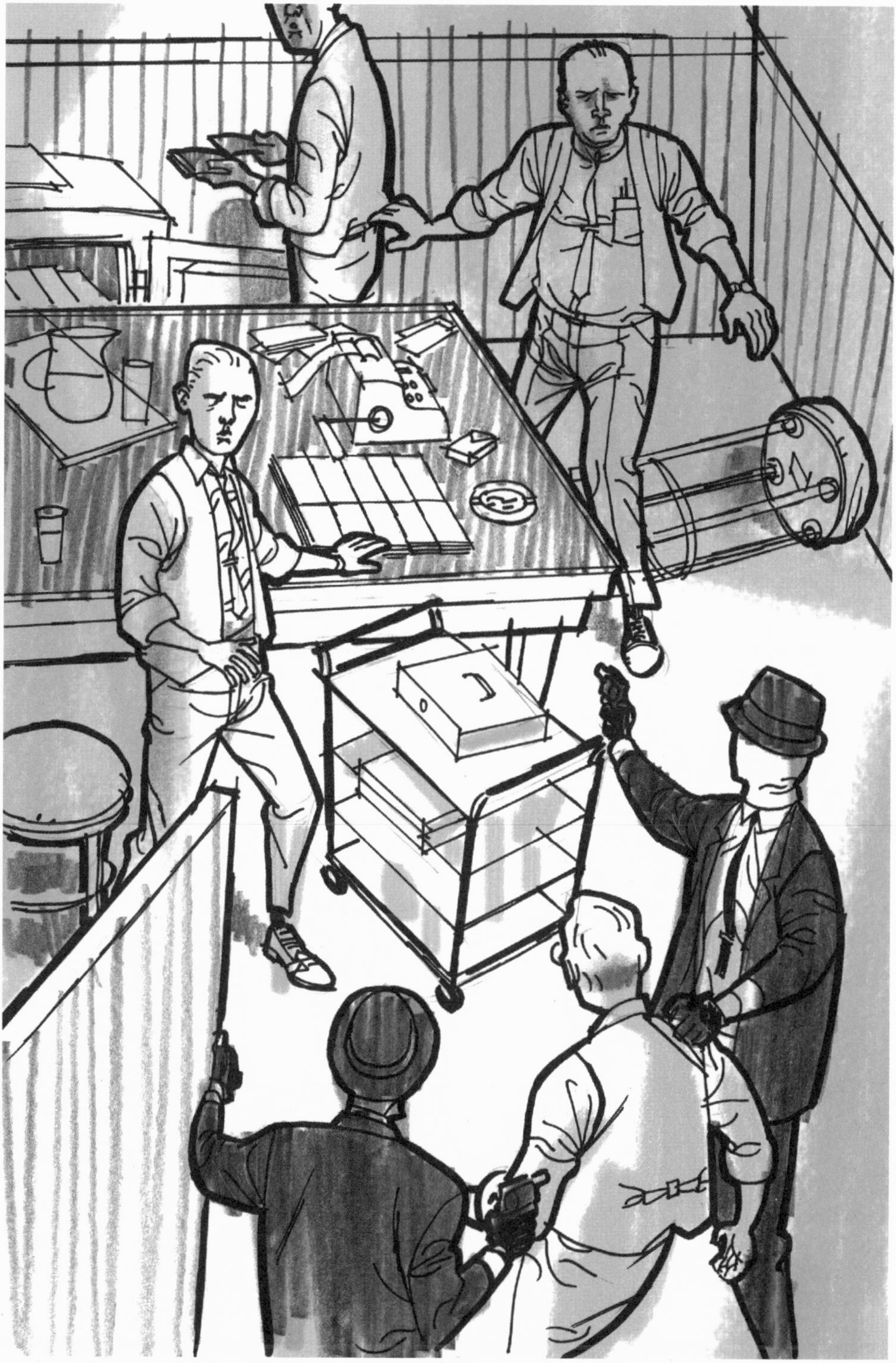

Stewart hurried back downstairs. His shoulders hunched, like he believed he would be shot anyway.

Rico and Terry went over and got into the Buick. Rico got behind the wheel and Terry sat beside him. The canvas sacks were on the floor between Terry's legs. Rico backed the Buick out of the slot and headed for the highway. They both still had the masks on.

Terry turned, looking back at the club. Just as Rico reached the road, he saw the side door open and four men come running out. Two of them pointed frantically at the Buick. Terry said, "They spotted us."

JUST AS RICO REACHED THE ROAD, HE SAW THE DOOR OPEN AND FOUR MEN COME RUNNING OUT.

"Good for them," said Rico. He spun the wheel and the Buick cut left, then leaped down the highway. Behind them, the four men were piling into a Chrysler Imperial. Rico accelerated and the Buick streaked along. He switched off the headlights as soon as he saw the station ahead. "Here they come, Rico."

"Sure."

Rico cut the wheel and switched off the ignition and the Buick slid silently up beside the orange Volkswagen.

They were out of the Buick before it had completely stopped. They grabbed the sacks and jumped out. The sacks they tossed behind the front seat of the Volkswagen. Hats and masks followed. Then they both got into the car, slamming the doors.

The Chrysler Imperial shot by, and went about a hundred yards further down the road before its brakes began to squeal. Rico started the VW, spun it around in a tight turn, and aimed it toward town. It didn't shift like a Volkswagen, and, above 60 miles an hour, it didn't sound like a Volkswagen any more. Two more cars came boiling out of the Club Cockatoo and roared by the little orange car without a glance. Everybody knows a VW's no good as a getaway car.

This wasn't the operation Rico had ordered the VW for, but just before he'd picked up the car he'd received the letter from Parker about hitting the syndicate. The Club Cockatoo had been bothering him for seven years, and he felt relieved when he discovered a justifiable reason for knocking it over. He combined the plan he had already with the car he had just picked up, brought Terry into the deal, and did the job immediately, before Parker could tell him everything had been straightened out. He drove along now pleased with Parker, pleased with the car, pleased with the operation, pleased with the world. By morning, they were nearly six hundred miles away from the club, so they stopped to see just how much they'd taken.

Del Mar

THE NEXT DAY

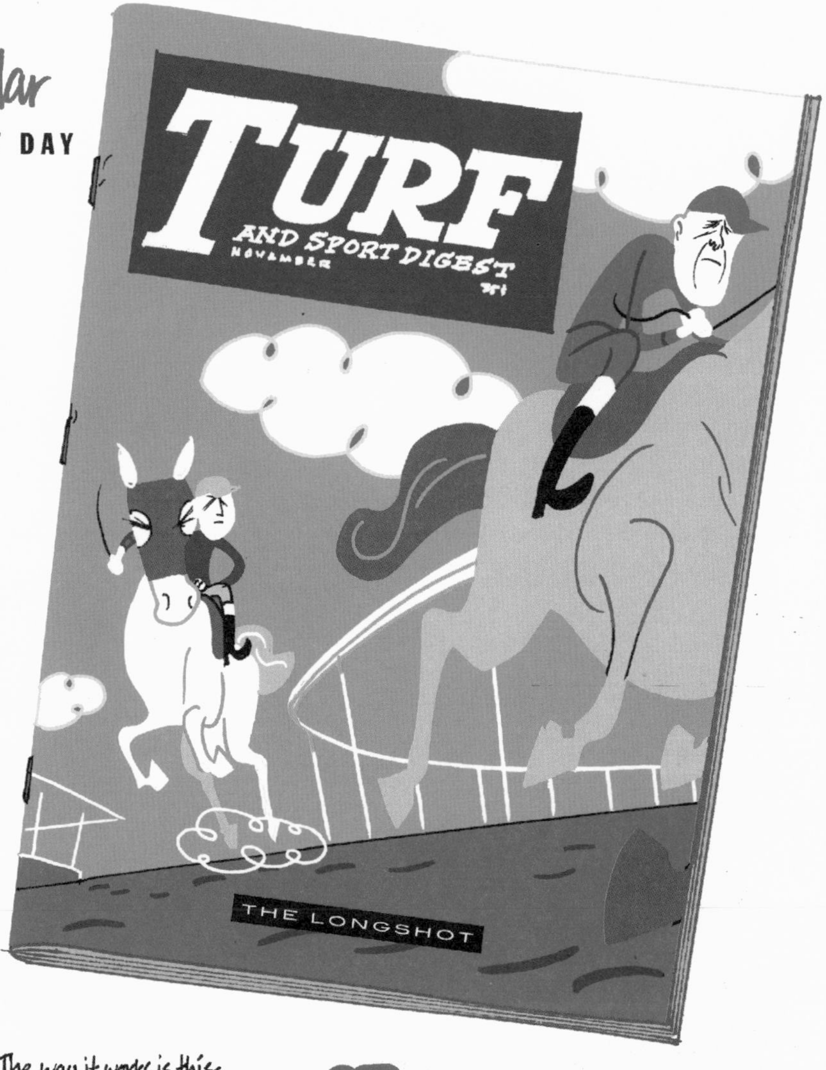
TURF
AND SPORT DIGEST
NOVEMBER
THE LONGSHOT

The way it works is this:

Racetracks use a complex array of factors to calculate each horse's chance of winning. These are the "odds" that the horse might win the race.

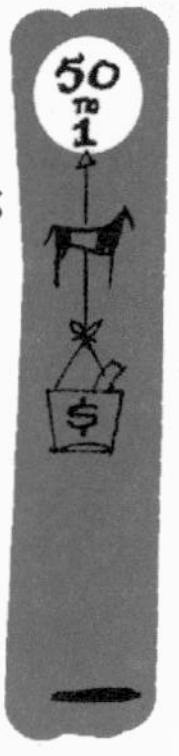
50 TO 1
$

A longshot is a horse with very high odds going into race day. If enough people bet on the longshot the odds and the potential payoff become lower.

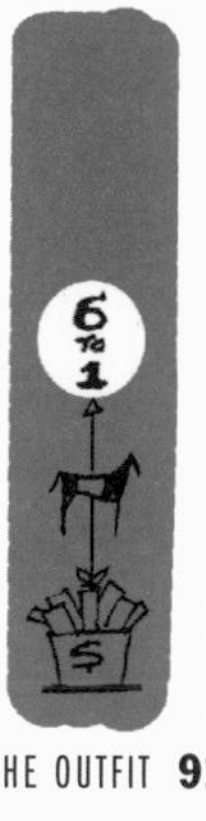
$

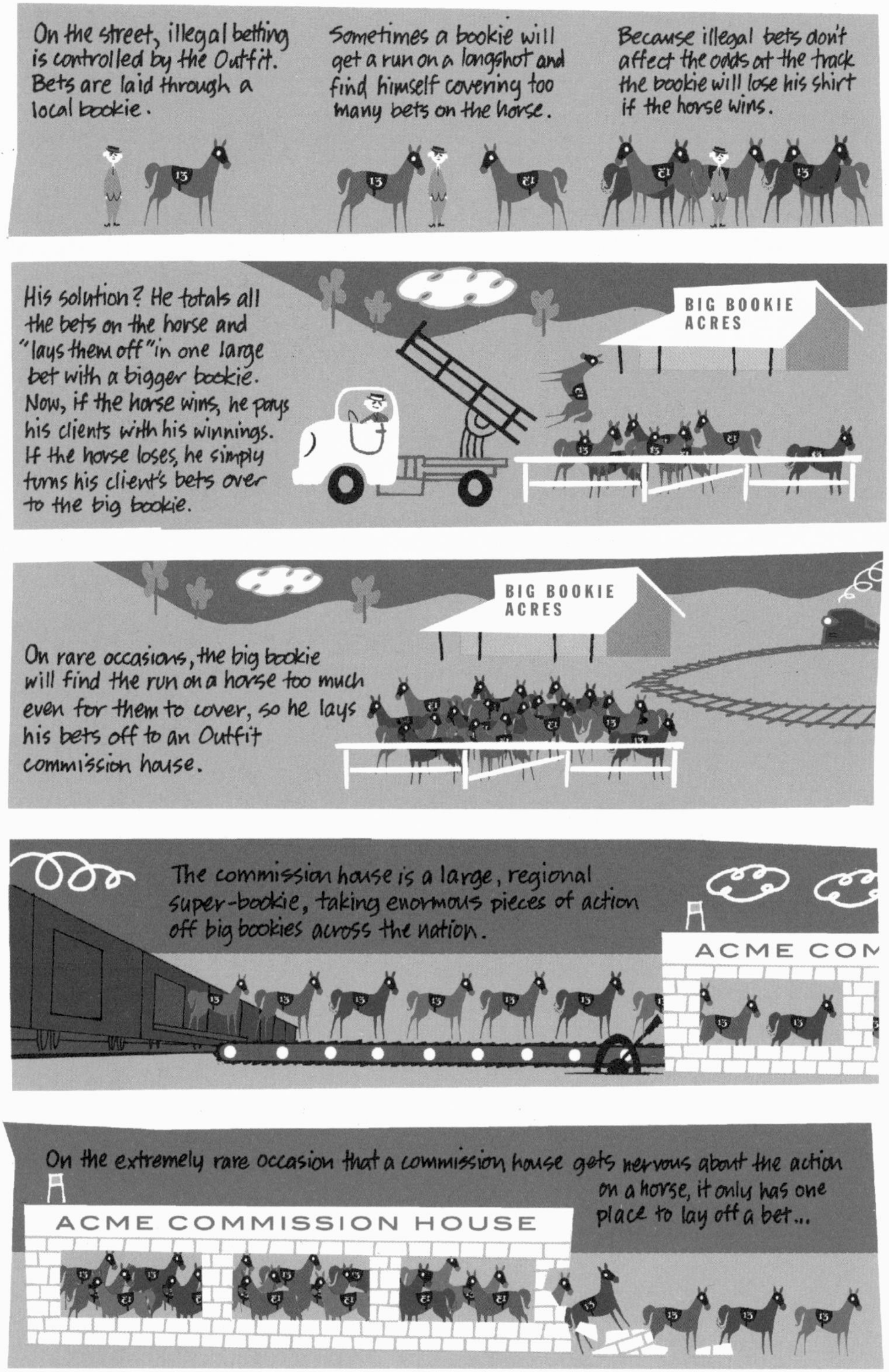

On the street, illegal betting is controlled by the Outfit. Bets are laid through a local bookie.
Sometimes a bookie will get a run on a longshot and find himself covering too many bets on the horse.
Because illegal bets don't affect the odds at the track the bookie will lose his shirt if the horse wins.
13
His solution? He totals all the bets on the horse and "lays them off" in one large bet with a bigger bookie. Now, if the horse wins, he pays his clients with his winnings. If the horse loses, he simply turns his client's bets over to the big bookie.
BIG BOOKIE ACRES
On rare occasions, the big bookie will find the run on a horse too much even for them to cover, so he lays his bets off to an Outfit commission house.
BIG BOOKIE ACRES
The commission house is a large, regional super-bookie, taking enormous pieces of action off big bookies across the nation.
ACME COM
On the extremely rare occasion that a commission house gets nervous about the action on a horse, it only has one place to lay off a bet...
ACME COMMISSION HOUSE

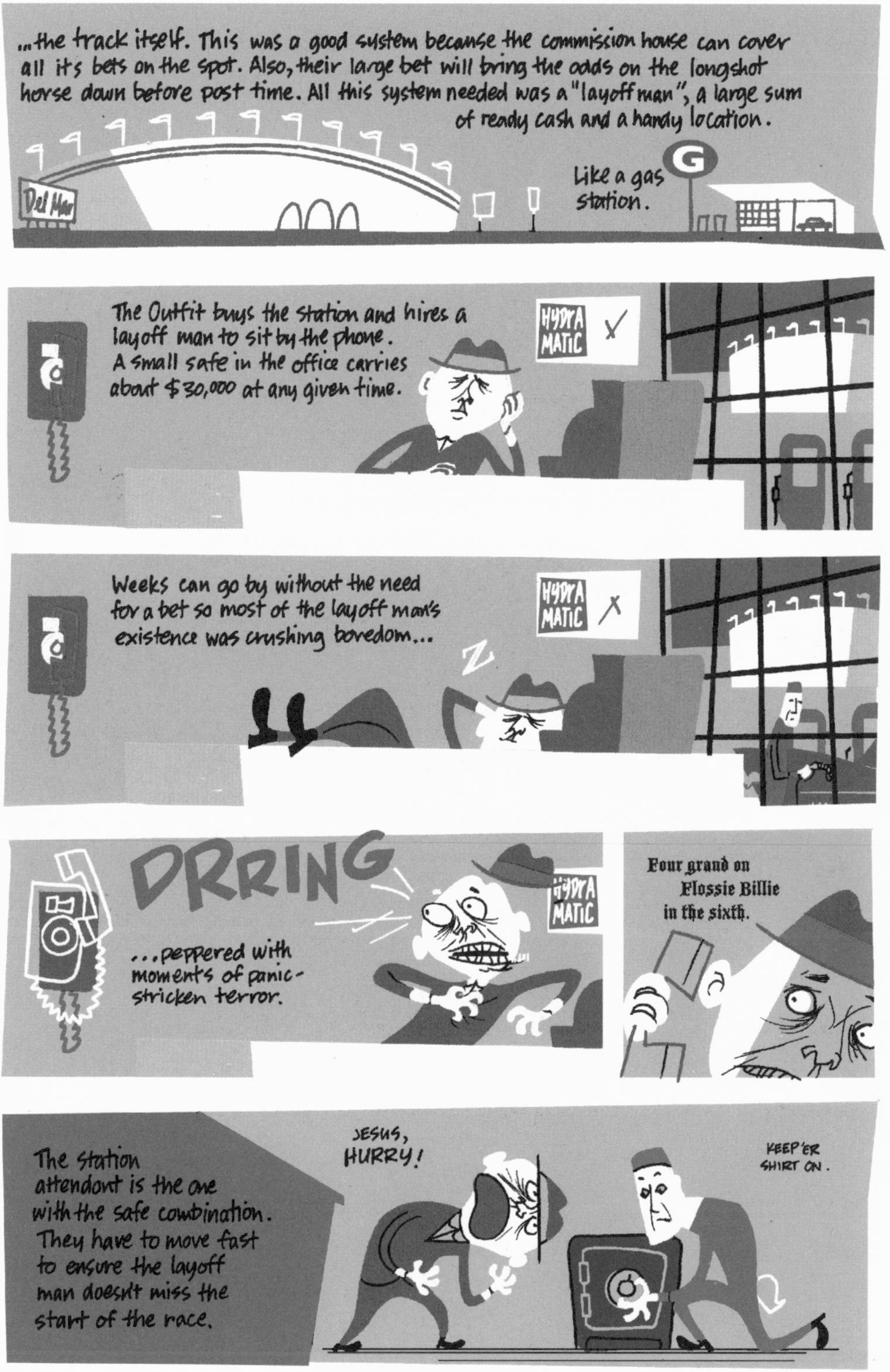
...the track itself. This was a good system because the commission house can cover all it's bets on the spot. Also, their large bet will bring the odds on the longshot horse down before post time. All this system needed was a "layoff man", a large sum of ready cash and a handy location.
Del Mar
G
Like a gas station.
The Outfit buys the station and hires a layoff man to sit by the phone. A small safe in the office carries about $30,000 at any given time.
HYDRA MATIC
Weeks can go by without the need for a bet so most of the layoff man's existence was crushing boredom...
HYDRA MATIC
Z
DRRING
HYDRA MATIC
...peppered with moments of panic-stricken terror.
Four grand on Flossie Billie in the sixth.
The station attendant is the one with the safe combination. They have to move fast to ensure the layoff man doesn't miss the start of the race.
JESUS, HURRY!
KEEP 'ER SHIRT ON.

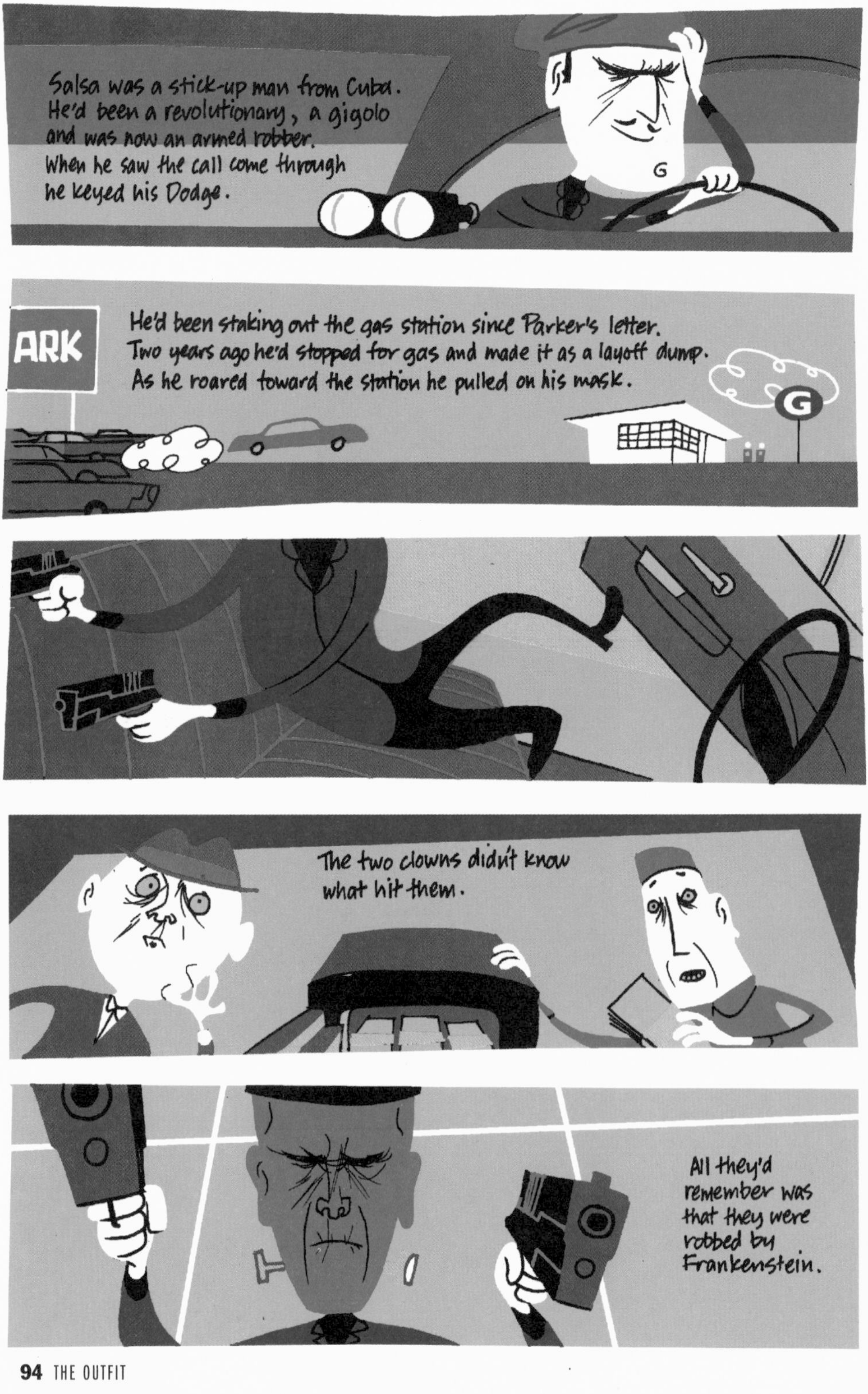
Salsa was a stick-up man from Cuba. He'd been a revolutionary, a gigolo and was now an armed robber. When he saw the call come through he keyed his Dodge.
ARK
He'd been staking out the gas station since Parker's letter. Two years ago he'd stopped for gas and made it as a layoff dump. As he roared toward the station he pulled on his mask.
G
The two clowns didn't know what hit them.
All they'd remember was that they were robbed by Frankenstein.

Queens

THE SAME DAY

The way it works is this:

The Outfit bought heroin from a concern in Miami. The actual heroin travelled by boat, but they needed a safe, easy way to move large sums of cash from New York to Miami. A man named Carter had the idea. He hired a very special tailor to make four very special suits.

Each suit was identical in every way including the hidden pockets stitched into the linings of the suit jackets.

Once a month Eric La Renne put on a brown suit with $75,000 cash sewn into the jacket lining and took a plane ride to Miami.

He'd get the call, pack and head to Argus Imports in his brown suit. Ten minutes later he emerges in the same suit. Or so it would seem.

Inside, La Renne switched jackets for the one with the money stitched into it. Then it was off to the airport. La Renne was ideal for this job.

Two years ago, La Renne fell ill with appendicitis followed by pneumonia, and was unable to make the Miami run for three months.

Arnie Strand was a 36 short and for three months he made the trips. Arnie was married and his wife's brother often visited.

Fred Parnell was a stock car racer. He thought his sister's husband was a loudmouth and a bragger. But when Arnie got tight on beer and started on about $75,000, Parnell was all ears.

Each moved out of his apartment. Wycza went to New York and got a room in a fleabag across from La Renne's apartment. Parnell went to Miami and got a motel near the airport.

Eight days passed and they were ready to give up. Every morning Wycza had to call the airline and reserve a ticket in another false name.

On day nine, La Renne appeared in the brown suit. Wycza made a quick call to Parnell to let him know they were on.

Wycza grabbed his coat and caught a taxi to the airport. His only luggage was his attache case.

He was an outfit boy, he lived in the right city and most important — Eric La Renne was a perfect 36 short.

The man at the other end was Marv Hanks and he had the same excellent qualities as LaRenne.

They would meet in the airport cafe or lounge and discretely switch jackets. Neither knew what the money was for and both were smart enough not to get curious. It had worked this way for over five years now.

Arnie laid it all out to Parnell and with a few questions he had the whole picture. Parnell raced cars, but he also had a sideline Arnie didn't know about.

A few times a year he drove for men like Parker. He used the money from the scores to finance his race cars.

When Parnell got Parker's letter, Arnie's setup sprang to mind. The problem was Parnell was a driver.

So he brought in Dan Wycza, an ex-wrestler and heavy Parnell had worked with on four or five jobs. Wycza was game so they made a deal and started to plan it out.

He beat La Renne there, bought his ticket, and then staked out the gate. La Renne arrived and Wycza stuck close as they began to board.

It was a crowded flight so there was nothing strange about him taking the seat next to La Renne. He kept his attache case in his lap.

Wycza dozed for most of the flight, coming awake as the pilot prepared to land. It was time to bait the hook for La Renne.

And that is where things got interesting.

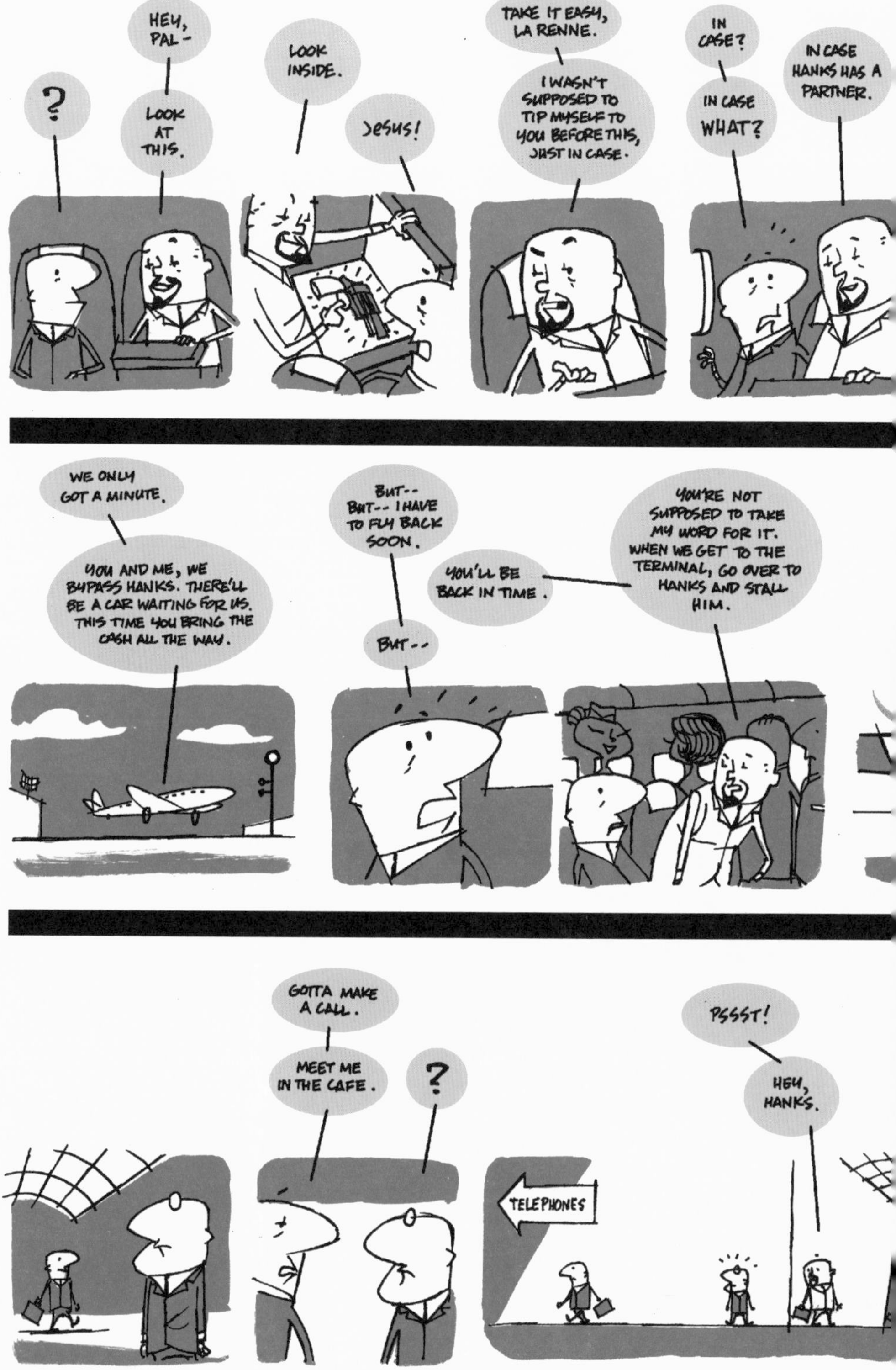
HEY, PAL -
?
LOOK AT THIS.
LOOK INSIDE.
JESUS!
TAKE IT EASY, LA RENNE.
I WASN'T SUPPOSED TO TIP MYSELF TO YOU BEFORE THIS, JUST IN CASE.
IN CASE?
IN CASE WHAT?
IN CASE HANKS HAS A PARTNER.
WE ONLY GOT A MINUTE.
YOU AND ME, WE BYPASS HANKS. THERE'LL BE A CAR WAITING FOR US. THIS TIME YOU BRING THE CASH ALL THE WAY.
BUT-- BUT-- I HAVE TO FLY BACK SOON.
BUT--
YOU'LL BE BACK IN TIME.
YOU'RE NOT SUPPOSED TO TAKE MY WORD FOR IT. WHEN WE GET TO THE TERMINAL, GO OVER TO HANKS AND STALL HIM.
GOTTA MAKE A CALL.
MEET ME IN THE CAFE.
?
TELEPHONES
PSSST!
HEY, HANKS.

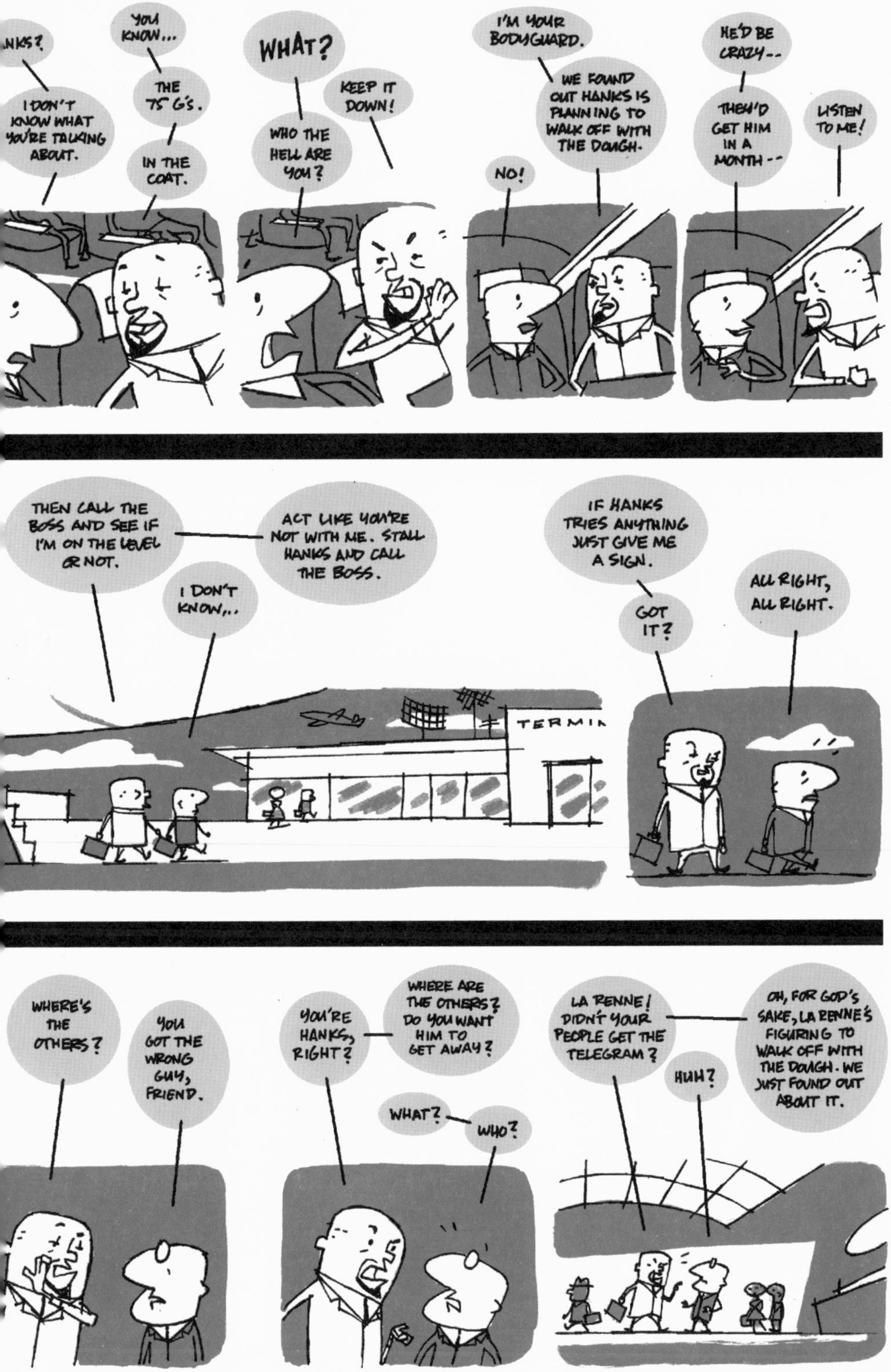
NKS?
I DON'T KNOW WHAT YOU'RE TALKING ABOUT.
YOU KNOW...
THE 75 G'S.
IN THE COAT.
WHAT?
WHO THE HELL ARE YOU?
KEEP IT DOWN!
I'M YOUR BODYGUARD.
WE FOUND OUT HANKS IS PLANNING TO WALK OFF WITH THE DOUGH.
NO!
HE'D BE CRAZY--
THEY'D GET HIM IN A MONTH--
LISTEN TO ME!
THEN CALL THE BOSS AND SEE IF I'M ON THE LEVEL OR NOT.
ACT LIKE YOU'RE NOT WITH ME. STALL HANKS AND CALL THE BOSS.
I DON'T KNOW...
TERMI
IF HANKS TRIES ANYTHING JUST GIVE ME A SIGN.
GOT IT?
ALL RIGHT, ALL RIGHT.
WHERE'S THE OTHERS?
YOU GOT THE WRONG GUY, FRIEND.
YOU'RE HANKS, RIGHT?
WHERE ARE THE OTHERS? DO YOU WANT HIM TO GET AWAY?
WHAT?
WHO?
LA RENNE! DIDN'T YOUR PEOPLE GET THE TELEGRAM?
HUH?
OH, FOR GOD'S SAKE, LA RENNE'S FIGURING TO WALK OFF WITH THE DOUGH. WE JUST FOUND OUT ABOUT IT.

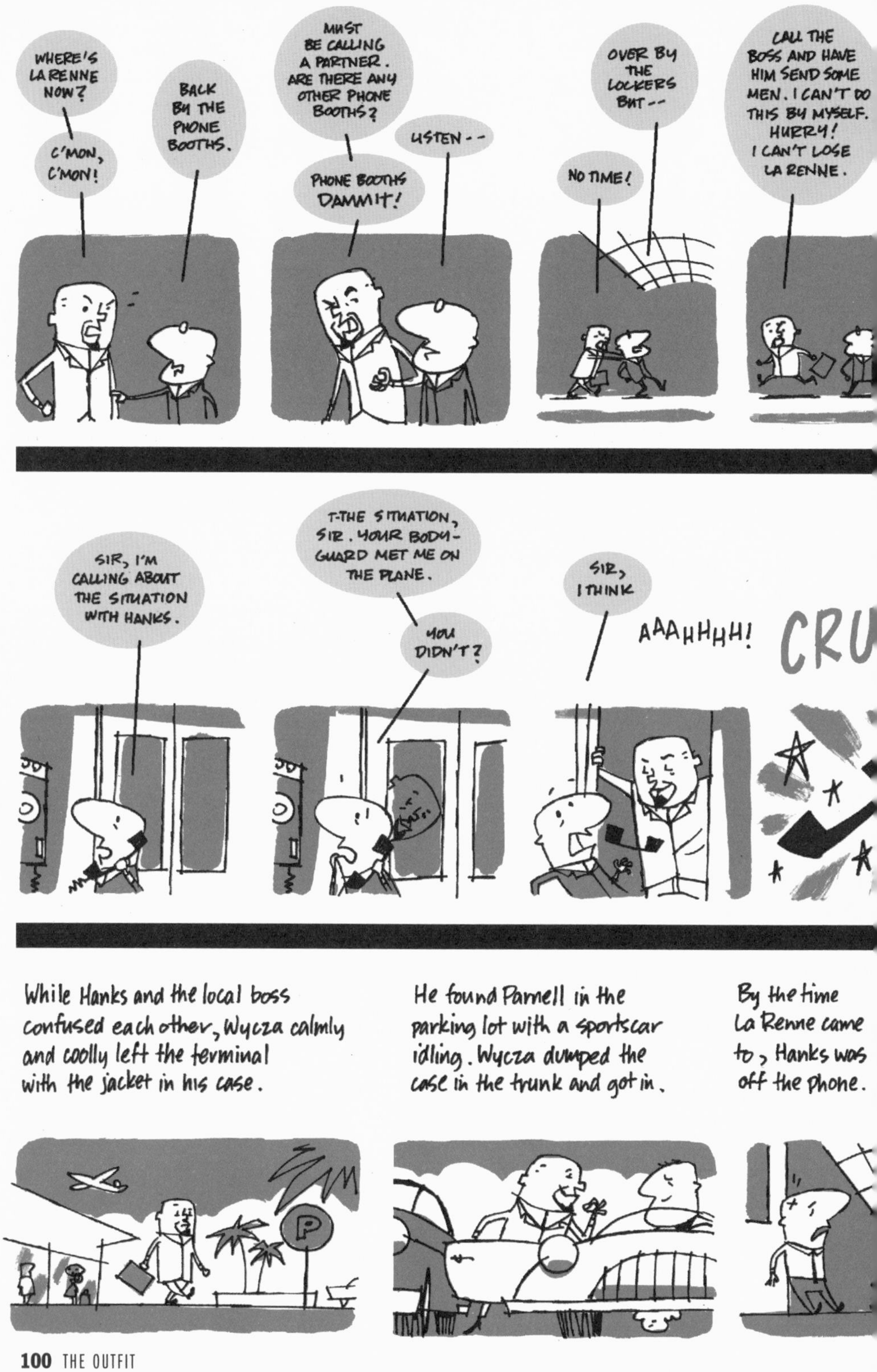
WHERE'S LA RENNE NOW?
C'MON, C'MON!
BACK BY THE PHONE BOOTHS.
MUST BE CALLING A PARTNER. ARE THERE ANY OTHER PHONE BOOTHS?
PHONE BOOTHS DAMMIT!
LISTEN --
OVER BY THE LOCKERS BUT --
NO TIME!
CALL THE BOSS AND HAVE HIM SEND SOME MEN. I CAN'T DO THIS BY MYSELF. HURRY! I CAN'T LOSE LA RENNE.
SIR, I'M CALLING ABOUT THE SITUATION WITH HANKS.
T-THE SITUATION, SIR. YOUR BODY-GUARD MET ME ON THE PLANE.
YOU DIDN'T?
SIR, I THINK
AAAHHHH!
CRU
While Hanks and the local boss confused each other, Wycza calmly and coolly left the terminal with the jacket in his case.
He found Parnell in the parking lot with a sportscar idling. Wycza dumped the case in the trunk and got in.
By the time La Renne came to, Hanks was off the phone.

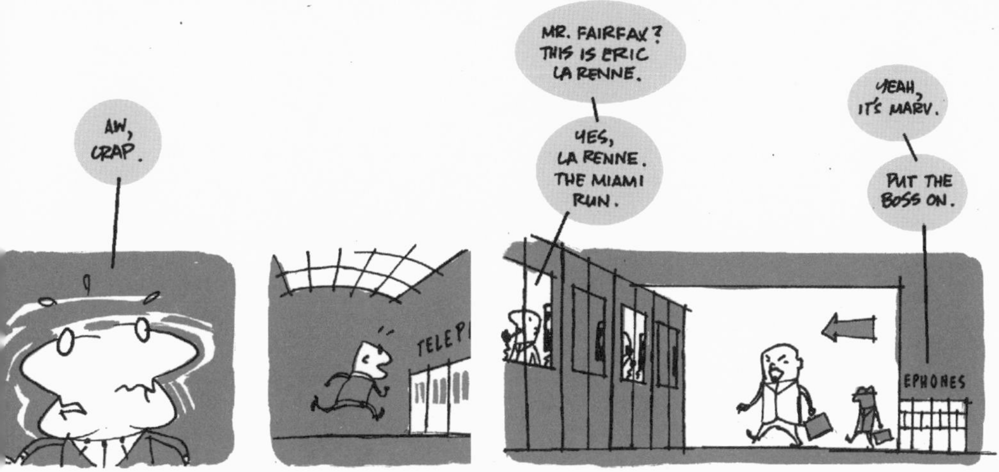
AW, CRAP.
TELEP
MR. FAIRFAX? THIS IS ERIC LA RENNE.
YES, LA RENNE. THE MIAMI RUN.
YEAH, IT'S MARV.
PUT THE BOSS ON.
EPHONES

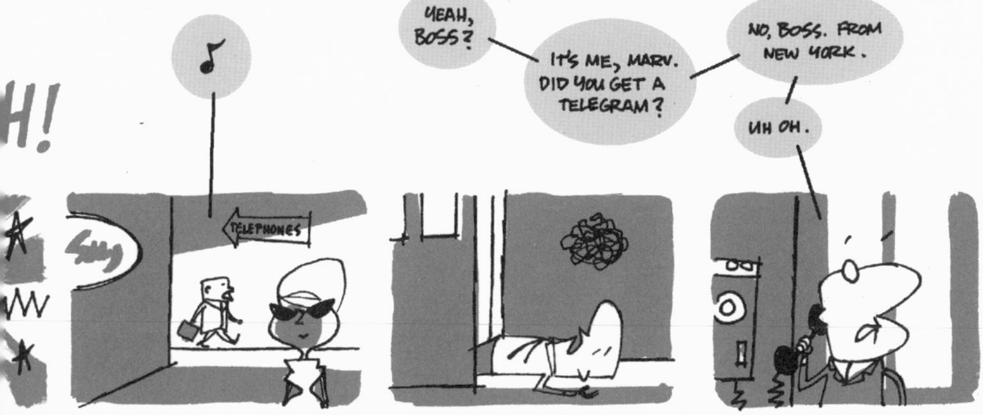
TELEPHONES
YEAH, BOSS?
IT'S ME, MARV. DID YOU GET A TELEGRAM?
NO, BOSS. FROM NEW YORK.
UH OH.

They searched the terminal but the stranger with the attache case was long gone.

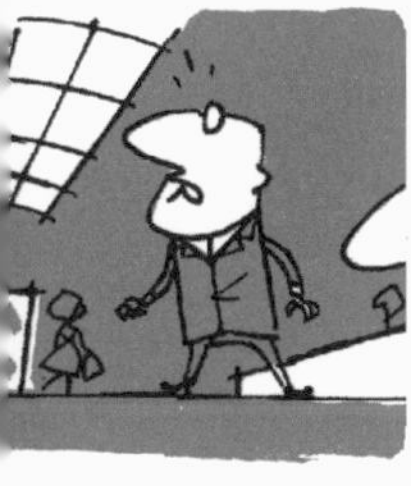

Parnell got them back to his motel without any troubles.

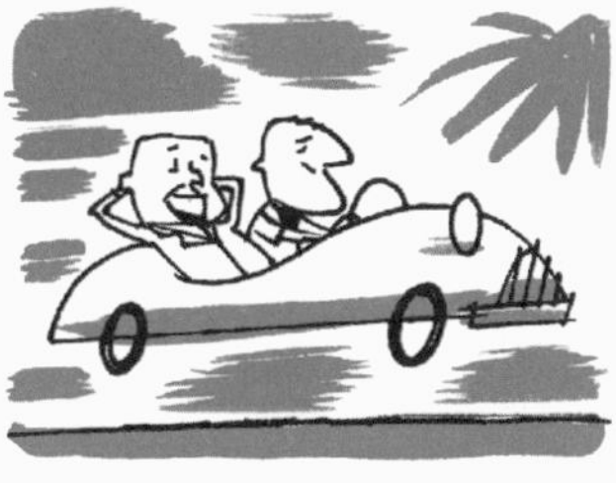

After a celebratory beer they split the coat and the take up the middle. Wycza spoke of travel. Parnell told Wycza about the new car he was going to build.

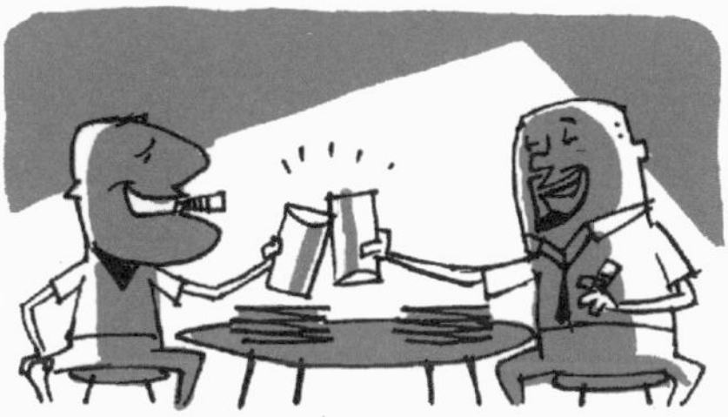

Manhattan

TWO DAYS LATER

The way it works is this:

All the money came in to the Acme Novelty Corporation. It started as small change, here and there throughout the city, and it all funneled into one central office, all the money bet every day on the numbers.

Take one dime.

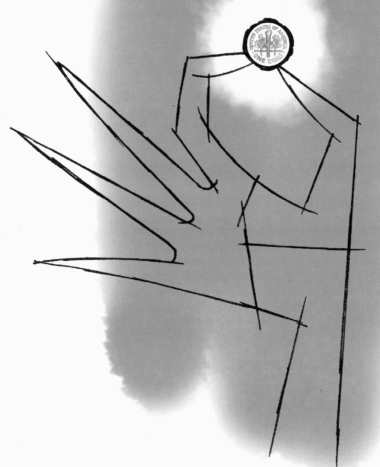

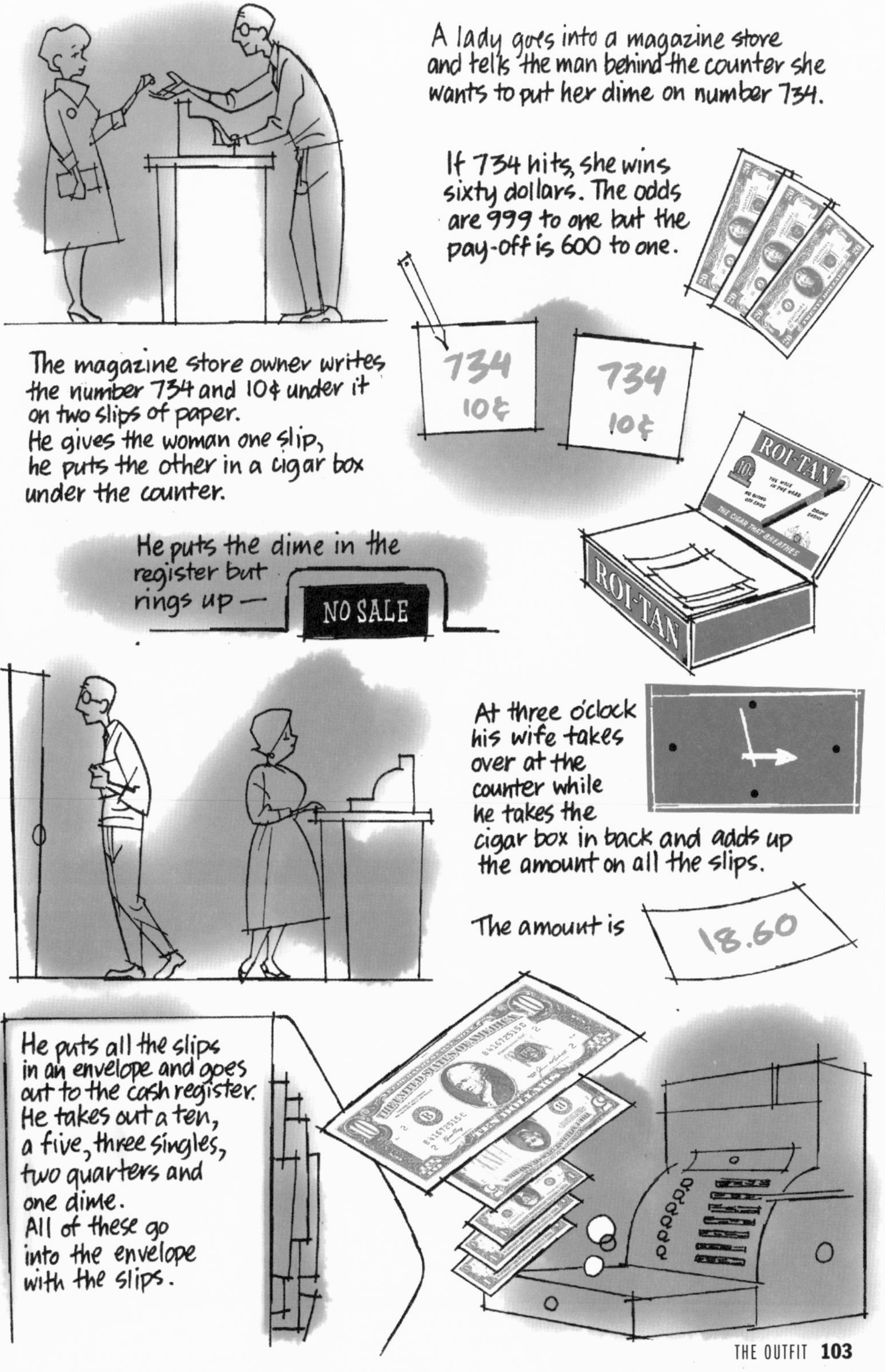
A lady goes into a magazine store and tells the man behind the counter she wants to put her dime on number 734.
If 734 hits, she wins sixty dollars. The odds are 999 to one but the pay-off is 600 to one.
The magazine store owner writes the number 734 and 10¢ under it on two slips of paper.
He gives the woman one slip, he puts the other in a cigar box under the counter.
734
10¢
734
10¢
ROI-TAN
THE CIGAR THAT BREATHES
ROI-TAN
He puts the dime in the register but rings up —
NO SALE
At three o'clock his wife takes over at the counter while he takes the cigar box in back and adds up the amount on all the slips.
The amount is
18.60
He puts all the slips in an envelope and goes out to the cash register. He takes out a ten, a five, three singles, two quarters and one dime. All of these go into the envelope with the slips.

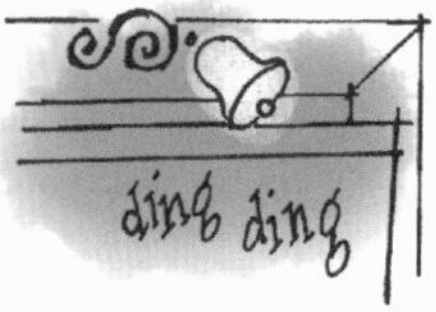
ding ding

At three-thirty, the collector comes. The collector is a plump young man with a smiling face, a struggling writer making a few dollars while waiting to be discovered by Darryl Zanuck or Bennett Cerf.

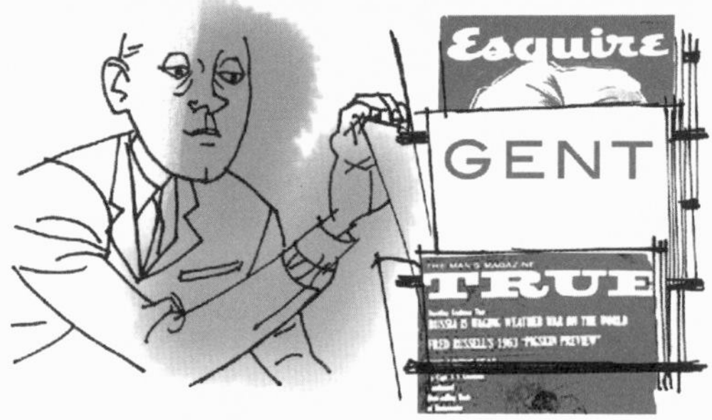
Esquire
GENT
TRUE

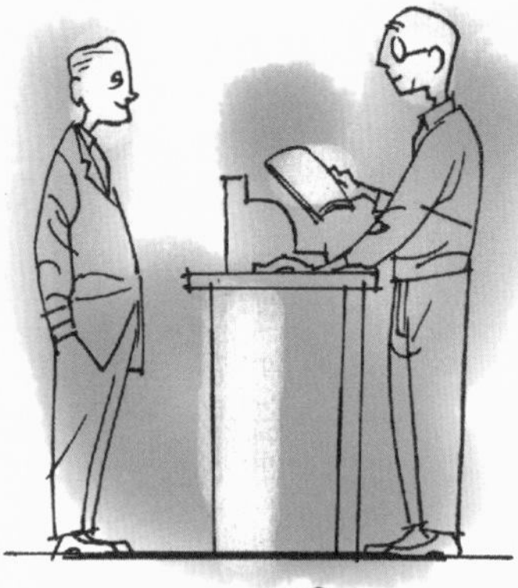

The collector selects a men's magazine. At the register the store owner puts the envelope into the magazine. He tells the collector the magazine costs $1.86. The collector pays this outrageous sum without protest.

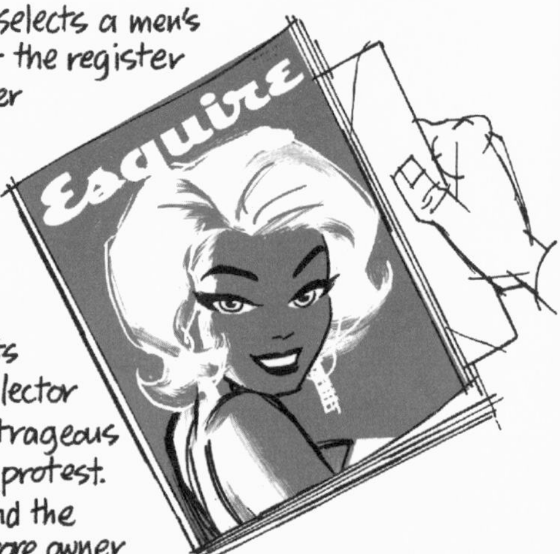
Esquire

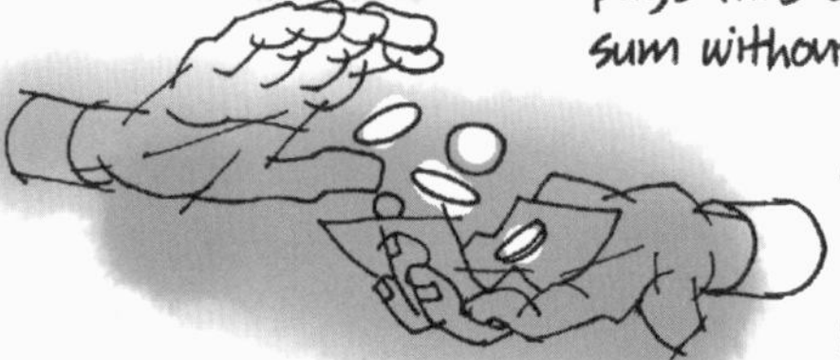

and the store owner pockets the $1.86 as his profits for the day's numbers.

The collector takes the magazine out to his car and removes the envelope. He throws the magazine onto the back seat and puts the envelope into a briefcase. He pulls out a small notebook filled with entries. He enters—

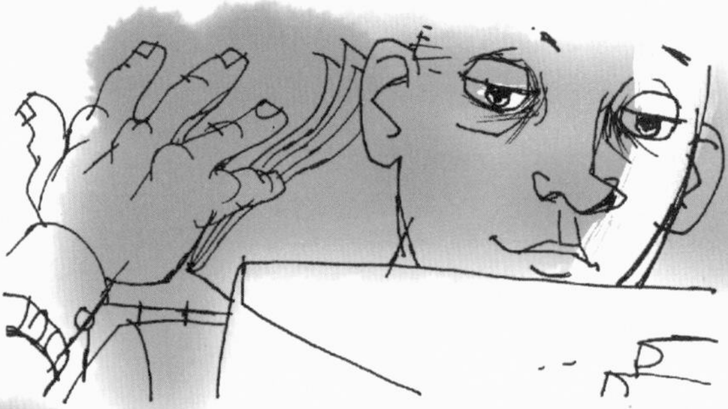

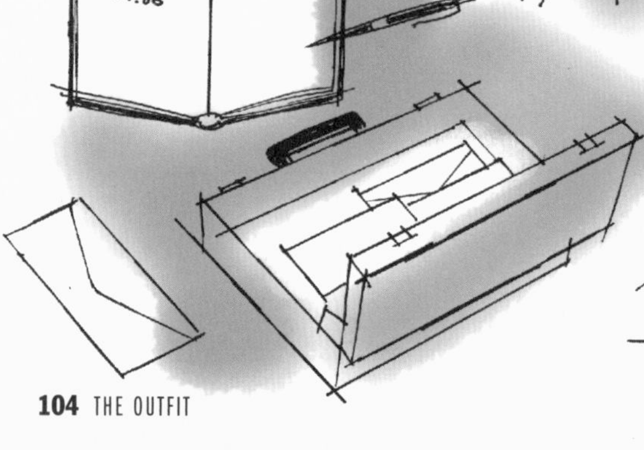
NAT.NEWS.SW
$1.86

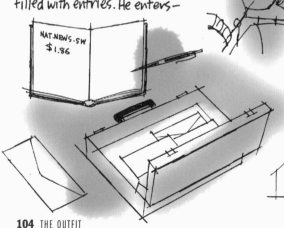

It takes just over an hour to cover his territory. All in all, he buys fifteen magazines.

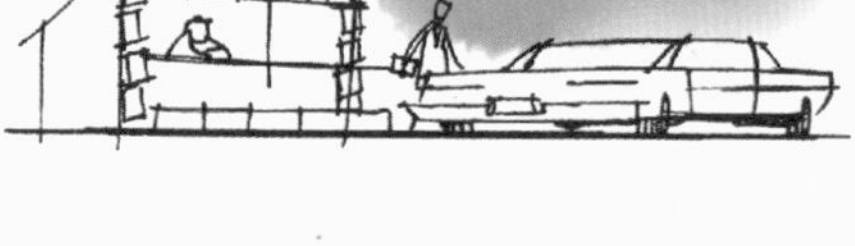
NEWS

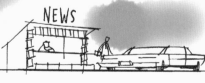

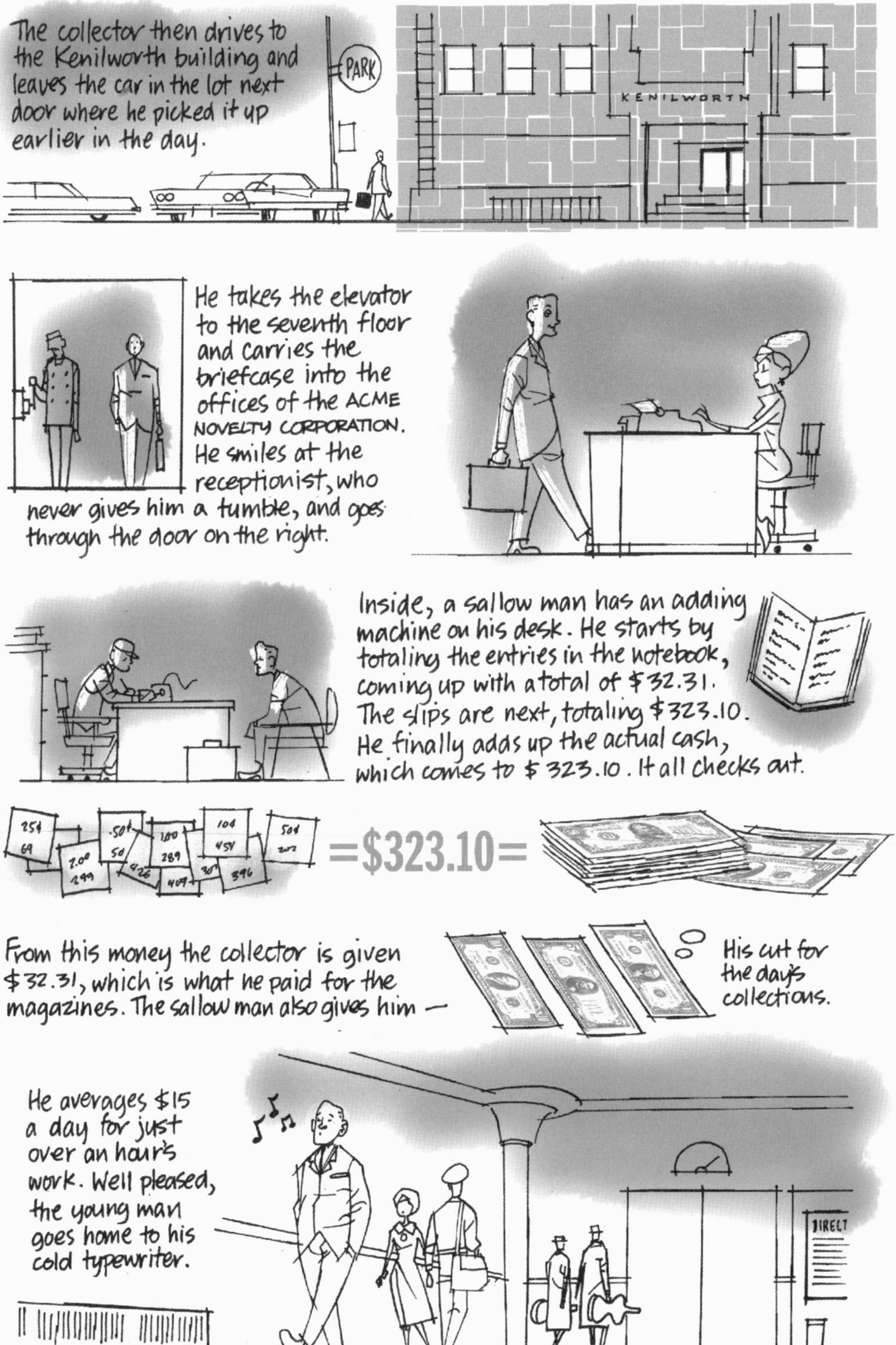
The collector then drives to the Kenilworth building and leaves the car in the lot next door where he picked it up earlier in the day.
PARK
KENILWORTH
He takes the elevator to the seventh floor and carries the briefcase into the offices of the ACME NOVELTY CORPORATION. He smiles at the receptionist, who never gives him a tumble, and goes through the door on the right.
Inside, a sallow man has an adding machine on his desk. He starts by totaling the entries in the notebook, coming up with a total of $32.31. The slips are next, totaling $323.10. He finally adds up the actual cash, which comes to $323.10. It all checks out.
=$323.10=
From this money the collector is given $32.31, which is what he paid for the magazines. The sallow man also gives him —
His cut for the day's collections.
He averages $15 a day for just over an hour's work. Well pleased, the young man goes home to his cold typewriter.

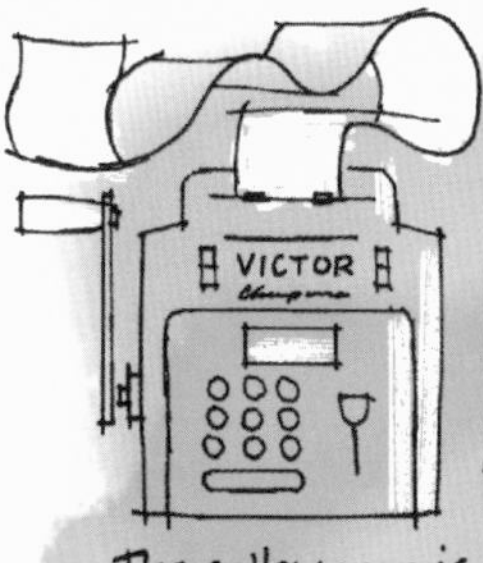
VICTOR

The sallow man now takes a ledger and enters in it the amount of, and the number of each bet according to the exact location where each bet is made. He adds his figures again to check his work and gets the correct total. By then another collector has come in.

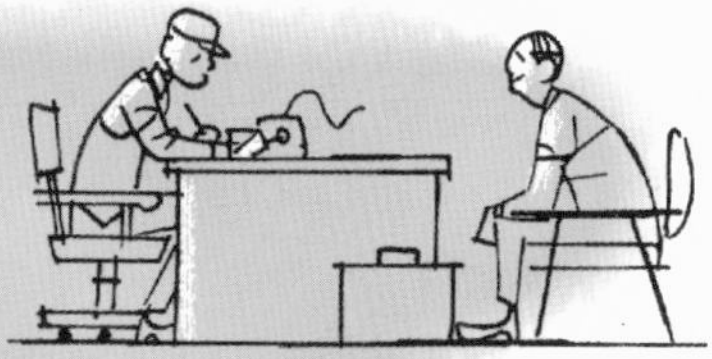

The sallow man is one of six at Acme Novelty who each take in receipts from five collectors.

They work at this approximately from four until six o'clock. Each of them clears roughly $1500 per day.

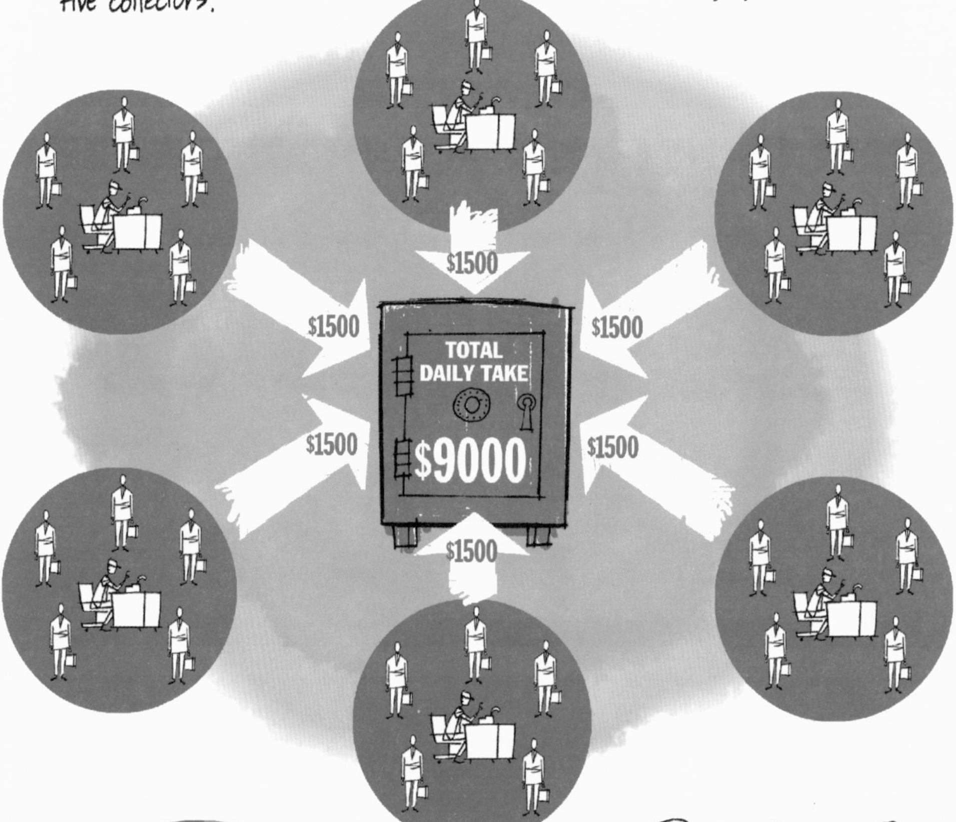
$1500
$1500
$1500
$1500
$1500
$1500
TOTAL DAILY TAKE
$9000

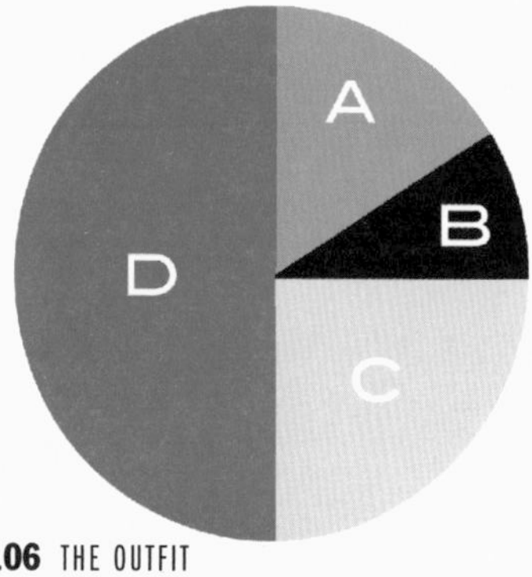
A
B
C
D

The $9000 is divided this way
↓

A VENDOR PAYOFF AND OVERHEAD.

B LOCAL LAW AND CITY OFFICIALS.

C LOCAL OUTFIT.

D NATIONAL OUTFIT IN CHICAGO.

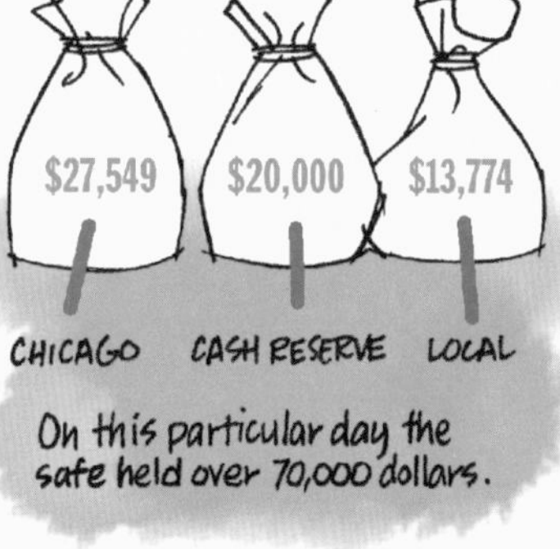
$27,549
$20,000
$13,774
CHICAGO
CASH RESERVE
LOCAL

On this particular day the safe held over 70,000 dollars.

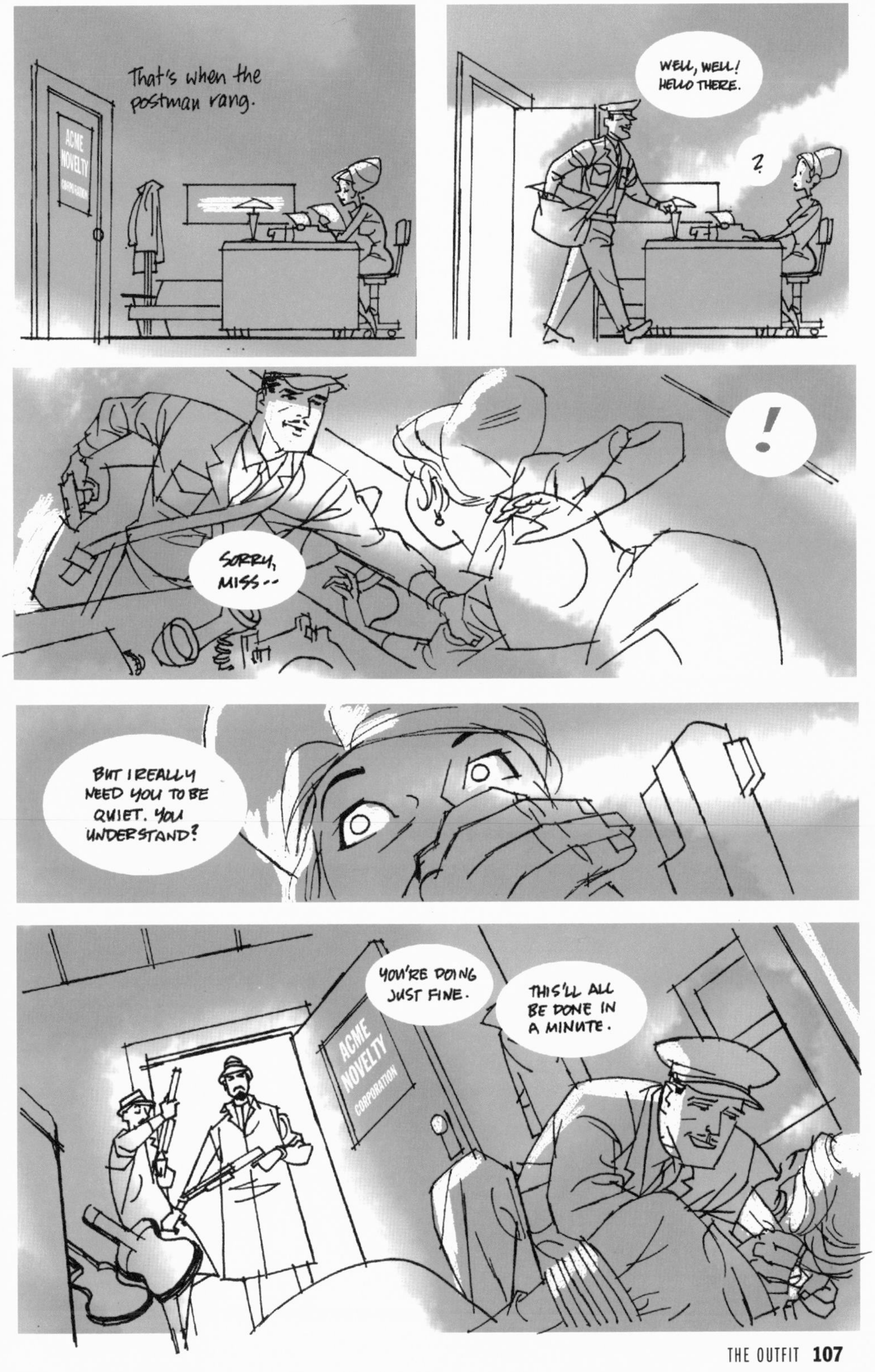
That's when the postman rang.
ACME NOVELTY CORPORATION
WELL, WELL! HELLO THERE.
?
!
SORRY, MISS--
BUT I REALLY NEED YOU TO BE QUIET. YOU UNDERSTAND?
YOU'RE DOING JUST FINE.
THIS'LL ALL BE DONE IN A MINUTE.
ACME NOVELTY CORPORATION

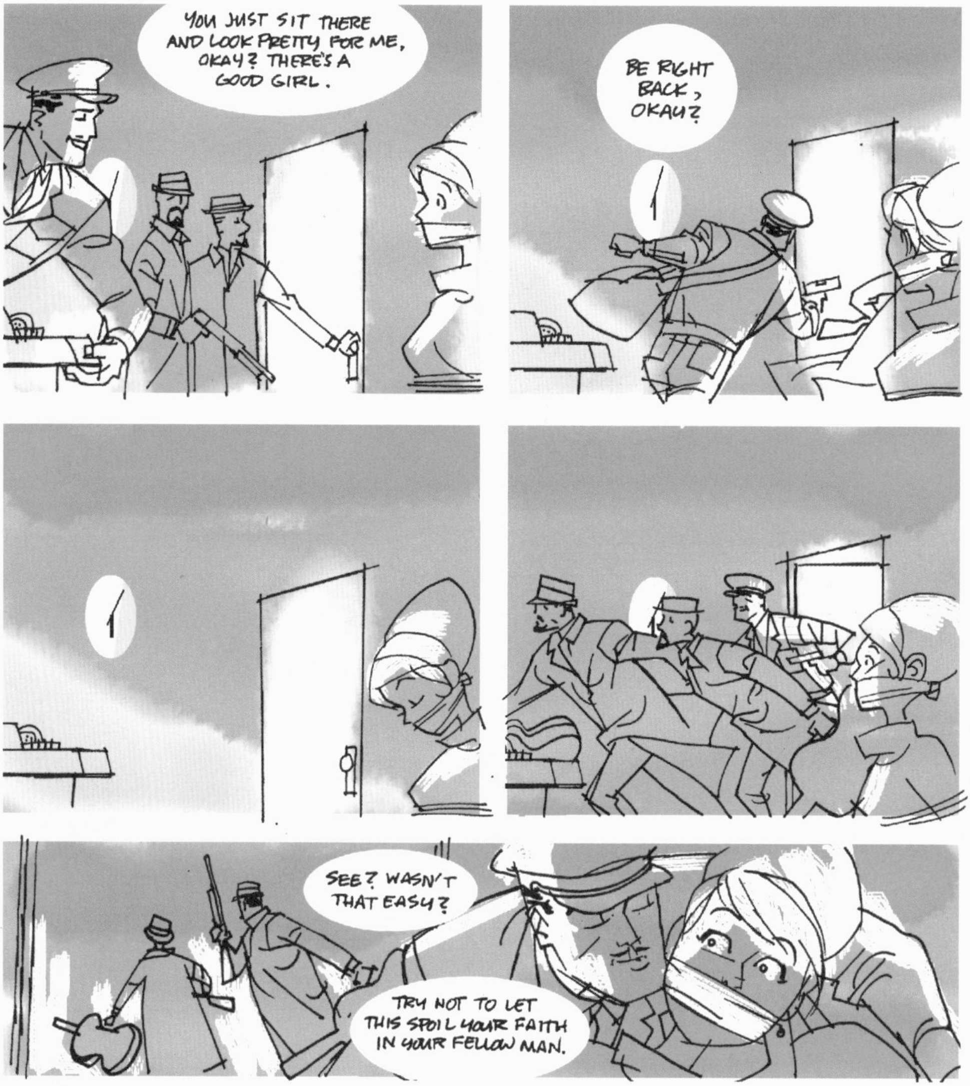
YOU JUST SIT THERE AND LOOK PRETTY FOR ME, OKAY? THERE'S A GOOD GIRL.
BE RIGHT BACK, OKAY?
SEE? WASN'T THAT EASY?
TRY NOT TO LET THIS SPOIL YOUR FAITH IN YOUR FELLOW MAN.

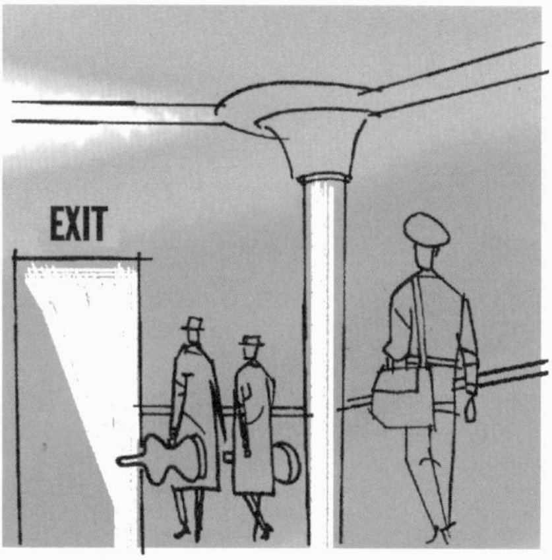
EXIT

They left with their cases and mailbag full of cash. They split up on the street and each one took a different route to a black sedan four blocks over. Forty minutes later, at a motel, the musicians took off their beards and the mailman removed his moustache. Then they got pencils and paper and split $61,323 between them.

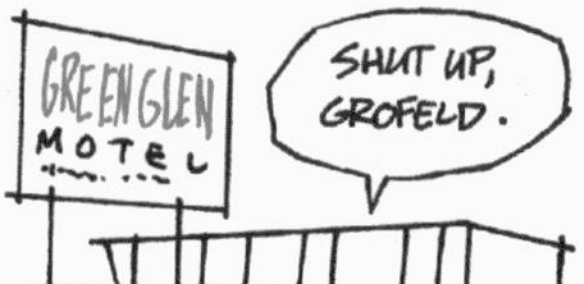
GREEN GLEN
MOTEL
SHUT UP, GROFELD.

They'd left five dimes in the safe.
One of them was our lady's dime.

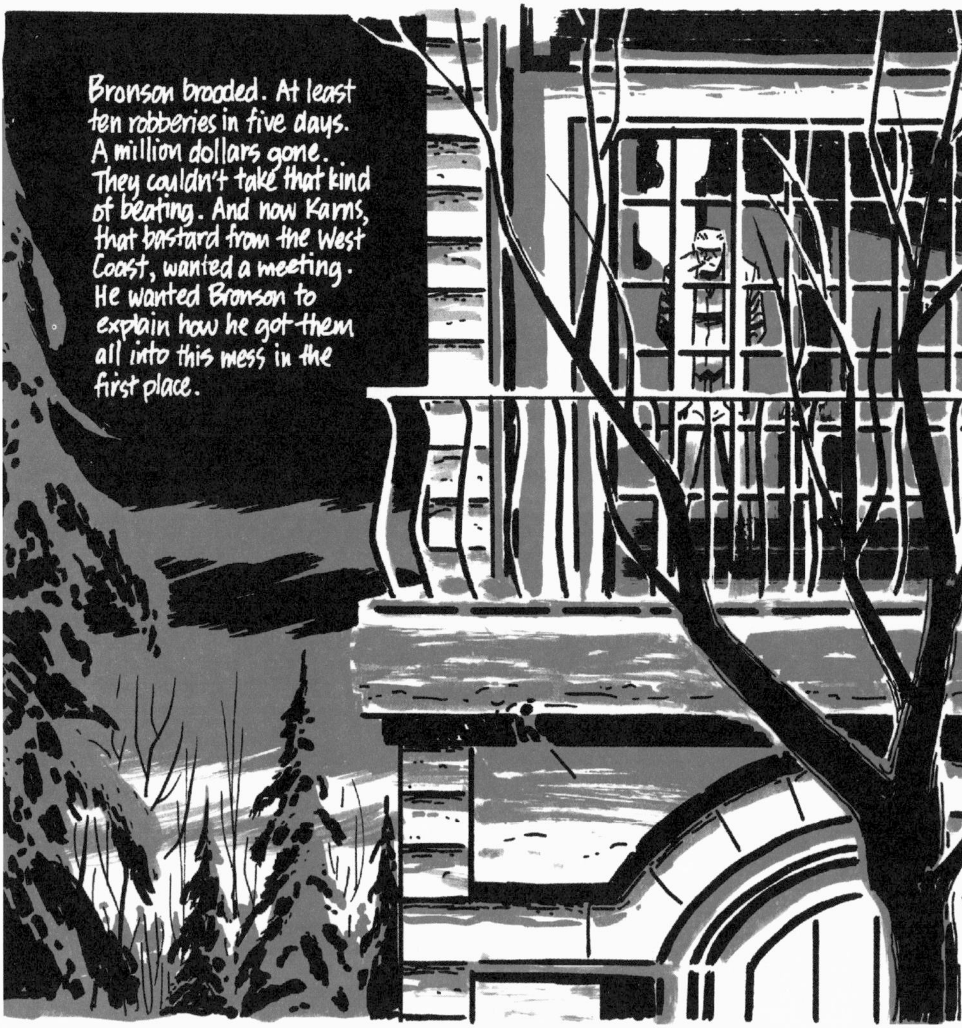
Bronson brooded. At least ten robberies in five days. A million dollars gone. They couldn't take that kind of beating. And now Karns, that bastard from the West Coast, wanted a meeting. He wanted Bronson to explain how he got them all into this mess in the first place.

A million dollars. It was a hell of an argument and Karns would use it until Bronson was out on his ass.

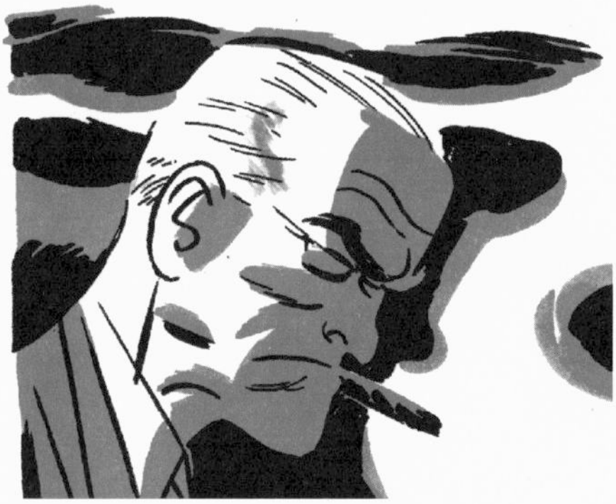

If it was only Parker, it wouldn't be that bad. Go to the meeting with Parker's head on a tray That would shut Karns' face. But it wasn't just Parker. Four jobs in one day, scattered across the country. It wasn't just Parker. It was Parker and all his damn friends.

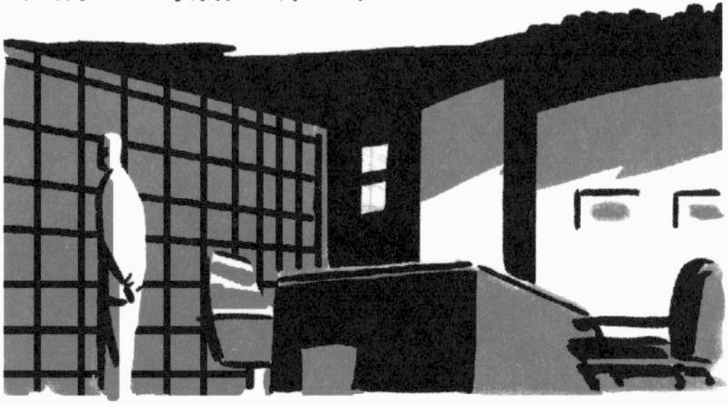

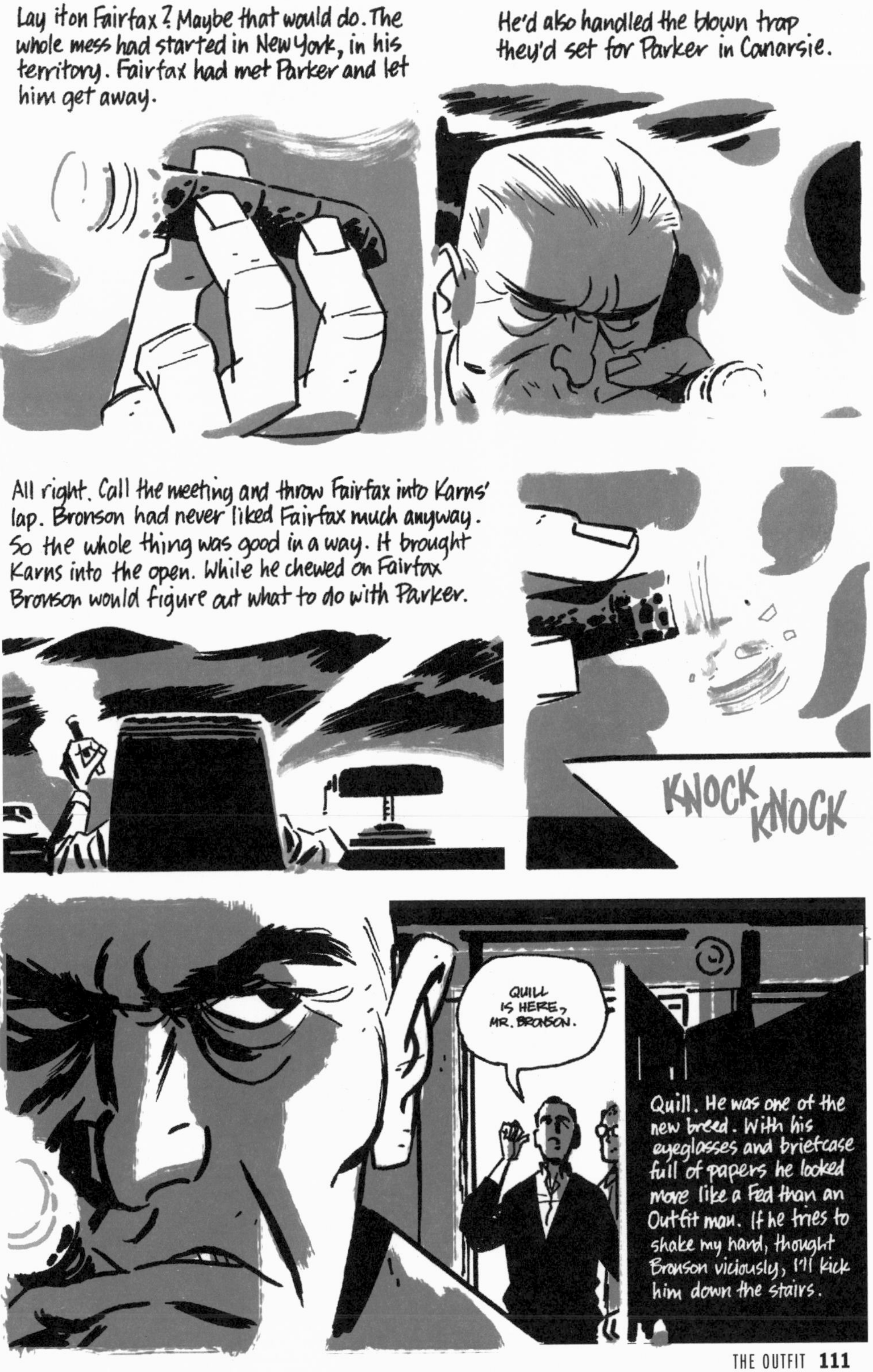
Lay it on Fairfax? Maybe that would do. The whole mess had started in New York, in his territory. Fairfax had met Parker and let him get away.
He'd also handled the blown trap they'd set for Parker in Canarsie.
All right. Call the meeting and throw Fairfax into Karns' lap. Bronson had never liked Fairfax much anyway. So the whole thing was good in a way. It brought Karns into the open. While he chewed on Fairfax Bronson would figure out what to do with Parker.
KNOCK KNOCK
QUILL IS HERE, MR. BRONSON.
Quill. He was one of the new breed. With his eyeglasses and briefcase full of papers he looked more like a Fed than an Outfit man. If he tries to shake my hand, thought Bronson viciously, I'll kick him down the stairs.

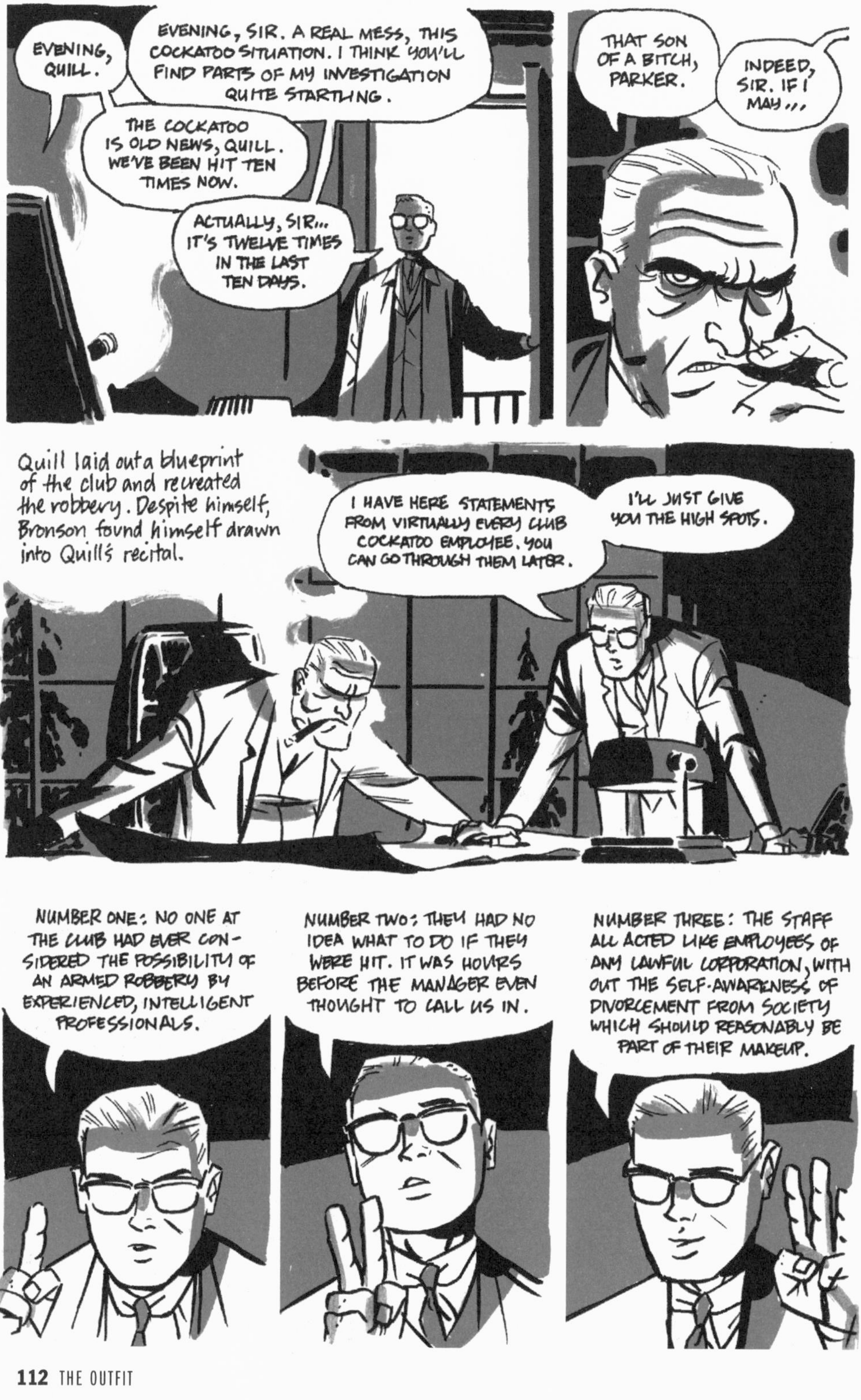
EVENING, QUILL.
EVENING, SIR. A REAL MESS, THIS COCKATOO SITUATION. I THINK YOU'LL FIND PARTS OF MY INVESTIGATION QUITE STARTLING.
THE COCKATOO IS OLD NEWS, QUILL. WE'VE BEEN HIT TEN TIMES NOW.
ACTUALLY, SIR... IT'S TWELVE TIMES IN THE LAST TEN DAYS.
THAT SON OF A BITCH, PARKER.
INDEED, SIR. IF I MAY...
Quill laid out a blueprint of the club and recreated the robbery. Despite himself, Bronson found himself drawn into Quill's recital.
I HAVE HERE STATEMENTS FROM VIRTUALLY EVERY CLUB COCKATOO EMPLOYEE. YOU CAN GO THROUGH THEM LATER.
I'LL JUST GIVE YOU THE HIGH SPOTS.
NUMBER ONE: NO ONE AT THE CLUB HAD EVER CONSIDERED THE POSSIBILITY OF AN ARMED ROBBERY BY EXPERIENCED, INTELLIGENT PROFESSIONALS.
NUMBER TWO: THEY HAD NO IDEA WHAT TO DO IF THEY WERE HIT. IT WAS HOURS BEFORE THE MANAGER EVEN THOUGHT TO CALL US IN.
NUMBER THREE: THE STAFF ALL ACTED LIKE EMPLOYEES OF ANY LAWFUL CORPORATION, WITHOUT THE SELF-AWARENESS OF DIVORCEMENT FROM SOCIETY WHICH SHOULD REASONABLY BE PART OF THEIR MAKEUP.

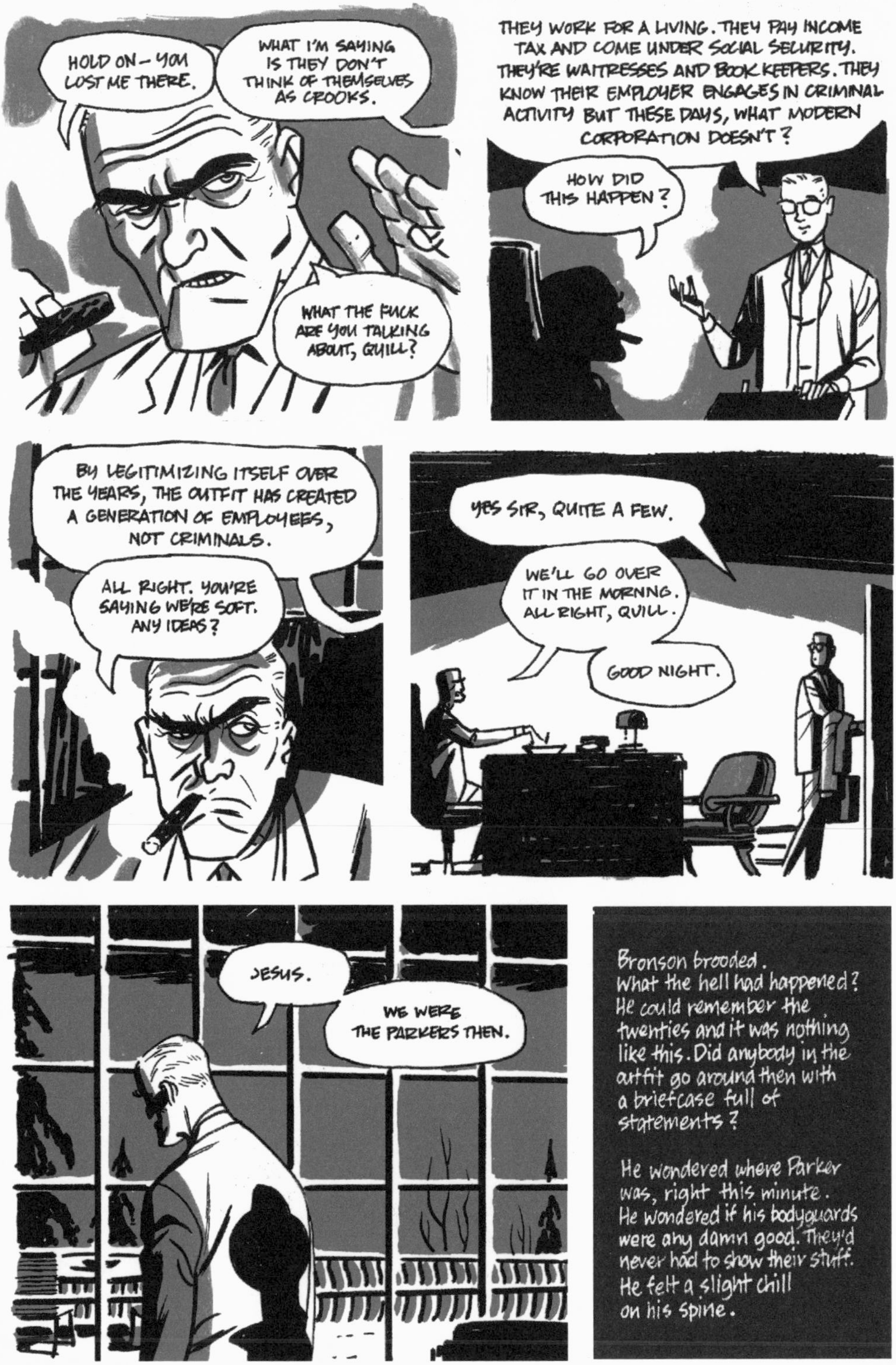
HOLD ON – YOU LOST ME THERE.
WHAT I'M SAYING IS THEY DON'T THINK OF THEMSELVES AS CROOKS.
WHAT THE FUCK ARE YOU TALKING ABOUT, QUILL?
THEY WORK FOR A LIVING. THEY PAY INCOME TAX AND COME UNDER SOCIAL SECURITY. THEY'RE WAITRESSES AND BOOKKEEPERS. THEY KNOW THEIR EMPLOYER ENGAGES IN CRIMINAL ACTIVITY BUT THESE DAYS, WHAT MODERN CORPORATION DOESN'T?
HOW DID THIS HAPPEN?
BY LEGITIMIZING ITSELF OVER THE YEARS, THE OUTFIT HAS CREATED A GENERATION OF EMPLOYEES, NOT CRIMINALS.
ALL RIGHT. YOU'RE SAYING WE'RE SOFT. ANY IDEAS?
YES SIR, QUITE A FEW.
WE'LL GO OVER IT IN THE MORNING. ALL RIGHT, QUILL.
GOOD NIGHT.
JESUS.
WE WERE THE PARKERS THEN.
Bronson brooded. What the hell had happened? He could remember the twenties and it was nothing like this. Did anybody in the outfit go around then with a briefcase full of statements?
He wondered where Parker was, right this minute. He wondered if his bodyguards were any damn good. They'd never had to show their stuff. He felt a slight chill on his spine.

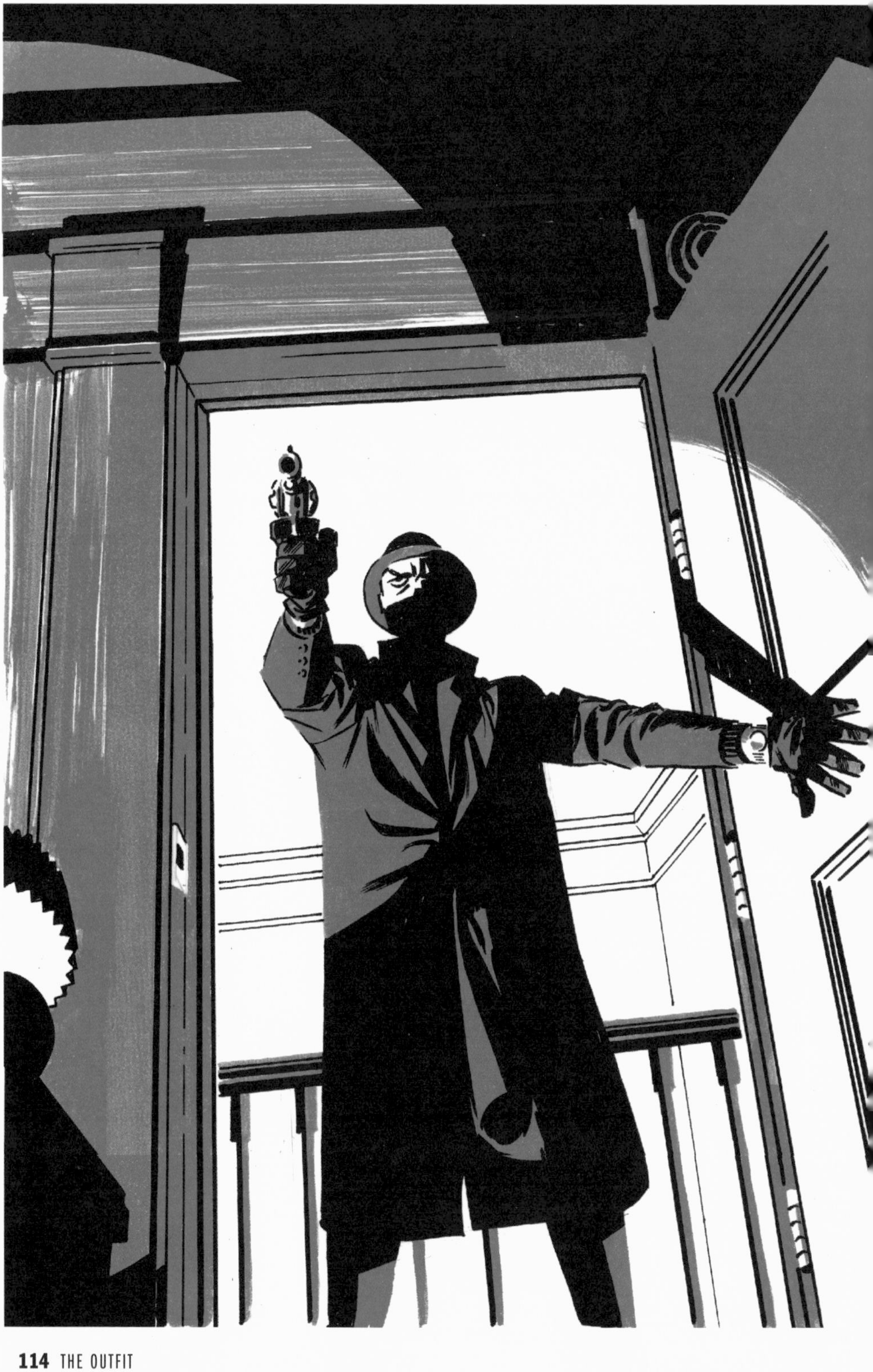

The hall door was open. There was a man standing there. Bronson had never seen him before in his life, but he knew right away it was Parker.

He wasn't even surprised.

BOOK FOUR

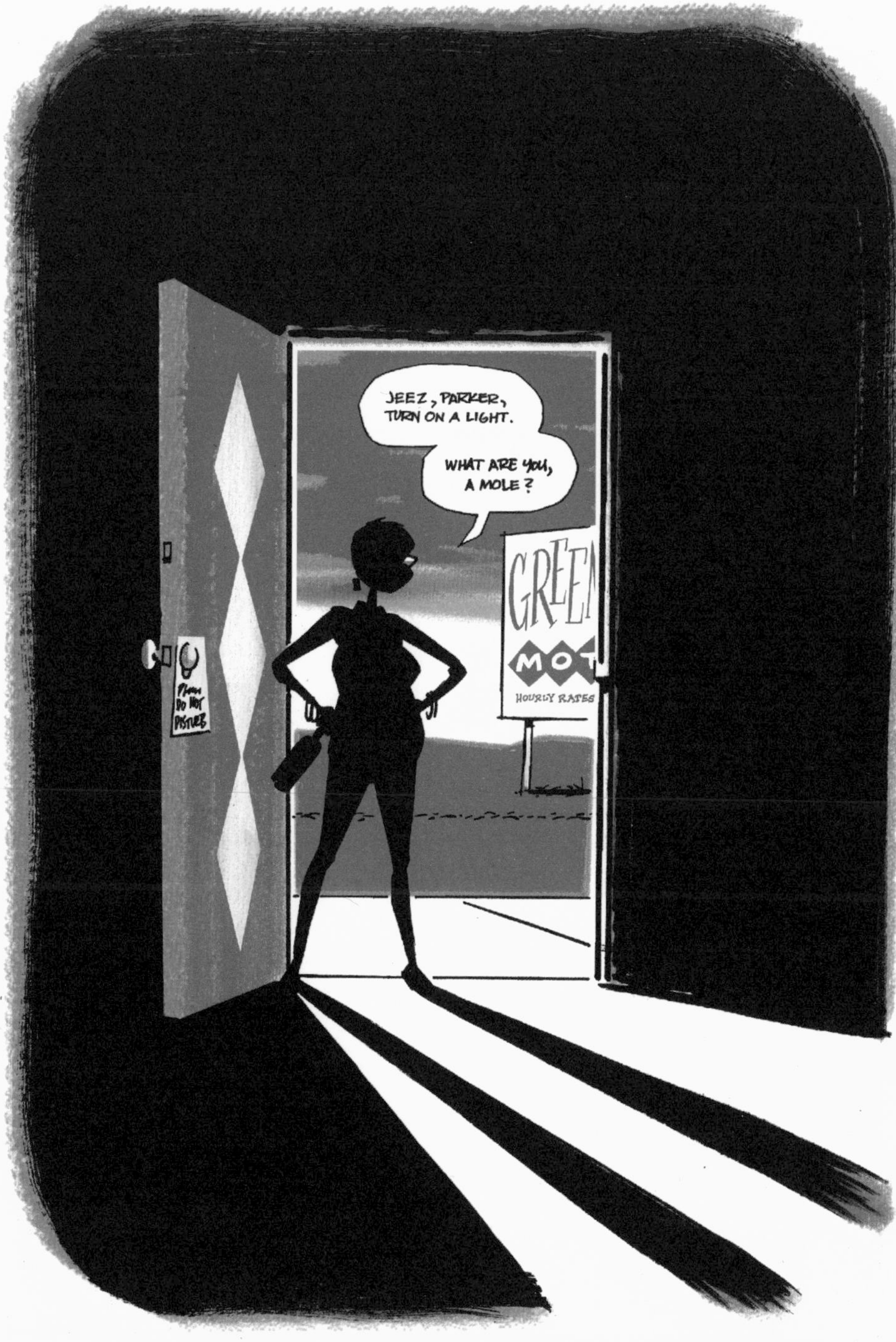
JEEZ, PARKER, TURN ON A LIGHT.
WHAT ARE YOU, A MOLE?
DO NOT DISTURB
GREE
MOT
HOURLY RATES

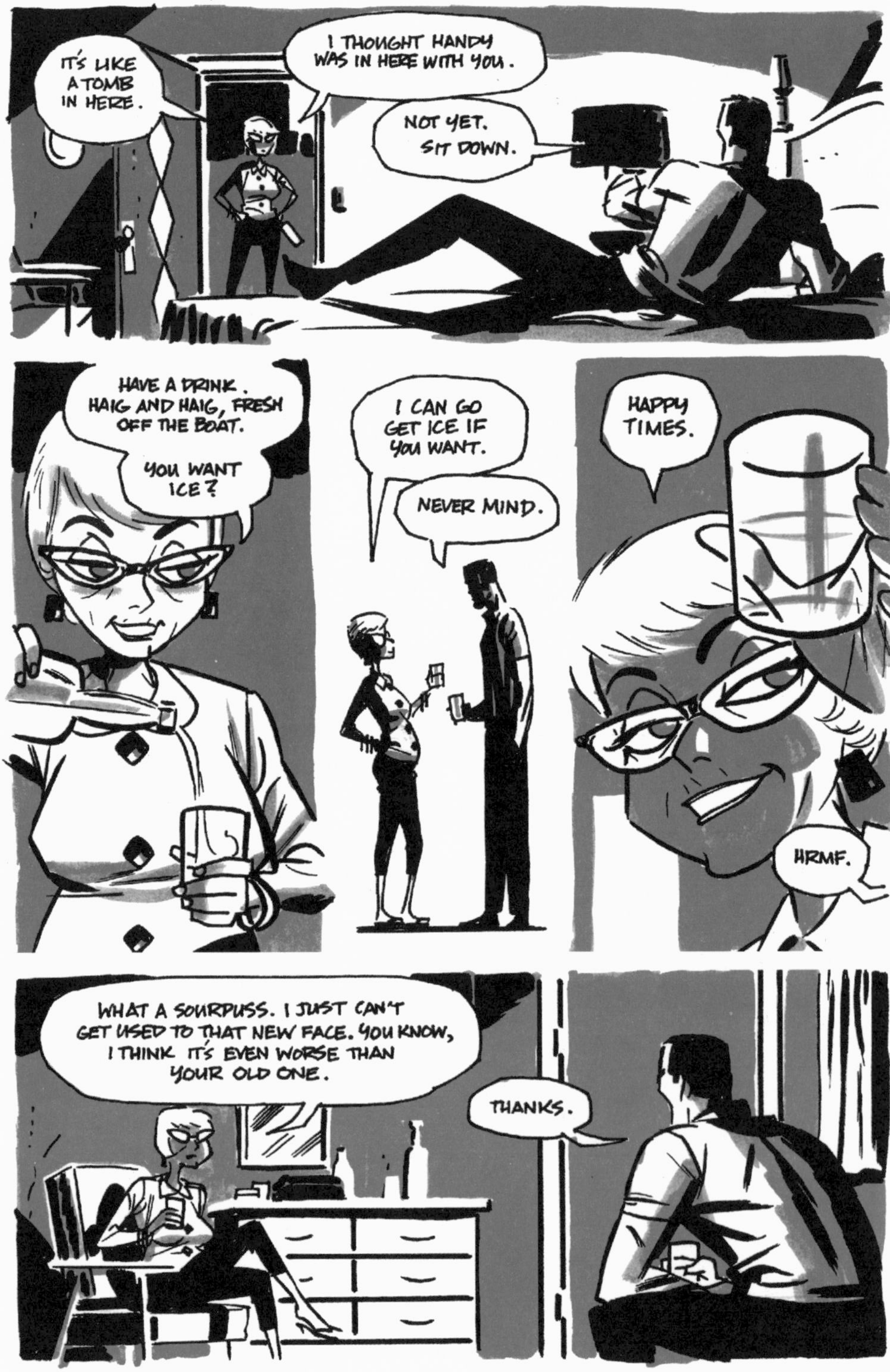
IT'S LIKE A TOMB IN HERE.
I THOUGHT HANDY WAS IN HERE WITH YOU.
NOT YET. SIT DOWN.
HAVE A DRINK. HAIG AND HAIG, FRESH OFF THE BOAT.
YOU WANT ICE?
I CAN GO GET ICE IF YOU WANT.
NEVER MIND.
HAPPY TIMES.
HRMF.
WHAT A SOURPUSS. I JUST CAN'T GET USED TO THAT NEW FACE. YOU KNOW, I THINK IT'S EVEN WORSE THAN YOUR OLD ONE.
THANKS.

Madge ran the Green Glen Motel. She was in her sixties now, one of the rare hookers that retired with money in the bank.

Running the motel brought her a modest living and gave her something to do. It also kept her indirectly connected to her old profession since most of the units were rented by the hour.

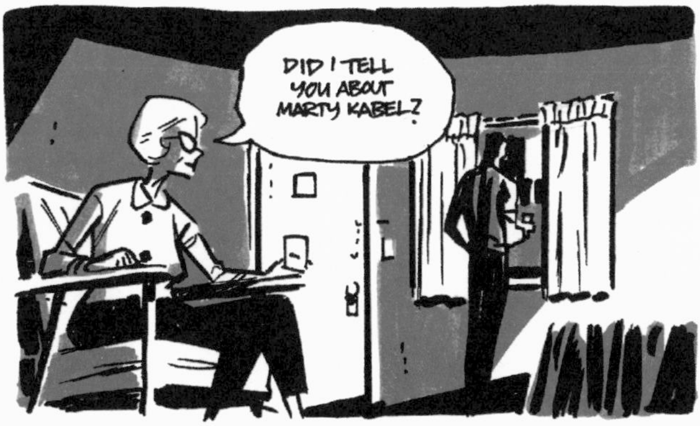
DID I TELL YOU ABOUT MARTY KABEL?

Parker, Handy and Grofeld had used the Green Glen as a base of operations while they set up the Acme Novelty job.

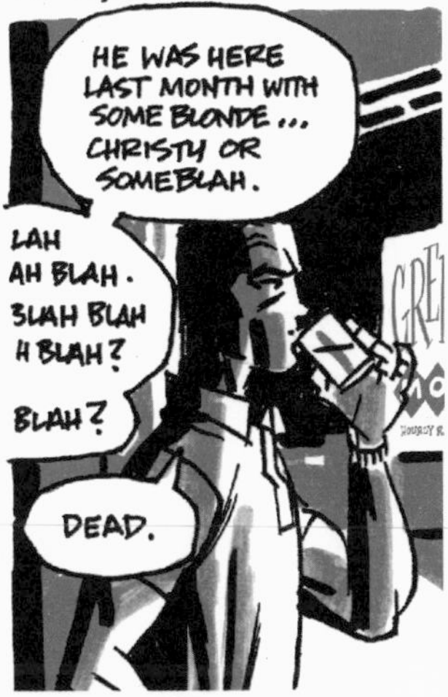
HE WAS HERE LAST MONTH WITH SOME BLONDE... CHRISTY OR SOMEBLAH.
LAH
AH BLAH.
BLAH BLAH
H BLAH?
BLAH?
DEAD.

The heist went perfectly and the take would leave the Outfit hurting. After the split Grofeld had started back for the foothills of Rocky Mount.

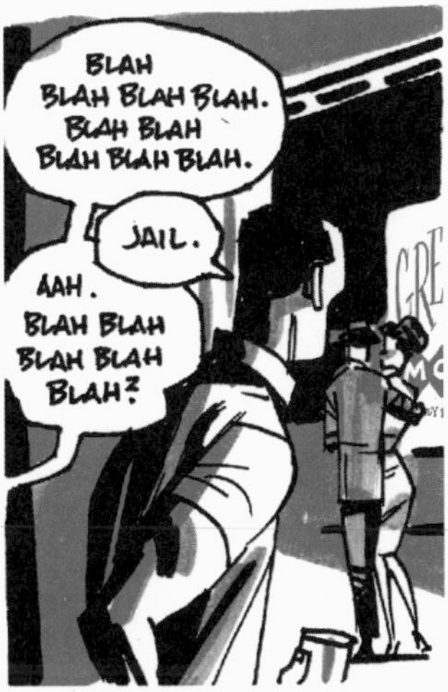
BLAH BLAH BLAH BLAH. BLAH BLAH BLAH BLAH BLAH.
JAIL.
AAH. BLAH BLAH BLAH BLAH BLAH?

Parker had asked Handy in on Buffalo but waiting for him now meant listening to Madge. He wondered, half-seriously, if it was worth it.

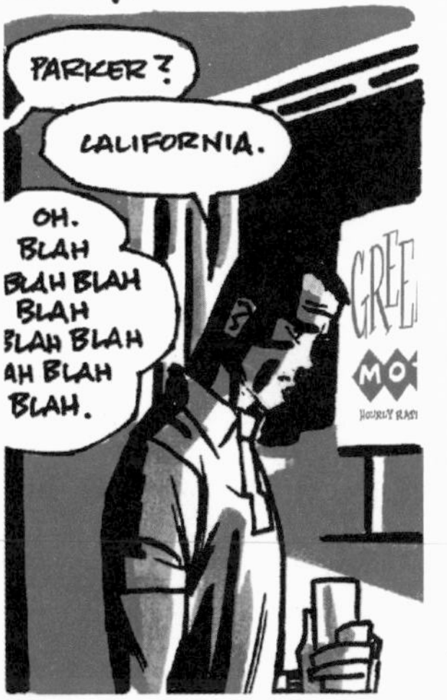
PARKER?
CALIFORNIA.
OH. BLAH BLAH BLAH BLAH BLAH BLAH AH BLAH BLAH.

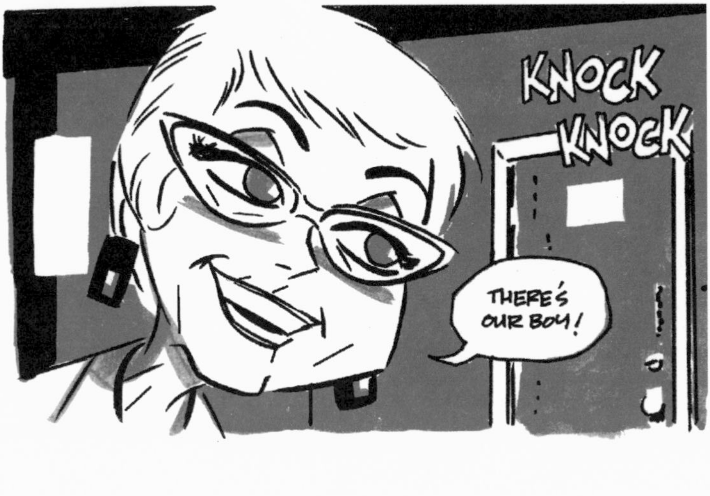
KNOCK KNOCK
THERE'S OUR BOY!

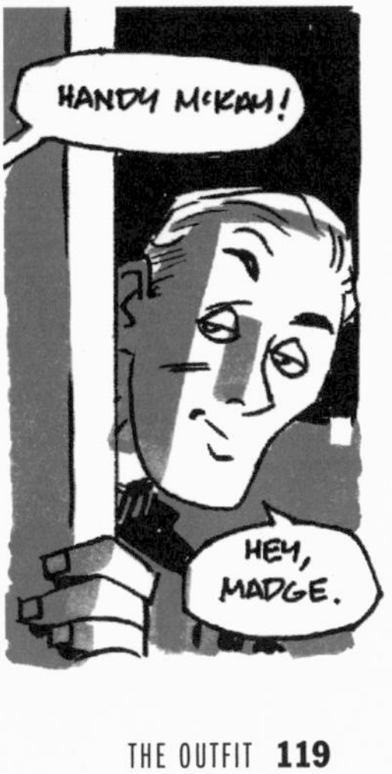
HANDY McKAY!
HEY, MADGE.

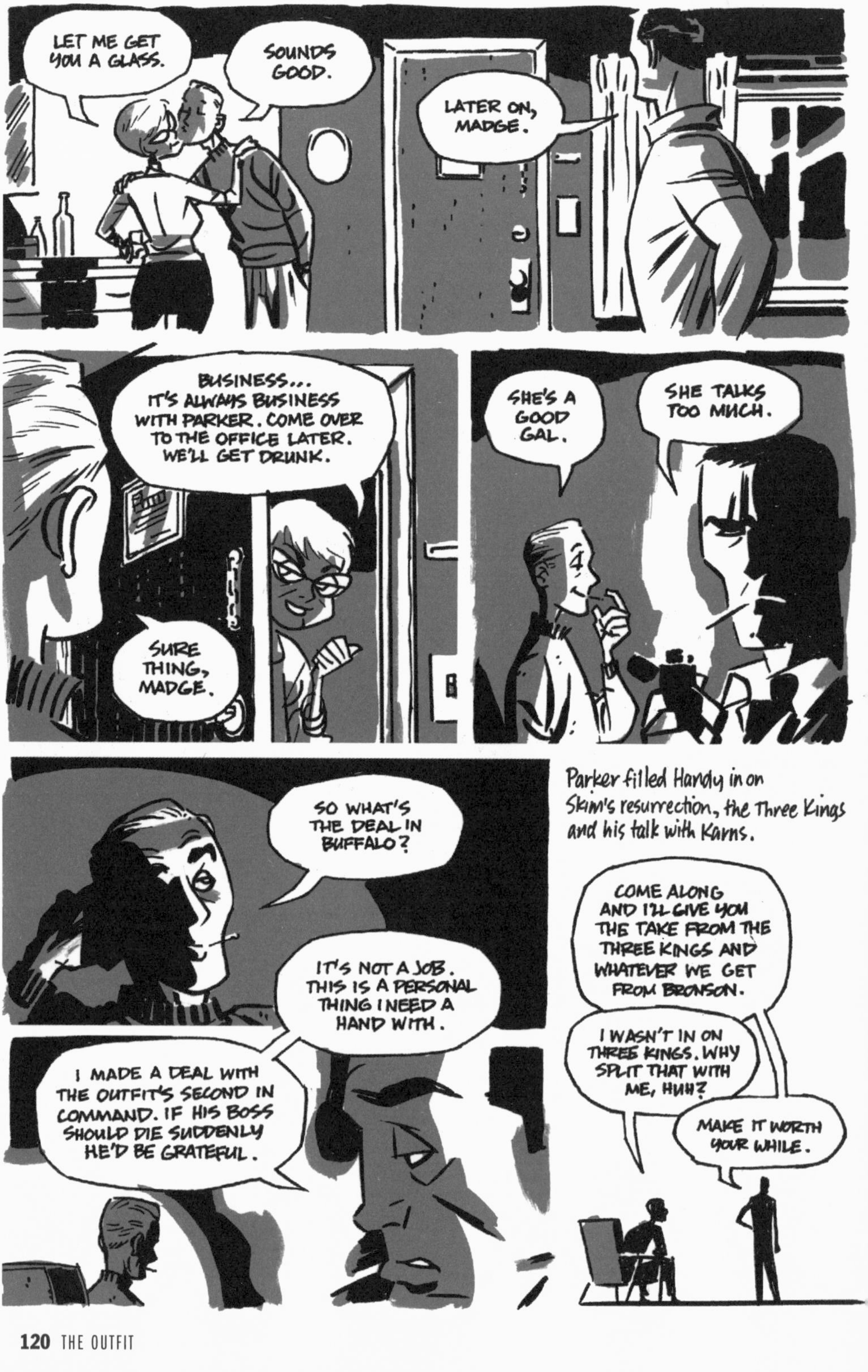
LET ME GET YOU A GLASS.
SOUNDS GOOD.
LATER ON, MADGE.
BUSINESS... IT'S ALWAYS BUSINESS WITH PARKER. COME OVER TO THE OFFICE LATER. WE'LL GET DRUNK.
SURE THING, MADGE.
SHE'S A GOOD GAL.
SHE TALKS TOO MUCH.
SO WHAT'S THE DEAL IN BUFFALO?
IT'S NOT A JOB. THIS IS A PERSONAL THING I NEED A HAND WITH.
I MADE A DEAL WITH THE OUTFIT'S SECOND IN COMMAND. IF HIS BOSS SHOULD DIE SUDDENLY HE'D BE GRATEFUL.
Parker filled Handy in on Skim's resurrection, the Three Kings and his talk with Karns.
COME ALONG AND I'LL GIVE YOU THE TAKE FROM THE THREE KINGS AND WHATEVER WE GET FROM BRONSON.
I WASN'T IN ON THREE KINGS. WHY SPLIT THAT WITH ME, HUH?
MAKE IT WORTH YOUR WHILE.

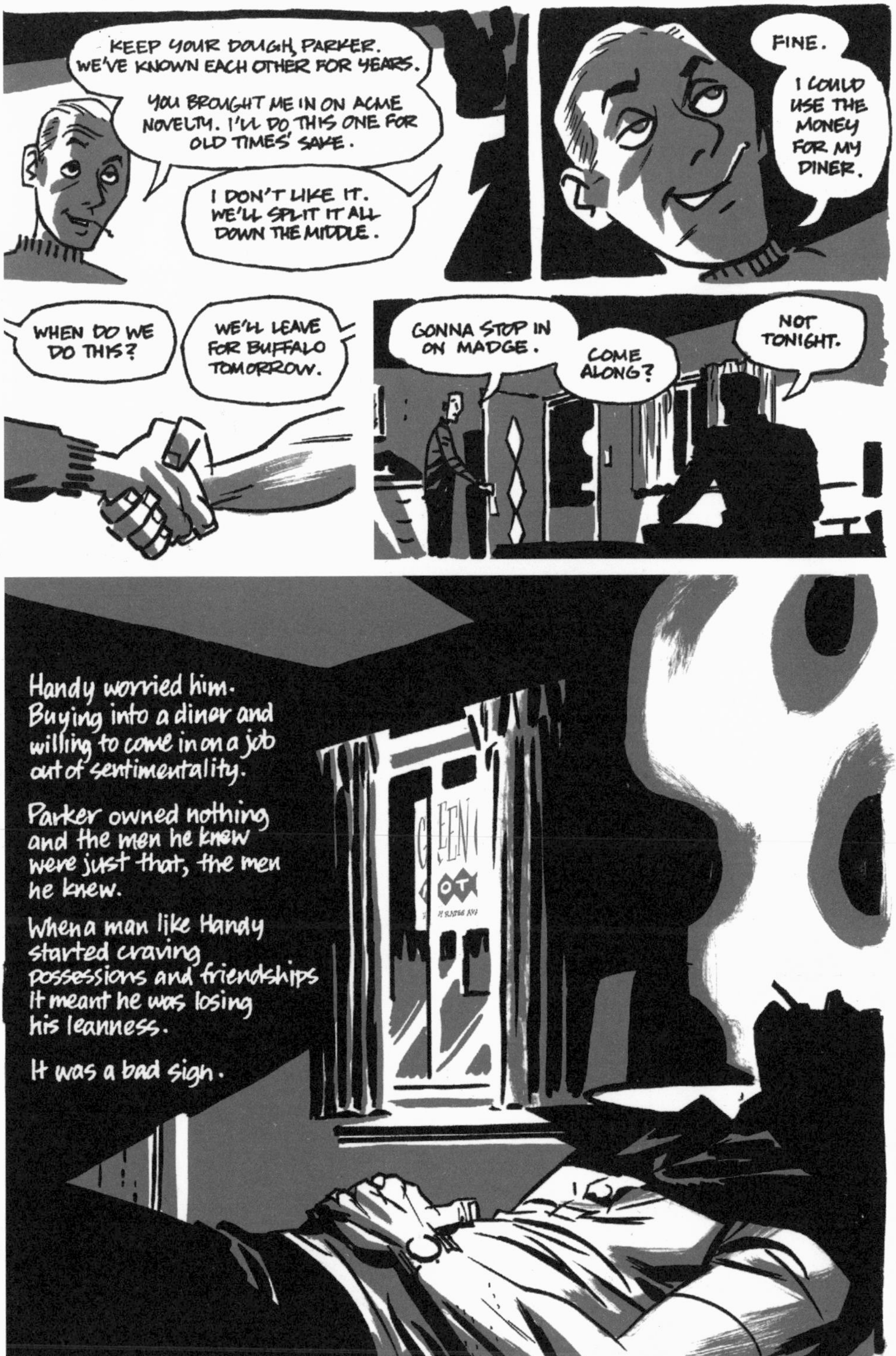
KEEP YOUR DOUGH, PARKER. WE'VE KNOWN EACH OTHER FOR YEARS.
YOU BROUGHT ME IN ON ACME NOVELTY. I'LL DO THIS ONE FOR OLD TIMES' SAKE.
I DON'T LIKE IT. WE'LL SPLIT IT ALL DOWN THE MIDDLE.
FINE.
I COULD USE THE MONEY FOR MY DINER.
WHEN DO WE DO THIS?
WE'LL LEAVE FOR BUFFALO TOMORROW.
GONNA STOP IN ON MADGE.
COME ALONG?
NOT TONIGHT.
Handy worried him. Buying into a diner and willing to come in on a job out of sentimentality.
Parker owned nothing and the men he knew were just that, the men he knew.
When a man like Handy started craving possessions and friendships it meant he was losing his leanness.
It was a bad sign.

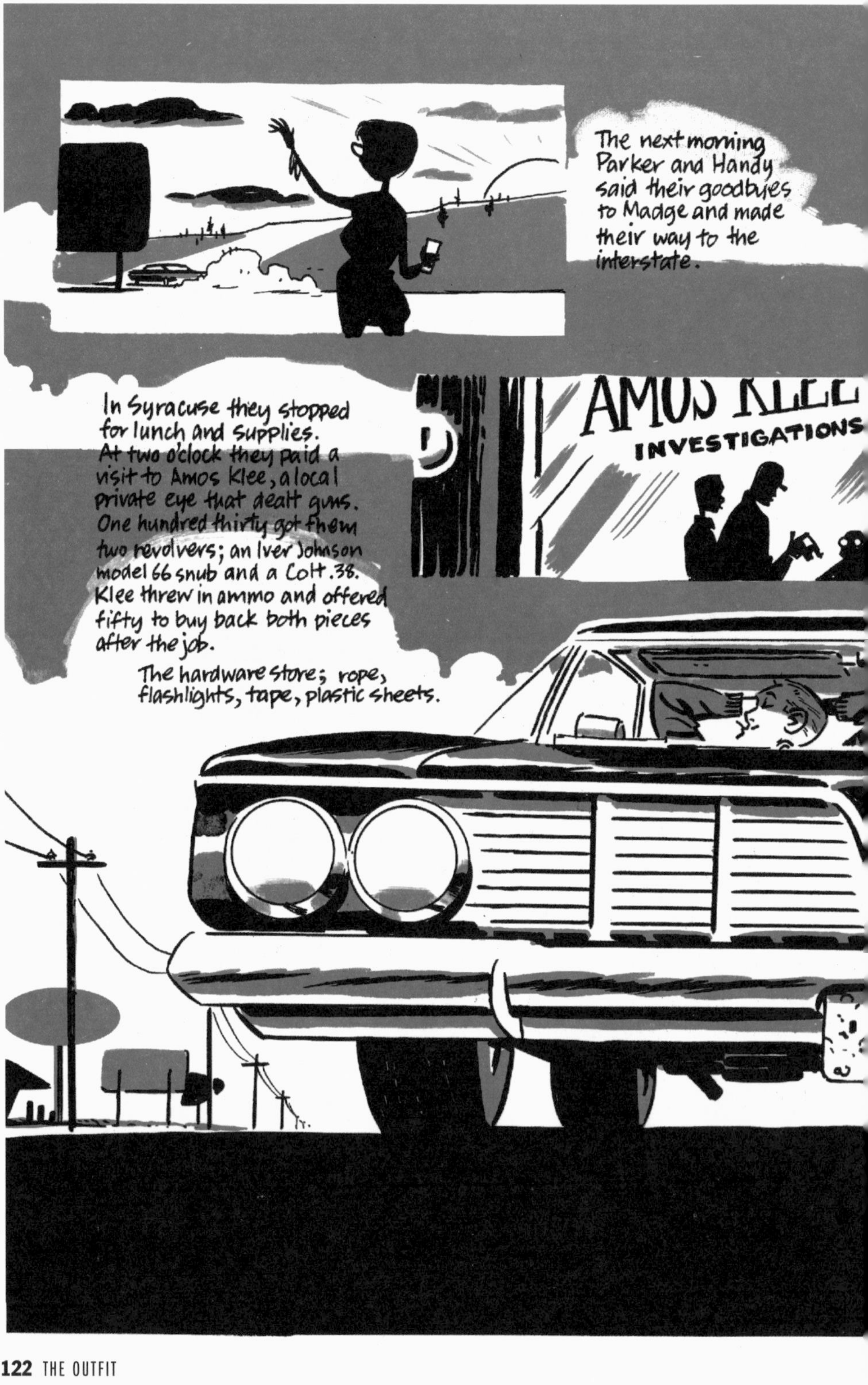
The next morning Parker and Handy said their goodbyes to Madge and made their way to the interstate.
INVESTIGATIONS
In Syracuse they stopped for lunch and supplies. At two o'clock they paid a visit to Amos Klee, a local private eye that dealt guns. One hundred thirty got them two revolvers; an Iver Johnson model 66 snub and a Colt .38. Klee threw in ammo and offered fifty to buy back both pieces after the job.
The hardware store; rope, flashlights, tape, plastic sheets.

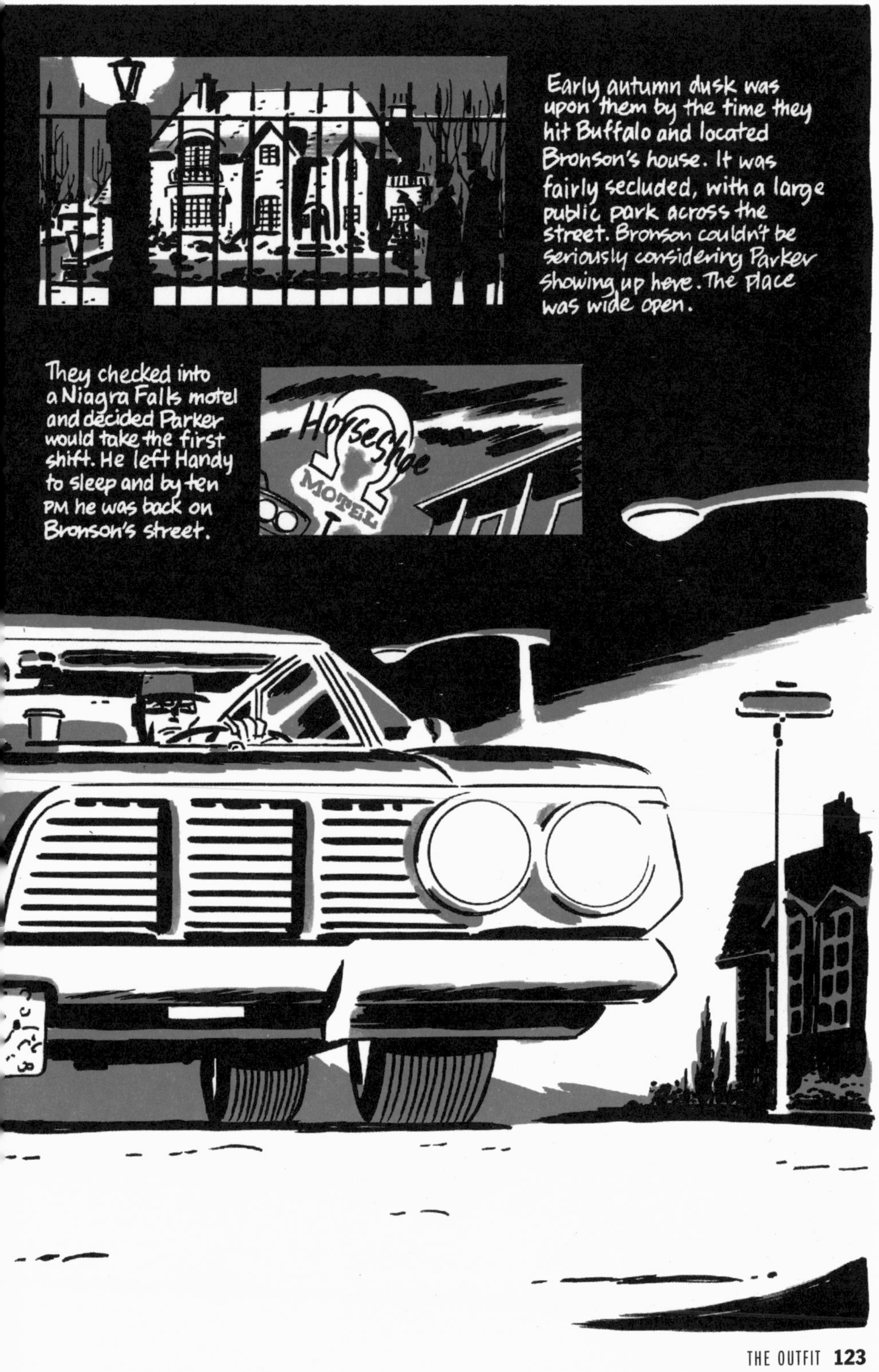
Early autumn dusk was upon them by the time they hit Buffalo and located Bronson's house. It was fairly secluded, with a large public park across the street. Bronson couldn't be seriously considering Parker showing up here. The place was wide open.
They checked into a Niagra Falls motel and decided Parker would take the first shift. He left Handy to sleep and by ten PM he was back on Bronson's street.
Horseshoe
MOTEL

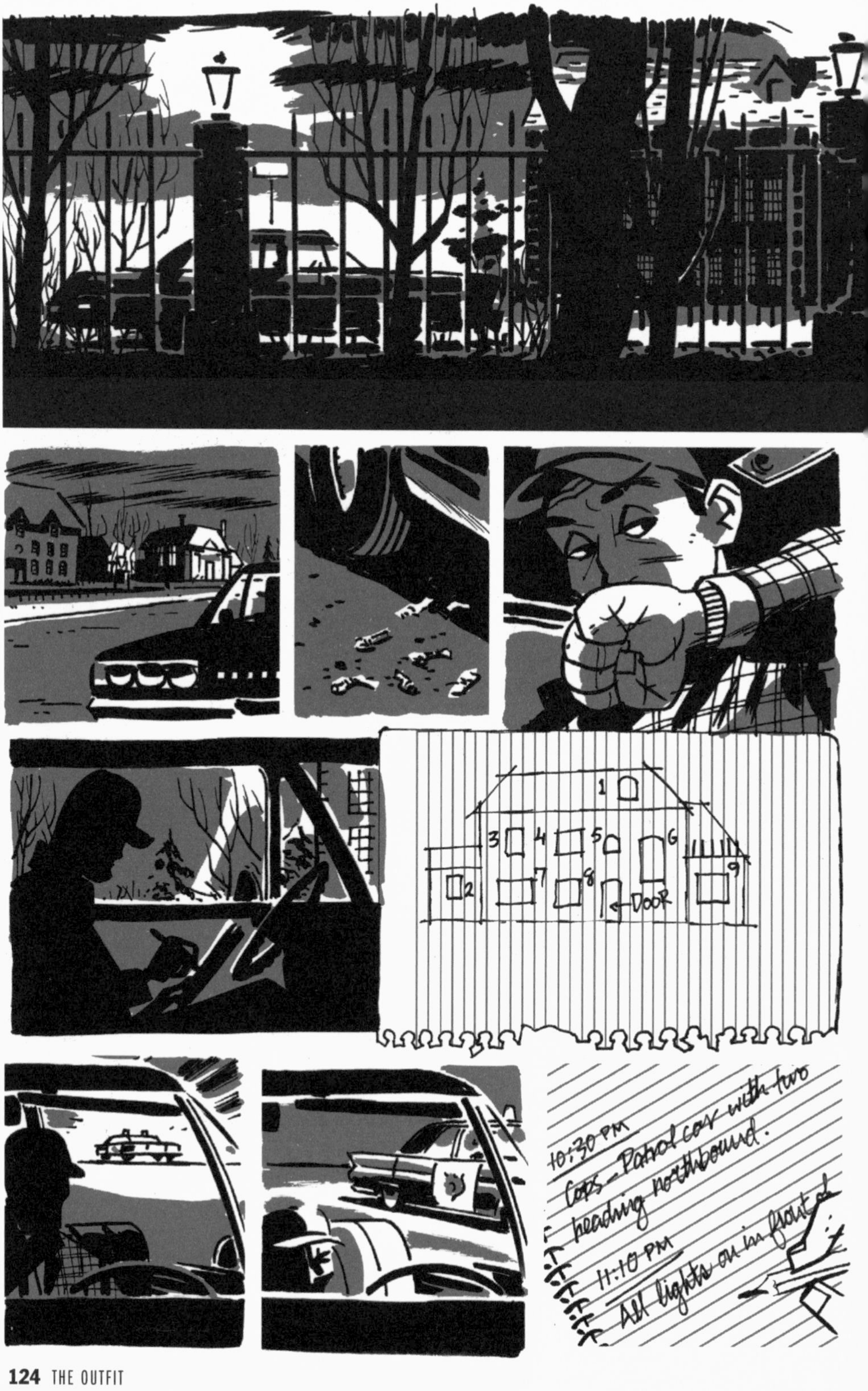
1
3
4
5
G
2
7
8
9
DOOR
10:30 PM
Cops - Patrol car with two heading northbound.
11:10 PM
All lights on in front

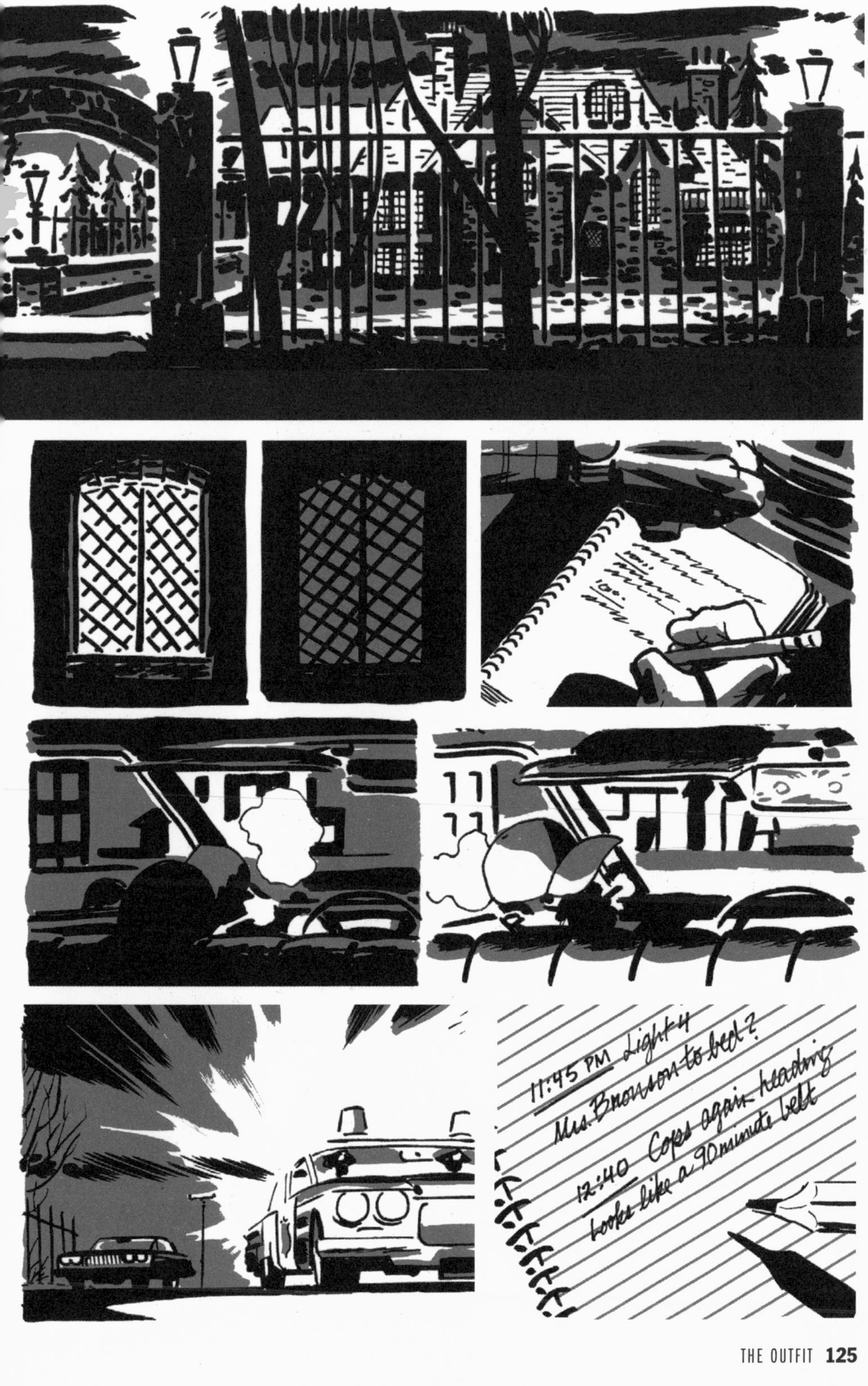
11:45 PM Light 4
Mrs. Bronson to bed?
12:40 Cops again heading
looks like a 90 minute belt

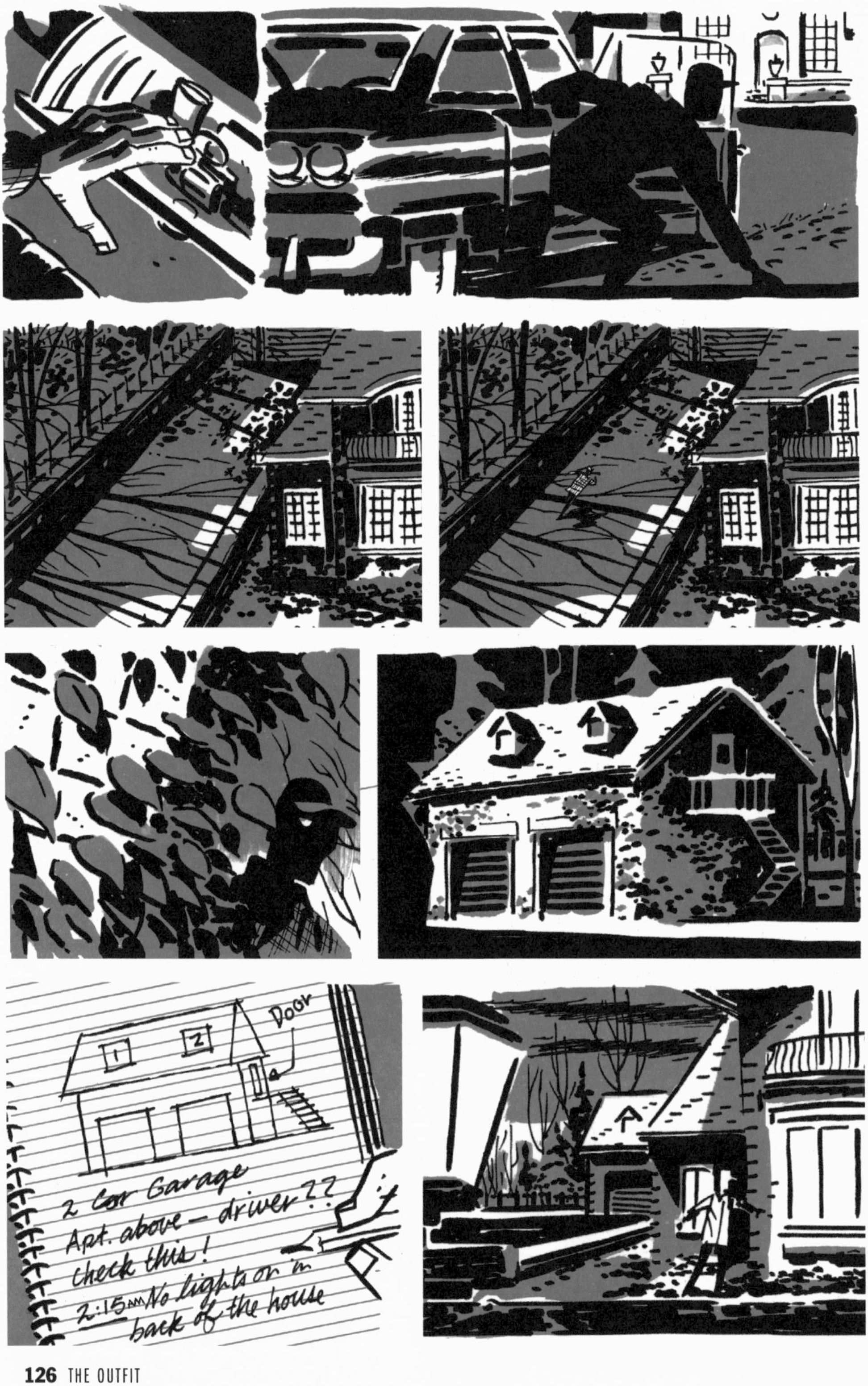
Door
1
2
2 Car Garage
Apt. above — driver ??
check this!
2:15 AM No lights on in back of the house

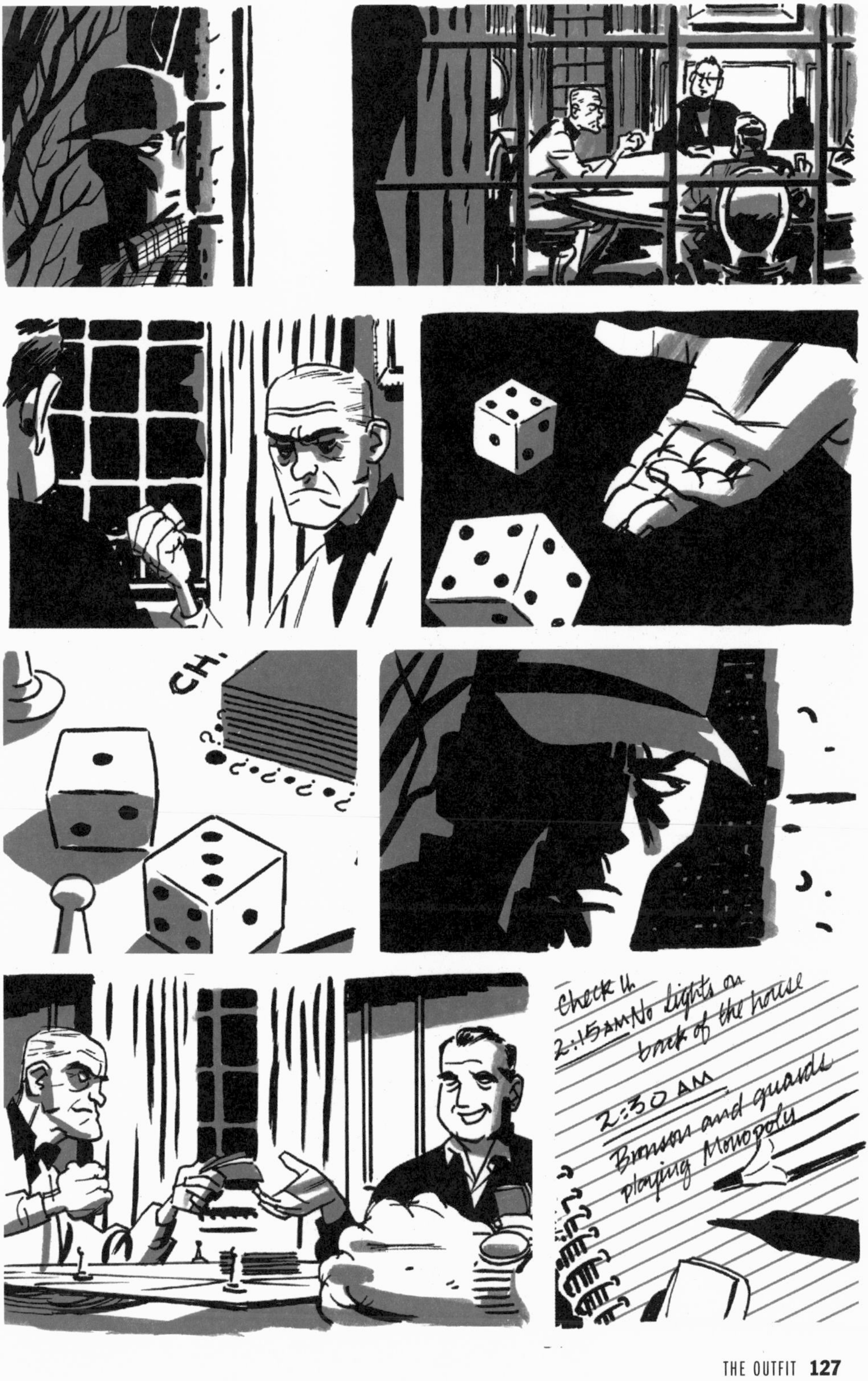
Check in
2:15AM No lights on back of the house
2:30 AM
Bronson and guards playing Monopoly

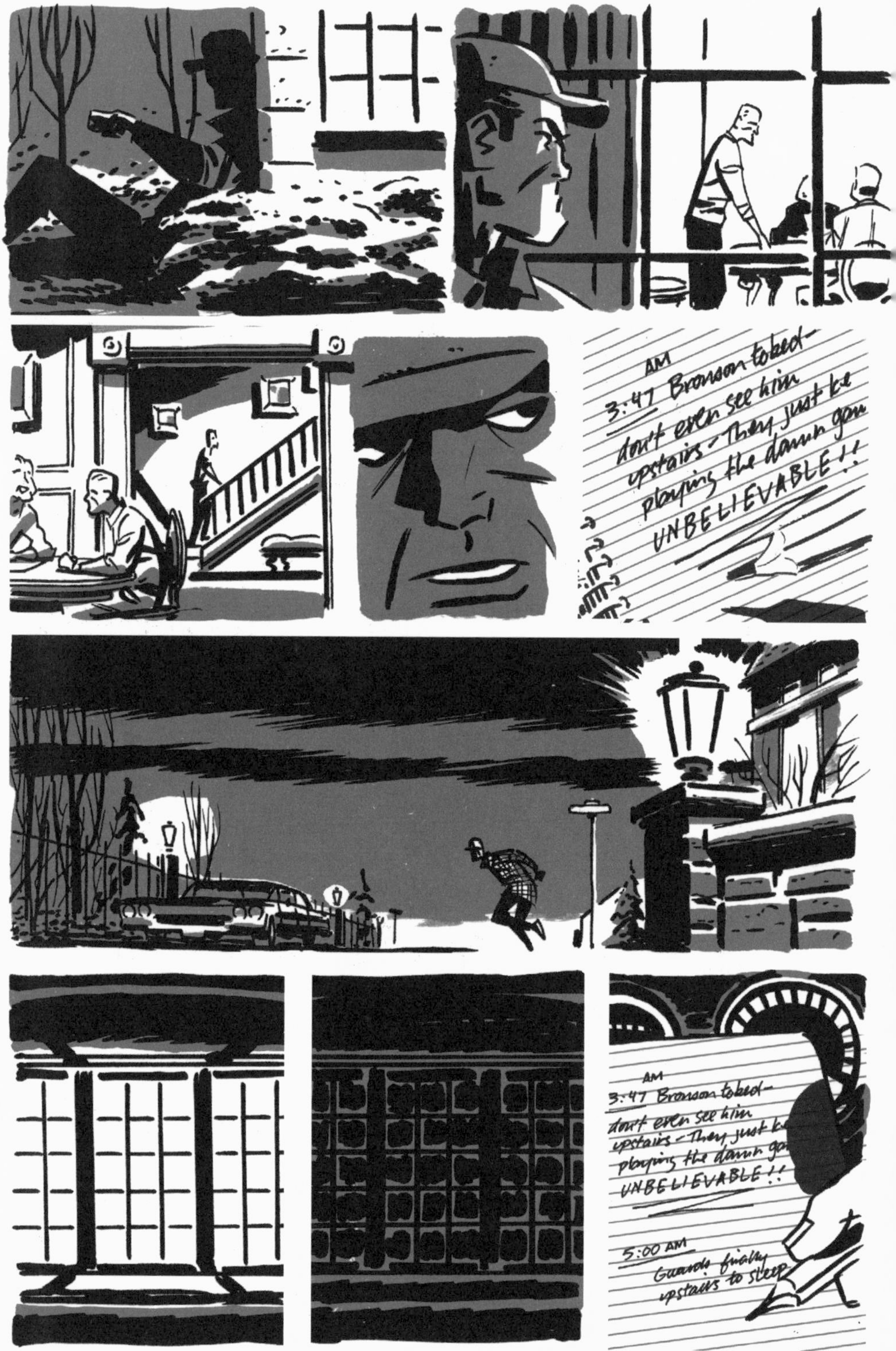
AM
3:47 Bronson to bed—
don't even see him
upstairs – They just ke
playing the damn gam
UNBELIEVABLE!!
AM
3:47 Bronson to bed—
don't even see him
upstairs – They just k
playing the damn ga
UNBELIEVABLE!!
5:00 AM
Guards finally
upstairs to sleep

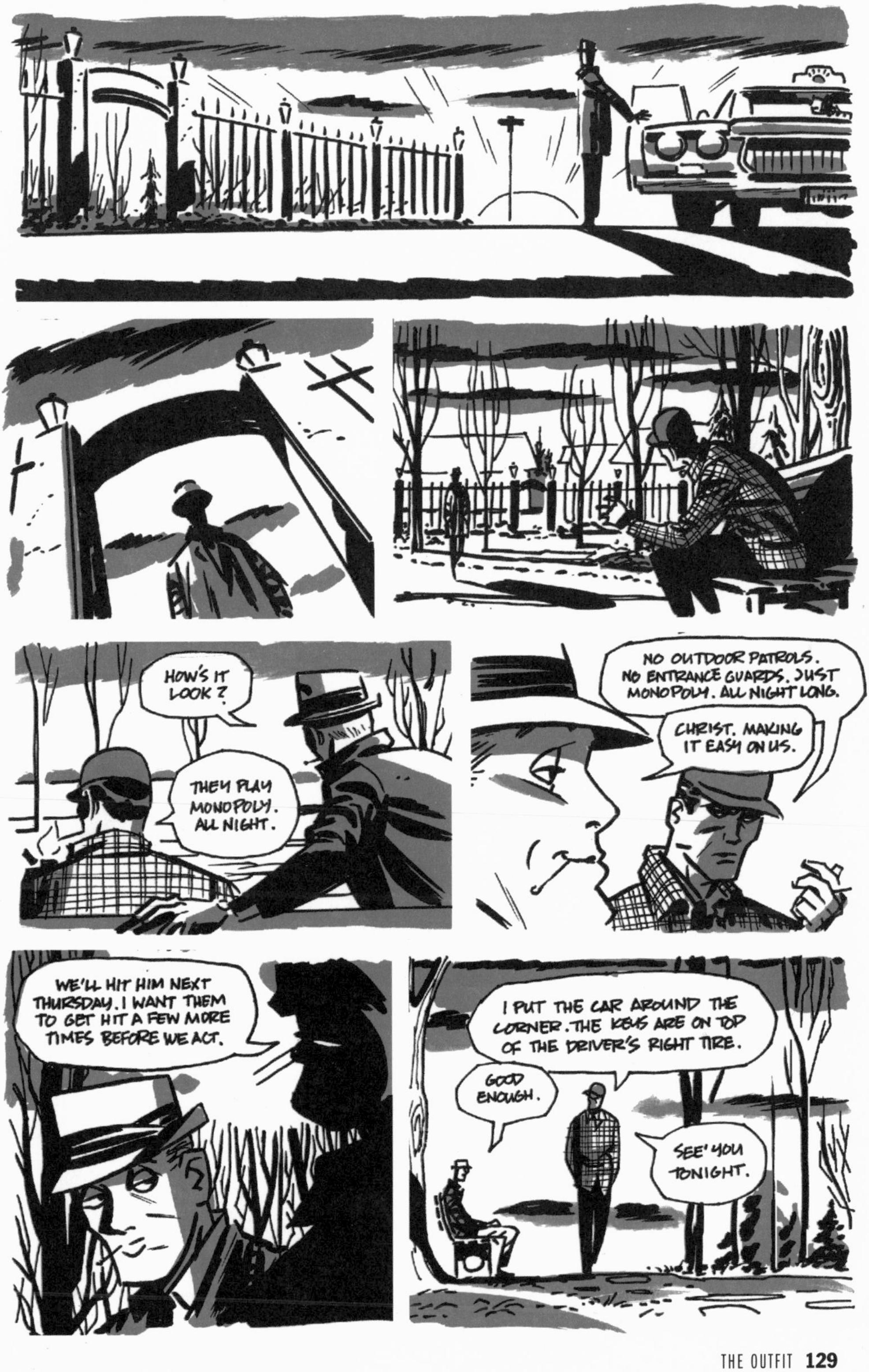
HOW'S IT LOOK?
THEY PLAY MONOPOLY. ALL NIGHT.
NO OUTDOOR PATROLS. NO ENTRANCE GUARDS. JUST MONOPOLY. ALL NIGHT LONG.
CHRIST. MAKING IT EASY ON US.
WE'LL HIT HIM NEXT THURSDAY. I WANT THEM TO GET HIT A FEW MORE TIMES BEFORE WE ACT.
I PUT THE CAR AROUND THE CORNER. THE KEYS ARE ON TOP OF THE DRIVER'S RIGHT TIRE.
GOOD ENOUGH.
SEE YOU TONIGHT.

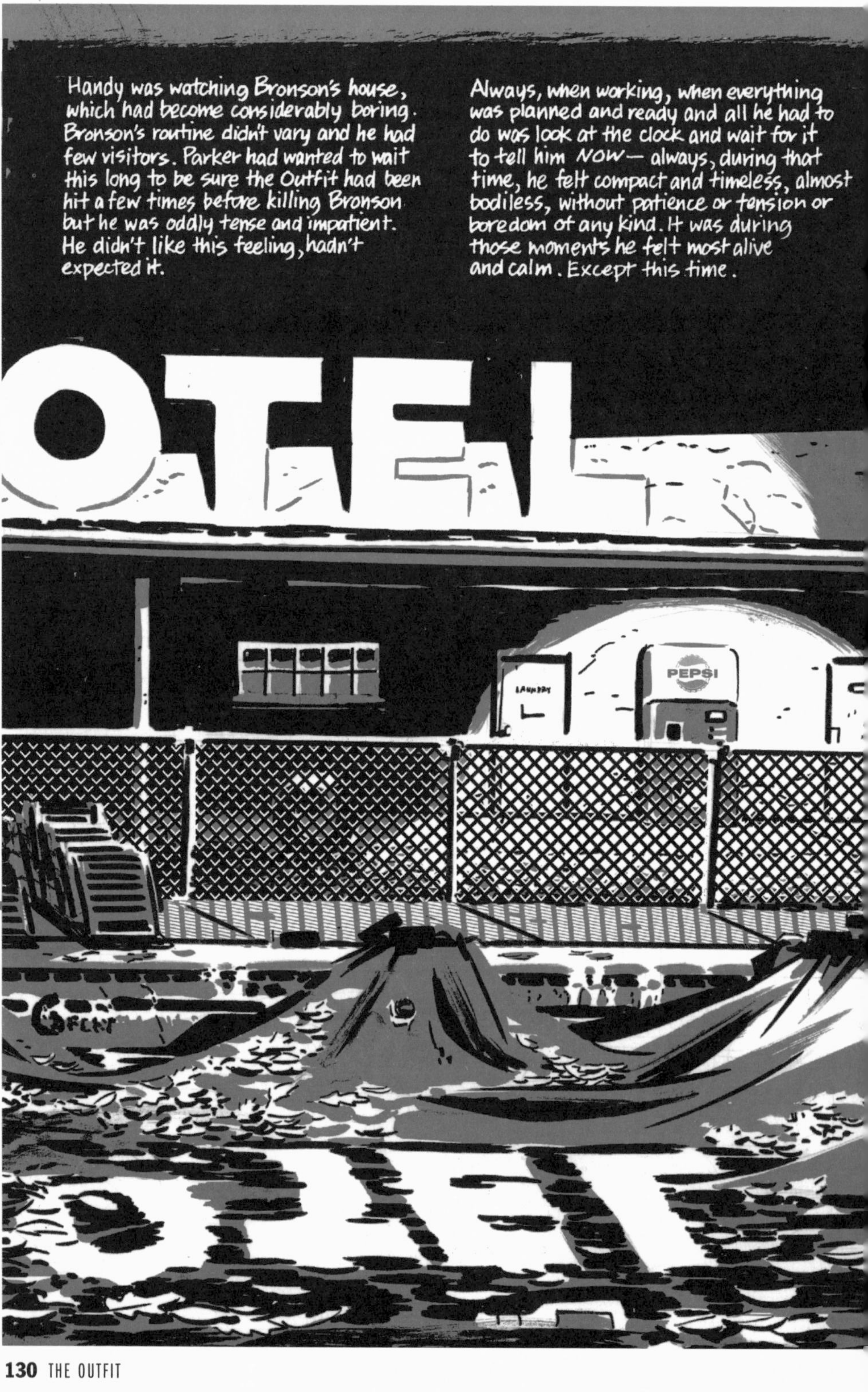
Handy was watching Bronson's house, which had become considerably boring. Bronson's routine didn't vary and he had few visitors. Parker had wanted to wait this long to be sure the Outfit had been hit a few times before killing Bronson but he was oddly tense and impatient. He didn't like this feeling, hadn't expected it.
Always, when working, when everything was planned and ready and all he had to do was look at the clock and wait for it to tell him NOW— always, during that time, he felt compact and timeless, almost bodiless, without patience or tension or boredom of any kind. It was during those moments he felt most alive and calm. Except this time.
OTEL
PEPSI

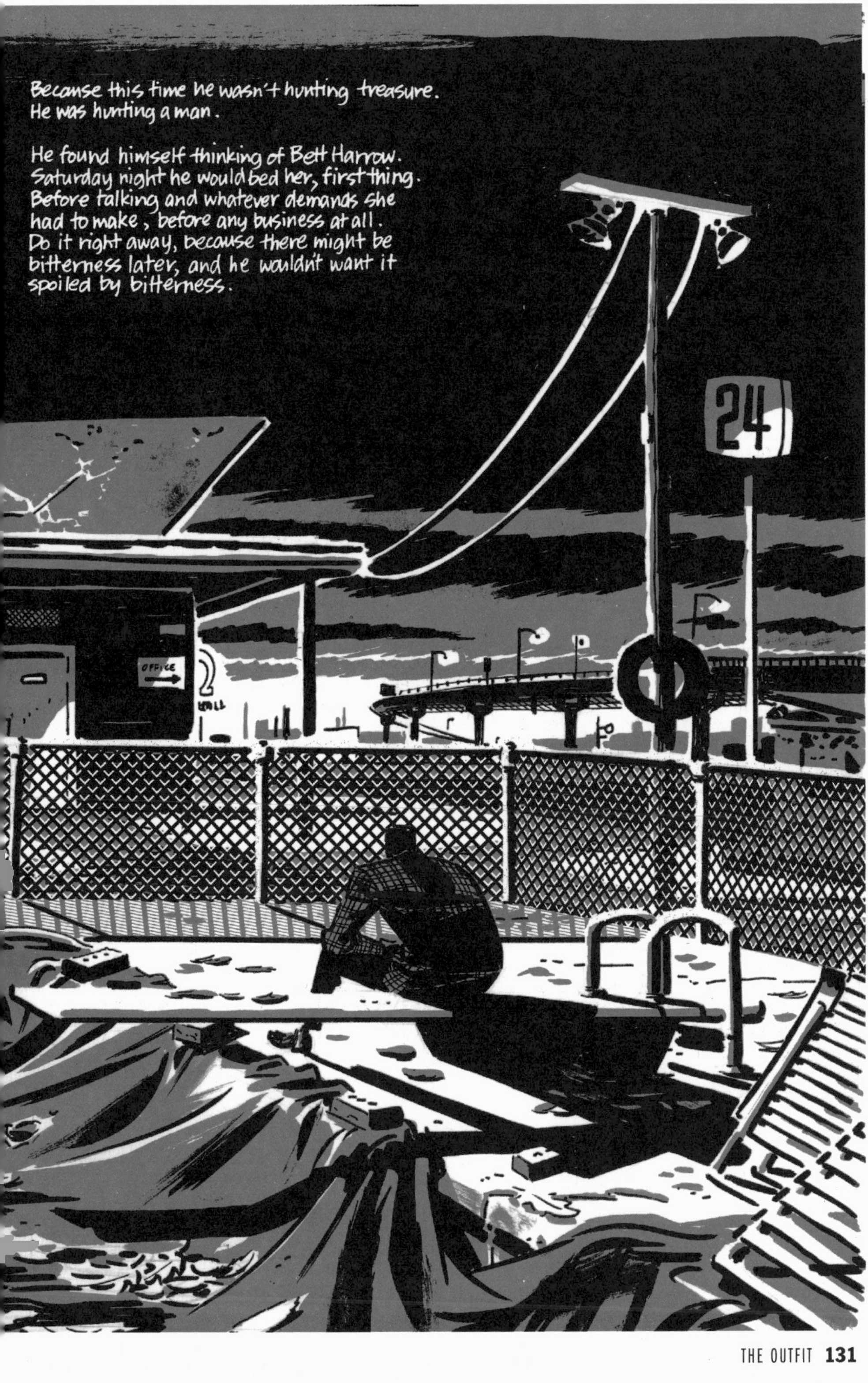
Because this time he wasn't hunting treasure. He was hunting a man.
He found himself thinking of Bett Harrow. Saturday night he would bed her, first thing. Before talking and whatever demands she had to make, before any business at all. Do it right away, because there might be bitterness later, and he wouldn't want it spoiled by bitterness.
24
OFFICE

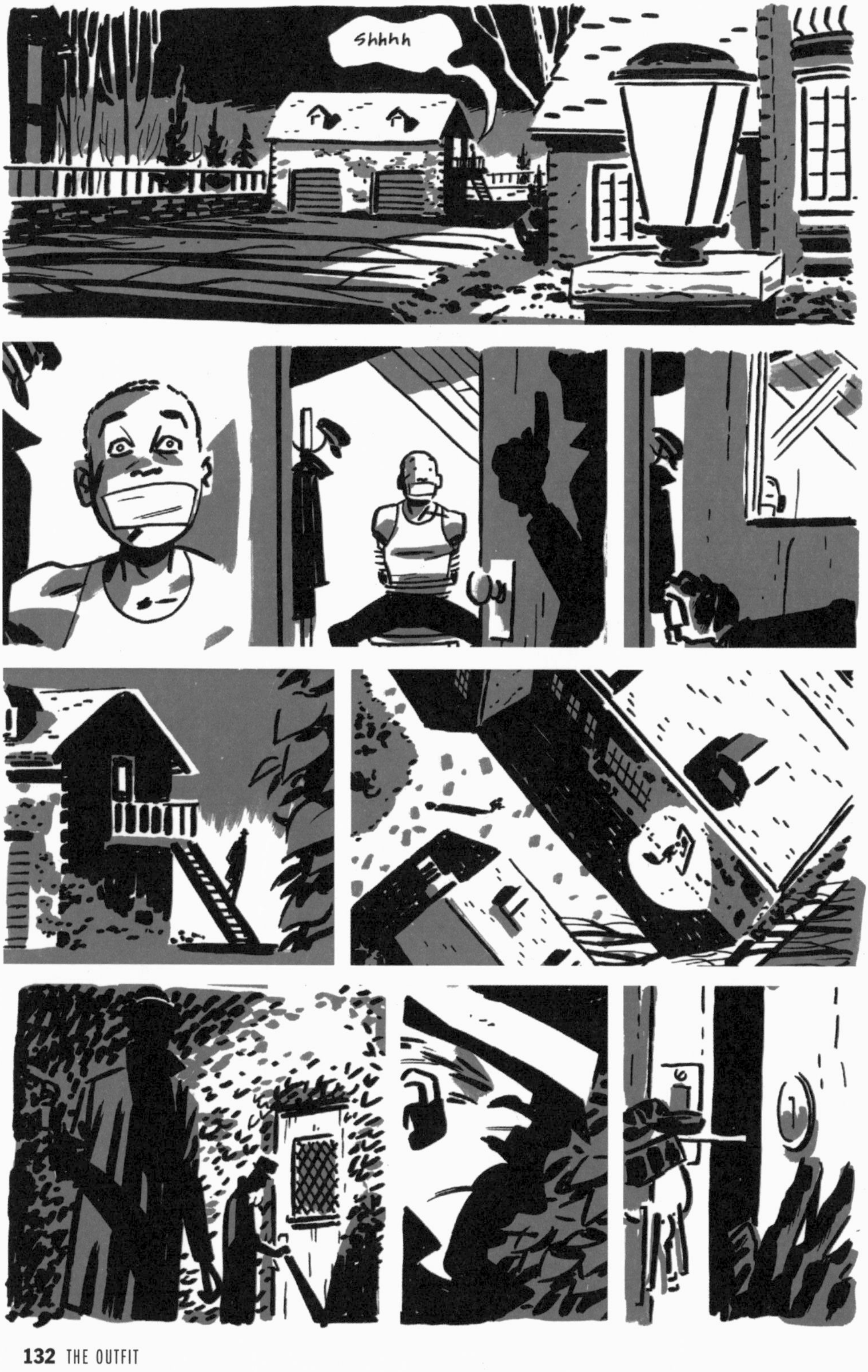
Shhhh

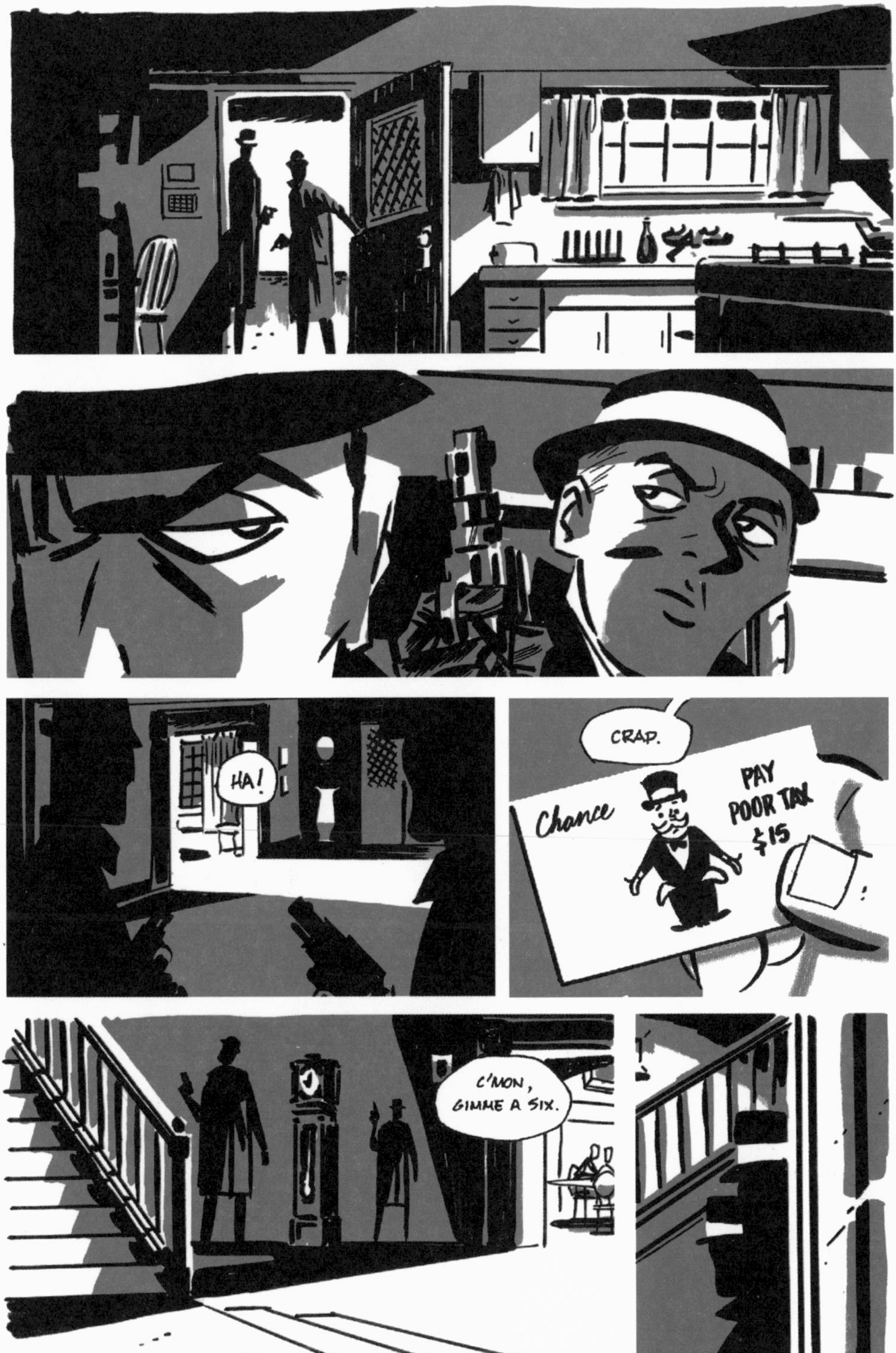
HA!
CRAP.
Chance
PAY POOR TAX $15
C'MON, GIMME A SIX.

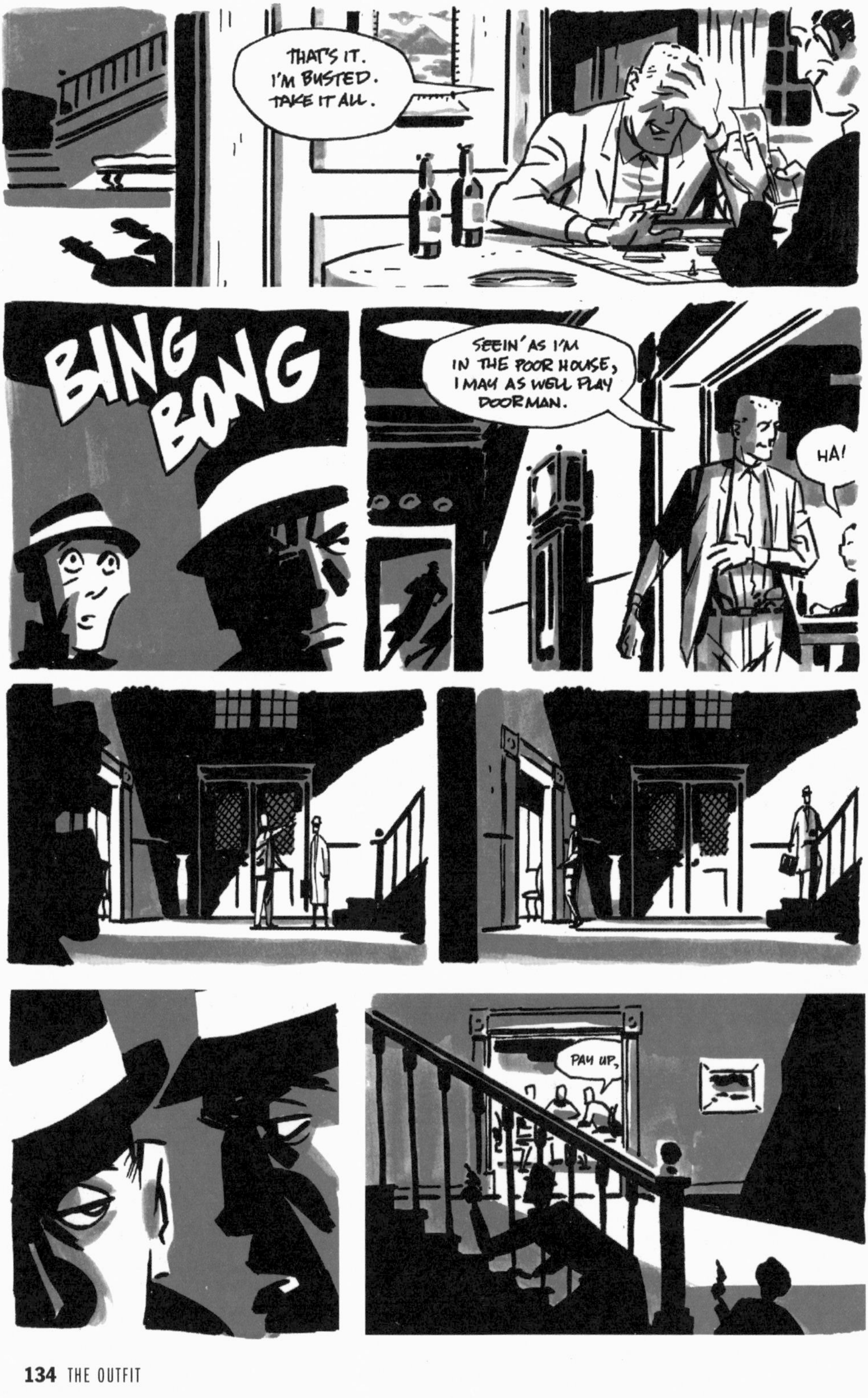
THAT'S IT. I'M BUSTED. TAKE IT ALL.
BING BONG
SEEIN' AS I'M IN THE POOR HOUSE, I MAY AS WELL PLAY DOORMAN.
HA!
PAY UP,

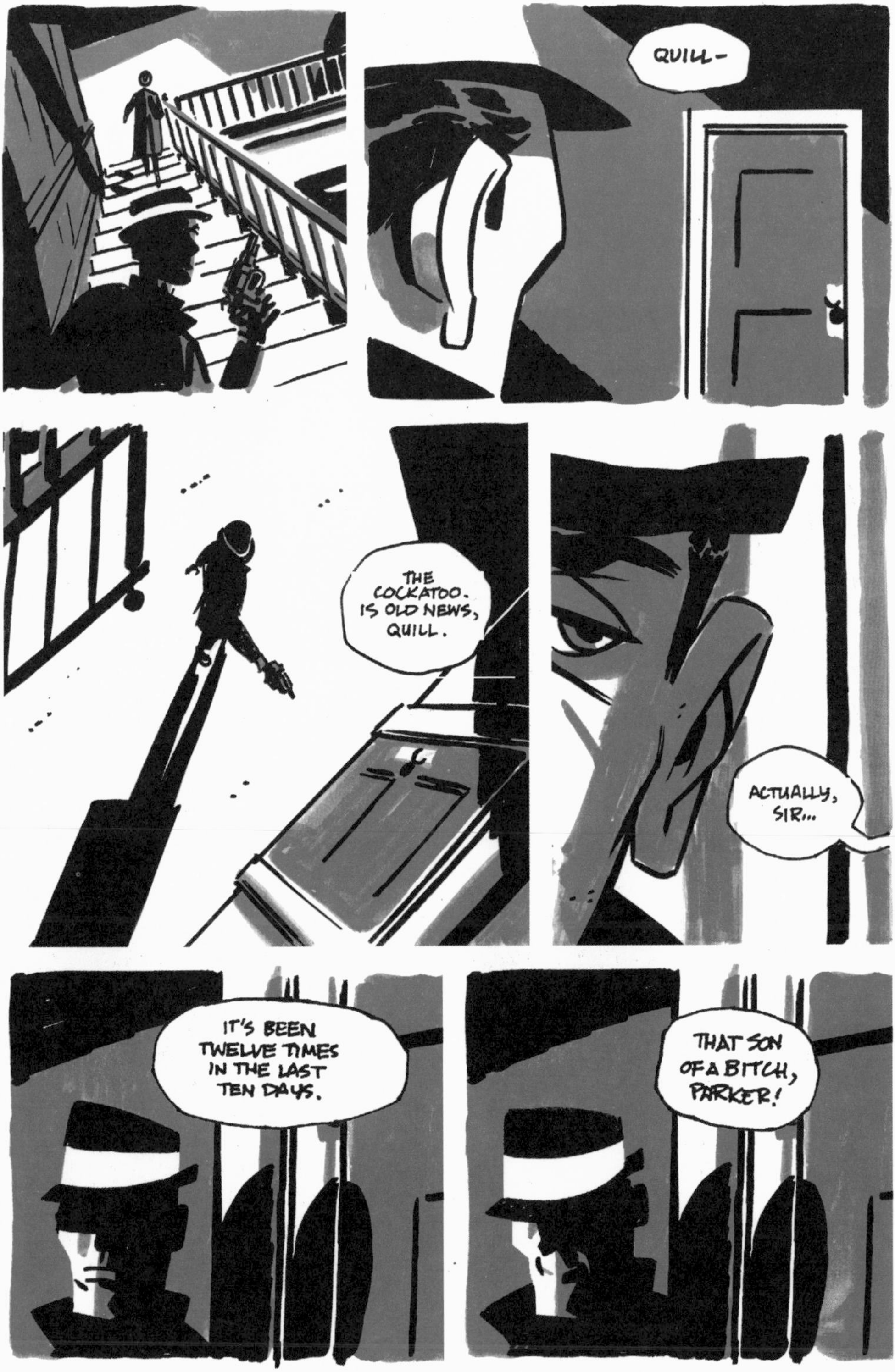
QUILL-
THE COCKATOO. IS OLD NEWS, QUILL.
ACTUALLY, SIR...
IT'S BEEN TWELVE TIMES IN THE LAST TEN DAYS.
THAT SON OF A BITCH, PARKER!

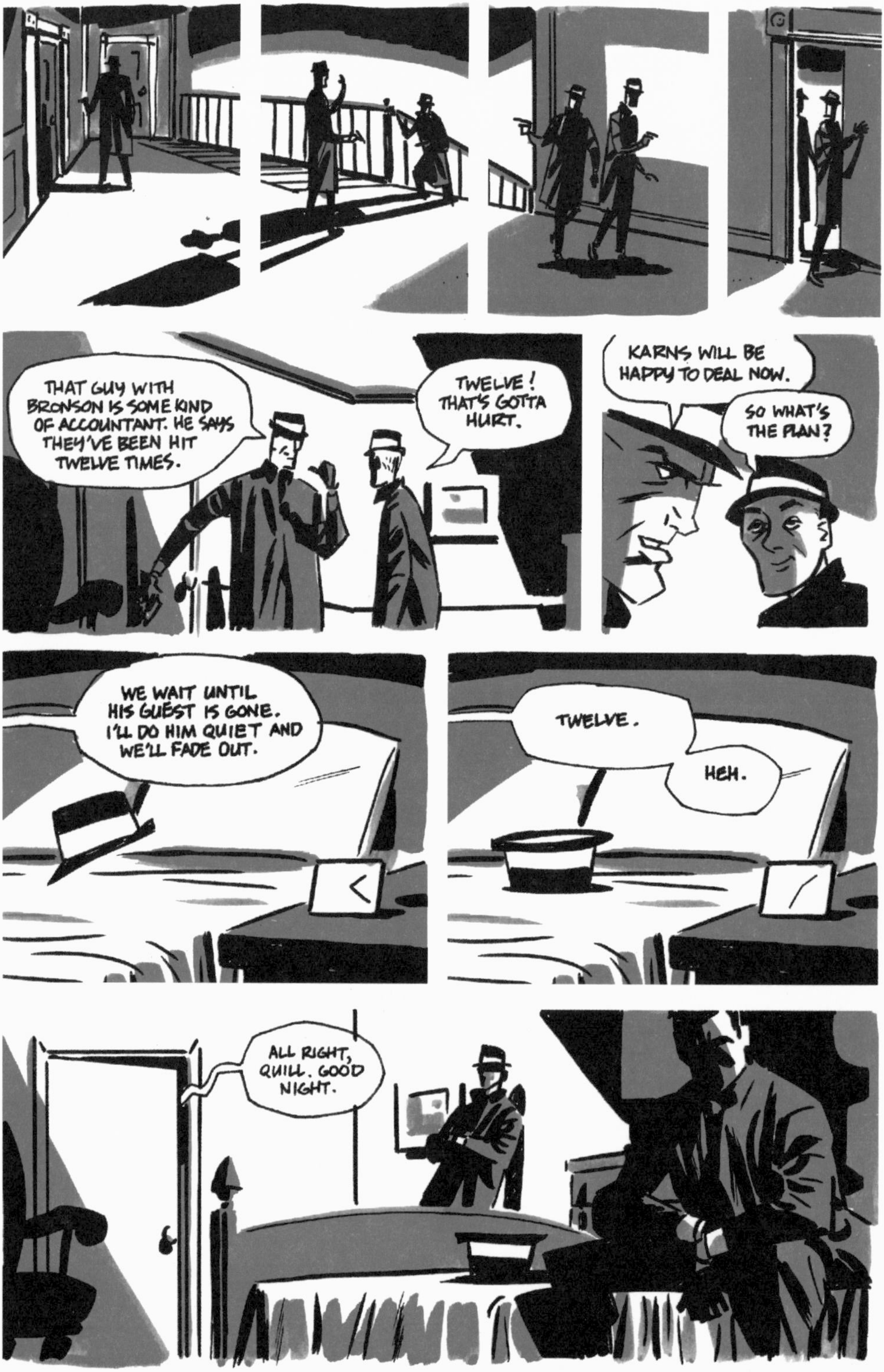
THAT GUY WITH BRONSON IS SOME KIND OF ACCOUNTANT. HE SAYS THEY'VE BEEN HIT TWELVE TIMES.
TWELVE! THAT'S GOTTA HURT.
KARNS WILL BE HAPPY TO DEAL NOW.
SO WHAT'S THE PLAN?
WE WAIT UNTIL HIS GUEST IS GONE. I'LL DO HIM QUIET AND WE'LL FADE OUT.
TWELVE.
HEH.
ALL RIGHT, QUILL. GOOD NIGHT.

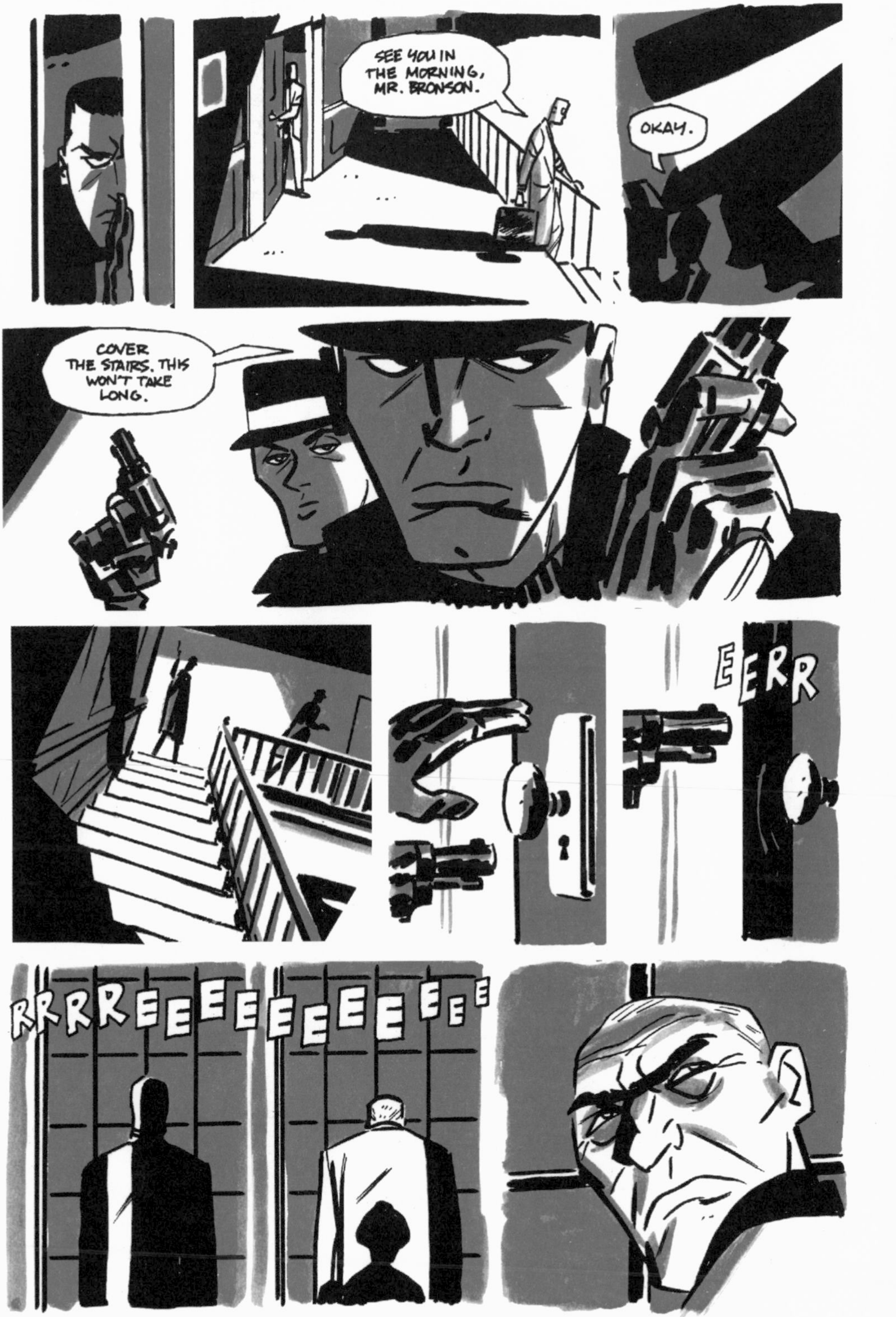
SEE YOU IN THE MORNING, MR. BRONSON.
OKAY.
COVER THE STAIRS. THIS WON'T TAKE LONG.
EERR
RRRREEEEEEEEEEEE

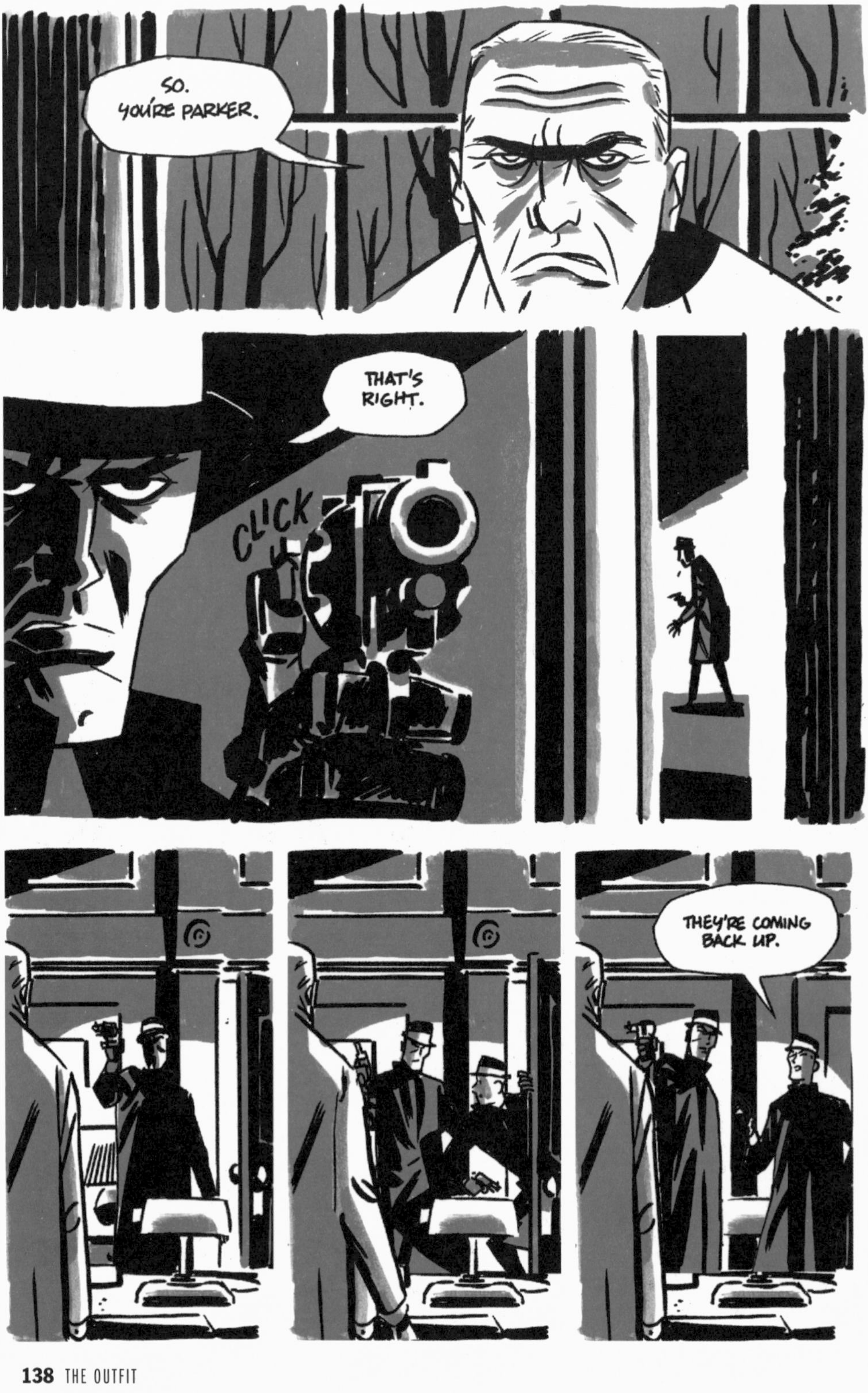
SO.
YOU'RE PARKER.
THAT'S RIGHT.
CLICK
THEY'RE COMING BACK UP.

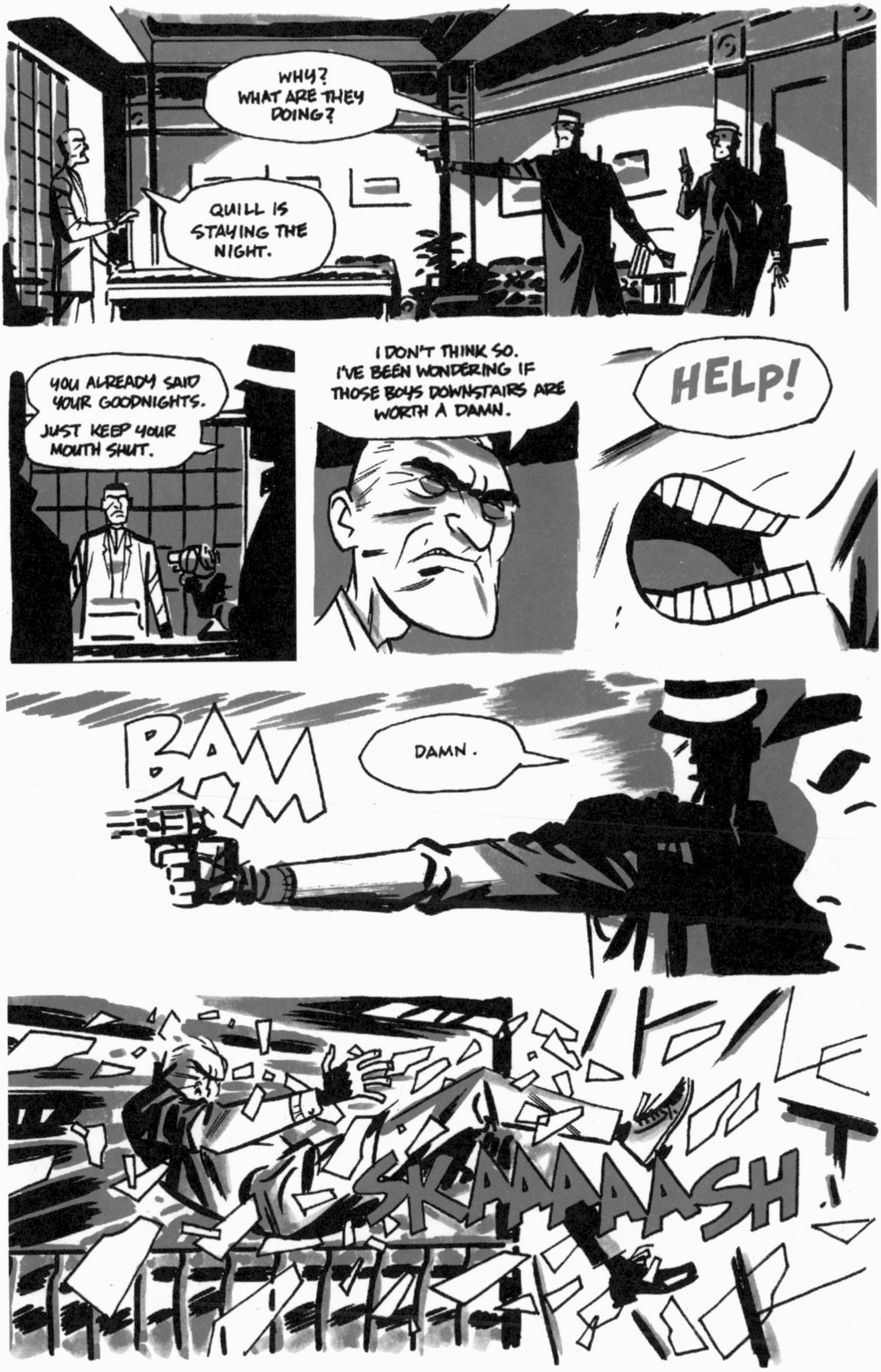
WHY? WHAT ARE THEY DOING?
QUILL IS STAYING THE NIGHT.
YOU ALREADY SAID YOUR GOODNIGHTS.
JUST KEEP YOUR MOUTH SHUT.
I DON'T THINK SO. I'VE BEEN WONDERING IF THOSE BOYS DOWNSTAIRS ARE WORTH A DAMN.
HELP!
BAM
DAMN.
SKAAAAASH

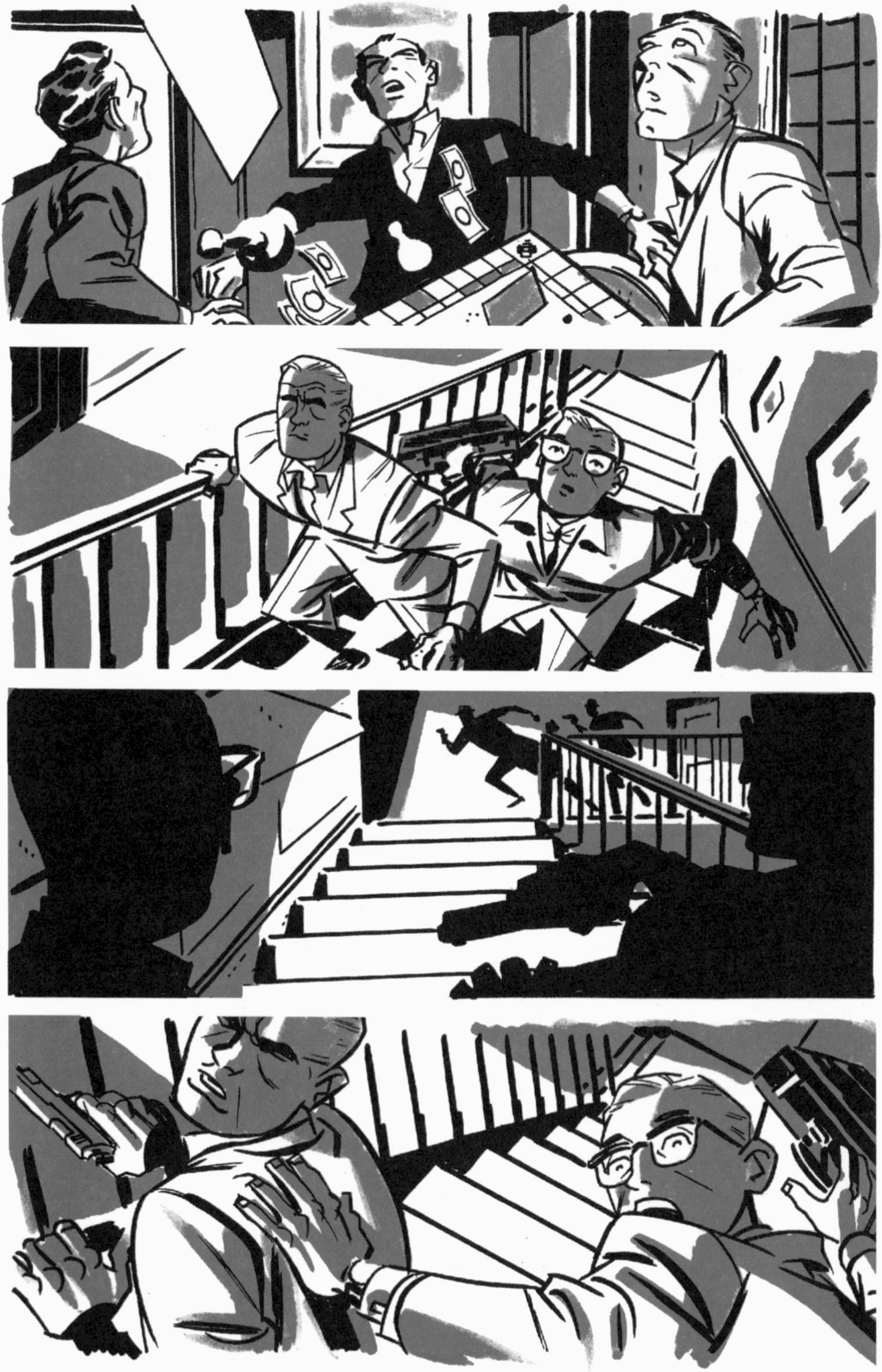

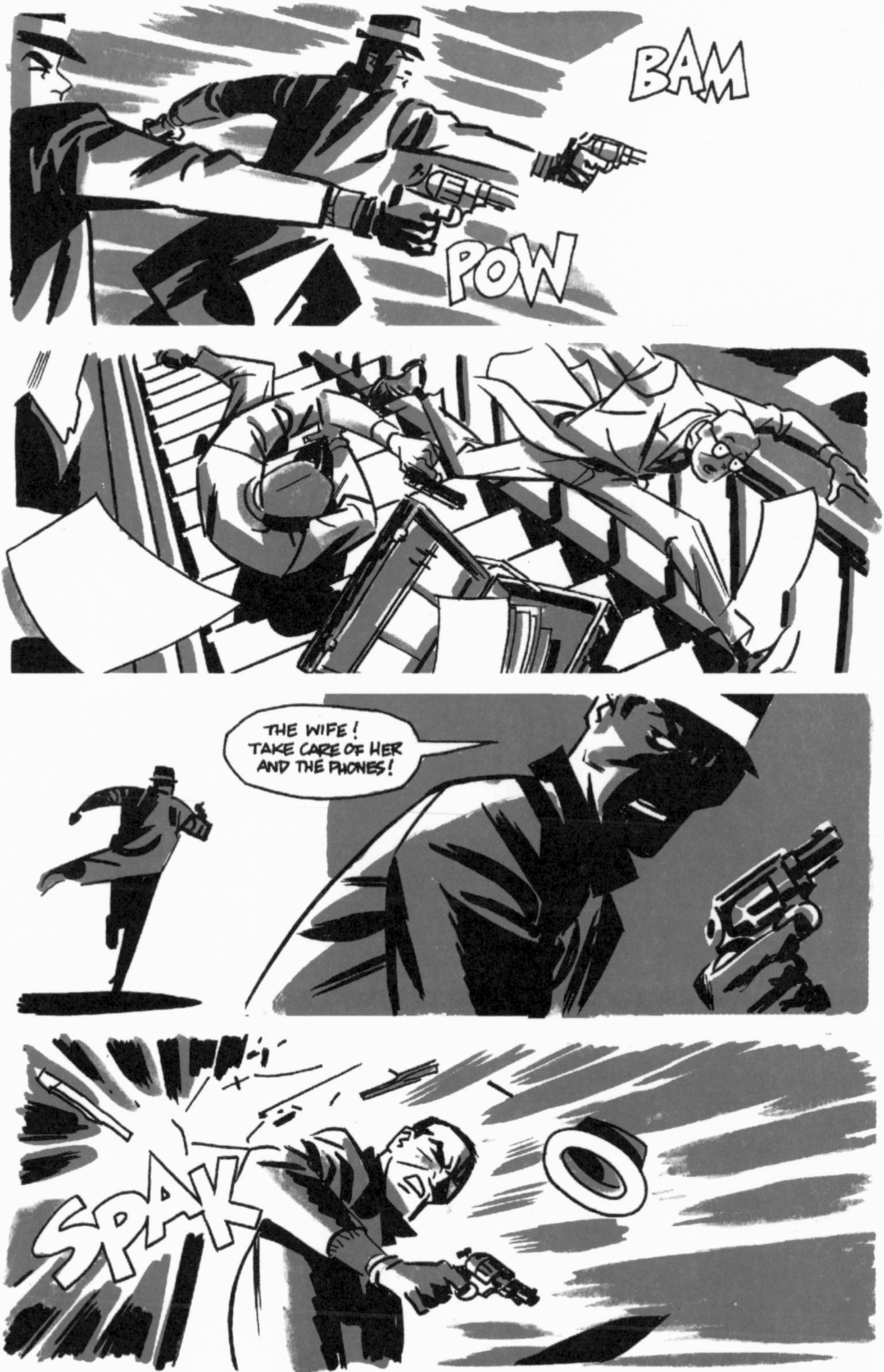
BAM
POW
THE WIFE! TAKE CARE OF HER AND THE PHONES!
SPAK

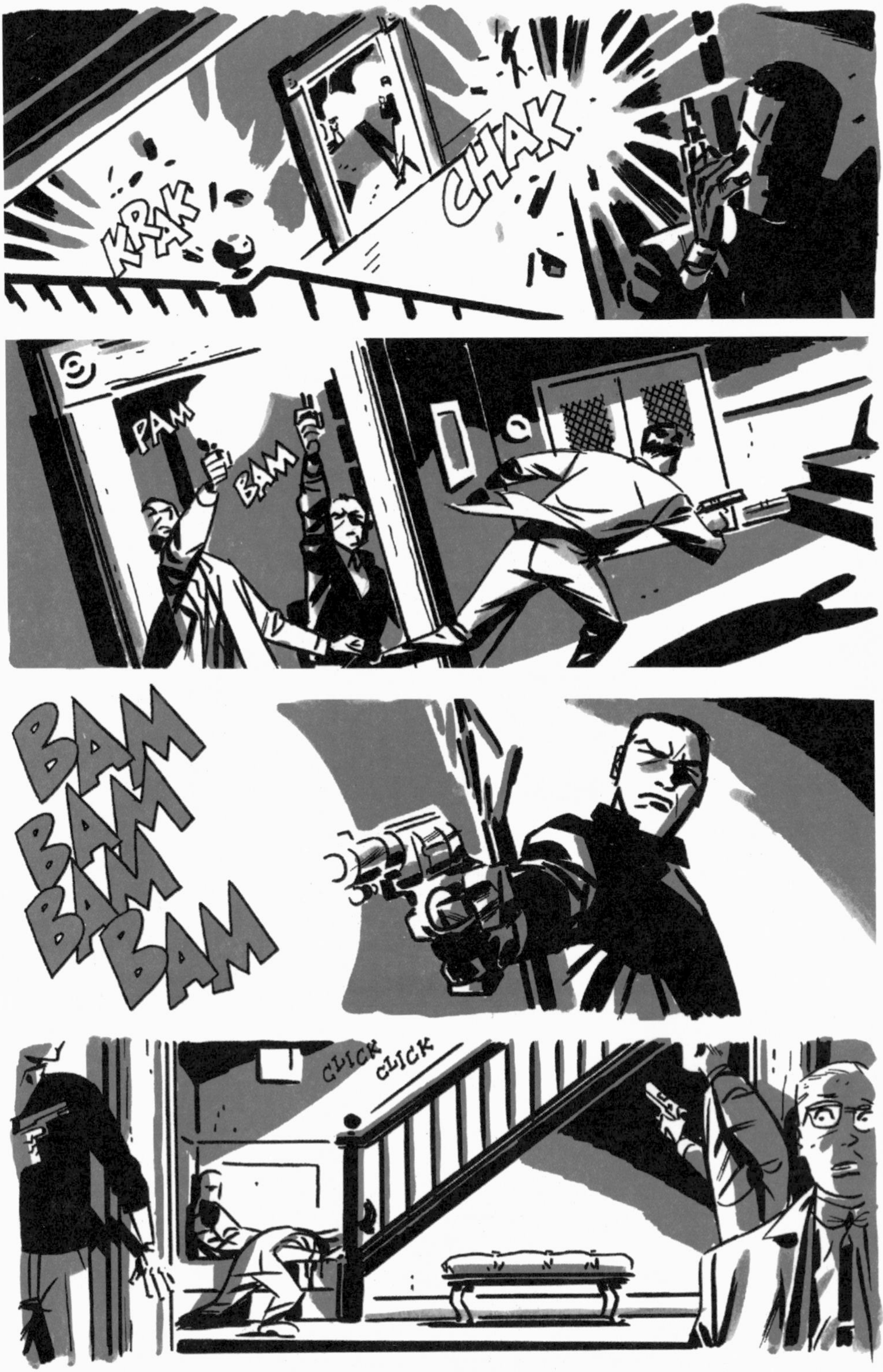
KRAK
CHAK
PAM
BAM
BAM BAM BAM BAM
CLICK CLICK

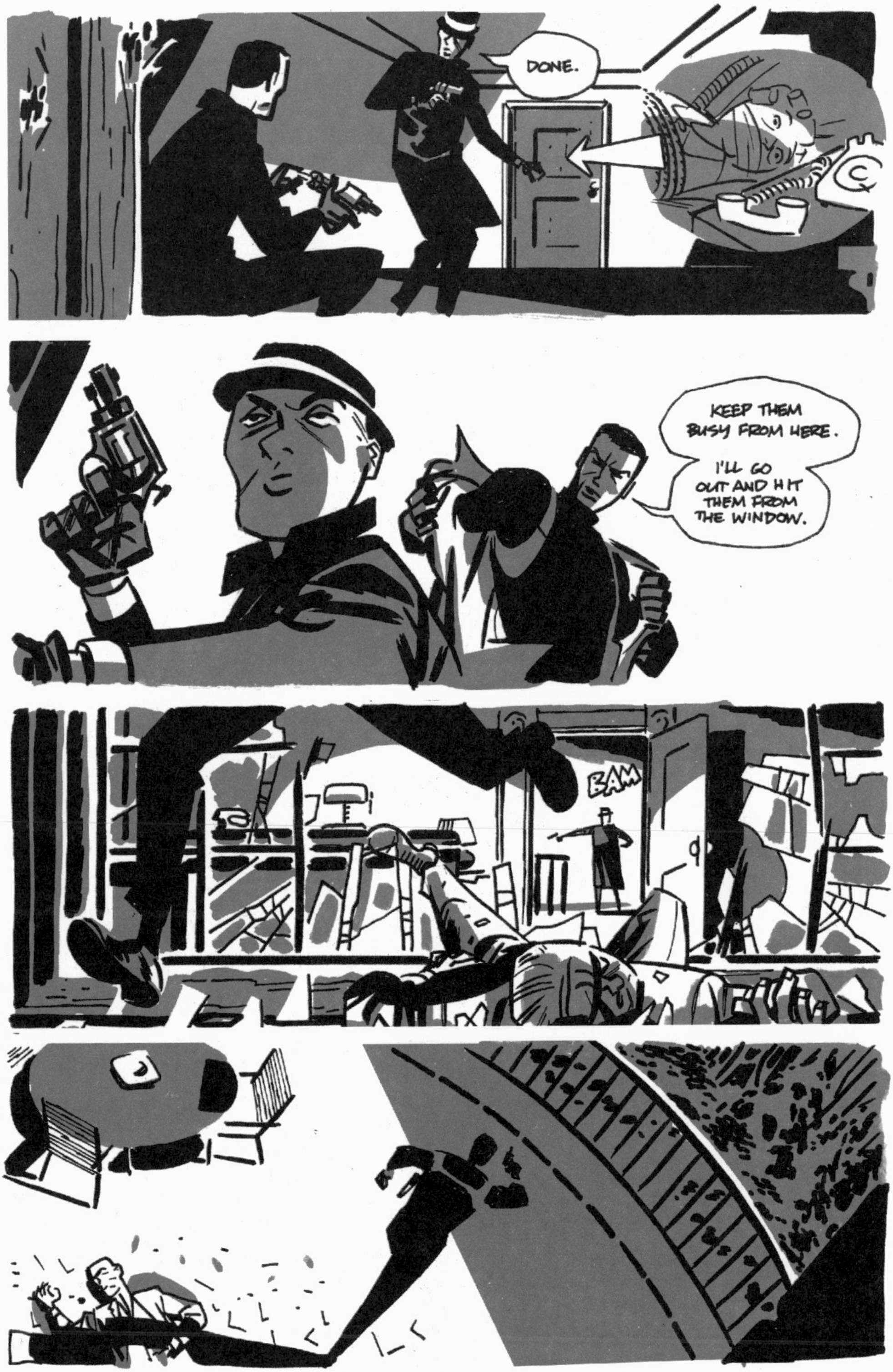
DONE.
KEEP THEM BUSY FROM HERE.
I'LL GO OUT AND HIT THEM FROM THE WINDOW.
BAM

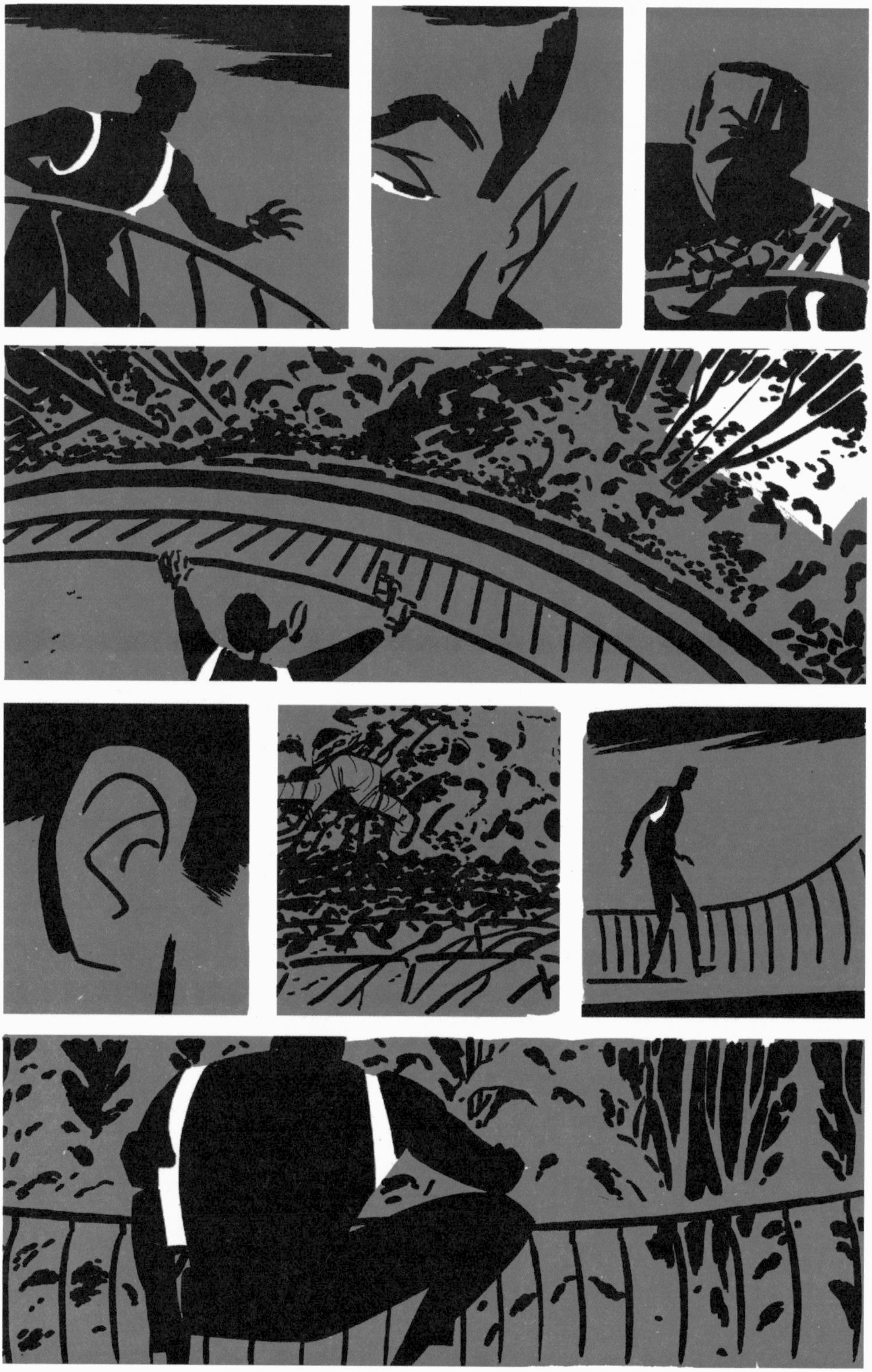

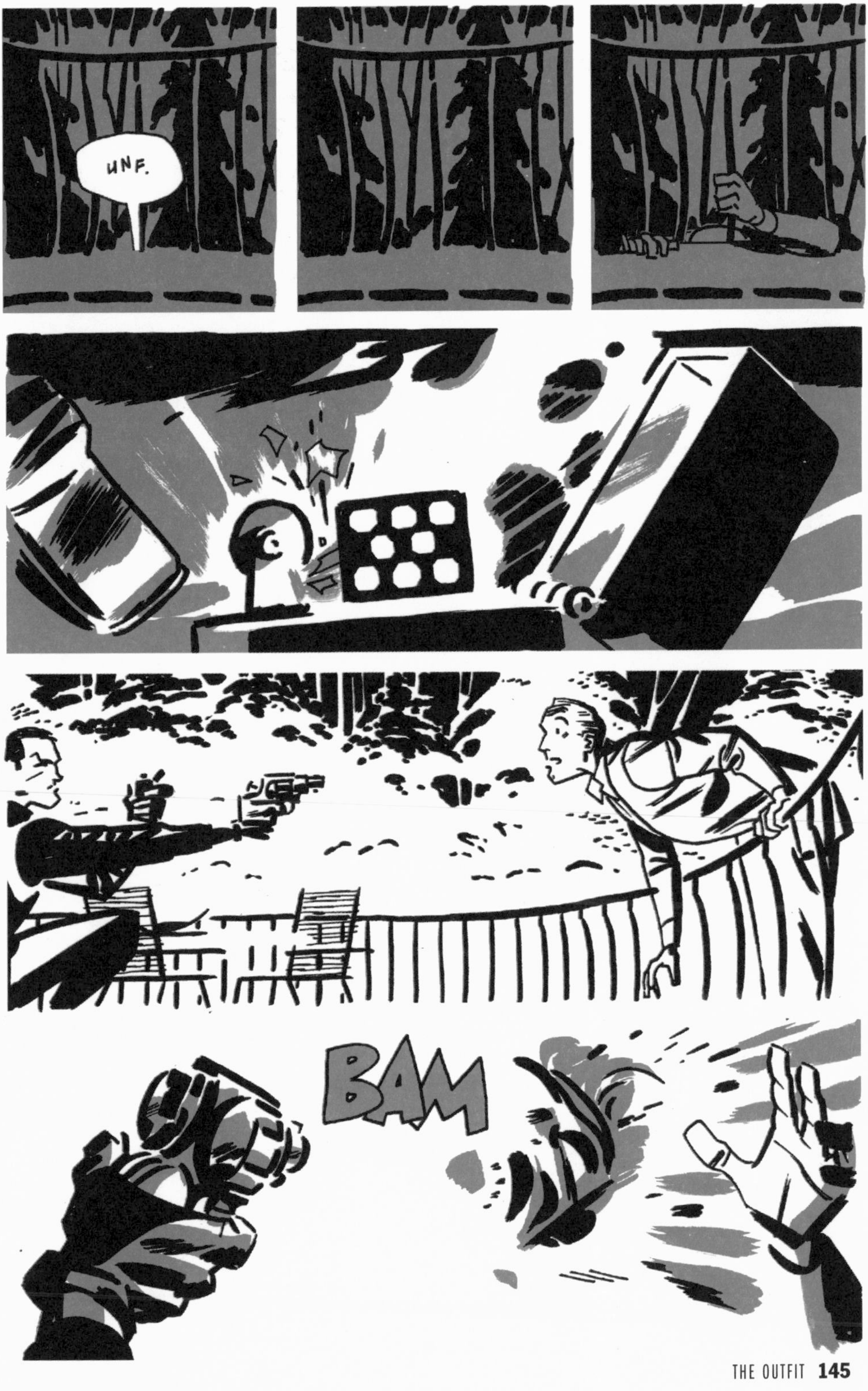
UNF.
BAM

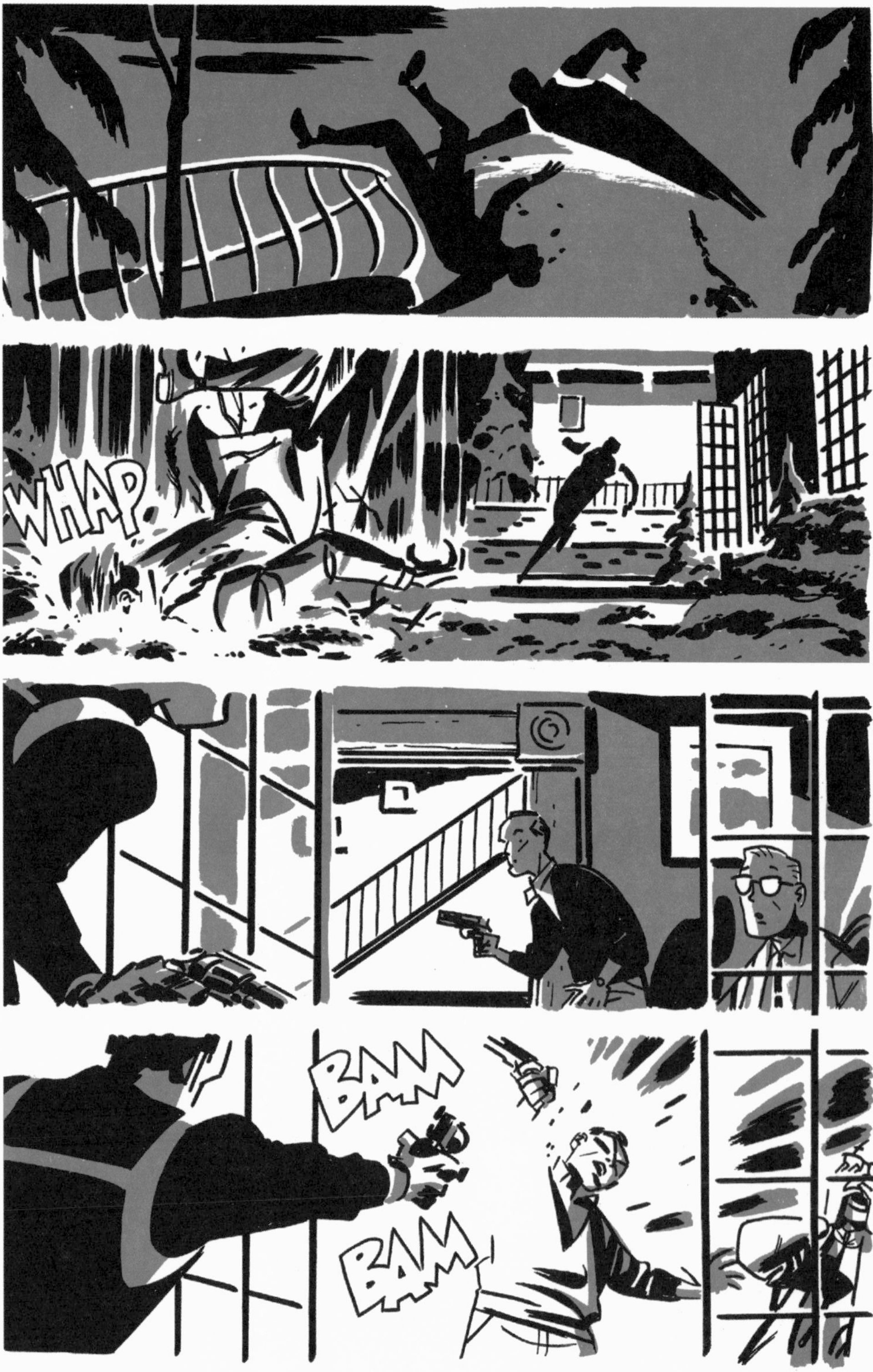
WHAP
BAM
BAM

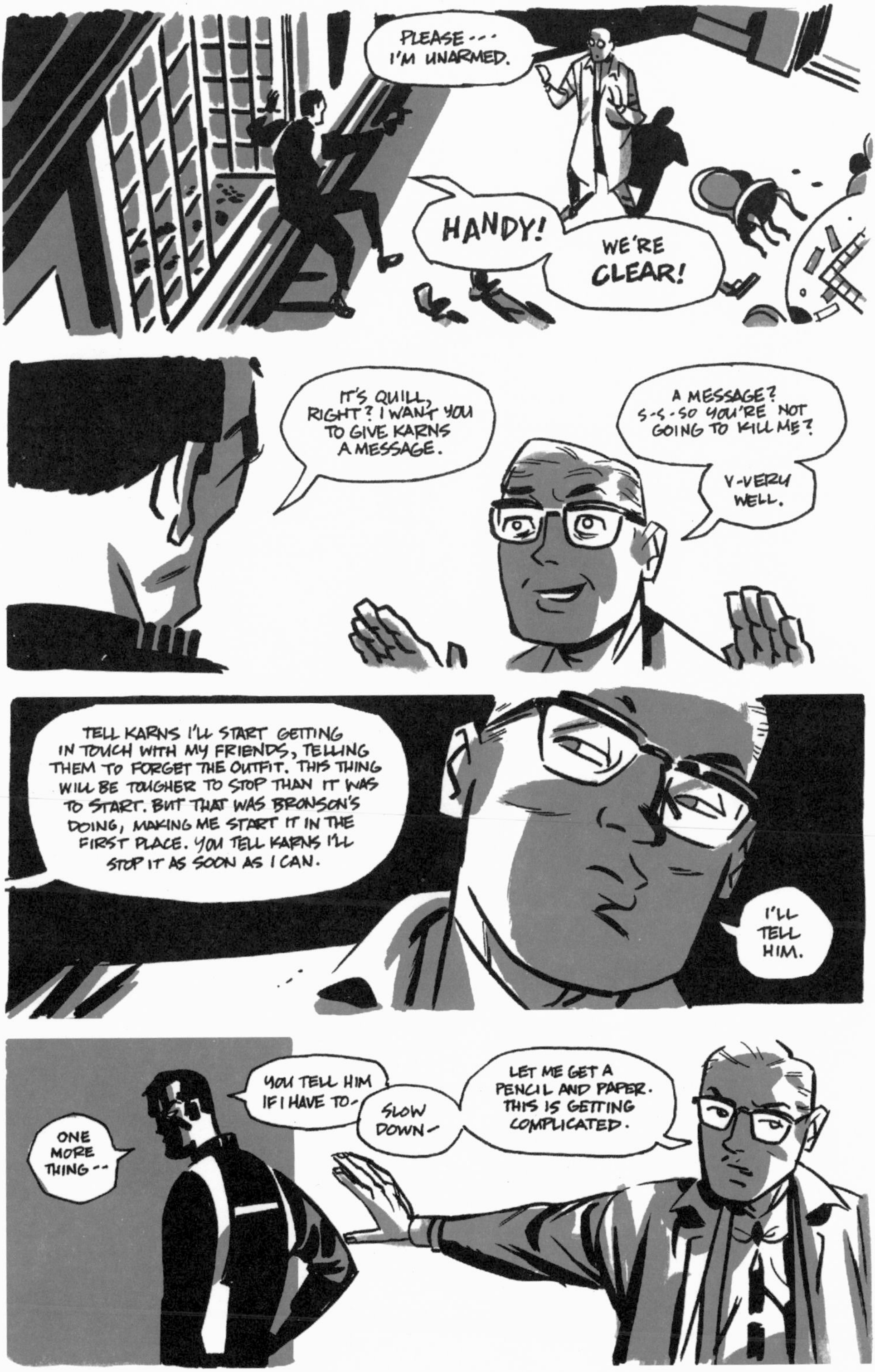
PLEASE--- I'M UNARMED.
HANDY!
WE'RE CLEAR!
IT'S QUILL, RIGHT? I WANT YOU TO GIVE KARNS A MESSAGE.
A MESSAGE? S-S-SO YOU'RE NOT GOING TO KILL ME?
V-VERY WELL.
TELL KARNS I'LL START GETTING IN TOUCH WITH MY FRIENDS, TELLING THEM TO FORGET THE OUTFIT. THIS THING WILL BE TOUGHER TO STOP THAN IT WAS TO START. BUT THAT WAS BRONSON'S DOING, MAKING ME START IT IN THE FIRST PLACE. YOU TELL KARNS I'LL STOP IT AS SOON AS I CAN.
I'LL TELL HIM.
ONE MORE THING--
YOU TELL HIM IF I HAVE TO-
SLOW DOWN-
LET ME GET A PENCIL AND PAPER. THIS IS GETTING COMPLICATED.

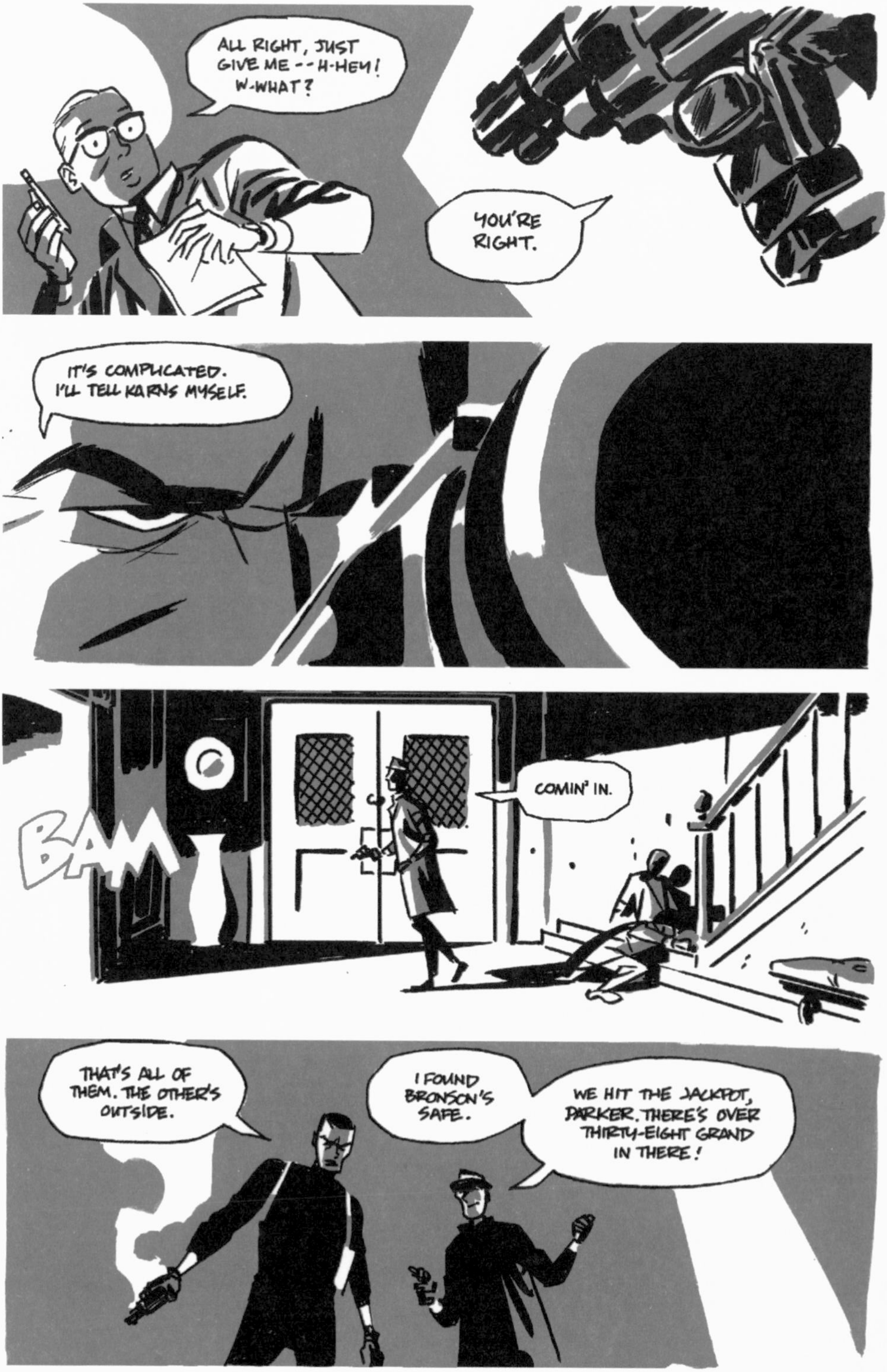
ALL RIGHT, JUST GIVE ME --H-HEY! W-WHAT?
YOU'RE RIGHT.
IT'S COMPLICATED. I'LL TELL KARNS MYSELF.
BAM
COMIN' IN.
THAT'S ALL OF THEM. THE OTHER'S OUTSIDE.
I FOUND BRONSON'S SAFE.
WE HIT THE JACKPOT, PARKER. THERE'S OVER THIRTY-EIGHT GRAND IN THERE!

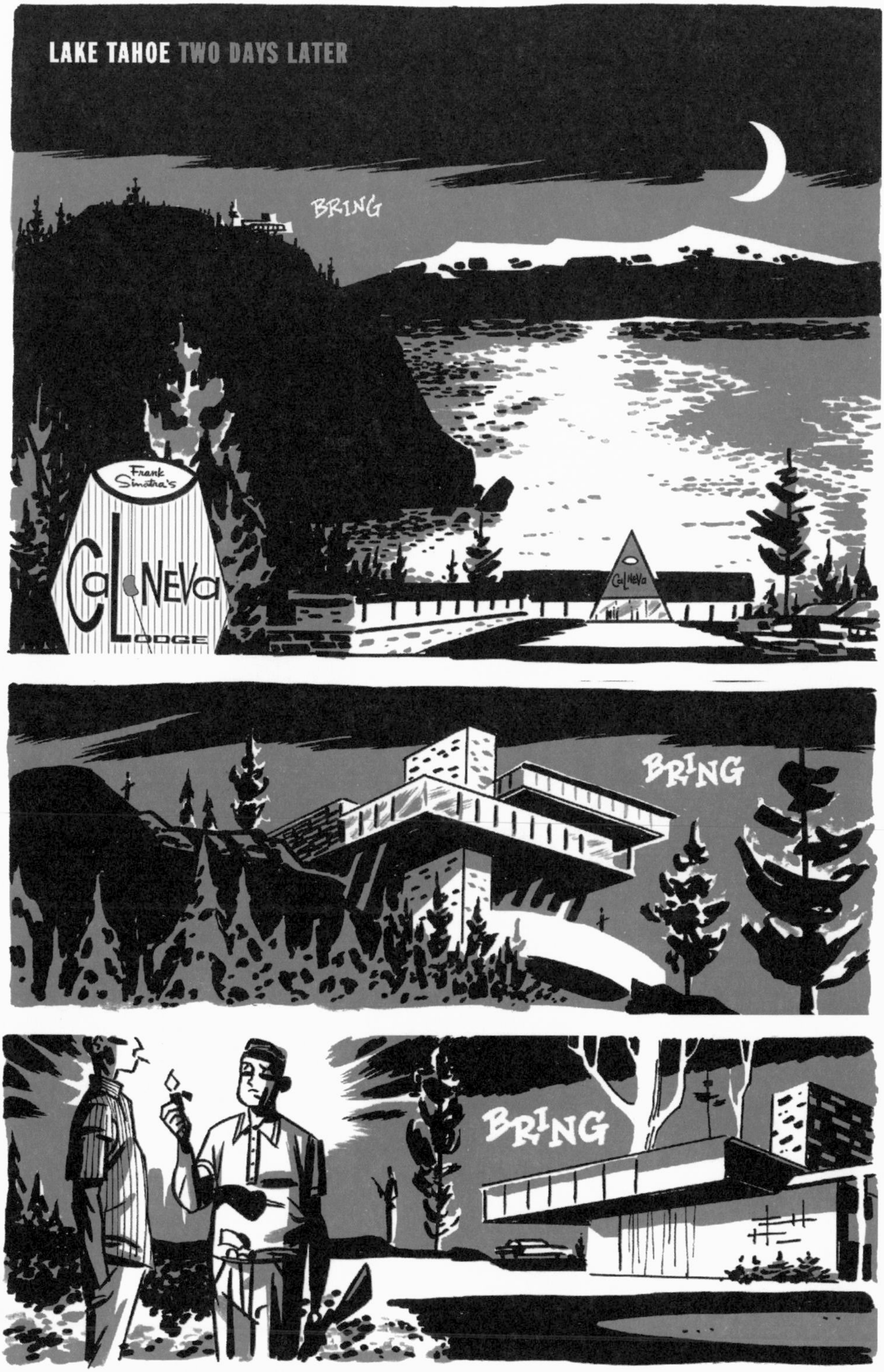
LAKE TAHOE TWO DAYS LATER
BRING
Frank Sinatra's
CalNeva
LODGE
CalNeva
BRING
BRING

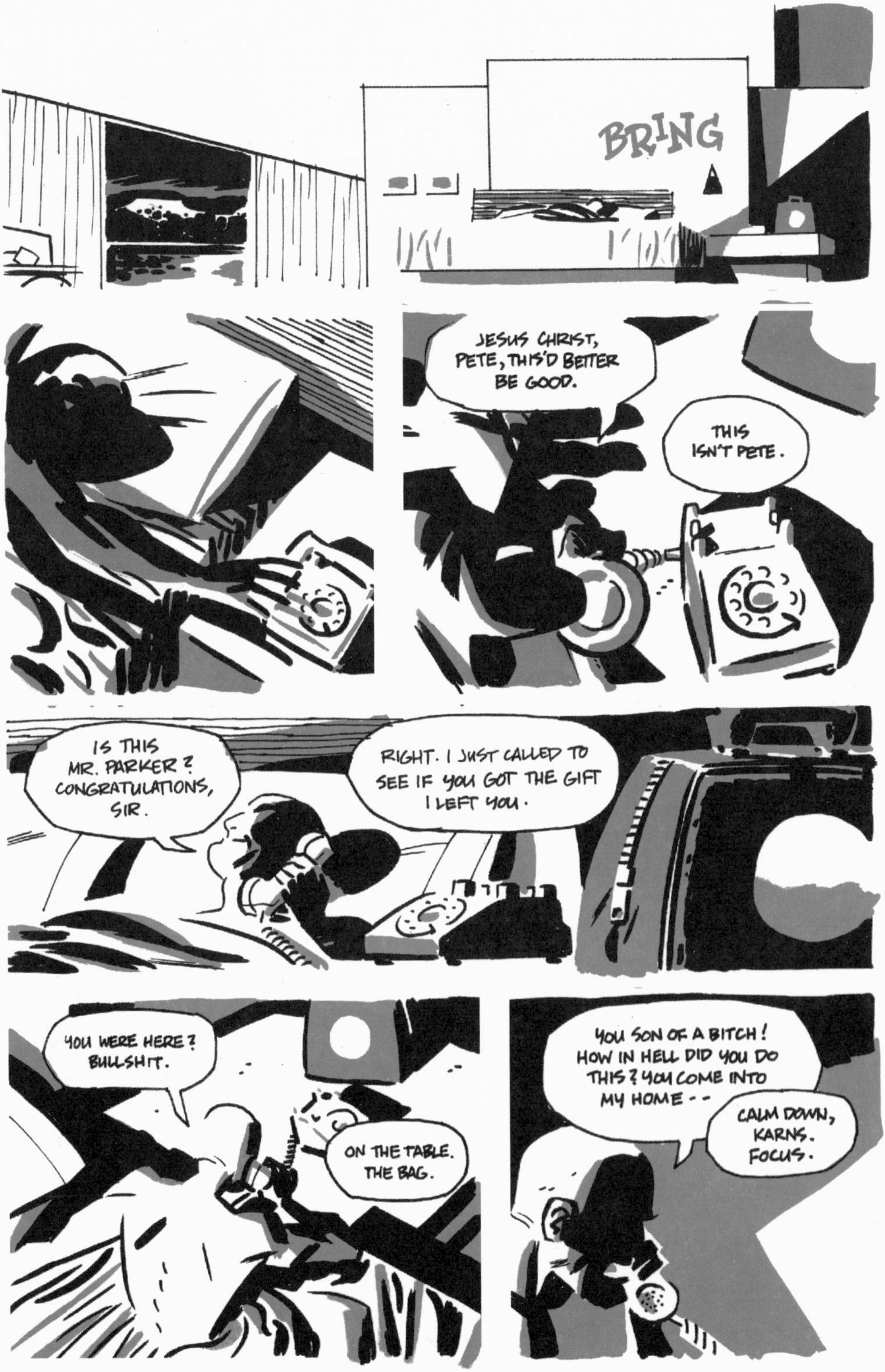
BRING
JESUS CHRIST, PETE, THIS'D BETTER BE GOOD.
THIS ISN'T PETE.
IS THIS MR. PARKER? CONGRATULATIONS, SIR.
RIGHT. I JUST CALLED TO SEE IF YOU GOT THE GIFT I LEFT YOU.
YOU WERE HERE? BULLSHIT.
ON THE TABLE. THE BAG.
YOU SON OF A BITCH! HOW IN HELL DID YOU DO THIS? YOU COME INTO MY HOME--
CALM DOWN, KARNS. FOCUS.

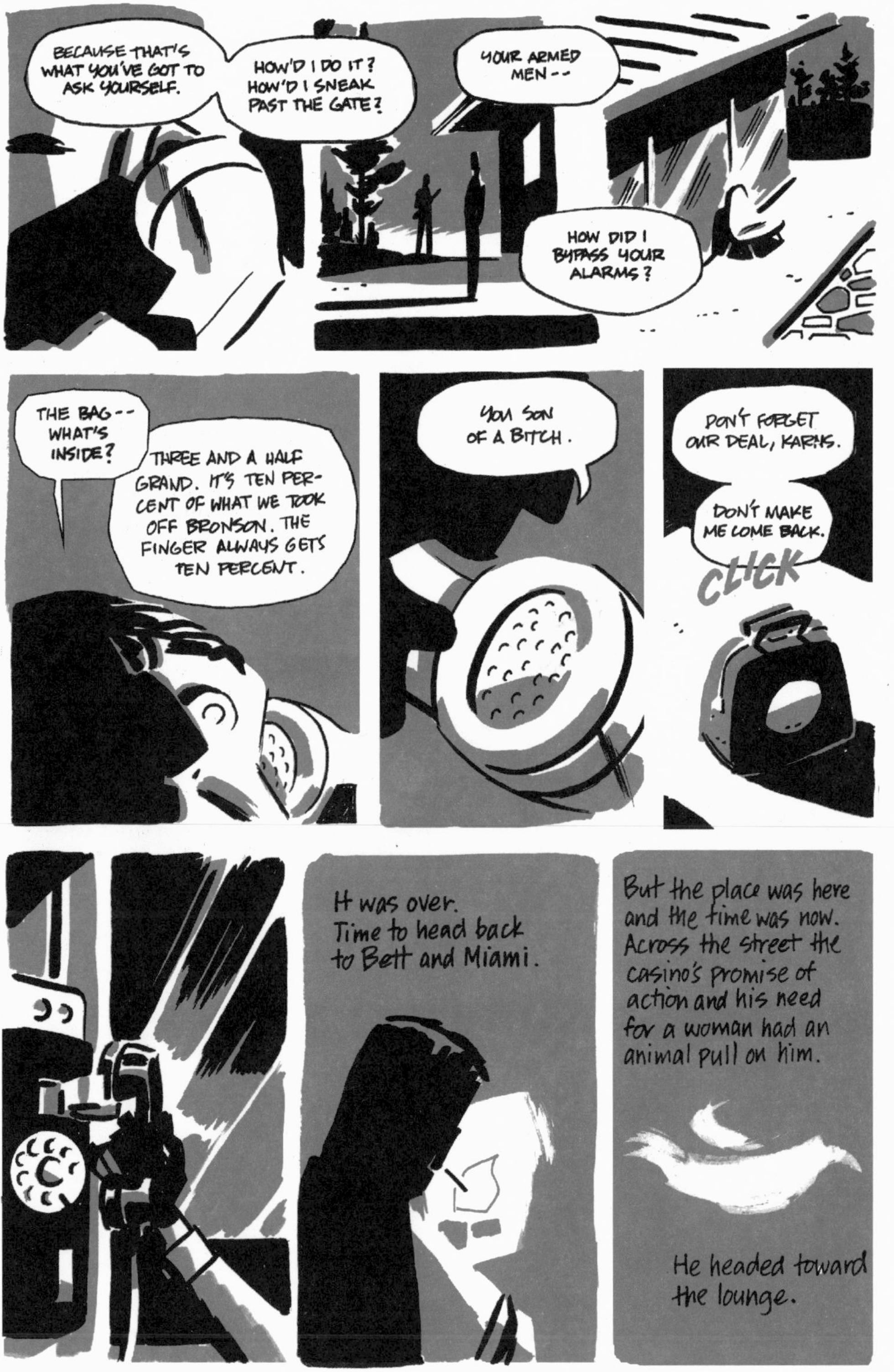
BECAUSE THAT'S WHAT YOU'VE GOT TO ASK YOURSELF.
HOW'D I DO IT? HOW'D I SNEAK PAST THE GATE?
YOUR ARMED MEN --
HOW DID I BYPASS YOUR ALARMS?
THE BAG -- WHAT'S INSIDE?
THREE AND A HALF GRAND. IT'S TEN PERCENT OF WHAT WE TOOK OFF BRONSON. THE FINGER ALWAYS GETS TEN PERCENT.
YOU SON OF A BITCH.
DON'T FORGET OUR DEAL, KARNS.
DON'T MAKE ME COME BACK.
CLICK
It was over. Time to head back to Bett and Miami.
But the place was here and the time was now. Across the street the casino's promise of action and his need for a woman had an animal pull on him.
He headed toward the lounge.

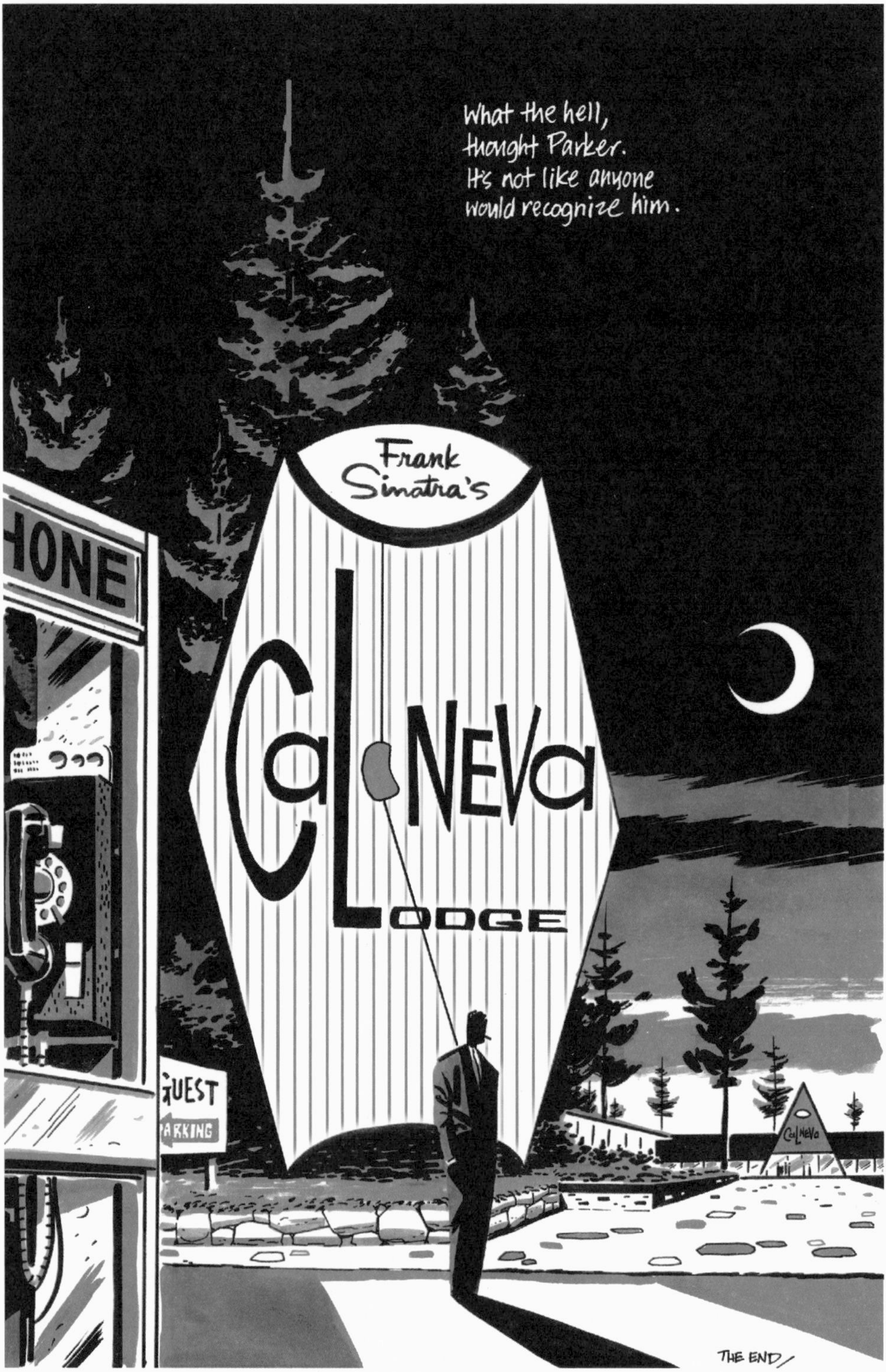
What the hell, thought Parker. It's not like anyone would recognize him.
Frank Sinatra's
CaL NEVa
ODGE
HONE
GUEST
ARKING
CaLNEVa
THE END/

Special Thanks:

Abby Westlake
Paul Westlake
Susanna Einstein (of LJK Literary Management)
Ted Adams
Robbie Robbins
Geoff Boucher
Cal Johnston
Marsha and Manda
Tom Spurgeon
Nona Martin (of the Smithsonian Institute)
Trent at violentworldofparker.com
San Francisco (you know who you are)
Josh, Conor and Ron

PARKER WILL RETURN IN

2012